Deanne Anders was reading romance while her friends were still reading Nancy Drew, and she knew she'd hit the jackpot when she found a shelf full of Harlequin Presents in her local library. Years later she discovered the fun of writing her own. Deanne lives in Florida, with her husband and their spoiled Pomeranian. During the day she works as a nursing supervisor. With her love of everything medical and romance, writing for Mills & Boon Medical Romance is a dream come true.

Shelley Rivers is a Bournemouth girl who spent most of her childhood reading. Married with a family, she now splits most of her time between reading, writing, and pandering to the whims of her hilarious greyhound. Her hobbies include lopsided sewing, holey knitting, and collecting old stuff that no one else sees the beauty in.

Also by Deanne Anders

From Midwife to Mummy
The Surgeon's Baby Bombshell
Stolen Kiss with the Single Mum

Tempted by the Brooding Vet
is **Shelley Rivers**'s debut title

Look out for more books from Shelley Rivers
Coming soon

Discover more at millsandboon.co.uk.

SARAH AND THE SINGLE DAD

DEANNE ANDERS

TEMPTED BY THE BROODING VET

SHELLEY RIVERS

MILLS & BOON

First Published in Great Britain 2020
by Mills & Boon, an imprint of HarperCollins*Publishers*
1 London Bridge Street, London, SE1 9GF

Sarah and the Single Dad © 2020 Denise Chavers

Tempted by the Brooding Vet © 2020 Shelley Rivers

ISBN: 978-0-263-27976-4

MIX
Paper from
responsible sources
FSC® C007454

This book is produced from independently certified FSC™ paper
to ensure responsible forest management.
For more information visit www.harpercollins.co.uk/green.

Printed and bound in Spain
by CPI, Barcelona

SARAH AND THE SINGLE DAD

DEANNE ANDERS

MILLS & BOON

This book is dedicated to all the donor families
who have chosen to give the ultimate gift.
The gift of life.

CHAPTER ONE

SARAH HENDERSON STUDIED the computer chart in front of her. She didn't like the way ten-year-old Lindsey's lab work was trending. With the child already in heart failure, what had started out as a cold had quickly turned into a respiratory infection. Now even with intravenous antibiotic treatment she seemed to be deteriorating daily.

"There you are," the deep voice of Dr. Benton boomed behind her.

Startled, she turned to see the older man standing next to another taller and much younger one wearing a hospital-issue white jacket.

"Sarah, I'd like you to meet Dr. David Wright. He's starting his fellowship here with our cardiothoracic surgery group this week."

Standing, Sarah held out her hand. As the new MD shook it she looked up into a striking pair of eyes that were an unusual blend of light green and gray, and an attack of déjà vu hit her as she took in the dark brown hair and the square chin that accompanied them. She was certain that she'd seen the face before, but where?

"Are you okay?" a warm, concerned voice asked. A voice she could swear she had heard before. Was it her imagination or had she met or seen this man before?

Sarah shook off the trace of an old memory that seemed just out of reach. Realizing she still held the new doctor's hand, she loosened her grip and withdrew her hand, then looked back into questioning eyes. Could she have made any more of a bad impression? The man had to think she was crazy. And maybe she was.

"I'm sorry," she said, as she tried to get her mind back on track, "I'm at least one cup of coffee behind my usual schedule this morning. It's nice to meet you Dr. Wright."

"Sarah's one of our nurse practitioners. I swear we wouldn't get anything done if we didn't have her. If you have any questions or needs, she'll be able to help you," said Dr. Benton. The gray-haired man looked down to his watch. "I hate to leave you, David, but I've got a budget meeting to get to."

With a heart that was beating way too fast, Sarah started for the door, anxious to excuse herself as well. Why was this man affecting her this way? Yes, he was a nice-looking man, but she met nice-looking men all the time and none of them had ever made her feel as if her heart was going to come out of her chest. No, it wasn't his good looks that were upsetting her, but there was something about the man that was ringing all her warning bells.

"I've got a great idea," Dr. Benton said, "how about you show Dr. Wright around for the rest of the morning, Sarah?"

Sarah stopped. She should have seen this coming as soon as Dr. Benton had begun giving his excuses. The chief of the department was good at volunteering her time and there was no way she could get out of this without appearing rude. Besides, if Dr. Benton followed his normal course when he had an intern or new fellowship participant, she would be helping with a lot of Dr. Wright's day-to-day orientation. She pivoted and turned back toward the two men and forced a friendly smile on her face. Her working relationship with all the staff was important and if she was going to be spending a lot of time with the new doctor she didn't want to mess this one up, no matter how he made her feel.

"Of course," Sarah said. "I'm rounding right now, but I'd be glad to take you along with me."

"That would be great," the younger doctor said as his face lit up with a smile that was too bright for Sarah to comprehend at this time of the morning.

Sarah waited for him to catch up with her, and then started down the hallway toward the PCIC unit.

"Are you from Houston, Dr. Wright?" she asked as she gave him a sideways glance, looking for anything that would help her remember where she might have seen him before. Maybe she was wrong. But still, there was something inside her that recognized this man.

"Please, call me David," he said. "No, I'm from Alabama, though I did my residency just east of here, in Beaumont."

"What was your residency in?" she asked. Maybe she'd seen him at one of the many state conferences she had attended.

"It was in pediatric cardiothoracic surgery, but they didn't have a transplant program there so—" he held his arms up in the air, then shrugged "—here I am."

"Our pediatric transplant center is one of the best in the country as I'm sure you know. It's always nice to see new doctors interested in the specialty," she said.

"Believe me, I'm very well aware of what a wonderful program you have here. I feel very lucky to have been given this opportunity with Dr. Benton. The residency in pediatric cardiac was great, but my main interest now is in transplantation. It's where I think I can make a real difference," he said. A shadow passed over his face, reminding her of a man from the past that she had never been able to forget. But then he blinked and the pain she had seen was gone.

She was being ridiculous continuing on this path. He couldn't be the man from the waiting room that day so long ago. David was much younger than the man she remembered.

But still…for just a second those haunted eyes—the color of fresh green pastures shrouded in the thick gray mist of early morning—had reminded her of a time she didn't want to remember. Not here. Not now.

"Well, we're glad to have you," Sarah said politely. She couldn't keep playing this game of detective. If she had met David somewhere she would eventually remember where. Till then she needed to concentrate on her job of helping him get acquainted with everything.

She stopped at the closed doors to the unit and swiped her badge, then waited for the doors to open.

They entered the unit and she headed straight to the nurses' station where only the unit coordinator was in attendance.

"Betsy, this is Dr. Wright. He's starting a fellowship with Dr. Benton and I'm going to be showing him around the unit today."

"Hello, Dr. Wright," Betsy greeted David, quickly taking the time to explain to him where the charts and miscellaneous equipment was kept in the unit.

Sarah picked up the chart with the records that had come along with a baby girl that had been transferred there during the night, turning to David once Betsy had finished.

"I want to start with a new patient we had flown in during the night. She was diagnosed at three days old with hypoplastic left heart syndrome after she became cyanotic. We have the results of the echocardiogram that was performed. It looks like the IV medications are working for now, but I want to see her first and have a talk with her parents," Sarah said as David joined her on her rounds through the unit.

"I'm glad they caught it this early. I've seen cases where it's only been diagnosed after the infant is critical and unstable," David said as they stopped at the door of a room where a young mother stood over a sleeping infant.

As they entered the room she saw a young man asleep on a cot that had been brought into the room as well, leaving her in no doubt that it had been a long night for this young family.

"Ms. Lawrence?" she asked as she held out her hand to the young woman. Her eyes were red and damp and Sarah's heart broke for the woman. She would never be able to forget the helplessness you felt as a mother unable to make your child whole again.

"My name is Sarah and I'm a nurse practitioner with the thoracic-cardio group, and this is Dr. Wright."

She watched as David shook the woman's hand and then led her to a group of chairs in the room.

"Shall we sit down?" he asked the young woman who looked close to collapsing.

"Let me wake my husband," the young mother said. "And please call me Maggie."

The young mother bent over and whispered into her husband's ear. When the couple joined them, Sarah began going over the tests that had been done on their daughter so far. Though she was sure the doctors had reviewed everything with them before their daughter had been transferred, Sarah knew that it was easy in these situations for parents to be overwhelmed with too much information. It was better to repeat the information they needed than to assume they had been informed.

"So, the IV medications that they've started Breanna on are working?" John, the young father, asked, looking hopefully across the room where his newborn daughter lay.

"For now, but it's only a temporary fix. Breanna still needs surgery and there will be more surgeries necessary later," David said.

As David went on to explain the procedures that were needed and the many surgeries that would be necessary, Sarah found herself impressed with how understanding and patient he seemed to be with the parents' questions and concerns.

Before they left the room, Sarah listened to the baby's heart and lungs, noting that even with the medications that were keeping the ductus open, the infant's color was still a sickly gray. She pulled out her phone and texted the cardiologist on call with her concerns, then used the computer at the bedside to order the tests that would be needed before they took the infant to surgery.

"I'm sorry. I haven't been officially assigned to the case, I shouldn't have taken over like that. I get a little carried away sometimes. It's just…" said David. "It's better that they know what they're up against from the beginning so that they can prepare themselves."

"We have a great team here and we stress the importance of making sure all our parents understand what is going on with their child, but sometimes they're in such denial that it just takes time for them to come to terms with their child's condition," she said. Sarah understood his frustration only too well. She remembered being on the other side of those conversations when her mind had been unable to wrap itself around what she was being told by the medical staff.

She forced the thoughts of those days away, and mentally shut the door to where she kept the memories of a life she'd had before locked away. There was only one place where she felt safe to take those memories out and it certainly wasn't here at the hospital. She'd always been very careful to keep her work life separate from the personal memories she had of this place.

"There's nothing that can prepare them for how their life is going to change. Right now it looks like they have a strong marriage. We can only hope that it will be up to the test that having a critically ill child brings," David said as they headed toward the next room.

Was that a hint of bitterness that Sarah heard? There was a story there, she was sure. Glancing over at David, she tried to catch a glimpse of the man she had seen earlier, the man with the haunted eyes. It seemed she wasn't the only one who had something she kept hidden away.

They made their way through the critical care unit and then continued down the acute pediatric cardiac floor, looking in on patients recovering from surgery and those who had been brought in for assessments for surgery or for placement on the transplant waiting list. They stopped at the room of a teenage boy, Jason, who had been brought in after collapsing on the baseball field at his high school a couple of days ago.

Sarah had tried to get the boy to talk to her on her last two visits, but he'd answered her with only one word responses then focused on his phone when she had tried to start a conversation with him.

"Jason's scheduled tomorrow to have a defibrillator implanted, but he's refused to agree to the procedure," she told David as they stopped outside the room.

"I know it would be best to have his agreement, but the fact is that he's a minor so we only need his parents' consent," David said.

"Well, yes, but that's not the point. He's the one who's going to be living with this for the rest of his life." A point she had made to Dr. Benton the day before.

"Do you mind if I see him alone?" David asked as he moved toward the room. "I'll leave the door open so that you can hear."

"Give it your best shot," she said. "He's certainly not responding to me or Dr. Benton."

David rapped his knuckles on the door and entered leaving the door partially open as he had promised.

"Hey, Jason, my name is Dr. Wright."

Sarah wasn't surprised when she heard the boy answer with a grunt and the sound of the boy's computer keys continuing to click. So far it was teenager one. Dr. Wright zero.

"Today's my first day here on the unit and I wanted to introduce myself," said David.

Another grunt came from the room now making it teenager two, Dr. Wright still zero, but she had to give it to David, he wasn't giving up.

"I'm a thoracic surgeon here to study transplantation," David said.

"I don't need a transplant," Jason said with an exaggerated sigh.

Sarah couldn't help but be impressed. That was more than she had been able to get out of the kid in the last two days. Still, from Jason's uninterested tone, she'd have to consider the point a tie.

"No, you don't," David said, his voice still patient. "Nice computer. The graphics are amazing."

"Yeah, they are. It's the best one I've ever had," Jason said. "You play any games?"

Sarah listened as David and Jason discussed computers and various aspects of computer gaming versus something called console games. After a couple minutes of computer terminology that she didn't understand, she heard David ask to see the teenager's computer.

"There are a couple videos I want to show you. It will explain a lot of what the doctors have been talking about as far as how they're going to fix your heart," David said.

As David explained the procedures alongside what they seemed to be reviewing on the computer, Sarah was amazed at the way the teenager was opening up with him. She would have to look into the videos available on the internet that could be used to educate their older patients.

"Is there anything on there that will tell me if I will be able to play baseball again?" Jason asked, and Sarah's heart sank. That was the real issue. His parents had explained to her that he had been playing baseball since he was able to hold a bat and it wasn't something that the boy would be able to give up on easily.

"There are actually some studies they've done in relation to athletes and defibrillators, but as of now they are recommending that anyone with a defibrillator doesn't play most competitive sports," David said. She could hear the regret in his voice and hoped that Jason could hear it too. David understood the loss the boy was feeling at knowing that he was going to have to give up his favorite sport. "There are other sports that you can participate in though."

"But not baseball," Jason said, his voice so low now that Sarah could barely hear him.

A few minutes later David walked out of the room. Sarah had heard him promise Jason that he would be around early the next morning to see him before he was taken to surgery and it seemed that the boy was finally going to accept that the surgery was necessary.

"That was hard," David said as he joined Sarah in the hall.

"I know, but you did get him to agree to the surgery and you were honest with him," Sarah said as they headed to see the last patient of the morning. "What did you play?"

"Basketball," he said. "I had great dreams of making it big in the NBA."

"What happened?" she asked as she knocked on the door of the next patient.

"I reached five-eleven and stopped growing," he said, smiling as he turned his full attention to the little girl they found lying in the bed surrounded by stuffed animals.

Sarah looked down at the little blond girl whose breathing seemed even more labored today than it had the day before. As with a lot of pediatric heart patients, Lindsey was small for her ten years. The little girl looked up at her and smiled, those baby blue eyes hitting Sarah right in the heart. The two of them had been on such a long journey together over the past two and a half years as they had waited for a heart to become available. Lindsey been moved up recently on the waiting list so it was just a matter of waiting for a match with a donor heart. Only now Lindsey had been exposed to a respiratory virus that was making her heart work even harder.

She looked around the room and found the child alone as was often the case. Lindsey's mother, Hannah, was very young, and a single mom without any support, and had to work long hours to provide for her and Lindsey. But Lindsey was very sick right now and her mother needed to be there. Sarah would touch base with Hannah and give her an update so that she understood exactly how critical Lindsey's condition could become. Hannah had fought beside her daughter for so long, Sarah knew the young mother wouldn't give up now.

As David walked over to the bed to introduce himself to the little girl, Sarah joined the nurse who was charting on the computer at Lindsey's bedside.

"Has Pulmonary been in today?" Sarah asked.

"Yes, Dr. Lorten wants to do a bronchoscopy, but I haven't been able to get Hannah to give us consent," the nurse said.

"I'll call her," Sarah said. Then crouching down on the floor next to Lindsey's bed, she asked, "How are you feeling, kiddo?" She pushed the child's blond curls off her forehead and was relieved to feel it cool. No fever. At least that was a good sign.

"I'm not going to make it to see the horses this week, am I?" Lindsey asked.

"Horses?" asked David. He'd pulled a chair up beside Lindsey's bed while Sarah had been talking with Kim.

Lindsey turned her blue eyes toward him and for the

first time in the last week she saw the little girl's eyes come alive.

"Oh, yes," Lindsey said. "Sarah has lots of pretty horses. I've seen pictures of them all. Maple is my favorite. Sarah let me name her myself when she first got her."

"And Maple will be waiting to see you as soon as you get better," Sarah said as she squeezed the little girl's hand in hers. "I'll tell you what—when I get home I'll take a picture of Maple for you and I'll bring it in tomorrow."

"I have to see this horse with a name like Maple," David said as he gave Lindsey a smile. The little girl's face turned pink and Sarah knew it wasn't from a fever. It looked like Lindsey might have her first crush, which was so sweet to see that Sarah couldn't help but smile up at the man who had made her special little girl happy when she was so sick.

She listened as Lindsey explained the therapy program Sarah ran at her father-in-law's ranch teaching young cardiac patients from the community how to ride. Or if their medical condition wouldn't allow them to participate in the riding lessons they could interact with the special therapy horses kept on the ranch. Sarah was proud of The Henderson Memorial horse therapy program that she had founded. Working with the children at the ranch wasn't only good for them, it had also been good for her.

"That sounds like a lot of fun," David said to the little girl.

"You can go too. Lots of times the doctors volunteer to help. Can he go, Sarah?" asked Lindsey.

"Of course he can come," Sarah answered. "And as soon as you get better, I'll take you out there to see Maple."

"I don't have any experience with horses, but I definitely know someone who would be interested in seeing them," David said as he gave Sarah a questioning look.

"We'd be happy to have them. We run the program on the second Saturday of the month and all the staff is welcome," Sarah said. A smile lit David's face and she couldn't help wondering who this someone was. A wife? She looked down at his left hand and saw that he wasn't wearing a ring. Maybe a girlfriend? It wouldn't be surprising that a man like David had someone special in his life.

As they left the room Sarah texted Hannah and asked her to call as soon as she had a minute. She didn't want to scare the girl's mother but she did need to get consent from Hannah and tell her that Lindsey's condition was getting worse. Hannah needed to know.

"How long has she been waiting?" David asked as they headed back to the doctor's workroom.

"Five years. She's been in and out, though mostly in, of here for the last two and a half years," Sarah said.

"Family issues?" David asked.

"Hannah's young and a single parent. I know this had been hard on her and I worry about her. She's been through a lot with Lindsey. She couldn't have been more than nineteen or twenty when Lindsey was born. When Lindsey gets a heart transplant—" she refused to consider that there was the possibility that the little girl wouldn't get a donor heart "—it's going to be a lot more responsibility."

"I hope for that child's sake that her mother is up for the job, but an overabundance of toys and the lack of a parent present is a sign... Let's just say I've had some experience as far as missing-in-action parents. It's a lot harder to be the parent at the bedside than the one that sends the prettiest packages." Again the hint of bitterness she heard in David's voice surprised her.

"Hannah's not like that. It will be a lot for her to handle, but she'll do it," Sarah asserted.

"About your ranch," David started as they turned back toward the nursing station.

"David? David Wright? Is that you?" Melody, one of the older staff nurses said as she jumped up from her seat and came around the desk to the two of them. "It is you. How's Davey doing? I've thought about him so much over the last few years."

"Mel! I didn't know if you still worked here or not. I meant to ask Dr. Benton, but I haven't had a chance," David said as he beamed down at the gray-haired nurse. "Davey's great. I'll have to bring him up to see you one day when I'm off."

Sarah watched as the nurse turned around and announced to the other staff members that were looking curiously at the three of them, "David was here with his son, was it three years ago now?"

Sarah's heart stuttered then sped up to a dangerous rate as she waited for David's answer. Had she been wrong to dismiss that feeling of familiarity? Was this truly the man she'd seen over three years ago in the waiting room?

"Davey's 'new heart birthday' was three years in January," she heard David say.

That was all the confirmation she needed. It was him she remembered seeing.

The shock sent her spinning backward toward another time. A time when her perfect life had ended, only it hadn't. Life hadn't been that kind. Instead it had been heartbreaking and life shattering, made only bearable because of the man standing in front of her now.

Suddenly she was back in that waiting room, running from the terrible news the doctors had just given her and hiding from a family that would be as devastated as she was at the news that her little boy's brain had lost the ability to function. How could she face them with this news? Then she had seen the dark-haired man hunched over in his seat appearing to bear a burden just as heavy as her own. Immediately she had felt a connection to him, a compassion that only someone who was traveling the same path as she could feel.

But was David really that man? The man she had seen that night in the waiting room, the one who had broken down when the organ transplant case manager had told him that they might have a heart for his son, the one that she had wondered about for the last three years, the one who may have been given back his son because of the gift of her own son's heart?

It had to be more than just a coincidence that this man's son had been given a heart in this hospital around the same time of her son's accident. Around the same time that she had chosen to donate her own son's organs. A decision she'd made because of that man in the waiting room.

It had been David's eyes that had first sparked her memories of him, but now she could see that there was more. While he certainly looked much younger than the defeated man she had seen back then, the build and dark hair matched what she remembered of that night.

Sarah forced herself to stand there while the rest of the staff excitedly asked him questions concerning his son and his recovery. While the staff knew that she had lost her husband and son due to a car accident, Houston General was a big facility. She had been working on the adult surgical floor at the time of the accident and since her transfer to the pediatric cardiology service she had never discussed the donation of her own little boy's organs with the staff here. It was too personal and still too painful.

And what did she do now? What was she supposed to say to a man who had helped make the hardest decision in her life? How was she supposed to work next to David and never mention that time in her life when just looking at him brought back such difficult memories for her?

There had been days she had wished she had died in the car crash along with Kolton and Cody, but then she would think of that young father who'd been so desperate for a heart for his son.

Later, when she realized she wanted to do more to help families like that young man's, it had taken only one trip through the pediatric cardiac unit for her to know this was where she was needed, where she could help the critical children that waited for a new life with their families. She'd finished her nurse practitioner program and found a place in Dr. Benton's practice. And now the man who had influenced her life so much was here on her unit.

And what about his son, Davey? She'd always imagined that it had been her son who had saved the son of the man in the waiting room. Knowing that David's son had received a heart transplant back then made the possibility feel only more real. Now she had been given an opportunity to find out if she had been right all along.

As the rest of the staff started to disburse back to their patients, she pulled herself into the present only to find that some of the younger nurses were giving the new doctor more than just a friendly smile. Not that she could blame them for their interest. Dr. David Wright was a very good-looking man with his dark brown hair curling around his face, those striking eyes, and a smile full of laughter as he talked to Mel.

But there was more to the man than his looks. She had immediately recognized that when she had first seen him. He had a strong, competent look to him that had quickly put the patients and their families at ease. And she remembered the way he had dealt with the news that there might be a last hope for his son. The anguish in his face had matched hers as she'd mourned the loss of hope for her own. He'd openly shed tears at the news that his son might be getting a new heart and still the man hadn't appeared weak.

Mentally shaking herself, she forced herself to put the old memories behind her again. It was not going to be easy to keep those memories away with David here, but she had to remember that it was the here and now that was important. Her past life was over, and she had patients that relied on her now. These were the children she was responsible for now. Later, when she could be alone, she'd take the time to deal with all of this and what it could mean for her.

She watched as Dr. Benton walked down the hall toward them and then as he and David walked away together. She had so many questions that she was desperate to find a way to ask, to tell him to wait so that she could ask the one question that was circling around and around in her head. It was a question that at some point she would have to ask, but it would have to wait.

Is the heart of my little boy, my Cody, beating in your son's chest?

CHAPTER TWO

DAVID PUT ONE of the cups of coffee he'd purchased at the trendy café across from the hospital on the desk in front of Sarah.

"What's this for?" Sarah asked as she looked up at him, those deep brown eyes questioning. It was a look he'd seen a lot lately when she looked at him. It was as if that intelligent mind of hers was trying to solve a complex puzzle, and for some reason he had a feeling that he was that puzzle.

"It's to say thank you. If it wasn't for you I'd have been buried in all this paperwork. I knew there was a lot of paperwork involved with the assessments for the transplant patients, but I never imagined that there would be this much," he said.

"Really? I guess I assumed that because you had been through this firsthand that you'd know all about the mountains of paperwork," Sarah said. And there was that look again.

Was that what she was curious about? It wasn't that he didn't understand why she would be curious about what he had gone through. After working with her for the last week, he had quickly discovered that she had a very inquiring mind, and with working on one side of the transplant process it was only normal for her to want to know what it was like on the other side.

"I'm sorry, I didn't mean to pry," Sarah said, then looked back to the computer screen in front of her, her golden-tan cheeks turning a pretty pink with a blush that he found surprisingly charming. The Sarah that he had been working with didn't seem like the type of woman that would be so easily embarrassed, but there was always more to a person that what you first saw. If anyone should know that, he should. He'd thought he had known his ex-wife until their son had been born and everything in their life had changed.

"It's okay, Sarah. I don't mind talking about it, most parts at least," he said, then regretted that he had added the afterthought. He had no reason to think that any of her questions would deal with the breakup of his marriage.

"Are you sure?" she asked.

"I'm sure," David said.

He took his chair next to her and waited. It was almost as if he could see the gears in her mind turning as she seemed to struggle with her question.

"What was wrong with Davey? Why did he need the transplant?" Sarah asked.

"Davey was diagnosed with hypoplastic left heart syndrome not long after he was born. It hadn't been caught on ultrasound so it was a shock. There were a lot of surgeries before it was decided that a transplant would be necessary. There wasn't anything else they could do for him."

"I'm sorry. That had to be hard for you and your wife."

Deep brown eyes seemed to bore into his, or was it

just that he felt uncomfortable discussing the situation with his ex-wife with Sarah?

"And he's okay now?" Sarah asked.

"He's great. He's done a lot of growing in the last three years. I keep a close watch on him and he still has a lot of follow-up testing that's necessary, but so far he's not shown any signs of rejection over the past three years."

David watched her as Sarah bit down on her lip, an act that caught way too much of his attention.

"Can I ask you one more question?" she asked.

"Sure," David said as he forced his eyes away from lips that looked way too dangerous right then.

"What did it feel like when you learned that there was a heart available for your son?" she asked, her eyes never wavering from his.

This was not the question he had expected. He had thought maybe she would want to know about the impact that a sick child had on someone's life or how he had gotten through the awful waiting period. But this? That moment had to have been the most emotional moment of his life. How did you explain the feeling of being lifted from a pit of despair and given the chance of a new life?

"It's hard to explain," he said, not knowing where to start. Though it might seem like an easy question to answer to Sarah, it was far from it. Someone would have to understand where Davey was in his life at that time. "Davey had so many surgeries before he was finally put on the transplant list. With each surgery, I kept thinking this will be the last one. But it never was, and when he was almost two it was determined that the only thing that would save him would be a transplant. I knew the odds that he would receive one in time were against us.

By the time I brought Davey here, his heart was failing and we were getting to the point where I was going to have to make some hard decisions on his care. I'd almost given up. I had walked out into the waiting room knowing that if there wasn't a miracle I would lose my little boy within the next few days. Then one of the organ procurement staff found me and told me that there was a good chance that Davey would be getting a heart very soon. Learning that there was a heart available for my son was the happiest moment of my life. I don't have another experience to compare it to. To have that hope of a future for your child when you are at the point of giving up is unimaginable. It was like going from the lowest point in your life to the happiest in two point five seconds and not knowing if you should laugh or cry."

"I'm glad that it worked out that way, that you were given that chance."

This was it. This was the moment she had been obsessed with over the last week. All she had to do was explain that she had been there that night and that she had suspicions that the case manager that night had been talking about her son when she had told David that there could be a heart available. All she had to do was open her mouth and the words would come, she knew they would.

"Hey, Sarah, Hannah's here and wanted to know if you had a second to talk to her," Melody said from the doorway.

She'd missed her chance.

Turning away from David she stood and headed toward the door before turning back. "Didn't you say you'd like to meet Lindsey's mother?" she asked.

"That's okay," David said, "I'm scheduled in surgery with Dr. Benton this afternoon."

"Okay," she said, then turned again toward the door before stopping a second time. "Did you say you wanted to come out to the ranch? This Saturday is therapy day for the kids enrolled in the program if you want to come and bring your son."

"Yeah, Davey would love that."

She could feel his searching eyes on her as she left the room. Instead of coming clean with David, she had just managed to make him think she was nosy. There had to be a better way to go about this. If only she didn't feel that gut-wrenching pain when she thought of that night maybe she could. She'd asked David to share his personal experiences with her, but she'd been unable to share with him her own experiences that day.

She'd been working one on one with David for a week now helping him to understand her side of the cardiac practice and she'd been impressed with how well he interacted with both the young patients and their parents. He'd been up-front with the parents when they'd had concerns about their children's diagnosis and risks of the many procedures that were necessary. She had no doubt that if it was David in her position that he would have come right out and told her.

But he hadn't been through what she had been through that night, she reminded herself. His child had survived that night, hers hadn't. Either way, she had to tell him. The next time she had an opportunity to tell David she'd do it, no matter how much it hurt.

* * *

David pulled his car off the highway and stared down the long dirt road. He'd been driving for almost an hour and had started to think he was lost.

"Are we there?" his son asked, trying to strain his neck to look over from his booster seat in the back of the car.

David looked at the metal sign hanging over the road that swung back and forth with the wind. He hadn't expected anything this big when Lindsey had been telling him about the horses Sarah had at her house, but from the size of the pastures that ran on both sides of the road he could see he had been mistaken. He looked back up at the sign that read "Henderson's Horse Farm."

"I think we are," he answered his son.

He eased his car down the clay dirt road until he saw the large stables surrounded by a high white livestock fence. He parked the car beside an old gray pickup truck covered in red dust and a new SUV that along with his car looked totally out of place.

After opening the back door to get his son out, he fought with the seat buckle as his son tried to help.

"Hurry, Daddy, I want to see the horses," Davey said as he pulled against the buckled strap.

"I know, son, but we're not going to get there any sooner if you don't let me get this buckle undone," David said. Somehow he could perform surgery on the smallest of hearts, but the talent for unbuckling the car seat was something he had never been able to achieve. Finally, he freed his son and he watched as Davey ran toward the open door of the stable.

"Woe, slow down partner," David said as he grabbed

his son's hand, "we talked about this. We don't run where there are big horses around, do we?"

By the time they had entered the door, Davey had stopped trying to pull against his dad and slowed to a stop as soon as he saw the other children and adults in the building. As Sarah made her way over to them, his son had grabbed him behind his leg and was trying to hide behind him. Davey had a tendency to be shy when he first met new people, but he was too inquisitive for it to last very long.

"Davey, this is Mrs. Henderson. She's the one who invited us to come see the horses," David said as he tried to pry his son from behind him. "Remember, I told you she had a horse named Maple."

"That's a funny name for a horse," Davey said, peaking around his father's leg at Sarah.

Unlike the always neatly dressed Sarah he was used to seeing, this Sarah wore a long-tailed chambray shirt that looked two sizes too big over jeans that had almost faded to white. Jeans that were tucked into a pair of scarred brown cowboy boots. Her hair, usually piled atop her head, was hanging down past her shoulders in thick brown waves and her warm brown eyes seemed to be captivated by his son who had finally come out from behind him, though he still hung onto David's legs.

"Maybe she's a funny horse. Do you want to go see her?" she asked as she bent down and held out her hand to his five-year-old son.

David followed the two of them over to where four other children and a short weathered man seemed to be studying a dark brown horse that stood in a rectangular stall.

"This is Davey," Sarah said as she started to introduce his son to all the other children.

"Hi, I'm Jack Henderson," the man said as he held out his hand. David put his age around sixty and figured this couldn't be Sarah's husband. He shook Jack's hand and then the man turned toward Davey.

"Hi, Davey. I'm Miss Sarah's father-in-law, Mr. Jack. Did I hear you say that our Maple is a funny horse?" the man asked as he bent down so that he could talk to Davey.

"I said it was a funny name. I didn't know horses could be funny," Davey said.

"Well, horses have all kinds of personalities, just like people. How about I introduce you to some of them?" Jack said as he held his hand to Davey. Davey stared up at him with eyes that pleaded for his dad to let him go explore the other stalls.

"You can go, but remember what I said about running and no leaving the stable without me," David said, then watched as his son headed off with the older man toward the end of the stalls. He could tell by how the man had interacted with Davey that he had spent some time around children, but Davey could be a handful at times and he really didn't like letting him go off with strangers. Hearing a loud snort, he turned to see Sarah opening a stall and leading out the large brown horse.

"Josh, you can take Maddie but stay in the north paddock where I can see you," she said while handing the reins over to an older teenage boy, who took the horse and led him out of the stable.

He watched as she handed the reins of a smaller horse to a young nurse he had seen at the hospital, who took the horse and the other three children out another side door. As Sarah walked toward him, he was aware of how much she looked like she belonged here, while he felt totally out of his element. He forced his eyes away from Sarah and back to Davey.

"He'll be fine," Sarah said as she appeared at his side, "Jack will watch him."

"I know," he said, though he couldn't help but check on the progress his son and the older man were making as they seemed to be stopping at each stall.

"I'm so glad you made it," Sarah said as she looked around the stable. "What do you think?"

"It's definitely not what I was expecting," he said, "I was thinking you had a couple of horses in your backyard. This is amazing."

"It is, isn't it," she said. Her eyes lit up with her smile and it was easy to see how much she loved the ranch. "It's a lot of work, but Jack has a small staff that helps with the horses and keeps up the grounds."

"Are all the horses yours?" David asked as he looked at the horses still in their stalls as they walked toward the door where the group of children had gone. He took a look back behind him and saw that Davey was still occupied with Jack as they continued going from horse to horse.

"Only three of them are mine, but we board a few for friends, or Jack does, but most of them are for breeding. This is all Jack's. I just help when I can. He's been great about letting me base a therapy program here. The kids love it out here and after spending as much time as they do inside hospital walls, it's good for them to spend time outside. I give some private lessons to the kids from the hospital that are interested and cleared medically by their doctors," she said.

"I'm impressed," he said. "And your husband? I thought I might meet him today. Is he not a horse person?" Though how he couldn't be if he was raised among all these beautiful animals he couldn't imagine.

"My husband, Kolton, passed away. We started the therapy program in memory of him," Sarah said, turning away from him and stopping to rub the neck of a beautiful white horse that was nudging her with his head. David stood and watched the two of them as he tried to think of something to say. But what was there to say? She was so young to have lost her husband. He had noticed that she didn't mention anything about her family, but he had assumed that she was just a private person when it came to her home life.

"I'm so sorry, Sarah. I didn't know," he said. It sounded so inadequate.

"It's okay. It's not something I talk about. It's in the past," Sarah said as she continued to talk quietly to the horse in front of her, which seemed to comfort both of them.

"And this, Davey, is Sugar," Jack said as he and David's son walked up behind them making it easy to change the subject from one that he could see made Sarah uncomfortable.

"So she's named Sugar because she's sweet?" Davey asked the older man. David could see the wonder in his son's eyes as he stared up at the large white horse. He'd heard of people getting horse fever and he could understand them now. He was sure it would be easy to fall in love with any one of the animals.

"She's named Sugar because she was the sweetest gift I was ever given," said Sarah. "Do you want to pet her?"

David tensed as Sarah lifted his son up on her hips

and showed him the proper way to touch a horse and explained to him how Sugar liked her neck rubbed in long strokes. He'd been a little apprehensive about bringing Davey around the big horses, but after talking with some of the nurses at work, he'd learned that Sarah had a good reputation for working safely with the patients from the hospital. Still, he'd have to buy Davey a safety helmet if he was going to spend more time here. And from the look on Davey's face, they would be back.

Looking over at the majestic animal, he had to admit he would like to learn more about the horses himself. Maybe this was something the two of them could do together; and Sarah was right, the fresh air was good for children.

"Can I touch her?" he asked Sarah.

She gave him a smile and a nod and he reached out to the horse and rubbed its neck. It was easy to see why his son enjoyed this as the horse leaned her head against him.

"I'm thinking this horse definitely deserves its name. What do you think, Davey?" he asked his son.

"You should see the big black one down there," his son said as he pointed to the other end of the building. "His name is Thunder. Mr. Jack says it's because he makes a really loud noise when he runs. Mr. Jack said I might get to ride him some day when I'm bigger. You want to see him?"

Letting Davey down onto the floor, Sarah explained where they would be and David let his son pull him down to where the large black horse whose temperament seemed to match its name stood with a look that seemed to dare the two of them to come any closer. He knew immediately that he would never be comfortable with his son riding such a big horse. As his son rattled off the names of other horses, they headed out to where Sarah was working with the other children.

"That was great, Ryan. Take him around one more time. Loosen up on the reins a bit," Sarah said as she directed a boy that couldn't have been over ten. "There, you see. She's not fighting against you when the bit's looser."

David leant against a fence and watched her as she took time with each child, making sure they felt comfortable with the horse as well as that the horse felt comfortable with them. He'd learned so much about Sarah today. He had assumed that Sarah was married after she had mentioned that she ran the therapy program with her father-in-law. He'd never imagined that she had lost a husband. Sometimes he forgot that he wasn't the only one who had things in their past that they didn't want to discuss with others.

When Jack returned with a small brown pony, he watched Davey's eyes light up and there was no telling him that he couldn't take a ride around the paddock on him. He pulled out his phone and started a search for a helmet with a good safety rating.

Sarah watched as Jack worked with Davey on the pony he had brought up from the small paddock they had behind the house. She could barely pull her eyes away from the child that looked so much like his father with his dark hair and those beautiful eyes. He had been shy at first, hiding behind his father. Cody had been the same way when he had first met strangers, though like Davey the shyness was short-lived. She couldn't help but smile when the little boy started giggling over something that

Jack had said to him, though inside she felt a sting of pain with the memory of her own son who had loved spending time with his grandfather.

She hadn't been surprised when her father-in-law had been drawn to the small boy. Though Jack rarely showed his grief of losing his only son and the only grandchild he would ever have, she knew that working with the kids from the hospital helped him as much as it did her and the kids. And though smaller than Cody would have been at Davey's age, the boy's excited nature around the horses couldn't help but remind them both of how excited three-year-old Cody had always been when his grandfather had walked him around the stable telling him about all of the horses he would be able to ride once he got bigger. Only Cody had never had the chance to get big enough to ride one of the horses.

"Thanks again, for letting us come," David said. "Davey will be talking about this for a long time."

"I'm glad he's enjoying it. He and Jack seem to be having fun. Let's give them a little more time," she said as she climbed the wood fence that circled the paddock so that she could see the little boy better.

As she had worked with the rest of the kids, she'd given a lot of thought about what she was going to say to David. A part of her desperately wanted to know if there was a possibility that her son's donated heart had been given to his son while another part just wanted to enjoy the day sitting beside David as they watched his son taking his ride. Once the rest of the children had left, she'd decided that taking small steps to see what she could learn would be the best course for now. She knew she was being a coward in not telling David just yet about the chance that Davey had received her son's heart, but she also knew that David was a private man and she couldn't just hit him with that information until she had an idea about how he would take it. She didn't want things to become strange between the two of them. They would still have to work together no matter what she learned about Davey's heart.

And she'd have to tell him about losing Cody and right now watching the healthy little boy that Davey had grown up to be, she didn't want to face the pain of the past. But she could use this opportunity to learn more about Davey.

"I saw Massey in the office with Dr. Benton for her checkup last week. She told me that you were giving her private lessons here?" he asked. She watched as he climbed the fence then slung his own legs across the top board.

"I offer to give all our patients private lessons when they're well enough to take them. She was cleared to start lessons six months after her transplant last year. She's doing really well. Are you thinking about letting Davey take lessons?" she asked. She watched as Davey broke out in laughter again. It was amazing how after everything the little boy had been through, he was still such a happy child. From things David had said she knew that he had worked hard to let Davey live as much of a normal life as possible. She couldn't help but wonder where Davey's mother fit into their life.

"Maybe, someday, but I was thinking maybe it would be good for me to take them first. That way I would know the risks," he said as he joined her in watching his laughing son.

"That would probably be good for you. It might make

you feel better to know how I teach, that is if you want me to teach him."

"It's not that I don't trust you, it's just…" David looked over at her as he rubbed the back of his neck with one hand as he held on to the fence with the other. "Okay, maybe I'm a little protective, but it's not personal. Besides, I can't have my son outdoing me."

"I understand, David," she said. She couldn't help but think of how Kolton had made fun of how protective she had been of Cody around the horses. "I'd be glad to give you some lessons, but I have to tell you that I'm used to teaching kids, not adults."

"The children you teach probably know a lot more than I do about horses. It would probably be good if we just start off with the basics like you would with them," David said.

The two of them sat and watched as Jack explained the parts of the saddle to Davey. He had always liked to start with the basics of horsemanship too.

"Can I ask you a question? You don't have to answer if you don't want to," Sarah said. Now that the two of them knew each other better she was hoping that she wouldn't offend him with one of the questions that had nagged at her from the time she'd learned that David was a single parent.

"Let me guess, you're wondering about Davey's mother." While he didn't seem upset by his comment, she could still tell that it wasn't something he liked to talk about.

"I'm sorry if…"

"It's okay. It's not the first time I've been asked about Lisa. There's not that many single dads raising a child who's had a heart transplant. Questions about my ex are kind of natural. Lisa… She didn't really understand what we were up against at first. I tried to explain it to her, but she…she seemed to think I was making too much of Davey's heart defect. She had this idea that there would be a surgery and then we'd get back to our lives," David said.

"A lot of times that's as far as a parent can think ahead. They're not really ready to deal with the future. They've made plans for their children's lives and then everything changes and their whole world falls apart. It's understandable that it might have taken some time for your wife to understand." Sarah knew only too well how it felt when suddenly your world was upended.

"Once Lisa realized what life with Davey was going to be like, she took off," David said. Anger dripped from every word, but if what he said was true, she couldn't blame him for being angry. How could any woman leave their child when they were the most vulnerable? She could understand why David didn't like to drag out memories of his wife. It had to be painful for him. And here she had been the one to cause him to relive those memories while she hadn't had the courage to share her own with him.

"I'm sorry, I know that couldn't have been easy for you. I know it might seem strange that I'm asking all these questions, it's just that I need to tell you…"

Suddenly Jack and Davey joined them at the fence, chattering animatedly. For a few minutes Sarah had forgotten that the two of them weren't alone. Now a bittersweet feeling filled her as she saw the light in her father-in-law's eyes. A light that had been missing for so long now. She looked down at the little boy at Jack's side. A miniature copy of David.

Jumping down from the fence she and David followed as Davey and Jack headed back to the stables, where Davey insisted on saying goodbye to all the horses individually.

And later as she watched David load a reluctant Davey into his car seat, she found herself pitying the little boy's mother who was missing so much by not being there with her son. She couldn't help but wonder about the woman who had walked away from a man like David. He had everything to offer a woman but somehow it seemed that hadn't been enough for his ex-wife.

And that was the problem when you became too involved in someone's life. Her obsession with knowing if Davey had her son's heart had her becoming more and more involved with David. She needed to mind her own business, but that was hard to do when she felt that her and David's lives had somehow been tied together that night three years ago. Still, she had no business being concerned about David's private life. It wasn't like she was interested in the man, at least not *that* way. She hadn't thought about another man since she lost her husband. She had accepted that that part of her life was over when she had buried her husband and son. There was no reason for her to waste her time thinking of the good-looking doctor. His being married or divorced wasn't important. The only thing she was interested in was learning more about Davey and finding out if he had been the recipient of her son's heart.

A tiny voice inside her head called her a liar, but she refused to listen. She and David had a good relationship as co-workers, and they were becoming friends and that was all the two of them could ever be. How that friendship would fare when he learned that she had been keeping her suspicions concerning his son's heart to herself she didn't know, but she would have to face it soon. She couldn't keep living this way, dodging every opportunity to come clean with David.

She made herself a promise that she would come clean with him the next time they were alone. She would open up to David about everything and somehow the two of them would work through this together.

Sarah walked into the unit early Monday morning to find the nurses rushing around the room of one of the toddlers that she had been involved with assessing for the transplant waiting list several weeks earlier. The eighteen-month-old had been diagnosed with cardiomyopathy are there had been little hope that there would be an available match in time to save him as he had been deteriorating at a faster pace than they had expected. And unfortunately, the little boy had antibodies that they knew would make it even harder to find a donor match. The call that there had been a match found had come unexpectedly and both the staff and the parents were thrilled.

Sarah took a minute to say hi to Tyler's parents then started her examination of the little boy.

"Hey," she heard from behind her. Turning she saw that David had arrived. Dressed in scrubs and with his hair bushed out wildly around his head, he looked as excited as a kid on Christmas morning.

"Hey," she said, relieved that David seemed to be as comfortable with her as he had been before she had started prying into his business.

She introduced David to Tyler's parents as they waited for the operating team to arrive to take the toddler to the operating room.

"How far out is the team?" she asked as she watched Tyler's parents say goodbye. Their fear for their son was almost palpable in the room and she and David stepped out of the room to give the family some privacy.

"They called a few minutes ago and they were loading the plane then. It's an hour flight. They're as surprised as the rest of us that they found a match for Tyler this soon," David said.

She saw David look back into the room. Was he remembering how he had felt the day he had turned his own son over to the operating team as she was remembering the day they had taken her son away to the operating room? She had learned to accept the loss of her son and over the years she had seen many young patients who had survived because of the gift of life another grieving mother and father had helped give, but there were times that the pain refused to stay buried. She would never regret that her son had been able to save other children, but it didn't ease the loss of her son.

They both turned and watched as the OR team arrived and the little boy was taken off on the stretcher. As David left to follow Tyler into the operating room, she watched as the couple began to gather their belongings so they could join the rest of their family in the waiting room.

Sarah, like the rest of the staff on the unit watched the clock constantly for the next few hours. News that the heart had been delivered and the surgery was going well so far filtered down through unofficial channels. As the hours passed and they waited for news that Tyler was coming off the bypass machine, Sarah forced herself to make her rounds. She'd stopped by Jason's room to find the teenager preparing to be discharged home. Unlike the boy she had seen the week before, he now was willing to talk to her as she discussed his post-op care and his need to return for a follow-up appointment.

After checking the clock again when she left Jason's room she turned and headed down to Lindsey's room. She'd checked on the little girl on and off during the weekend and she'd been happy to learn that there had been some improvement in her condition. Opening the door to her room she was greeted with a smiling Lindsey who sat up on her bed playing with a pink unicorn with a long flowing tail.

"Now, that is a pretty horse," Sarah said as she moved some of the child's other toys off the bedside chair so that she could sit down.

"It's a unicorn. My momma brought it for me this weekend," Lindsey said. "Isn't she pretty?"

"She is," Sarah said as she reached over and stroked the long rainbow-colored main. "Maybe we could dye Maple's hair this color."

Lindsey laughed, and then covered her mouth as she coughed. Sarah bent over and listened to her lungs with her stethoscope, then moved back to her chair.

"I'm much better," she said to Sarah. "I told my momma that I might get out of the hospital this week."

Sarah let her hands run through Lindsey's long curls. She hoped that Hannah had been able to see that the child was being overly optimistic. Even with the improvement from the antibiotics she was getting it would be several days before they would move her out of the critical care unit. Lindsey's condition was just too fragile to not take every precaution.

Her phone beeped and she looked down to find a message from Tyler's parents. After she gave Lindsey the promised picture of Maple, Sarah headed down a floor to where Tyler's parents waited in the surgical waiting room.

"Oh, Sarah," Tyler's mother said as she rounded the corner and found both the child's parents standing in the hallway. "They said they would give us an update in an hour but that was over an hour and a half ago and no one has been out. The last update they gave us they said they were almost ready to take Tyler off the bypass machine. Can you find out what's going on?"

"Let's go over here," Sarah said as she led the distraught mother back over to the area of the waiting room where she recognized some of Tyler's other family members.

"I tried to tell her that they were just running a little behind," Tyler's father said reassuringly, though Sarah saw the way the man's hands trembled as he gently rubbed his wife's back.

"Let me go see what I can find out," Sarah said, praying that nothing had gone wrong in the OR.

Before she could turn from the couple, though, she heard the voice of Dr. Benton as he entered the waiting room, David just behind him. The smile on both their faces told her all she needed to know.

As Dr. Benton discussed the surgery with Tyler's parents, Sarah walked over to where David stood.

"So how did it go?" Sarah asked, as the two of them moved away from the group that surrounded Dr. Benton.

"It was amazing," David said, "that moment when we removed the heart was one of the scariest moments of my surgical career so far, but after the new heart was attached and we waited for the new heart to start up...

then that first beat and then another. It was like experiencing a miracle."

"Weren't you?" Sarah asked as she smiled up at him. They headed back to the doctors' workroom where they could start requesting all the lab work and other tests that would need to be done on their newest transplant recipient. Sarah was impressed with the questions David had concerning the care Tyler would receive over the next twenty four hours. She had met many doctors in her years working as a nurse and then as a nurse practitioner and she felt that she had enough experience with both really good doctors and some not-so-good doctors to be able to tell the difference. She was already sure that David would be one of the best doctors due partly to his enthusiasm and partly to the empathy he showed for his patients.

While most of the doctors she had worked with showed their patients and their families' empathy, David had experienced exactly what these families were going through which made him able to help them in ways that other doctors wouldn't understand.

"By the way, I was thinking maybe I could start those riding lessons next week. That is if you have the time," David asked as he set a cup of coffee on the desk in front of her.

They had fallen into a pattern of working together where the two of them ended each day discussing their plans for the next day. She was going to miss this when David finished his time learning the part of the practice that she handled.

"Sure," Sarah said. "How about next Saturday? I'll check with Jack, but if he doesn't have anything scheduled I'm sure he'd be happy to watch Davey for you.

That is if you are okay with that." Her father-in-law had mentioned the young boy several times in the last few days and she knew he had enjoyed the time he's spent with Davey.

"Jack seems like a nice guy," David said. "If you don't mind me asking, does he have any other children?"

Sarah knew that David was being only curious about a man that his son had enjoyed spending time with, but that didn't keep her from feeling the pain that was always present when she discussed her husband.

"Kolton, my husband, was an only child," she said.

"I'm sorry. It's easy to see how good Jack is with kids. He would have made a great grandfather," David said.

This was the opportunity for her to tell David about Cody. If she could get through this maybe she would be able to approach the subject of Davey's donated heart.

Little steps. Just take this little step and everything will be okay.

"He was a great grandfather to our son, Cody. When we lost Cody and Kolton, it was really hard on him," she said.

"Oh, Sarah, I'm so sorry. I didn't know," David said. He reached out and covered her hand with his. A small gesture but somehow it helped ease the pain that always came when she was forced to talk about the loss she had experienced.

"It's not something I talk about. It's hard, you know?" she said. She took a deep breath and forced the air out.

"I'm sorry. I can't imagine what you must have gone through," David said as his hand tightened on hers. "How long ago did this happen?"

"Sometimes it feels like it was a long time ago and others it feels like it was just yesterday, but it was actually just over three years ago January," she said. Would the time ring a bell with him? Was there a possibility that he would put things together without her having to tell him?

"There was an accident, a car accident," she continued. Just that one statement drained her. There was a reason she didn't discuss this with other people. It was still too raw. She wondered if she would ever be able to speak about her son and husband without feeling that way. Her mother had wanted her to go to a counselor, but she hadn't been able to make herself go even after her mother had made an appointment for her.

"I'm sorry, Sarah. And I've sat here telling you how hard it is to live with the emotional rollercoaster of waiting for a heart donor," David said before he withdrew his hand from hers.

She knew David was feeling uncomfortable now, which was another reason for not discussing the loss of her family with others. The conversation always became awkward later.

"If you ever need to talk, just let me know. I can be a good listener," he said, then gave her a small smile before he returned his attention to the computer screen and she knew her chance to tell him everything she needed to was gone.

CHAPTER THREE

DAVID WAS UP early Saturday morning at his son's demand. Davey had been so excited the night before when he learned that they would be going back to see his friend, Jack, that he hadn't been able to sleep. He had gone to bed talking about all the horses he was sure he would get to see the next day, surprising David with all the names of the horses that he remembered.

If David had had any sense he would have waited until that morning to tell his son. Then he would have gotten a good night's sleep. Marking it down as just another lesson learned in the single parent department, he made himself climb out of bed.

There was a slight nervousness in the middle of his stomach as he made breakfast for his son. Was it the excitement of starting something new and spending time around the horses or was it fear of looking a fool in front of Sarah that was making his stomach feel like it was doing summersaults? She made it look so easy when she was up on a horse but with his luck he'd fall off the minute he climbed up on one which would most definitely injure his manly pride along with his backside.

And then there was that strange attraction he felt while watching this new Sarah around the horses, an attraction that shouldn't have been there. They had taken their relationship out of the work environment and with Sarah that felt a little dangerous now. He had no business thinking of Sarah as anything other than a colleague when his life was already full with the new fellowship and taking care of his son. Any kind of relationship other than friendship with Sarah was a complication that he didn't need in his life. His first priority would always be taking care of Davey. Just the time and planning it took to make sure that all his medications were taken on time and all his follow-up appointments were made was a lot more than anyone who hadn't lived with a child with a heart defect would understand. Lisa certainly had never understood.

But wouldn't Sarah?

He picked up the phone to cancel his lesson then looked over to where his son was struggling to get his new cowboy boots on and cancelled the call. He couldn't disappoint Davey. He was reminded of his promise to the little boy when he had lain surrounded by tubes and monitors that the two of them would have a life full of adventure. Even now he had no idea what the future held for his son. He had seen too much already while working with the young transplant patients at the hospital to not know that there was always a chance that Davey could go into rejection or that his new heart could go into heart failure.

He knew all the numbers, the percentages and the years that he could expect for his son to live with his new heart, and he wasn't going to let the two of them miss out on any of the time they had together. Not that he was taking any chances with Davey. He'd already bought a helmet to wear when he was on one of the horses, something that had not made Davey happy as he had insisted that cowboys wore cowboy hats, not helmets. He knew he had made a mistake when he had pulled up a video of a bull rider with a helmet on to show Davey which had set his son into wanting to ride "cows" too.

By the time they had arrived at the horse stables, though, David was sure he had made the right decision. He was taking what was surely just Davey's safety too seriously. Being around the horses had brought more pleasure in his son's life than he'd had in a long time and just watching his son's eyes light up was worth falling off a horse a dozen times. At least that was what he had thought before Sarah had led out a horse much bigger than the one he'd seen the kids riding the last time he had been there.

"It's okay, Daddy, Mr. Jack says Sarah teaches kids all the time."

David looked down to where his son was gently patting his hand, something David had done to him countless times when Davey had been nervous about a procedure, and he smiled down at his son. How had he gotten so lucky to have been given this little boy?

"Come on, Davey. Let's go find someplace where we can watch your daddy," Jack said as he took the boy's hand and they walked out of the stable.

"You do what Mr. Jack tells you, Davey. No running off," David said as he watched them walk away.

"He'll be okay," Sarah said, then turned back to the horse she had brought out for him.

"This is Fancy," Sarah said as she ran her hands over the horse, a movement that seemed to calm the horse. "She's the queen of the farm right now, or at least she thinks so."

"I don't know what makes her a queen, but she is certainly a beautiful horse," David said as he walked up to where Sarah was standing and reached his hand out to touch the stately animal whose coat was solid brown except for her two front feet that were snowy white. Was she what they called a painted horse? He didn't know anything about the different types of horses, something he planned to change by stopping at a bookstore on the way home.

As his hand replaced Sarah's on the horse's neck, Fancy turned her head and looked down at him with a haughty glare that was surely meant to put him in his place.

"I'm not sure she likes me," David said as he slowly removed his hand.

"She's just trying to intimidate you," Sarah said with a laugh. Looking over at her he was once more reminded of how comfortable she appeared here on the farm. It was like she shed her no-nonsense air along with the starched white medical coat she wore at work. Not that she was some stuffed shirt at work. He had been amazed by the way she interacted with the children at the hospital, but here, with the horses, it was like her whole body relaxed. She seemed to have an intimate relationship with each one and he found himself wondering more about her—how she got to be here. Had she always had a love of horses? Or had she married into this family and the horse life?

"Fancy, this is David. He just wants to be your friend," Sarah said as she moved back to the horse and started making some nonsense sounds that seemed to comfort the horse so that the horse stopped giving him the evil eye.

Sarah took David by the hand and then dropped it quickly.

"I'm sorry," Sarah said, a sheepish smile tugged at her lips. "I'm just so used to working with kids."

"Don't apologize," David said. "Please, teach me just the way you would one of your kids. They probably know more about horses than I do right now."

"Okay, then," she said as she took David's hand and placed it under hers. "Every horse has their own way of wanting to be patted. Your job is to watch how the horse responds.

"Fancy here thinks she's above all that patting and scratching. She likes a smooth rub from here—" she placed his hand on the top of the horse's neck "—to here," she said as she brought both of their hands down the horse's neck to where the saddle sat then moved it back up slowly, then down again. They stood there, close together, for what could have been only a minute with their hands joined together, neither talking as they comforted the horse, the only sound their breathing.

As Sarah removed her hand from his, David took a deep breath he hadn't known he needed. His body stirred with an arousal that surprised him. He hadn't responded to the touch of a woman's hand in he didn't know how long.

Okay, this was stupid. He'd asked Sarah to teach him as she would any of her other students, but that didn't mean he had to act like some teenage boy with a crush on his pretty teacher. He wasn't an inexperienced kid. He'd learned the hard way that you couldn't let attraction override your brain. His whole relationship with Lisa had been built on physical attraction and look how that had ended. And he had even more to consider now. He had Davey.

"Well, I think you'll be okay with her now," said Sarah as she stepped back away from him. What exactly had just happened between the two of them? Or had it just been him that had felt that spark of attraction?

She handed him a rope she called the leads and he led the horse out into a small fenced area she referred to as a paddock. As Sarah went on to explain all the parts of the saddle and what their uses were, he wished he had made that stop at the bookstore sooner. He'd make a point to take the time to study before his next lesson.

"Now that Fancy is a little more comfortable with you, I think that you should be safe to mount her," Sarah said as she walked back up to the horse and took hold of the lead rope.

"Safe?" he asked as he swallowed down the dread he had felt earlier that morning. He could already picture himself lying on his backside in the dirt with Sarah standing over him.

"You'll be perfectly safe," Sarah said, then gave him a mischievous smile. "I've never lost a student yet."

David put his leg in the stirrup as she had shown him how to do earlier, then with a leap of faith born from the knowledge that Sarah knew what she was doing, he lifted his other leg over the horse.

"Relax, David. Fancy can smell fear a mile away, relax your seat and take the reins," Sarah said as she handed him the leather straps.

As Sarah explained the use of the reins and the other parts of the bridle, both he and Fancy began to relax and by the end of the lesson he had managed to take the two of them in a circular walk around the yard with Fancy protesting only mildly.

"You did great," Sarah said as they led Fancy out to a bigger paddock.

"Are you talking to me or the horse?" he asked. He felt a bit silly about his first reaction to the horse. He'd had a good time learning how to interact with the beautiful animal.

And it hadn't hurt that he'd had a beautiful teacher too.

He thought of the feeling of her hand on his again. No, that didn't mean a thing. It was strictly male appreciation for a lovely woman and no more.

He looked over to where he'd last seen Davey standing on a small bench outside the paddock and froze.

"Where's Davey?" he asked, not trying to keep the panic out of his voice.

"It's okay. He's with Jack. I saw them walk toward the house. I'm sure they'll be back in just a minute," Sarah said.

He looked down the road where he knew the house had to be. How had Sarah seen Davey leave when he hadn't?

"The lesson isn't over, cowboy, till we put the tack up," Sarah said, trying to get David's attention back to the horse. She knew her father-in-law would never let anything happen to Davey. She hoped that David would know that too. She could see the time away from David was good for Davey and hanging out with Davey was good for Jack too. Not that she could blame David for being so cautious. She was the last person to judge David's parenting. He had been through a lot with Davey and you could see what a wonderful job he was doing with the happy little boy.

Sarah removed the saddle and bridle from Fancy then shut the paddock gate. She watched as the horse headed across the large yard to where a water trough waited for her. Looking over at the man standing beside her, she could see the same look of wonder she'd seen on most of her students after their first lesson. When it came to horses, the beauty and excitement they generated was enough to enchant all ages. Except it hadn't been just David that had been enchanted, for that moment when they had been alone in the stable, their hands touching, their bodies so close, she'd felt as spellbound herself. She'd had to remind herself that she was there to teach David about horses, not flirt with her student. What had gotten into her? This was not how she allowed herself to respond to men. She was a mature widow who had lived without a man in her life for three years now. She had no business responding to one of her colleagues. She'd made sure to keep her distance during the lesson itself, but it still ate at her as David came to stand next to her to watch Fancy as she cantered off to the other side of the fenced yard.

"Let me take that," he said as he reached out for the horse tacking in her hands. As he took the saddle from her she was careful to make sure that she kept her hands away from his, and then she laughed at the ridiculousness of her reactions.

"What?" he asked as he heaved the saddle up on his shoulder as they walked back toward the stable.

"Nothing," she said. She wasn't about to explain how stupid she was acting. She was sure the man had seen more than his quota of women that had fallen all over him. She wasn't going to give him any ideas that she was like those women. Because she wasn't. She had just been being silly about something that she had done with plenty of her students, she just wasn't used to having a man's hands on hers, not anymore at least.

The sight of Jack and Davey coming toward them with her late husband's dog, Pepper, in tow swept away any thoughts she had left of her reaction to David. It was her reaction to Davey that was the problem she needed to concentrate on. Part of her wanted to scoop the little boy up in her arms and hold him close while another part warned her that becoming too involved with the little boy could only lead to heartache when he and his father left Houston after his father's fellowship was complete. And always there was that question in the back of her mind that she found herself wanting to ask. The one question she had no business asking.

Does my son's heart beat in your chest?

Of course she would never ask such a thing of the little boy, she couldn't even come up with a way to approach the subject with David. No, it was best if she just treated this child as the adorable little boy that he was instead of asking herself all of these *what if* questions.

"You two look like you've had fun," she said to Jack and Davey.

"This is Pepper, Daddy, he knows a lot of tricks," Davey said as they all headed back into the stable. "Mr. Jack says it was his son's dog, but his son isn't here anymore because he died and went to heaven."

"I'm very sorry to hear that," David said as he looked over to her and Jack. He rubbed his hand behind his neck and Sarah could see he was worried about her and Jack's feelings with what could be an awkward conversation.

Bending down she petted Pepper. Kolton had gotten the black lab while the two of them had still been in college. Though now more gray than black, the dog was still up for a game of fetch when she had the time.

"I'm sure Kolton would be happy to know a little boy like you was playing with Pepper," she said to Davey then gave the dog a last scratch behind its ear.

"That's what Mr. Jack said," Davey said as he took up the petting of the dog.

"Davey, would you like to help me put some of this tack up?" She held out her arms and showed him the equipment she was carrying. "Jack, can you show David what to do with that saddle?"

As they put away Fancy's equipment, Sarah listened to the little boy talk about the time he had spent with "Mr. Jack." It was plain to see that Davey was enjoying the time he had spent on the farm and she was reminded of all those dreams she and Kolton had for their own son when they'd watched him running around the grounds of the farm. They'd planned to fill their house with children and had looked forward to sharing their love of horses with them. But those dreams had ended in just one second by a driver trying to make it through a yellow light. There wouldn't be children filling her home or running around the farm now. That dream had died with her family. There would be no more children for Sarah. Even if she met a man she wanted to have a relationship with it would never be the same as she had with Kolton. And she would never risk having children again. She wouldn't be able to live with the knowledge that she could lose them at any second. She wasn't even sure what Jack would do with the farm once he was too old to keep it up.

"And then Mr. Jack showed me all the trophies his son had won in the rodeo and he said some of them were yours, too," Davey said as he turned toward her. Sarah blinked. She hadn't thought about those old trophies in years.

"What is that?" David asked as he and Jack joined them again. "You've won trophies?"

"She was a champion barrel racer," Jack said, smiling over at her with pride. "You've never seen anything like the way she could get her horse to respond to her."

"Really? I had no idea you had so many hidden talents," David teased as he looked back over to her.

"It was many years ago." Heat flooded her face, "I haven't raced since I finished college."

Her days of racing were long gone but after Kolton and Cody's death, she had discovered the only place she felt like she was in control was on the back of her horse, far away from people where she could cry and scream and not have to worry about what other people thought of her.

By the time David and Davey had left the farm, Sarah was ready for a good long ride. The tension of being around the little boy and the pain and joy that it brought to see him enjoying himself around the horses had confused her. The thought of all her son would miss made her heart raw with emotion. But Davey's laughter was like a bandage to her soul.

When she and Sugar made it to the back pasture, she let the horse run. It wasn't until they topped the hill that she realized where she had come. Looking down across the field she saw the large white stone and mortar house with its covered windows and locked doors. Hers and Kolton's forever house where they had planned to raise Cody and later his brothers and sisters. Only now her forever family was gone and her dream home was as empty and lonely as she was herself.

She dismounted the horse and sat down on the green grass. There should have been good memories there, memories of all the firsts they had experienced: Cody's first words, first steps and the first night she and Kolton had spent the night making love in that big king size bed that he had insisted they buy. Had she let the pain of their loss steal all the good memories away from her?

The field was full of the new growth of spring. The flowers around the front entrance that she had planted with Kolton would be starting to peak their heads out of their winter beds by now. Soon there would be scarlet sage and hummingbird mint filling the garden. They'd picked the white stone of the house so that the flowers would be showcased against the stark color. They'd spent hours planning everything in the house. It was the only one they'd ever planned to build and they hadn't wanted to have any regrets.

But now she did have regrets. Her life was full of them and she instinctively knew that if she didn't share with David her suspicions as far as her son and his son were concerned that she would just be adding more regrets to her life. She didn't want that for her or for David. She had to find a way to tell him before it was too late.

Sarah stopped in front of Breanna's hospital room door. Inside she could hear someone crying. There were a lot of tears shared on the pediatric cardiac floor, some were happy, but there were a lot of sad tears too. While Sarah wanted to give her patient's family their privacy, she had to see if there was anything she could do to help. She knocked on the door and entered to find the young mother she had met only the week before in a rocking chair crying while her little girl slept surrounded by tubes and machines. Maggie looked up at Sarah as she entered, her face streaked with tears that she was too tired to wipe away. Sarah had once been a young mother all alone waiting at the bedside of her child waiting to see if her son was going to wake up, too tired to hide the sight of her tears from others.

"Hey, Maggie, I just wanted to check on you. Is there anything I can do to help?" Sarah said. "I know all of this is very scary, but I've spoken with the cardiologist and the cardiac surgeon and they say Breanna's doing really well after her surgery."

Maggie looked from her child to Sarah. "I know she's better. She's so pink now, just like a normal baby, but she isn't normal. She's hooked up to all those tubes and I can't even hold her except when the nurses are there to help. I don't even think she knows who I am," Maggie said as she started to cry again. "And I know I should be happy that she's doing so much better, but I just can't help it. It wasn't supposed to be like this. John worked so hard on the nursery and we haven't even been home since I went into labor. And now John's left because he has to go back to work."

Sarah moved over to a chair beside Maggie where she sat hugging herself then wrapped her arms around the young woman. She didn't have the answer to all of Maggie's worries right now, but she could at least give her some company.

"I know it's hard going through all of this, especially now that John is gone, but we are here to help."

"I know," Maggie said as she grabbed a tissue from a half-empty box. "Everyone's been great. It's just I never

dreamed this would happen, you know? You always hear
of things like this happening to other people, but you
never think it could happen to you."

Sarah felt her heart squeeze for a moment. She knew
only too well how it felt when you realize that the horrendous things that happen to other people have happened to you.

"How about we move the rocking chair over to the
crib and I'll help you hold Breanna?"

Sarah left the room after sharing her number and the
number of another mother who lived in the Houston area
whose child had been born with the same congenital defect as Breanna and who was happy to help with other
families. Maggie had promised she would call one of
them if she needed to talk, but Sarah would check back
with her before she left for the day. It was hard for some
people to reach out to others as she well knew.

Speaking with Breanna's nurse, she shared that she
had helped Maggie get Breanna from the crib and the
two of them were doing fine though the nurse would
need to check on them shortly.

Sarah turned to see David talking to another nurse,
before he waved at her and headed her way.

"What's up?" she asked as he joined her on the way
out of the unit.

"I saw you come out of little Breanna's room. Is everything okay?" he asked.

"Breanna's doing great. It's her mother that's a mess
right now. Her husband, John, had to leave to return to
work and she's all alone. Add to that the fears of any new
mother and it's just a lot. She's really worried about losing the bonding time that most mothers get with their

baby. I think we just need to work harder to get her involved with Breanna's care."

The overhead speaker squawked then a monotone voice started to speak. "Code blue, PCIC room ten."

As the speaker repeated the information, the two of them ran back down the hall.

"It's Lindsey," she said to David as they pushed past the rest of the staff. As the charge nurse assigned jobs, she rushed over to the nurse performing compressions on the small chest.

"What happened?" David asked as he moved behind the bed with the respiratory tech and prepared to intubate.

"She suddenly desated down to the sixties. By the time I got in here she was in PEA," the nurse said as one of the patient techs took over the compressions.

"Have you given her any meds?" David asked as he expertly inserted the endotracheal tube with a skill that she would have expected from an older, more experienced doctor.

"Giving epinephrine now," said Mel as she pushed the medication into an IV line.

David moved back and the respiratory tech quickly hooked up the Ambu bag to the ET tube and started squeezing the bag that would force the air into her lungs. Sarah watched as Lindsey's chest began to rise up and down. Checking the monitors she could see that the oxygen saturation was rising.

"It's time for a rhythm check," the charge nurse called out. The room turned silent as they all turned to look at the monitor.

"See if we have a pulse with that," David said as he

checked the carotid and Sarah checked the femoral. She held her breath.

Please let them get this sweet girl back.

Then she felt the weak beat under her fingers that told her that Lindsey was back with them again.

"We have a pulse," David announced to the room. It was as if the room itself let out a deep sigh, then the world returned to normal with everyone talking at once.

Sarah moved with David to check the monitor.

"She's still not oxygenating well," David said.

"She was doing so much better before this respiratory infection. Her heart's just not strong enough to handle the extra work," Sarah said as she started looking through her phone for Lindsey's mother's number.

"Dr. Benton is in the OR. I'm going to call into the room and talk to him. She's a perfect candidate for ECMO," David said as she looked over to where Lindsey lay.

Gone was the laughing little girl who had excitedly shown her the pretty unicorn. Now hooked to even more monitors and drips to keep her sedated she lay still and quiet. Too quiet. Lindsey had always been a fighter, but now it was up to Sarah and the staff to fight for her.

"You go talk to Dr. Benton. I'm going to call her mother," she said.

"She should've been here. Doesn't she realize how sick her child is? We'll need her to consent to take Lindsey into the OR."

"She's probably at work. I have the number. I'll get her here even if I have to go get her myself," Sarah said as she started going through the contacts on her phone.

"If she can't do any better than this, how is she going

to do when her daughter gets a transplant?" David said angrily before he walked out of the room.

As Sarah began to go through the numbers she had listed for Lindsey's mother, she wondered why David, who was usually so patient with his patients' parents, seemed to have none for the single mom. Sarah knew that David was just concerned about Lindsey, but he had to understand that Hannah, like Breanna's father, had to go to work to make a living to support both herself and her daughter. Although Sarah had to admit that it seemed that Hannah had been spending less time than usual with Lindsey. There was definitely something going on with Hannah and she planned to find out what it was before things went any further. If the mother needed their help she wanted to know. No one should have to go it alone in a situation like this. Only David himself had once done just that.

CHAPTER FOUR

SARAH STAYED IN the waiting room with Hannah while Dr. Benton and David took Lindsey back to the operating room to insert the needed catheters to start the child on the ECMO system that would help her heart and lungs rest while she recovered from the respiratory infection that was making her already failing heart work harder than it could.

The doctors had explained to Hannah that Lindsey had stopped breathing, causing her heart to quit pumping, and that even though they had gotten her heart beating again they couldn't promise that she wouldn't arrest again and that this was the best hope she had to recover.

Now they both waited together, a young mother who was barely holding it together and Sarah who had let her heart become involved with another child who she could lose. Sarah cared for all the children that she took care of in the hospital, but Lindsey was special. The girl had a passion for life and had fought her way through every trial her failing heart had given her. Sarah had shared her love of horses with Lindsey and hadn't been surprised to find that the girl had quickly made friends of all the horses in the stable, which reminded her of another child, a little dark-haired boy who was quickly becoming a favorite around the stable and finding a way into her heart.

For years she had protected her heart from the pain of losing another child she loved and now she sat here knowing that she was dangerously close to knowing that pain again. Only neither child belonged to her. She had to remember that. Right now what she needed to be doing was helping Lindsey's mother as much as possible.

"Hannah, is there anyone you want me to call?" she asked. As far as Sarah could remember there had never been anyone except for Hannah visiting Lindsey.

"No, thank you," Hannah said as she pulled at the cuffs of her sleeves.

"Are you cold? I can get you a warm blanket. These waiting rooms are always too cold," Sarah offered, then looked back over at the young woman who stared at the entrance to the waiting room as if in a trance. Reaching for Hannah's hand she squeezed it.

"It's okay, Hannah. You're not alone," Sarah said as they sat there with their hands joined as they waited for news of Lindsey's condition.

Moments later David and a very tired-looking Dr. Benton came into the waiting room.

"She made it through," Dr. Benton said, taking a seat next to Hannah.

Sarah stood and left as Dr. Benton explained the plan they had for Lindsey's care to her mother.

"I know that this was the best thing for Lindsey right now, but do you think her heart will be strong enough after she gets over this respiratory issue to come off the machine?" she asked David.

David rubbed the back of his neck, something that she was beginning to notice he did often when he was worried which didn't make her feel any better about Lindsey's chances.

"To be honest, I don't know. We discussed it before we spoke with Hannah and we all agreed that it was the only choice we had right now. If her lungs get better she'll have a much better chance. Dr. Benton's going to see about getting her moved up on the transplant list as soon as she starts turning around. Till then, we let her rest and we hit her with everything we have to wipe out this infection," said David as he rubbed the back of his neck again. "I wish I knew something else to do, but for now we just have to wait."

It seemed to Sarah that Lindsey had been waiting most of her life for a chance to live a normal existence, instead of one that was spent having one medical procedure after another, being in and out of the hospital, and never getting to be the little girl that she deserved a chance to be. Sarah knew life didn't always work the way it was planned. Her own life was proof of that, but she had to believe that Lindsey would someday have the life that she deserved. She just needed to hang in there until a heart could be found for her. Until then all they could do was wait.

Sarah watched as David once again tangled the reins as he tried to apply the bridle. She held back a laugh when Fancy turned and gave him one of her haughty looks that plainly said she wasn't impressed. David had arrived with a new air of confidence until Sarah had told him that he would be tacking his own horse that day. It might have been that distraction that had made him agree for Jack to take Davey up to the house to see one of the smaller ponies; though it hadn't been enough for him to not insist that they come back as soon as they finished. She had expected her father-in-law to balk at that instruction, but Jack seemed to understand that David wasn't trying to be rude. He just felt the need to watch over his son a little more than the normal parent.

"It looked so easy in the book. I don't understand what I'm doing wrong," he said as he let go of the tangled reins and moved away from the horse.

Jumping down from the gate she had been sitting on, Sarah reached out and took the bridle from him and once more showed him how to make sure that it didn't tangle with the other straps. Taking pity on all three of them, she finished putting on the bridle. With the bit safely in Fancy's mouth, she handed the reins to David and mounted Sugar.

"Come on, let's go have some fun," Sarah said as she made a clicking sound with her tongue and started across to where she'd opened the gate to a large pasture. After a minute of a very one-sided conversation, Fancy decided she'd let David follow behind Sarah.

"Remember feet all the way in the stirrup, turned in like you're hugging Fancy with your legs," she said as she rode up to him then reached over and placed her hands on his lower back and abdomen.

"Shoulders back and back straight," she said as felt his abdomen tighten under her hand. She ran her other hand up his back to his shoulders.

"There. That's perfect," she said, then cleared her throat as she moved her hands away from him. Why did this have to be so awkward? She was just trying to teach him the correct way to sit. There was no reason for it to feel so intimate every time they touched. She whipped

Sugar around so that he couldn't see her face and waited for him and Fancy to catch up with her.

For a minute there was only silence between the two of them.

"This is beautiful," he said as they reached the end of the pasture then turned around to face the stretch of green they had just ridden across and the white stables beyond that. "You must love living here."

There had been a time when the answer to that would have come easily. She had grown up not far south of Houston on a much smaller farm where her father and brother raised cattle, so she'd felt right at home after she had married Kolton and they'd moved to the farm to live with Jack. It had been a busy time in their life with Kolton starting his first job after he had graduated with an architect degree and her starting her first job as a nurse. They'd both come home exhausted but excited about their new lives together. They'd been married a year when Jack had given them the land to build their own home, declaring that the house was just too small for the three of them though they both had known Jack was trying to push them out the door so that they could start a family.

After Kolton and Cody were gone she'd known that she could never live in the house that had been so full of promises. She'd planned to move back to the city until Jack had invited her to move back in with him. She couldn't have said no to the man who she had come to love as a second father who was hurting as much as she was.

"It is beautiful," she said, thinking of the house that lay just over the next hill.

"I'm sorry. I didn't think," David said as he began

rubbing a hand down Fancy's neck. "You lived here with your husband and son?"

"Yes," she said as she climbed down and looked back away from the pasture to where the woods hid the home the three of them had shared. "We made a life here together. It was all we ever wanted. Kolton was just as horse crazy as I am and we couldn't think of a better place to raise our family. But that part of my life is gone now."

David dismounted, being careful to hold Fancy's reins as Sarah had taught him so that he could still control her. He could tell that Sarah needed to talk to someone about the loss she'd suffered. She was still holding so much pain inside of her that it couldn't be good for her.

"I don't talk about my ex-wife or my divorce either. Not that I'm comparing the two. But sometimes I do wish I could talk about it. It's like by keeping it inside I don't have to deal with it, but I know that's not healthy," he said as they both started walking across the field.

"You can talk to me," Sarah said as she looked over at him, "if you want to, that is."

Surprisingly, he found that he did want to talk to her. If anyone would understand the stress a new baby—a sick new baby—could put on a marriage, she could. She dealt with not only the young patients they saw, but also their parents.

"When Davey was born with a heart defect we didn't know what to expect. By the time he was two he'd had four surgeries. He went on the transplant waiting list after the last one."

"A lot of marriages have trouble when they have a

chronically sick child. You know that," said Sarah. "Did your wife have any medical experience?"

The only thing Lisa had experience with had been manipulating men, though he hadn't known that until it was too late. The woman had made a fool of him long before Davey had been born. He could have forgiven her that, but he would never forgive her for running out on their son when he had needed them the most. A part of him had known from the beginning Lisa didn't have it in her to accept what life with Davey would mean, but he had hoped that for the sake of his son that she would be able to change.

"No. Lisa blamed a lot of her problems with dealing with Davey on the fact that he was always sick. She even blamed the time he spent in the hospital for the reason she hadn't bonded with him." He remembered the anger he had felt at that remark.

"She finally decided that she didn't have the time for a sick child like Davey in her life and then she was gone. Davey seldom mentions his mother, but then why would he when he hasn't seen her since his second birthday when she had arrived expecting a birthday party to only find Davey back in the hospital." And instead of staying with their son till he was well enough to leave the hospital she'd laid a fancy wrapped present on the bed and left.

"Are you afraid that she'll come back one day and want to be part of Davey's life?" Sarah asked.

She unexpectedly reached for his hand then squeezed it. When she began to pull it away, he held it tighter. He had started this conversation to help Sarah be able to talk to him, to help her deal with the pain that he suspected was holding her back from moving on with her life, but here she was helping him instead. Holding her warm hand in his seemed to ease the pain and anger that he felt whenever he talked about his ex-wife.

"A part of me is afraid she'll come back and another part of me is afraid that she won't. Davey deserves to have a mother in his life." Right now all he knew was having a father, but someday that little boy would ask him why his mother wasn't there and he didn't know what he'd say to him.

As they neared the paddock, David was surprised to see his son sitting on top of a squat pony being led by Jack. He dropped Sarah's hand before they got closer. It wouldn't do for either Jack or Davey to get the wrong idea about their relationship.

"Daddy, look at me," Davey said as they got closer. "Look Miss Sarah, I'm riding just like my daddy."

"I see," Sarah said as they both stopped.

"The boy's a natural and Humphrey needed some exercise. I hope you don't mind," Jack said.

David started to assure the older man that he didn't have a problem with Davey on the pony when he realized that Jack hadn't been talking to him. It was Sarah that he'd wanted to make sure was okay that Davey was riding. Did her father-in-law think that Sarah didn't trust him with Davey? But that didn't make any sense at all.

"It's fine, Jack. Humphrey is perfect for Davey right now," she said, then turned away and went inside the building.

Then it hit him. Humphrey must have been her son's horse. How old had the child been? The pony was a good fit for Davey partly because he was much smaller than most of the children his age. Had her son been younger?

There were so many questions he had and none of them were his business he reminded himself.

"He was your son's pony? I'll understand if you don't want Davey on him, again," he assured her, though right now he wasn't sure how he would be able to talk his son off the pony.

"It's fine," she said as she looked back over at him. "I mean it. Let's get this tack up and I'll show you the proper way to brush out a horse." A small smile crossed her lips, but it didn't reach her eyes.

They worked in silence till they were joined by Davey and Jack.

"That was the best!" said Davey as he led the small pony inside with Jack walking beside him. "And Mr. Jack says I can take him back to the house and tackle him."

"I think he meant that you could put up his tack—that's the saddle and reins, like me and your dad are doing here," Sarah said as the three adults laughed at his son's expression. This time he was relieved to see that her smile touched her eyes.

"Okay. He said I could do that tack thing and then we're going to eat some beans like the cowboys used to do," Davey said, then smiled at Jack. David had never gotten that reaction from his son when he'd tried to get him to eat his beans.

"I said we'd have to ask your dad, Davey," Jack said as he rubbed the top of Davey's head affectionately.

"Ah…" David looked at Sarah, obviously not sure how she would feel having the two of them suddenly to dinner.

"That sounds like an excellent plan," she said as she took the pony's lead in one hand and his son's hand in the other and started down the road that led to the house.

* * *

That night Sarah was unable to sleep, struggling with the knowledge that she hadn't taken her chance to tell David about her suspicions. That Davey had been given her son's donated heart the night she had seen him in the waiting room. She'd had the perfect moment when they had been alone on the horses, but then David had brought up the subject of his ex-wife and she couldn't deny that she was curious about what had happened between the two of them. Once again, he had shared more of himself than she had. It only made the guilt of keeping everything from him worse.

When Jack had invited the two back to the house for dinner, she had felt herself being drawn in even more by the charming little boy. And then there had been the question that always ate at her when she was around the little boy.

Does some part of my Cody still live on in you?

She found herself wanting to hug the little boy to her and to rest her head on his chest just to listen to the beating of his heart.

She knew she should have come clean with David the first time she had met him and realized who he was.

But she hadn't been ready to deal with the possibility herself. Only now that she had waited till she was ready, she was afraid that David would be angry with her for not sharing this earlier.

She'd finally fallen asleep after she had come to the decision to share what she knew with David as soon as possible and let him decide if he wanted to learn the truth. Only when she awoke the old doubts were back. What if David didn't want to know his son's donor family? There was a reason why Organ Procurement didn't allow them to communicate unless both parties were in agreement. And what if he decided not to bring Davey to the ranch anymore? She hadn't seen Jack enjoy himself as much as he did with Davey after his son and grandson had been killed, and Jack didn't even know yet about the circumstances of Davey's heart transplant.

Arriving at the hospital early, she wanted to spend some time with Lindsey before she started her regular rounds. She'd gotten a message from the cardiopulmonary perfusionist that they had decreased the sedation that morning and that Lindsey was responsive. Entering the room, she was overwhelmed by the amount of machinery that was keeping such a little girl alive. A cacophony of beeps, clicks and occasionally a high-pitched alarm greeted her. In among all the machines she was surprised to see Hannah sitting in a small chair at the side of the bed asleep with her head resting next to her daughter. Trying not to wake her, Sarah spoke quietly to one of the nurses that was assigned to keep all the machines working properly as another nurse continually monitored Lindsey.

"How is she?" she asked Jose, who sat the farthest away from the sleeping mom.

"She's holding on. She got too anxious when she saw her mom so we had to increase the sedation again," he said.

Sarah left the room and headed for the doctors' workroom where hopefully someone had started a large pot of coffee. She'd need the caffeine. Sleepless nights were not something that she could afford to have when she was dealing with critically ill patients and their families. The doctors she worked with depended on her to keep her eyes and ears open for anything that could go wrong with their patients and right then her eyes were not cooperating.

She'd finished her second cup and had reviewed several of her patients' new lab work by the time David and Dr. Benton showed up.

"We just left Lindsey," David said as he poured himself a cup.

"I just checked this morning's X-rays and there is some improvement," she said as she pulled them up on her computer. David bent over her as they both reviewed the newest film that showed a small amount of improvement in her lungs. As he reached around her to point at a whited-out part on her right lung, Sarah found herself tensing as the warm heat of his body surrounded her.

At once she was overcome with a desire to curl up inside the arms that encased her. The need to be held and loved filled her body making it difficult to breathe, to think. Surprised by the deep longing that almost had her turning into David's arms, she pushed away from the desk forcing him to step back away from her.

What was wrong with her? It wasn't like the man had been making a pass at her. Thankfully he hadn't seemed to notice her reaction to his closeness. It had to be the guilt of holding back the information about her son that was making her feel so uncomfortable around him. That was it. All she had to do was have a conversation with him and all these uncomfortable feelings would go away.

"David, if you have a minute—" she looked over to where Dr. Benton was working on his own computer "—I need to talk to you."

"We've got a few minutes before we head back to surgery," he said as he took the seat beside her. "What's wrong? Is there something else about Lindsey?"

"No, it doesn't have anything to do with work. It's something else I need to tell you," she looked back over at Dr. Benton hoping that he would take the hint that she didn't want to talk in front of the other MD. David's eyes followed hers and then he seemed to understand.

"If it's about Davey and the pony, you don't need to worry about it. You know how children are, he'll have forgotten about him in a day or two. Next time we're at the ranch he'll fall in love with another animal," he said. "Actually I wanted to talk to you. Dr. Benton has offered to let me take his place at the UNOS conference in Dallas this weekend so I'm going to have to cancel my next lesson."

David was going to the conference instead of Dr. Benton? That meant that they'd be there together. "I'd meant to cancel the lesson myself as I'm going to be out of town at the conference too."

"I'm sorry, Sarah," Dr. Benton said from behind her. "I meant to tell you I was going to have to cancel. The wife is insistent that I stay in town till the next grandchild is born, though between the three of us I'd much rather be at the conference. I hate all that waiting in the waiting rooms. It seemed a shame to waste the registration fee and it's a great chance for David to meet some of the board members."

"What about Davey?" she asked. She was torn between hoping that she would finally have a good opportunity to talk to David about her son and concerned about being alone with the man after the way her body had just reacted to his.

"His nanny has agreed to stay over. Ms. Duggar's a retired nurse and is great with him. I'll have all his medications ready for her with a timer set and I can be back in an hour by plane if I need to be," David said as he raised one of his hands toward the back of his neck.

"I'm sure he'll be fine," she said. It had to be hard to leave his son alone in a new city, especially after all that Davey had been through and how protective he was of his son. Though she should probably do Ms. Duggar a favor and have a talk with David, she knew by watching him with Davey and Jack at the ranch that he could be a little overprotective.

"So it's settled," Dr. Benton said as he started back toward the door. "It's a very informative conference and the two of you will have a great time."

"Oh, wait," David said. "You said you wanted to talk to me. What's up?"

"It's nothing that can't wait till later," she said. It had waited this long, after all.

"How about we share a ride? I know you had been planning on riding with Dr. Benton to Dallas. We can talk then," David said.

"Sure," she said, then watched as the two men headed back to the surgical department. For the first time that day she felt as if she was free to relax. She'd been given a reprieve from having to come clean with David, at least for a few days. She would clear the air between them. She'd come clean about the night that she had seen him in the waiting room and her son's donation. By the time they returned from Dallas everything would be settled as far as whether they wanted to find out about their donor and recipient relationship or not and she'd be able to move on from there. There would be no more of these pangs of guilt or the butterflies when she was around David. They would be able to return to the comfortable friendship that they had enjoyed earlier.

CHAPTER FIVE

By THE TIME the two of them had set out for Dallas, David and Sarah both had put in a full day at the hospital. Lindsey had improved to the point that some of the sedation was being weaned down and her lungs had improved enough that Dr. Benton had called a meeting of the whole transplant team from the social worker to the cardiologist so that they could all work together to make a case on why Lindsey needed to be moved to the top of the transplant list at this time.

It had fascinated him to see all the parts of the team work together. It reminded him that it had once been his son's case that had been discussed at length while he waited for the outcome. What if they hadn't agreed to ask to move Davey up on the transplant list? It had been a miracle that a heart had become available when it did.

"He'll be okay," Sarah said from the passenger seat next to him.

"It shows, huh?" David said as he rubbed at the back of his neck.

"A bit," she said with a mysterious laugh.

"What's so funny?" he asked. Did she find the fact that he was worried about his son funny? He sure didn't think so. "It's the first time we've been separated like this."

He opened his mouth to say something about her not understanding, and then stopped. He had no idea what had happened to her son and husband. If he had learned anything in the few years that he had worked in the medical field, he had learned to appreciate the fact that there was always someone out there who was going through more than you. He had no right to assume that his path with his son had been harder than the path she had taken with hers. He still had Davey but her son was lost to her forever.

"You don't realize, do you?" she asked.

"Okay, tell me. What is it?" he asked. He couldn't help but smile at the playfulness in her voice.

"I don't think I should," she said. "It would just make it worse if you knew you were doing it."

"Doing what?" he asked. He wasn't doing anything except driving. He looked over at Sarah where she sat curled up in the seat next to him looking more relaxed than she had all week.

"It's just that you have this telling sign when you're worried. Hasn't anyone ever told you?" she asked.

What was she talking about? He looked back from the road to her. "You're kidding right?" he asked as he returned his eyes to the road. Traffic on I-45 was beginning to get heavy.

"No. I can't believe no one's ever told you. I would have thought at least your wife—I mean ex-wife—would have mentioned it," she said.

"Lisa? She had a tendency to be more wrapped up in herself," he said.

"I'm curious. Where did you meet her?"

"I met Lisa in medical school at Tulane, a year before I was supposed to graduate," he said. He rubbed the back of his neck again then turned toward Sarah to see her lips curve up into a smile. What was with the woman today?

"But you said she wasn't clinical," Sarah said.

"She was an art history major, with a couple minors I can't remember now, but no she didn't want anything to do with the medical field," he said. "She was smart and pretty and before I knew it was happening we were moving in together."

He remembered that first day when they'd moved into one of the small shotgun houses in the not-quite-respectable part of New Orleans. While not happy with the location, Lisa had been thrilled with the architectural details of the old house.

"It wasn't till later that I realized I had given Lisa the wrong idea about my situation." He'd never dreamed that she had assumed that he had a well-off family bankrolling him through college just because he drove a vintage sports car that he and his dad had fixed up. "It's silly really. I should have seen the signs, but I guess no one wants to think that someone is only interested in their bank account. By the time she figured out that the only thing I was going to have when I finished school was several hundred thousand dollars of tuition debt, she was pregnant with Davey."

"I'm sorry. You must have felt hurt," Sarah said.

The sun had begun to set and the shadows were beginning to fill the car as they drove in silence for a few minutes.

"I don't remember to be honest. I was so busy with school and getting my residency set up that I really didn't have the time to feel much of anything. By the time Davey was born I was deep in my last year of medical school." His whole life had revolved around his education until Davey.

"By the time we discovered that something was wrong with Davey, our marriage was already a mess. Lisa made it clear from the beginning that she wasn't willing to wait around until I got established to have all the things she wanted. She had a certain lifestyle planned for herself and I don't think me and Davey had a place in it. I came home one day to find her packing, with a woman I had never met in the house taking care of Davey. He'd had his first operation by then and we had him on a strict schedule with his medication. I couldn't believe that she was just going to leave him. I mean what kind of mother does that?" He didn't give Sarah a chance to respond. What was there really for her to say that he hadn't already said himself?

"It seemed that while our son was recovering from cardiac surgery, his mother had been job hunting via the internet and had taken up an online relationship with a very well-off art gallery owner. So while I'd been at work, thinking that she was taking care of our son, she'd been planning a new life with a French guy named Marchard. He had the status and money that Lisa wanted and that was all that was important to her. A month later the divorce papers showed up. She didn't even file for visitation rights with Davey."

The car was quiet when he finished. Filled with his anger for the way Lisa had treated their son. It had been years since she had left them. How long was he going to let it affect him?

"I don't want you to think that I resent raising Davey by myself," he said. "I don't."

"I'd never think that. The way you've managed to care

for Davey is amazing. It's plain to see how much you love that little boy," Sarah said. "What will you do if she comes back and wants Davey?" asked Sarah.

"I'll never let that happen. I promised Davey when he was waiting for a heart that it would always be just the two of us together. I'd never let someone break us up."

He had done all the talking and now Sarah knew all of his past. Maybe she would be ready to share some of her past with him. "What about you? Where did you meet your husband?" he asked.

"The rodeo community isn't as large as you would think. It seems as if we had known each other forever. We started dating in high school and were married before we graduated from college," she said. Only the interior lights lit the car now, but he could see that she hadn't turned away from him as she had at other times when she'd discussed her family.

"So it was a good marriage?" he asked, surprised by the small tinge of jealousy that filled him.

"It was a very good marriage," she said. "We both had goals for our careers and of course we both loved horses. By the time we were married we had become best friends."

"I'm glad. I know you didn't have a lot of time together, but at least it was good." He knew he had gone too far when she moved farther to the other side of her seat and then she surprised him.

"Would you ever consider getting married again?" she asked.

"I don't know. I really don't think much about it. Right now my first priority is Davey. I have to put him before everything. What about you?"

"No," Sarah answered as they arrived at the convention hotel. Somehow the answer didn't surprise him. Sarah was willing to give everything of herself to the people she cared for but it seemed to him that she didn't ask much for herself.

"Don't think that I've forgotten that you still haven't answered my question about what this *telling* sign I have is when I'm worried," he said, changing the subject, as he opened his car door.

As the valet opened the door for Sarah, she reached over and rubbed her hand up the back of his neck, the motion taking his breath away as she moved even closer, till all he could see was the smile on her all too kissable lips.

"This," she said, then climbed out of the car to help with the luggage that the bellboy had begun unpacking.

David reached his hand to the back of his head where she had touched him, then pulled it back. What did you know, the woman was right, he did have a telling sign when he was nervous. And being this close to Sarah was making him very nervous.

David was trying to listen to what Sarah was saying, but he kept being drawn back to the flickering light of the candles as it reflected off her deep brown eyes. Her touch the night before had caused something in him to go haywire. When he should have been taking in all the information in the seminars today, his mind had continually wandered back to that touch, that smile that had lit something inside him, which he was having a problem understanding. Now he sat here like a wide-eyed sap.

His only consolation was that Sarah didn't seemed to have noticed. He knew she had no idea how beautiful she looked tonight dressed in a violet dress with her hair left down to fall past her shoulders. She wasn't a classic beauty like Lisa. No, Sarah's beauty was deeper. It was those deep brown eyes that lit up when she talked about the kids at the hospital or the horses at the farm. Her smile was infectious and the compassion she showed for the parents she dealt with showed him that she was as beautiful on the inside as she was on the outside.

They'd both been required to dress up tonight as one of the organ procurement vendors was hosting a special dinner for the attendees and now that all the ceremonies for the night were finally over and the others from their table had left to mingle, the two of them were alone. Leaving a sense of intimacy that reminded him of the time they'd shared in the dark car driving into Dallas.

But there was something different tonight. Whether it was the atmosphere or just the change their relationship seemed to be going through, he didn't know, but he was becoming more aware of Sarah as a woman then as a co-worker, a very attractive woman who had his body reacting in ways that it hadn't in years.

"What about you?" she asked as she finished informing him about the last seminar she had attended that afternoon, a talk by a group of doctors that were involved in a new research program that hoped to help them determine which chemotherapy drug was the right medicine for their patients' specific cancer. He should have found it fascinating. He did find it fascinating; he just found this woman in the short violet dress more fascinating.

"David?" she asked again as she reached over and took his hand. "Are you okay?"

He looked down to where her hand lay over his. This intimate touch should have bothered him as he wasn't one of those touchy-feely people, but it didn't. Something had changed between the two of them in the past weeks. That was the only way he could explain why he would have bared all the unpleasantness of his marriage, of the hurt he had felt of not being enough, of him and Davey not being enough for the wife who had carelessly left the two of them.

"Why don't you call and check on him?" she asked as she moved her face close to his trying to get his attention. It was the closeness of her lips that brought him to his senses.

"Call who?" he asked, then realized there was only one person that he needed to check on. "I called before he ate his supper to make sure his medicine was given on time. I'm going to call back at bedtime. I've set an alarm."

"So, what do you think of the conference? What did you find out at that statistics seminar as far as this year's numbers?" she asked as she pulled her hand away from his.

"Basically what we all know. The need is great and though the numbers of donations have been rising, there's still a shortage," he said. "I did run into someone from our local procurement office, I think her name is Heather."

"Yes, Heather Long. She's great isn't she," Sarah said as she looked out over the room at the other attendees as if to locate the woman.

"She seems to be. We had a moment to discuss some of the patients we have listed right now and she seemed to think that we should be able to get Lindsey moved up once she stabilizes. Not that it will make much of a difference if we don't get a donation match soon," he said, then glanced back down at his watch. "What are your plans for tomorrow?"

"I'm attending the forum on donor and recipient relationships and privacy," she said, as once more she looked away from him and scanned the other people in the room. "I'm really looking forward to it. Do you want to go with me?" she asked though she still seemed to be looking over his shoulder.

He glanced back over his shoulder and wondered what it was now that had *her* preoccupied, then turned back to see her eyes had now returned to him. Was she feeling that same strange sense that something was changing between the two of them? Was that what seemed to be making her uncomfortable now?

"I promised Heather I'd attend her talk on how to create a closer community relationship between the local hospitals and the organ procurement programs," he said.

"Oh, okay," she said. He could tell she was disappointed, though he wasn't sure why.

"I thought maybe you'd be interested. You know, because of Davey," she said. She was back to looking past him again. "Do you ever wonder about the donor?"

"I do, sometimes. It's strange. I mean at first I was really busy taking care of Davey, but it was still there in the back of my mind. It's almost like a survivor's guilt. You know when you get a transplant of any kind, unless it's a living transplant of course, that someone lost someone that they loved very much and because of their loss, now someone that you love very much has a chance at life." Just talking about receiving the gift of donation, the gift of another one's child, tore at his heart. How had Sarah managed to live through losing her son as well as her husband?

"I remember one of those first nights after Davey's transplant I was just watching him sleep, just watching how much more comfortable he breathed and marveling at how fast his pale gray cheeks had turned a healthy pink after his surgery. It must have been about two or three days post-op and I couldn't help wondering if somewhere there was another family standing over a casket where their child now lay," he said. He looked up and saw the color blanch from Sarah's face.

"I'm sorry. I know that must sound a bit morbid," he said, relieved when he saw that the color was returning to her face.

"No. I appreciate you sharing that with me," she said, though he noticed the excitement she had shown for the next day seemed to have faded. "Have you ever thought of contacting them?"

He thought for a minute about those first few days and of the guilt he had felt. Had he ever considered contacting his son's donor's family? "No, I guess I always figured that if the donor wanted to contact me I would hear from them. I wouldn't want to cause them any more pain. I really haven't given it as much thought as I should have, I guess."

"Maybe they thought the same way you did," she said her voice a soft whisper across the table.

His phone beeped an alarm and after giving Sarah an apologetic shrug, he made his evening call to Davey. As always his son's happy voice made him feel better and calmed the fears that he always suffered from when he was away from his son. He could be accused of not thinking anyone could care for his son as well as he could and he wouldn't argue with that. He'd spent hours learning the best way to give Davey his medications, how to tell when he wasn't feeling well, what to look for if he ever started going into heart rejection. But after saying goodbye three times and then having a short conversation with Ms. Duggar who assured him that Davey's voice was not scratchy sounding just tired from playing rodeo that day, he had ended the call feeling satisfied.

He noticed that the crowd had been clearing out as he'd been on the phone and Sarah was alone, lost in her own thoughts now.

"I guess we better leave before they shut the doors on us," he said as the wait staff started cleaning off their table. Then he added, "What about tomorrow after the forums we take in some of the sights? I've never been to Dallas."

He didn't want the evening to end while Sarah appeared so unhappy.

"I was thinking about going over to Fort Worth, it's only a half hour away. The weather is supposed to be nice and they have a beautiful park that's made up of water gardens. I went there with a group from school one day," she said, smiling now presumably from an old memory. And if a walk in a park was what would keep that smile on her face, a walk in the park was what they would do.

"I think you'll like it and if we have time we could visit the stockyards. It's more of a tourist place now, but it does have a very colorful history."

"Then it's a date. I mean—" He stumbled over the words. "It's a plan."

Sarah was next to David as they walked to their rooms. For weeks, she'd wanted to know how David would feel about learning that the donation of Davey's heart could have come from her son, Cody, and even after their conversation tonight she had no idea how he would take the news. Would he be angry that she hadn't told him earlier? She knew that was a possibility that he could feel that she was being untruthful by holding back the information she had. She'd have to explain to him that it had taken time for her to come to terms with the possibility herself. If anyone would understand the mixed feelings she felt, he would. He'd admitted himself that he wasn't comfortable trying to approach the donor's family.

"Are you okay?" David asked her as they stopped at her door.

"I'm fine. It's been a long day," she said as she inserted her key card and opened the door to her room. "I'll see you at noon? Downstairs after the forums?"

"That sounds great," he said as he looked up and then down the hall. "I'll wait for you to lock the door."

"Okay, good night," she said, then shut the door and latched it.

It had been a long time since someone had worried about her safety, not that she didn't feel safe when Jack was around. The man had a shotgun that could take down any rattlesnake or intruder. And it wasn't as if she couldn't take care of herself—Jack wasn't the only one who knew how to shoot that shotgun. But it was kind of nice to have someone care about her.

David was that kind of man. He wouldn't be as good of a doctor as he was if he didn't care about his patients. And she had never seen a more caring father. It was only to be expected that he would care for his friends.

Just friends, she reminded herself. He had taken her hand while they'd left the dinner with the rest of the crowd. A crowd that had threatened to separate the two of them, and it had made her feel an excitement that she hadn't felt in years. There had been no one since Kolton whose touch had affected her the way David's touch did. There had been a few men that had asked her out over the last couple of years, but she'd never been tempted by any of them.

We're just friends...we can be only friends, she reminded herself again as she fell asleep.

CHAPTER SIX

THEY DECIDED TO hit the stockyards first as they both wanted to eat at a small barbeque shop there that Sarah had looked up online. They ate their sandwiches and toured the museum before heading outside to watch the daily cattle drive of longhorn steers.

"I love the longhorn steers. Aren't they pretty?" Sarah asked.

"They're awful big and those horns are massive, but I don't think pretty is the right thing to call something that could trample you to death in seconds," David said as he moved closer to hear over the noise of the animals as they were herded in front of them.

"Davey would love it here," she said, though she could see the doubt in his eyes.

"He'd love it, all right. I'd be chasing after him while he chased those steers down the road. He's taken a big interest in the rodeo since I started taking lessons."

"Jack once told me that Kolton was in love with the rodeo by the time he was three, so Davey's a little bit of a late starter." They moved off the main road and followed the walkway that let by the specialty shops. "Hey, I want to look in here for a belt buckle for Jack. It's his birthday next month."

As she paid for the oversized silver and golden buckle with the Texas flag displayed on it, she saw David pick up a small toy steer.

"Davey will love it," she said as he showed the toy to her. He quickly paid for it then rejoined her, both of them heading back out onto the walkway.

"He thinks that he's going to grow up and ride one of those bucking broncos like he sees the cowboys do on TV. I don't have the heart to tell him that it's not something that he'll ever be able to do," David said as he put the toy back into its bag.

"He'll change his mind a thousand times before he's grown," Sarah said, though she knew that there could be a lot of limitations on what Davey would be able to do when he got older.

"My brother's little girl wants to ride a bronco too and she's only four. His wife caught her out in the pasture trying to climb a cow the other day and almost had a heart attack," Sarah said.

They walked back through the shops then out to where the steer were corralled. She told David about being raised on a cattle ranch and then about her time barrel racing on the rodeo circuit. She found herself mentioning Kolton in a story of the days he was on their high school steer roping team. She had spoken so little of her deceased husband except when she and Jack were alone, but it seemed that the more she talked about him the easier it was becoming. Maybe her mother had been right. Maybe she did need to talk to someone, only for now the only person she wanted to talk to was David.

She felt the pressure of his hand against her lower back as they moved through the crowd and she buzzed with excitement as a shiver raced through her body. It was like it was so in tune with his that just the merest of touches was enough to weaken those walls she had put up against feeling anything more than friendship for him. She felt the temptation to move back into him so that she could feel what it would be like to be held in his arms. It wasn't until he'd moved his hand from her back that she felt her heart rate return to normal. Did he know he was doing this to her?

"Weren't your parents a little afraid that you'd get hurt riding that fast," he asked after Sarah explained how the sport of barrel racing was timed.

"Not really. I mean barrel racing is a lot safer than steer roping or bull riding. It was just part of our life," she said as they headed back through the cloud of dust that still hung in the air after the steers had gone through.

"Thanks for sharing that with me," David said as he started the car.

"I'm glad you enjoyed it," Sarah said as she buckled herself in. She was enjoying her time with David but she couldn't continue to be a coward. She had to tell him about Cody, about that night. She couldn't live with this between the two of them any longer.

"No, I mean you sharing your memories with me. I know you don't talk about Kolton very often. I appreciate that you trust me enough with those memories," David said, then reversed the car.

She felt the heat of embarrassment as it flushed through her body. If she trusted David like he believed she did she wouldn't be holding back from telling him about that night. She had to make things right between the two of them.

* * *

After the noise of the stockyard, she was relieved to see that the water gardens were as peaceful as she remembered.

It had been Kolton who had first been so amazed by the gardens when they had made the trip with their junior class to Fort Worth. He'd already been fascinated with building things and had made up his mind to major in architecture at Baylor University by then so it wasn't a surprise that the architecture of the fountains would interest him.

"Let's go this way," she said as they turned a corner and headed toward the meditation pool.

"I came here with my high school one year and fell in love with this part of the park," she said as she took his hand and led him down the path.

While the other kids had rushed off to the larger terraced falls where they could wade down the steps to the pool below, she'd found the private meditation pool surrounded by cypress trees as a respite after the noise of the bus crowded with her friends. It was there that she would tell David about her son. Their sons.

"It's beautiful, isn't it?" she asked as she led him to a spot where they could sit. The lights had come on across the park and the sun had begun to set as they had walked through the collection of fountains that covered part of the grounds.

"It is," David said as he sat next to her. "It's very peaceful."

She looked around the area to see that very few people were remaining now. Now the time had come, she didn't know where to start. She decided on the beginning when she'd first seen David in that waiting room over three years ago, or maybe more appropriate was to start with the ending of a young life that was taken too soon from this world.

Sarah turned toward David, noticing that instead of looking at the fountains he was staring at her.

"What's wrong?" she asked.

"There's nothing wrong," David said as he moved closer to her. "It's been a great day. There's only one problem."

"What problem?" Sarah asked. The only problem she was aware of was the fact that she was sitting talking nonsense with David when she should have been leveling with him.

"Sitting here surrounded by this beautiful park and earlier when we were at the stockyards, the only thing I've been able to think about is how much I'd like to kiss you," David said. While his voice contained a teasing note, there was no laughter in his eyes.

She tried to make her mind concentrate on what he was saying, but all she could think about was the deep longing she could see in eyes that now appeared more of a smoky gray then their usual mix of green. She knew that feeling. She had felt it ever since he had touched her earlier that day as he had laid his warm hand against her. And before, when his innocent touches at the stable had sparked a long-forgotten desire in her.

"I don't know if it's the magic of tonight or something more, but I won't cross that line if you don't want me to," David said as once more he rubbed the back of his neck.

Sarah couldn't believe what David was saying. Did he feel it too? This connection that seemed to flicker to life every time they touched. His touch had sent her hormones into overdrive today, but she had thought it was only her feeling that way. How was she supposed to keep ignoring the desire she felt whenever he was close now that he had admitted his attraction for her?

"It's okay, Sarah, if you're not interested in taking things between us any further," David said as he slid away from her.

Deep inside her a desire that had lain dormant protested against his withdrawal. She felt torn between what her body wanted and what her heart was telling her. She hadn't been kissed since the morning she had kissed her husband goodbye for the last time as she had left for work. Even now with her body driving her to say yes, she felt the fear of the unknown bearing down on her.

But it's only a kiss...one kiss. Would it be so bad to let yourself feel what it's like to be alive for just one moment?

"Yes," she said, the word coming out loud as it seemed to echo across the park. She cleared her throat and tried again. "Yes, I'd like you to kiss me."

She felt stupid as she knotted her hands together in her lap. Could she feel any more awkward? She'd shared kisses only with Kolton and she wasn't sure what it was that she was supposed to do right now. Then David moved in closer to her, closer than he had been earlier and everything suddenly felt okay. This was David, a man who she knew she could trust.

He hesitated a moment, then bent down and brushed his lips across hers before pulling back from her. His eyes opened and suddenly her own body was lit with the same fire she saw reflected in David's eyes. The force of the desire that claimed her body had her wanting to take a step back, but the need that David had kindled with just one small kiss held her in place.

He pressed his lips against hers again, this time teasing until they parted for him. His tongue met hers and her breath caught. When his arms came up around her, she instinctively moved into them. She forgot the park, the water, the night sky that surrounded them now. There were only the two of them, their bodies straining to be closer. What had started as a simple kiss was quickly turning into much more.

Then she remembered why she'd brought him here.

Pulling away from him, she straightened her clothes. What had just happened? It had been a long time since she had been kissed, but even that couldn't explain the way that kiss had made her feel. She had come here to tell David of her memory of that night in the waiting room and about her donating Cody's organs and now instead, she had just complicated things even more. She couldn't let things continue like this—but, oh, how she would have liked that kiss to continue. She had to set things right between the two of them.

"I need to tell you something. Something that I should have told you a long time ago," she said, then cleared her throat. "It's about the first time we met, well that's where it starts, I guess."

"At the hospital?" David asked, his eyes searching hers.

"Yes, but no," she said, and then held her hand up a moment before he could speak. "Well, actually we didn't meet exactly. I'm doing this all wrong. Let me start again."

"Okay," he said. She watched as his hand started toward his neck, then following her eyes he lowered it back down to the bench.

"That day in the hospital when Dr. Benton introduced

you wasn't the first time I had seen you." She forced her eyes away from his troubled ones. She was doing such a bad job of this.

"No?" he asked. "Where could you have seen me? At another conference?"

"No, it was at the hospital, just not that day. It was earlier. Over three years earlier. The night before Davey's transplant."

"I'm sorry. I don't really remember a lot of the people that night. Were you part of the team then? Dr. Benton told me you'd only been working with the cardiac group for a couple years," he said. She could see a trust in his eyes now that she was going to shatter.

"That's right. It wasn't till after I lost my family, after that night I saw you that I decided I wanted to change my focus to the transplant team."

"I don't understand," he said as he moved closer to her. She felt the heat of his body before he took her hand in his. The night was turning cool and she turned into him, finding comfort in his touch as he placed his other arm around her. Even through her nervousness she could feel that connection to him that had begun to form. He'd known she needed his touch even though he hadn't understood why.

She took a deep breath, and then let it out. A cleansing breath they had taught her in birthing classes and that was exactly what she needed. She needed to be cleansed from this secret she had been carrying around with her since he had come back into her life. There was something changing between the two of them, something that scared her as much as it fascinated her, but this had to be dealt with first. Suddenly she knew where to start the story that had changed all her life and maybe David's too.

"I was at work on the surgical hall of the hospital when I got the call from the emergency room that my husband had been in a car accident and they needed me to come as soon as possible. Of course I didn't believe them at first. No one wants to believe that something like that can happen to them. They'd taken Kolton to another hospital, a hospital closer to the accident, so I had a friend drive me. I knew it was bad. I'd given bad news to family members enough myself that I knew, but I didn't think he'd be gone. Not like that. He was so young and alive. And there he was lying so still on the stretcher." She wiped a tear that had streaked down her face. She'd never shared the whole story of that day with anyone, not even Jack.

"I didn't think about Cody, at least not at first. Kolton was to drop him off at day care that morning on his way to work. I'd assumed the accident had taken place afterward. And then a police officer came into the room and told me that my son had been taken to the children's hospital. The one I'd just left. I don't remember much after that. I think it was the police officer who drove me back, I'm not sure.

"The next thing I remember was seeing Cody lying in the hospital crib. He was so quiet, so still. Just like Kolton. The doctors and nurses were great, but there wasn't a lot they could do. The car had been T-boned by someone who had tried to make the yellow light. I guess Kolton didn't see them when the light turned green. It was a useless accident that shouldn't have happened." She stopped and paused for a second trying to gather her thoughts. "And that's how I ended up in the hospital waiting room the night that I saw you there."

"You're the woman who almost passed out," he said,

his voice a little shaky. Was it possible he had figured out where her story was going?

"Yes. I'm not surprised you didn't recognize me. I'd been at the hospital for three days by then and they'd just told me that Cody was brain-dead." Oh, God, it hurt to say those words. Even after all this time it physically hurt. Her stomach churned with the pain that griped her and she fought against the nausea.

"Sarah, stop. You don't need to put yourself through this," David said as he pulled her even closer till her back rested against his chest and both of his arms.

"No, I want to tell you. I need to tell you so that you'll know," she said as she willed her stomach to relax so she could continue.

"Like I said, I had just been told that Cody…was gone. I knew of course, but I didn't have to face the reality of it until the doctors had run all the tests. I'd held out for a miracle, but I didn't get one."

"Of course I knew the people from Organ Procurement would be notified by the staff and then they'd want to talk to me about donation and even if I didn't want to donate, the doctors were going to want to talk about the next step. I already knew the next step. They were going to talk about taking my son off life support. I did the only thing I could do. I ran and hid." It had been useless, but at the time it had seemed that it was the only thing she could do. Jack had been waiting for her in the trauma waiting room with her parents and she couldn't face them. She had needed some time alone, so she'd found the waiting room as far away from the trauma unit as she could.

"And that's when you saw me?" he said, his voice low and soft now.

Night had fallen as she'd been talking and the stars were starting to come out, adding their sparkle to the lights that reflected off the waterfall in front of them.

"Yes, you were talking with one of the transplant case managers. I shouldn't have stayed there listening, but I couldn't make myself face my family. Jack had already lost his son and now I had to tell him his grandson was gone too. I couldn't do it, not yet, so I stayed where I was and then I heard her talking to you about Davey's chance at a heart."

"She said that it was just a possibility, nothing for sure, just that there was a possible donor that they believed was the right blood type. I remember. It was the first good news I'd had in a long time," David said.

"It was the first piece of good news I had heard in days too. I remember feeling happy for just a few seconds as I thought of your child being saved. At least there was one family that wouldn't have to suffer the pain of losing a child. It wasn't until later that I started to think that maybe the two of us had become connected that night. That maybe I was in the right place at the right time as I considered what to do about my dying son while I thought of other children, like your son, that Cody could help save." She felt David tense against her. "Hearing about how much your son needed a donation helped me make my decision to donate my son's organs."

"What are you saying, Sarah? Do you think there's a possibility that Davey got Cody's heart?" David asked.

Running his hands through his hair he moved away from Sarah. He needed to think about this more rationally. This whole conversation had taken a turn that he hadn't seen coming. One minute he had been sharing what had to be the best kiss of his life, then suddenly

Sarah was talking about how she had been in the waiting room the night he had learned that there was still hope for his son.

If he'd known the story, the timing of the death of Sarah's family, maybe he would have put things together, but he hadn't. Not that he blamed Sarah for not talking about the death of her husband and son. She was certainly due the right to keep that to herself and he could see the pain it caused her to talk about that time in her life. But why hadn't she come to him with this information earlier?

"I don't know for sure, but I think that it's a possibility. We both know that by the time the neurologist told me about the brain death determination, Organ Procurement had already been involved in the background. The nurses that took care of Cody would have been required to call them when Cody had first come in unresponsive and ventilated," Sarah said.

"What was Cody's blood type?" David asked.

"O positive," she said shakily, then looked up at him. "Davey?"

"O positive," he said. Like he'd told Sarah earlier, he hadn't given Davey's donor family a lot of thought since those few months after the transplant. And he'd thought of them only abstractly. The idea of it being Sarah's family seemed surreal. "It's just a start, but there definitely is a chance, a good chance, that Cody could have been Davey's donor. I don't understand why you didn't tell me? Why wouldn't you have told me about this as soon as you remembered?" If it had involved his son, he had the right to know.

"At first I didn't want to make things awkward between us at work and I wasn't even sure that I wanted to know myself. Then, when I got to know you, I didn't want you to think that I was spending time with you and Davey just because of the possibility of the donation," Sarah said as she wrapped her arms around herself.

"Is it difficult? Seeing Davey? Knowing that Davey could have Cody's heart?" he asked. It had to be, didn't it? It was hard just asking the question.

"At first it was, at least until I got to know him better and I'd be lying if I said that the possibility that my son's donation could have made a difference in Davey's life didn't make me happy. He's a very special boy, just like my Cody. When I first saw Davey with Humphrey, I admit that it hurt a bit. Cody had only been two and a half when Jack and Kolton came home with that pony. Cody had loved him immediately and when I saw how taken with Humphrey Davey was, it shocked me that I felt a moment of resentment. But then I saw that smile on Davey's face and I knew that he loved that pony as much as Cody had."

"I'm glad you told me. Whether Davey was the recipient of Cody's heart or not, I'm glad you shared this with me, but you should have told me sooner."

It hadn't been an easy tale for her to tell, but he still felt as if he had been betrayed.

The park was deserted now and the walk back to David's car was quiet, the silence stretching between them. The laughter they had shared earlier that day had been replaced with too many emotions. He was torn between wanting to hold Sarah and tell her he understood why she hadn't told him and wanting to holler out, *Why didn't you trust me with this before?*

He knew neither of those reactions would help them work through this and no matter what, he knew that was what he wanted. That was what was important for them right now.

* * *

David's mind was full of more questions than answers as he walked Sarah to her hotel room. So much had happened over the last few hours. What would it mean to the two of them if Davey had received Sarah's son's heart? There was no way for that not to affect Sarah or her relationship to Davey. And what if it turned out that Cody's heart had been donated to someone else? Would that make a difference? No, he was sure it wouldn't. He'd seen how Sarah cared for the other children on the unit, showing them all the love and attention possible.

"So, what do you want to do?" Sarah asked as they stopped in front of her room.

Remembering the kiss that the two of them had just shared, there were a lot of things that came to mind with that question. None of which he thought Sarah was speaking of.

"Did you ever write a note to your donor?" she asked. "The privacy policy of organ procurement states that if a recipient and a donor both want to meet they will contact them."

"No, I'm afraid I didn't. I should have, I'd planned to…" he said.

"You were busy taking care of a sick child all by yourself. It's understandable that any family, especially a single parent, wouldn't have had the time for writing a note," Sarah interrupted as she turned to insert her key card into the slot. "Would you like to come in?"

David thought about all the reasons he shouldn't enter Sarah's hotel room, none of which seemed important right then. She stopped and turned to him, a look of concern shadowing her face.

"I don't mean to pressure you. I know this is a lot to take in," Sarah said as she opened her door.

"You've had weeks to think about this, Sarah. I've only had a few minutes," he said interrupting her. He would never feel anything but thankfulness for the family that had given his son a new heart, but it was going to take more than a few minutes for him to consider where the two of them went from here, especially if that family was Sarah's.

He watched as she slid her shoes off then walked over to the window where the lights of the city shone before her before turning and smiling at him. She had no idea what it did to him seeing her there, memories of their kiss still fresh, her dress still wrinkled from their embrace.

All that day he had thought of nothing but kissing Sarah, but he had never imagined just how wonderful sharing that one kiss with her could be. And now that he knew just how sweet those lips of hers tasted all he could think about was tasting her again. But this time he wanted to taste all of her, to feel every part of her against him, but he knew this wasn't the time for that. He needed to process everything Sarah had told him and he needed to come to terms with the fact that she hadn't been forthcoming with him. But while his mind might know that he needed to take a step back, unfortunately his libido did not seem to want to take the time that he felt they needed and he knew if he didn't leave right then, he was going to do something that both of them might regret.

"I have to go," he said as he turned away from her, not stopping even when he heard her call his name.

CHAPTER SEVEN

DAVID STARED OUT the window into the city below him. He didn't know how long he'd been standing there, but the road in front of the hotel was empty now. Looking out at the building across from him, he had watched the lights go out one at a time and now most of the building was dark. He glanced at his watch. A quarter past eleven. It had only been ten minutes since the last time he had looked.

He'd called and checked on Davey when he had first returned to his room and had found that his son had already gone to bed. Ms. Duggar had sounded half-asleep herself when she'd answered the phone and had seemed a bit put out when he had questioned her about Davey's medication. He knew he had a bit of a problem with control as far as Davey was concerned but he'd born all the responsibility in taking care of Davey since almost the day he had been born. Unlike him, Ms. Duggar had seen Davey only as the healthy little boy he was now. He knew that things could change quickly and Davey could be fighting for his life again.

Unlike most people, Sarah understood his concern for his son's routine and his need to check on his son often. The couple of times he had tried to date, the women had not been that understanding. Sarah had taken him and Davey into her home and her life just the way they were. Was it because of the possible tie Davey had to her son, Cody? He knew that she had worried about that, had been afraid that he would accuse her of such things, but Sarah wasn't like that. She was a genuinely good person. Maybe at first it might have been part of what drew her to him and his son, but he knew that she felt more for them now.

The fact that he'd walked away from her tonight was a miracle. He'd wanted her more than he'd ever wanted a woman before, including his ex-wife. There was something between the two of them that made him forget everything but her. He'd never felt this deep a need, this hot a desire or this chaos of emotions that would not let go of him.

Yet he'd walked away from her. And why? Because she had hurt his feelings by not being totally forthcoming with him? He couldn't deny that hurt, but he knew it hadn't been easy for her either. Whether or not it was Sarah who had donated Davey's new heart or another family, there was no way to explain to someone what that gift had meant to his son. And now instead of thanking Sarah for that selfless act, he was sitting here alone in his room brooding because he hadn't had the nerve to stay and see where tonight would lead the two of them. Yes, he did need to take the time to think about everything Sarah had told him, but what if this was the only night the two of them had to spend together? He had promised his son that they would live each day as if it was their last together, but here he sat spending his time worrying about things that were in the past. Was this how he wanted to spend his life?

He looked over at the bed where a staff member had turned down the covers for him. He had no desire to climb in that bed alone. He had no desire to spend the night alone at all. He thought about going back to Sarah's just to spend the time with her. Only he knew it wouldn't stop at talking. They'd only skimmed the surface of the attraction they felt for each other and it had left the two of them wanting more. Besides, she had probably already gone to sleep.

But what if she hadn't? What if she was suffering through this lonely night just as he was? Making a decision, he grabbed the key card off the entry table and headed out the hotel door before he could change his mind.

He tapped on Sarah's door quietly and waited. He would leave if she didn't answer the door in a minute or two. If she'd managed to fall asleep, he didn't want to interrupt her. But he heard the lock click and Sarah opened the door. She'd changed into a long sleep shirt, but her face showed no signs that she had been awakened.

"Is something wrong?" she asked as she moved aside for him to enter the room.

"No, nothing's wrong," he said. He looked through the door that led to the bedroom and saw the bed was undisturbed. Instead, he saw a pillow and blanket on the couch which looked out the window. Had she been spending the night watching the same lights go on and off as he had?

"Then…" she asked, looking at him expectantly.

"I couldn't sleep," he said as he motioned to the couch. "I take it you couldn't either?"

"No. But that doesn't explain why you came back,"

said Sarah. She had invited him inside, but she still stood next to the door.

Had he made a mistake coming here? Maybe she had been glad he had left when he did and now here he was looking like a fool arriving on her doorstep in the middle of the night.

Not able to stand the distance between them any longer, he walked back over to her and pulled her up into his arms. "I'm sorry I had to leave."

"I'm just happy you're back. I'm sorry I didn't tell you everything at first," Sarah said as she rested her head on David's chest.

"What's wrong?" David asked as he held her tight in his arms.

"It changes things between us, you know," she said as she buried her head deeper into his chest.

Putting a hand under her chin he brought her eyes to his. "Sometimes change is good, Sarah, and sometimes it's something we can't avoid. If this isn't what you want…"

She answered him with a kiss, slow and hot that pulled against every bit of his control.

"Can you feel it, too?" she asked him, her eyes feverish, telling him she wanted this as much as he did. He didn't have to ask what she meant. There had always been something between the two of them since the first time they had met. Not that slow burn of desire that had been building over the last few weeks, but that connection they had felt immediately as their friendship had built into more. He didn't understand it, nor did he want to at that moment, but he couldn't deny it either.

"Yes, I can feel it," he said before bringing her lips to his.

Her hands roamed over his body and heat spread through his veins with every touch. He palmed her breast then answered her moan with his own. His hand slid lower, his palm cupping her sex as she pressed against him.

"I want more," she said, panting as she arched against his hand. "I want you."

David loved the way Sarah responded to him and there was nothing he wanted more than her right now, but he didn't want to make a mess of this.

"Are you sure, Sarah?" he asked, "I don't know where this is leading and I don't want you to look back on tonight with any regret. Right now we can go back to just being friends, but once we cross into that bedroom things will change between us."

"No matter what might happen between us later, I want to take that chance. I want to be brave for once. I'm tired of being afraid of taking chances. For just a little while I need to feel alive. I want you to make love to me, David."

Picking her up, he carried her into the bedroom and laid her on the bed. He watched as she pulled the long shirt over her head then crawled across the bed to help him with his own shirt. The sight of Sarah in nothing but a small pair of panties overwhelmed him, making his fingers clumsy as they tried to work the buttons on his shirt until Sarah brushed his hands away. Opening his shirt, she pressed a small kiss to his chest and then started on the button and zipper of his pants. Unable to wait, he took her breasts in his hands and caressed them. Her skin was so soft. Bending down he took one nipple in his mouth and sucked.

In one night he'd already become addicted to the taste of her, the perfect mix of Texas sugarcane and the spicy heat of a jalapeño. He heard a moan, but he wasn't sure if it had come from her or him. He switched nipples then released it when she pulled away from him as she tried to push his pants down.

Stepping out of his pants and briefs, he followed her onto the bed as she crawled backward to the top.

"I'm really glad you came back," she said. She reached out and ran a fingertip down his chest to his lower abdomen and stopped at his erection.

"So am I," he said. A shudder ran through him as her hands encircled him. He bent back over her breasts and took a puckered nipple into his mouth as his hands worked off her panties. He was already addicted to the taste of her.

He parted the curls of her sex with one hand. He pushed a finger inside her and found her hot and wet. He ran his thumb over her core as she pushed against his hand. He heard the rustle of foil then tensed as Sarah rolled on the condom.

"I want you," she said as she raised her hips to him. "All of you."

He slid deep inside of her and caught her gasp with his mouth as he lowered his lips to hers. When he thought he couldn't take any more, she took him deeper still. Her moans filling the room as she drove him to give her more.

He tried to hold back, wanted to make it last, but the heat of her was too much. She opened herself to him, taking each thrust until he felt her body clench and spasm around him. He let her body take the control he'd held tight and let himself follow her over the edge.

* * *

Sarah quietly closed the door to Lindsey's room so as not to disturb the sleeping girl. It seemed they were finally making some headway with the infection that had attacked her lungs. They'd managed to decrease her sedation to the point where she could respond to people in the room, but she was still sleepy the majority of the time.

"How is she?" David asked as he came up behind her startling her.

For a moment she was frozen remembering the day before that they had shared. They'd enjoyed a late breakfast in bed at the hotel that had quickly led to a languid few hours of love making that she wouldn't be forgetting any time soon. It had been a magical weekend, but they both had their reasons for not wanting anything more. They had enjoyed each other and that was all. But why then did her heart still race when he looked at her the way he was right now?

Sarah gave her head a small shake. What would David think if he realized where her mind had gone? "She's doing better. Have you heard anything about when they are planning to take her off the ECMO?"

"Dr. Benton spoke to the pulmonologist this morning and they're hoping it will only be a few more days," he said. "I made rounds last night before I left and I didn't see her mother. I've spoken with Dr. Benton about my concerns about her being able to take care of Lindsey after a heart transplant."

Sarah stopped and stared at him. No, Hannah hadn't been there all the time, but she'd explained to him before that Hannah had a job and had to split her time between the two places. Speaking with Dr. Benton could cause big problems for Hannah if the older doctor decided to take his concerns to the ethics committee or the social worker.

"Look, I know that it seems as if Hannah isn't here very much, but I have no doubt that she will be there for Lindsey after her transplant. She's been taking care of her daughter by herself for a long time now. I realize you don't know Hannah, but you need to give her a chance."

"I've just seen this before, Sarah. You see the best in everyone, but not everyone is willing to be there for their child when they need them," he said. "Right now the most important thing for Lindsey is to have someone to take care of her. I just don't see her mother doing that right now."

"You can't judge everybody by your ex-wife, David. You have to see that. Hannah will be there for Lindsey. I know she will," she said making sure her voice was too low for anyone else to overhear. She understood how hard it was for David to trust and maybe he saw something in Hannah that she didn't, but the young mother deserved for him to give her a chance.

"I hope you're right," he said before turning away from her.

Sarah knew this went deeper with him than just Hannah. But she needed to make him see that most parents were not like his wife. He had made a good life for himself and Davey and he needed to let the anger of his wife go. He deserved better than to continue being burdened by her betrayal.

Only as she'd stood there telling David that he needed to move on, she'd realized that she fought against moving on without Kolton and Cody every day.

* * *

It had been two days since he had spoken to Sarah except for when they were rounding on patients together and he was getting tired of it. Maybe he was being a little too hard on Lindsey's mom, he had seen her come in the hospital the night before as he was leaving and from the uniform she wore he could tell that she had come from work. But Sarah's insinuation that he was judging Hannah by the actions of his ex-wife were wrong. Weren't they? He would never purposely do that.

The two of them needed to get together and talk things out. The silence between the two of them was not good for their working relationship. Okay, he could be more honest with himself than that. The truth was he missed his conversations with Sarah. He missed the way her eyes would light up when she told a story about one of the horses on the ranch or how she'd listen to him describe a surgery in detail and never get bored.

And he'd missed the feel of her in his arms every night since the one they'd shared at the hotel. He missed his friend and his lover and he didn't like it one bit.

Making up his mind to set things right with Sarah, he left the doctors' workroom where he had been reviewing Lindsey's X-rays and went to look for her.

Spotting her at the end of the hallway he watched as she gowned up before entering the room. He looked down at the app on his phone and saw that the patient's room she had entered was a readmission that Dr. Benton has asked him to check on.

Noting the isolation sign on the door and remembering that he had seen that the little boy's wound cultures had come back positive for a resistant bacteria, he gowned and gloved as he had seen Sarah do earlier before entering the room.

Sarah looked up from where she sat beside the boy's parents as she went over the paperwork on a clipboard in front of her, while the eight-year-old boy lay bundled in a blanket sleeping.

"Hi, I'm Dr. Wright," David said as he hunched down beside the mother. "You might not remember me but I assisted Dr. Benton with Bailey's last surgery."

"Is Dr. Benton here?" the boy's mother asked as she looked up from the paperwork she was signing. "Sarah says that Bailey is going to need to go back to surgery."

"Dr. Benton asked me to come see Bailey this morning, but he does plan on seeing him today."

"I'm glad you came in," Sarah said. "I was about to text Dr. Benton, but you might want to call him yourself. I don't think the doctor that transferred him back to us last night had looked at Bailey's latest lab work. He's showing signs of sepsis. Both his white count and his lactic acid are up."

"You don't see a lot of this in children but it happens. We need to get him back into surgery. I'll call Dr. Benton and see when we can get an operating room, but do you have a minute?" David said as he moved to the door to pull off the disposable gown.

"Sure, just give me a minute to talk with Bailey's parents. I've already discussed with them the possibility that he would need to go back to surgery," Sarah said.

David hung up after speaking with Dr. Benton to find Sarah exiting Bailey's room.

"Dr. Benton is on his way over from the office to talk with Bailey's parents, then we'll get him prepped for surgery," David said as they both headed toward the nurses' station.

"His mom says he hasn't had anything to eat since yesterday so that shouldn't be a problem," Sarah said. There was an awkwardness in their conversation that reminded him of the reason he had gone in search of her to begin with.

"I was wondering if you'd like to have dinner with me and Davey tonight," David said.

"Dinner? Tonight?" Sarah asked stopping in the hallway and looking up at him.

"It's spaghetti night and I know Davey would love to see you. I know it's a work night but I should be out of the operating room by five so it won't be a late night."

David caught himself about to rub at the back of his neck then stopped. He had expected a simple yes or no from Sarah, it was just spaghetti after all, but by the look on her face she was taking the invitation more seriously.

"So, is this like a date?" Sarah asked looking up at him.

"A date?" He hadn't thought of it quite like that, but he guessed it could be considered a date. "Is it okay with you if it is a date? I mean we won't be alone, Davey will be there, but it could be considered as a date."

"What time?" Sarah said, though he could still see some hesitation which he could understand. Accepting that they were actually having an official date, with or without Davey as chaperone, was a step toward a change in their relationship that they might not be prepared for. The night they'd spent together had been more spontaneous where this would be an intentional agreement.

"How about six thirty? I'll text you the address," he said as he went to his contacts on his phone.

"Sure, six thirty would be great," Sarah said as a nurse started toward them. "There's Bailey's nurse, I'll give her an update on him. Good luck with the surgery."

"Thanks," he said, then turned back to see the next patient on his list. He'd have to skip lunch to get finished before surgery if he hoped to make it out on time, but with the promise of spending time with Sarah and Davey tonight he knew it would be worth it.

Sarah looked around the kitchen and couldn't help but laugh. Among the dishes and vegetables laid out on the counter, two handsome young men, one considerably younger than the other, were busy working together as if they were chefs on the latest television cooking show.

"Do the two of you usually dress for dinner?" she asked as she took in Davey in his dress shirt and pants then turned to check out David as he stood chopping onions with his own dress shirt sleeves rolled up to his elbows.

"Davey insisted," David said as he looked up from the cutting board and gave her a smile. "According to him, this is how you dress when you have company over for dinner."

"It's when you have a girl over, Dad, and you're supposed to tell her how pretty she looks," Davey said in a loud theatrical whisper, then looked over at her with a mischievous smile.

"My dearest, Sarah, you look lovely tonight," David said with the same ridiculous theatrics as his son which sent Davey into a fit of giggles.

"Well, thank you, Dr. Wright," Sarah said, playing along with them. She was glad she'd changed into a nice dress after work though she was still dressed a lot more casually than David and Davey.

"Nice kitchen," Sarah said as she moved around to the other side of the large island.

"Thanks," David said as he raked the onions into a large pot. "I lucked out finding this place when I got accepted with Dr. Benton, especially since it came furnished."

"And I have the best room ever, wanna see it?" Davey asked as he jumped down from the stool and ran down the hall.

"I've got this," David indicated with a nod toward the stove where scents of garlic and onions were pouring out of the pot. "Would you like a glass of red wine?"

"That would be great. I'll be right back," she said as she followed the sound of footsteps to Davey's room.

The room was large with a window that overlooked a small manicured yard. With the exception of college she had never lived on a piece of land this small. She'd grown up with open pasture surrounding a large farmhouse and wasn't sure that she'd ever be able to get used to having neighbors so close that you could hang out the window and shake hands with them.

"Look what Daddy brought me back from that trip you went on," Davey said as he picked the toy steer off the ground where he had built a fence from plastic building blocks. "He said that I could go with you next time and see those steers with the big horns at the yards where they keep them."

Sarah felt a slight panic when she realized that she was being included in their family plans. She'd taken a big step agreeing to a date, she wasn't ready to start planning family vacations, if ever.

"We'll have to see if Sarah can come when we plan to go to the stockyards. She could have other plans," David said from the doorway where he held out a glass of wine to her. "Davey, go wash your hands."

"I love the big window," Sarah said as she took the glass of wine.

"His room is usually more of a mess, but he decided to clean it up before you got here. I'm sure if you look you'll find a thousand of those plastic blocks under his bed."

"Wow, flowers?" Sarah asked as they made their way back downstairs and into the kitchen where she now noticed a small table for four sat in a corner.

"Davey insisted that we had to have flowers on the table. Fortunately there were still a few azalea blooms left in the backyard."

"How did the surgery go?" she asked as she took a seat at the island and watched David toss the pasta with some olive oil.

"Good. The infection wasn't that deep, but he did have more blood loss than we expected," David said as Davey ran in the room and held his hands out for inspection. An alarm went off on David's watch and he looked over at his son with some unspoken message in the look.

"Okay," Davey said as the boy moved to a drawer in one of the cabinets and pulled out a medicine dispenser.

"Davey's been learning how to make sure his medications are on time," David said to Sarah. She could see that this wasn't the best part of the day for Davey, but she had to give it to David for sharing some of the responsibility with his son.

"That is great, Davey. Did you know that sometimes we have to give pills to the horses?" They ate while Sarah shared some of her best tricks to get the horses to take their medicine and Davey asked questions about how Pepper and Humphrey were doing since he hadn't been to see them the week before, something that he pointed out to David with emphasis. They'd just started to clear the table when another alarm sounded from David's watch.

"More medications?" she asked looking over at Davey.

"No, it's the hospital asking me to call urgently," David answered as he moved into the hall to make the call. By the time he returned she and Davey had loaded the dishwasher.

"What's up?" she asked as she dried her hands on the dishcloth.

"It's Bailey. He's bleeding and needs to go back to surgery. Dr. Benton's daughter is in labor so he's signed off to Dr. Sherwood who is asking for me to come in to assist since I assisted with the surgery today," David said. "Dr. Benton knows about Davey so it's not been a problem…"

"It's not a problem now. Go. Davey and I will be fine," she said. She could see his hesitation and understood that he was torn between his responsibility to help Bailey and his responsibilities with Davey. "It's okay. I'll take good care of him."

"Okay," David said before he rushed off down the hall, then returned seconds later. "He's already had his medicine and he took a shower before supper.

"His bedtime is in—" David looked down at his watch "—thirty minutes, though he'll try to stretch it for as long as you let him."

"Can't I stay up a little later tonight since we have company?" Davey pleaded with eyes so like his father's that she knew she would never have been able to deny his request.

"No. Bedtime is nonnegotiable tonight," David said before leaning down and giving his son a hug. "Be good for Sarah and this weekend instead of one movie I'll make it two. Deal?"

"Deal," Davey said with a smile.

"Thanks," David said to Sarah as she walked him to the door. "I'll be back as soon as I can."

"Just take care of Bailey. Davey and I will be fine," Sarah said before she shut the door.

"Now, Davey. What do you want to do for the next thirty minutes?"

"Can you help me with the book Daddy bought me about horses?"

"Sure, I can. Go get into your pajamas and bring back the book," Sarah said as she headed for what looked like a comfortable spot in the family room.

Half an hour later, Sarah had answered every one of Davey's questions concerning how to tack a horse and the different names for each part of the saddle and bridle, watched him brush his teeth and given him a drink of water. She'd missed this ritual of putting a child to bed. She'd spent hours of her life reading bedtime stories to Cody and hearing him plead for "just one more" before she turned out the light. How she regretted all the times she'd told him, "No more stories tonight."

Closing her eyes she let her mind wander to her memories of her little boy all dressed up in his dinosaur pajamas that had been his favorite as he begged for just one more story.

David knelt down beside the large recliner that sat in his family room. He felt a bit like the bear that came home to find Goldilocks asleep in his bed, except his version of Goldilocks had dark brown waves instead of golden curls.

Leaning down he brushed a strand of hair back from Sarah's face. Sighing, she turned her face into his hand then opened her eyes. Dark chocolate eyes blinked open then closed again. He had a couple choices here. He could let her sleep where she was or he could carry her off to his bed, which would be his first choice except for the fact that his son was asleep in the room next to his.

"Give me a couple minutes," Sarah said as those beautiful eyes blinked open again. He watched as she performed a full-body stretch that had him wanting to crawl into his recliner with her.

"How is Bailey?" Sarah asked, yawning then sitting up in the chair.

"He's stabilized. They'd already had him in the OR by the time I got there," he said. "I appreciate you taking care of Davey. Did he give you any trouble?"

"No. He wasn't any trouble at all. I had no idea how bright he was. He showed me the book you got him on horses and he had a lot of good questions," she said as she tried to climb out of the deep chair. David pulled her up from the chair and steadied her. "Thanks. I didn't mean to fall asleep."

"And I didn't mean to be so late," he said as Sarah moved into his arms. The warmth of her body against his had him pulling her closer until their bodies aligned perfectly. The feel of her breast brushing against him had him wishing he had gone with his first choice of action when he'd first found her sleeping. They would have been snuggled in his bed together by now.

"Look, I owe you an apology. I checked on Lindsey before I left the hospital and you were right, Hannah was there with her. I spoke with the night nurses and they said she has been there every night since her daughter went on ECMO," David said as he let Sarah pull back from him.

"I'm sorry too. I certainly don't have the right to tell you that you need to move on from what you went through with your wife. If anyone should understand how hard that is then it should be me. I've spent the last three years trying to work through my own issues," Sarah said. "We both have some baggage and I shouldn't have told you that your time for working through it was up."

He pushed the hair back from her face. Did she realize that in some ways she did have the right? Or at least the power? He'd taken what she had said and given himself a long hard look and realized that she was right. That it was time to get rid of the bitterness that he had carried around with him for the last six years. When he'd stepped in to check on Lindsey and saw Hannah at her bedside he knew that he had let his bitterness toward another woman influence his opinion of a young mom he didn't even know.

"I'm glad you did. I do have some issues. Lisa leaving like she did was rough. I suddenly had a sick young son to take care of and I'm sure that there were people who didn't think I was going to be able to make it on my own with Davey. I should have given Hannah the same benefit of the doubt that I needed with Davey."

"Thank you for that," Sarah said as she leaned in and placed a kiss on his cheek.

"And thank you for staying with Davey," he said as they moved to the front door.

"It was my pleasure," she said as she stepped outside the door then hesitated. "You don't have to do everything alone. It's okay to let others help you. It's not a sign of weakness as much as an act of sharing."

He stood there watching her as she walked to her car and he let her words sink in. There were times when he felt that Sarah could see through him into his soul. It was that connection again. That wonderful connection that had him wanting more with Sarah then he'd ever wanted from another woman. A connection that if broken he didn't know if he would survive it.

CHAPTER EIGHT

"But why can't I go too?" Davey asked for what had to be the fifteenth time since they had left the house. His son had been clingy all day. David had been afraid that Davey could be getting sick so he'd taken his temperature, but it had been normal. He was wondering if he should have just canceled the night he had planned with Sarah. Jack had certainly proved that he could handle his son, but Davey in the mood he was in right then was a different matter.

"Sarah said that Jack was really looking forward to spending some time with you. You wouldn't want to let him down, would you?" he asked as he parked the car in front of Sarah's house.

"No," Davey said with an impudence that he had never heard from his son.

"Davey, if you can't be polite we'll go home," said David. Turning around he saw the tears and Davey's quivering chin. He should have cancelled.

"I'm sorry. I'll be good. I promise," Davey said.

To David's relief, his son was back in his normal high spirits by the time he got him settled with Jack and Sarah had brought the horses up to the house.

"I packed some food. There's a nice spot just off the trail that's perfect for watching the sunset," Sarah said as she threw some type of bag across the back of her horse.

Why hadn't he thought of bringing some food? When he'd overheard one of the nurses talking about a sunset trail ride she'd taken with her family on the ranch, he'd thought that it would be a great idea. When he'd asked Sarah about taking the trail ride with him she'd made him clarify that he was asking her as a date, not as her student, which made him wonder what she had planned for the night.

He eyed Fancy, who was pretending to ignore him until he started to climb onto her back. From the haughty look she gave him, he knew that she was no more impressed by his mounting form now than she had been the first time he'd climbed on her.

"Ready?" Sarah asked him as she turned Sugar toward the end of the road that led past the house.

They took the orange clay dirt road for a few minutes then Sarah took a trail that led into a thick covering of trees.

"I don't know that I could have found that trail if you hadn't shown it to me," he said as they wound themselves through the thick woods.

"It's one of the more hidden trails," she said as she stopped at a spot where two trails shot off from the one they had taken. "We'll take this one on the left and it will take us back down the one on the right."

They rode silently, neither wanting to talk. The only sound was the horses' hooves on the trail. Sarah pointed occasionally to a squirrel in the underbrush searching for a nut that had survived the winter. The woods demanded a reverence that David would have compared to that of an old library. They saw several birds, cardinals and gray doves that were getting ready to roost in the trees and he knew that at some point he would have to bring Davey on the trail. The thought of his son had him worrying if he had done the right thing leaving him with Jack. He hoped that he was behaving for Sarah's father-in-law.

The path took a turn and he started to notice the trees thinning out. A few minutes later they stopped atop a hill overlooking a bright green valley of new grass. With the covering of trees he'd not been able to see the sky at all except for small patches where the tree tops had thinned out, but from this spot they had a clear view of the sun as it started its path below the skyline. Pinks and oranges blended with blues and violets.

"This is amazing," David said as he dismounted from Fancy. Sarah took the reins from him and walked back into the trees where he watched her tie the reins to a low hanging limb.

"Come on," she said, as she led him farther up the hill, stopping where the view was even better.

"Let me help," he said as she started to unpack the bag she had brought with her. He took the small blanket and laid it out, and then took a couple bottles of water from her. Sitting down on the blanket, he exchanged a bottle of water for the sandwich she handed him. They ate in silence as the sun slowly sank and the colors of the sky darkened.

"Look over there," Sarah said as she pointed to the dark sky behind her where the stars were starting to come out and a big full moon had begun to rise.

"It's beautiful," he said, then turned to her. "Almost as beautiful as you."

When Sarah turned back to him there was laughter

in her eyes and he had no doubt that she wasn't taking his compliment seriously. He watched as she lay back on the blanket and looked at the sky.

Lying beside her, David reached for Sarah's hand as they stared at the darkening sky. He had never been to a more peaceful place. The falling night had brought a cool breeze that brushed over the two of them.

Letting go of Sarah's hand he rolled toward her. He fingered a lock of dark brown hair that had fanned out from Sarah's head, then bent to touch his lips to hers with the same reverence he had felt for the woods they'd traveled through. "Thank you for sharing this with me," he said.

Sarah looked up into David's face and tried to will him to kiss her again. He'd made her feel as precious and fragile as a newborn foal, but she wanted more. She released the breath she hadn't known she was holding then sucked in another one with a gasp as David's lips grazed her cheek then traveled behind her ear then down her neck as he rolled over her. Her hands reached for him as his mouth found the peak of her nipple through the thin denim shirt she wore.

"I've missed you," David said when he pulled away from her.

"You've seen me every day at work," she said, then let out a frustrated moan as he pulled away from her.

"I've seen my friend Sarah and my co-worker Sarah. I've missed my lover, Sarah," he said as he began unbuttoning her shirt and removing her bra. His hands were cool as they touched her warm breast and then he replaced his hand with his mouth and she wanted to scream to the sky with the pleasure. But she wanted more. Squirming against him, she reached between them for the zipper of his jeans. Her breath caught as his hand skimmed inside her jeans and panties. He circled her most sensitive spot then dipped inside her with long, deep strokes that sent her hurdling into a climax that caught her off guard, but it wasn't enough—she wanted more. She needed more.

"You have on too many clothes," she said as she tried again to undo the pants that were keeping her hands from him. She wanted to feel the hard length of him so she could guide him deep inside her. She wanted him to fill that empty place that ached for him. She wanted to feel him come deep inside her while her body squeezed every bit of pleasure from him. But she'd never get what she wanted, needed, if she couldn't get the clothes that were between them off.

David rolled away from her then wrestled off his boots then stood to take off his pants. For one second she caught sight of his heart-stopping naked form against the darkened sky as he covered himself with a condom. Then he was kneeling down in front of her as he worked her boots off and then her pants. She'd never felt so needy in her life. When he finally came back to her she lifted her hips up to meet him, her body unable to wait any longer.

As Sarah felt her body reach for their climax she understood what her body had known before she had herself. She'd needed David to fill not only her body but also her heart. It had been empty for so long. As they rode out their climax together she let go of all the pain inside her. She opened herself up to David and let him see the woman who had held back so much of herself for the last three years.

Her scream of triumph swept through the trees and

seemed to echo over the valley. Tears filled her eyes but she didn't bother to brush them away. Whatever it was that the two of them shared right there in that moment was more than sex, more than intercourse. For the first time since the day she'd lost her family, she felt whole again.

They lay there together and stared up at the twinkling stars above them. They could have been the only two people in the world right then and that would have been all right with her.

"We have to go back," David said, though he made no move to stand.

"I know," she said as she turned toward him. "Thank you for tonight."

"It was my pleasure," he said as he turned so that they were facing each other.

She had never screamed during sex before and she would have thought she would feel embarrassed, but she didn't. Maybe she'd run out of feelings after purging so many from herself tonight.

She heard the buzz of a phone from the pile of clothes that lay scattered across the grass. "It's Jack," she said recognizing the ring tone as the one she had set up for him and hoping she hadn't worried him because they had been out longer than they had planned.

They both stood and started searching. She located her jeans and slid them on before she pulled her phone from the back pocket. It just didn't feel right talking to her father-in-law while she was undressed even if he was a couple miles of trail away and there was no way he could see her.

"Hey, Jack. What's up?" It took a minute for his words

to cut through the pleasant haze that had formed in her brain. "Are you sure? Yes, we're headed back right now. We're on our way. It's okay. We'll find him."

She ended her call then looked up into David's eyes. She knew he had heard the conversation and had to have realized what had upset Jack, but she made herself say the words out loud. "Davey's disappeared."

David tried to fight down the panic that had gripped him as he had listened to Sarah on the phone with Jack.

Davey had to be safe. It wasn't like he was lost in the mall where someone could have stolen him. He had always loved playing hide-and-go-seek when he was younger. He had to just be playing with Jack. By the time they got back to Sarah's house, Jack would have found him.

Fortunately, Fancy seemed to pick up that there was an urgent need for them to return to the ranch. Following behind Sarah, she'd sped up to keep pace with Sugar, but with only the moon to light their path they were unable to travel very fast. Finally they reached the road.

"Hold on," Sarah hollered back at him as Sugar took off in a run. He had just enough time to grab the saddle horn before Fancy followed her. He hugged the horse with his thighs and bent low as he saw Sarah do. He could see the reflection of light in the dark night and knew that they had to be close to the house.

Finally they topped a small hill and he could see the house in front of them. It was lit as bright as an airport landing strip with flood lights shining from each corner of the house.

His horse came to a stop so fast that it almost sent him toppling off. They were both off their horses and running for the door when they saw Jack coming around from the backyard with a large flashlight in his hand.

"Humphrey's gone too," Jack said as they sprinted up to him. "I'm so sorry, David. I only left him for a minute. I can't imagine where he's gotten off to."

The older man's hands shook, sending the beam from the flashlight skittering across the yard. Sarah took the flashlight and handed it to David, then took both of Jack's hands in her own.

"Tell us what happened," she said, as she walked Jack up to the front porch and sat him down in the closest rocking chair.

Jack looked pale and David could see that the man was visibly shaken by Davey's disappearance, but right then they needed to be out looking for Davey. As if reading his mind Sarah turned back to him.

"We need to figure out where Davey might have gone," she said, then turned back to Jack. "Start from the beginning. What did the two of you do after David and I left?"

David tried not to fidget as he listened to Jack tell them about the supper of hot dogs and chips and then how Jack had taken Davey down to the big stables.

"We came back up to the house as soon as I finished locking the doors. I could tell that Davey didn't feel well, but all he complained of was his throat hurting. He was in the family room, I'd put on a movie for him, and I left him there while I went into the kitchen to get him a teaspoon of honey. I thought maybe it would soothe his throat a bit." Jack turned back toward him, his eyes full of pain. "I'm so sorry, David."

"It's not your fault, Jack," he said as he let his hand rest on the older man's shoulder. It wasn't this man's fault. He wasn't responsible for Davey's disappearance. If the blame rested anywhere it was on David. He'd known his son was acting out of character and that something had to be wrong, but he never would have thought Davey would run off from Jack.

"You said you locked the stables. Did Davey know that they were locked? Would he have gone back there to see one of the horses?" Sarah asked.

"I told him I was locking it up and he saw the keys I had," Jack said. "At first I thought he was just in the bathroom. When he didn't come back I checked the bathroom downstairs and then the one upstairs."

"We played a lot of hide-and-go-seek when he was younger. Did you check under the beds?" David said as his mind searched for any explanation for his son's disappearance.

"But that doesn't explain Humphrey being gone," Sarah reminded him. "Jack, you go back and clear the house. Maybe the two things don't have anything to do with each other. Either way we need to know for sure that Davey's not in the house. I'll check out the stable behind the house with David."

He followed Sarah around the back of the house then down a hill where a much smaller building stood. Like the house, the building's bright lights shone from each corner. He could tell Jack had been in a hurry to meet them as he had left the double doors to the building wide open.

"Davey," Sarah called out as they entered the building. Though smaller, this building was set up much like the bigger one with a short aisle running between stalls that faced each other and a larger room at the end where tools and horse tack hung.

"Davey, are you in here?" David called as he went from stall to stall to make sure his son wasn't lying alone in one of them hurt and unable to call for him. Several of the stalls were empty, their floors swept clean. An older horse eyed him warily as he climbed up the metal bars of the stall door and looked past him, but the only thing besides the horse in the stall was a bed of fresh hay.

"David," Sarah called to him. Jumping down for the gate he ran toward her with visions of his son lying bleeding on the ground flashing through his mind, but when he made it to her all he could see was Sarah staring at a spot on the stable wall.

"Humphrey's saddle is gone," she said as she turned to him.

"I don't understand," he said. "Davey doesn't know how to put the saddle on the pony."

Sarah face fell. "Remember the other night when he was asking me questions about the horse book you had bought him? We went all the way through on how to get a horse ready to ride and he already knew the name of most of the tack parts." She headed back to where the stall doors stood open. Inside the stall he saw a small two-step platform.

She turned toward him, her eyes wide with fear that hadn't been there when they had been talking to Jack, and then she pushed past him running out of the building. He found her at the edge of woods that ran behind the building.

"Davey," she called out into the dark trees, and then ran blindly into the woods. He followed her, calling out his son's name. And soon was unable to tell which way led back to the stable and house. If Davey had gotten lost so easily, how was he supposed to find him? How was

Davey supposed to find him? He saw the light from the flashlight Sarah still held and used it as a guide back to her. What had he been thinking to leave his son alone? Davey was a precocious little boy who was always pushing the boundaries. And now his son was lost in the dark because his father hadn't been there to keep him out of trouble.

"I thought I'd lost you too," Sarah said as she threw her arms around him and waited for him to pull her closer, to comfort her like she was trying to comfort him.

"It's my fault," David said, his eyes staring out into the dark woods behind her. "My son is lost out there because of me."

"You can't think that. He's just a little boy who's fascinated with horses who decided to go an adventure," she said as she once more tried to get David to look at her. "We'll find him."

"He wanted to go with us and I told him he couldn't. He was tired this afternoon and I should have kept him home, but I was looking forward to spending time with you. I should have kept him home, Sarah. I'm his father, I'm supposed to put him first," he said before he turned away from her and headed back toward the house.

CHAPTER NINE

As DAVID TOOK his car and headed back to the stable to look for Davey, Sarah sat Jack down and they went over the night again. She tried to not let the things David had said bother her. He was scared for his son and it was natural that he would blame himself, but it hadn't been his words that had hurt. It had been the way he'd pulled back from her. He'd shut her out with his actions more than his words.

She made herself concentrate on what was important right then. There would be time for her and David to talk later. Right now they needed to find Davey. She would have to call the police and ask for help, something she didn't want to do if the boy was just hiding nearby.

"The only thing that makes sense is that Davey took Humphrey to go look for David," Jack said. "I just don't understand why that pony hasn't brought him home by now. Most of the time all he does is meander around in the yard. The only time he's ever been out of the backyard was…."

"You said that he should have come home," she said as she jumped up and looked for the keys to the ATV. "Remember where he went a couple months ago when someone left the gate open?"

"Yeah, he'd gone back to that little stable you and Kolton built," Jack said as he started to stand, realizing what Sarah had as well.

"Exactly. Stay here. I'll call you as soon as I get to the house. Tell David I know where Davey is."

Why hadn't she thought of this earlier? Kolton had built a two-stall stable after they had bought the pony for Cody. It was where they had kept Humphrey until Sarah had moved back in with Jack. It had been Humphrey's first home with them, it only made sense that he would head there if he was let out.

Sarah turned the key and hit the gas. The four-wheeler jumped to life, hit the corner of the front ditch in her urgency then righted itself as she turned it up the clay road. She remembered to turn the lights on after a close call with a tree-lined curve.

She left the ATV running with the lights on as she grabbed her flashlight and jumped out. She ran toward the house then stopped. She'd had the utilities turned off after a few months of living with Jack. The idea of walking back inside the house after losing her family had been too painful. Her momma and her brother's wife had packed up her clothes and a few other things that they felt she needed and Sarah had chosen to leave the rest of things where they had been that last day that Kolton and Cody had left the house. She stood staring at what was supposed to have been her forever house. She wanted to turn her back and walk away, but there was a little boy lost and she had to make sure that he wasn't here.

"Davey," she called as she walked up the driveway, then followed the sidewalk up to the front door. She checked it even though she knew she'd find it locked.

"Davey, can you hear me?" she yelled as she headed to the back of the house where Humphrey's stall had been.

Davey, please be here.

The door to the tiny stable stood open and she pointed her flashlight inside. A large shadow moved startling a scream out of her that quickly became a laugh. Standing in the dark, was the pony giving her a very put-upon stare. "Davey, where are you? It's okay, you can come out."

Pushing past Humphrey, she searched the stall then ran around to the other stall. He wasn't there? That couldn't be right. Davey would surely have stayed with the pony. Unless he had fallen off. What if he had fallen off? What if he was lying out in the woods hurt? Would the pony have left him? She didn't think so, but she never would have thought that Davey would have taken off on the pony either.

She left Humphrey in his stall and retraced her way back to the ATV.

"Davey," she hollered louder now. "Davey?"

She listened for an answer as she checked behind the overgrown hedges that lined the front of the house. As she passed one of the windows she thought she heard something. She checked both sides of the bushes, then heard a soft cough. It was coming from inside the house. She ran back to the front door but it was locked just like the first time she had checked it. She sprinted to the back door.

"Davey?" she called as she turned the knob. The door opened easily. Using her flashlight she checked each room as she came to it, flashing the light into each corner. Another cough came from the end of the hall. She entered the room for the first time since she'd lost Cody.

Her light hit the blue curtains that hung over the window and then came to rest on the little boy curled up on a bed way too small for him. She bent down and picked the boy up and wrapped him in the animal-covered comforter.

"Davey, it's Sarah." She touched her hand to his forehead then checked his pulse. He was warm and his heart rate was a little fast which could be explained if he had a fever, and though his respirations were even they did seem a little labored. She carried him out to the four-wheeler and laid him on the seat, then pulled out her phone, her fingers trembling as she went through her contacts. She'd managed to hold the tears off until David answered and she heard the desperation in his voice.

"David, I've got him. I've got Davey," she cried through the tears.

David took his first deep breath since Sarah had received Jack's call telling them Davey was missing. He'd been about to dial the emergency number after he hadn't found Davey anywhere around the stables when Sarah had called. He still didn't understand why his son would have gone off like that, but he did know that it wasn't something he would be taking a chance with ever again.

Pulling his car up to the house, he could see the lights of the ATV as it topped a hill on the road and he held his breath as he watched it headed toward him, then stop in front of the house.

"Hey, Daddy," his son said as Sarah lifted him off the bench of the vehicle and handed him to David. "I'm tired. Can we go home now?"

"Hey, buddy. Let me check you out first," David said as he hugged his little boy tight to him. There had been so many times in his son's life that he had thought he might lose him, but he had never imagined that he could lose his son like he had tonight.

"Let's get him inside. He's a little warm. I've got a thermometer in the house," Sarah said as she opened the door for them.

"We found him, Jack. Humphrey went back to the house, just like you said," David heard Sarah shout as she entered the house.

He followed her, then stopped when he saw the man that Sarah considered a second father sitting at the table looking tired and older than he had ever seen him.

"It's okay, Jack," Sarah said as she went to the man David knew she loved as much as she had loved his son. "Davey's okay."

Only David knew exactly how Jack felt, and he wasn't sure how easy it would be to get back to being okay.

David fixed the faded blanket decorated with cartoon animals so that it covered his son better as he watched Davey sleeping on the bed in the ER. He wondered exactly how many times he had sat in emergency rooms just like this one while he waited for Davey's lab tests and X-rays to come back. Ten? Twenty? More?

He should have been more in tune with what was going on with his son. He knew that Davey wasn't usually such a fussy child. He should have known that he was getting sick. He of all people knew how fast a small infection could turn into something worse where his son was concerned.

The night's growth of stubble scraped against his hand as he rubbed at his face, trying to remain awake. He'd spent many long nights sitting with Davey and even more on his rotations through his residency, and he'd still been able to function the next day, but the stress of the night was taking a toll on him. He jumped up as the door to Davey's room opened and the petite blond doctor that had seen Davey when he had first arrived came back into the room.

"You've got the X-ray back?" he asked before the women could speak.

"We did, and the labs too. If you want to go see them, we can walk back to my desk," she said.

David looked down at Davey. He wanted to see the labs and the X-ray film for himself but what if his son woke up while he was gone? Davey had been alone for hours in the woods; he couldn't leave Davey alone now.

"That's okay. I'll look at them later. What did the radiologist report say?" he asked. He couldn't remember the doctor's name though he was sure she'd introduced herself earlier.

"There is a small pleural effusion in the left lower lobe, but from the rest of the lab work I think Davey might have a slight case of pneumonia. I've sent all the results to Dr. Benton for a second opinion, but from the complaints that he had earlier that's my professional opinion. His white count is just above thirteen so I'll start him on some antibiotics. There's a nasty respiratory infection going around the schools right now. Whether exposure to that is the cause of Davey's infection or if it's his increased risk due to his transplant, I can't tell you. But I'm going to start him on an IV infusion and I'd like to admit him for observation at least for the next forty-eight hours just to be safe. Do you have any questions?"

"Not right now, but I would be interested in seeing his labs and of course I'll talk to Dr. Benton when he comes in this morning," David said. He didn't want the woman to think he didn't trust her opinion, but he was glad that she had consulted Dr. Benton.

"If you think of anything else you'd like to ask me or if there are any other tests you feel we should run just have the nurse let me know," she said before she left the room, shutting the door quietly behind her.

She'd done everything to put David at ease and more, but it was the fact that he hadn't listened to his intuition when he had first thought that his son was sick that still stuck with him. He'd known something was wrong when Davey had come home from school, but he ignored all the signs because he had wanted to keep his date with Sarah. What kind of father did that make him? He'd put his own desires ahead of his son's needs. That was exactly what Lisa had done. And he wouldn't make that mistake again. From now on Davey would be his only priority.

"It's going to be okay, Davey," he said as his son stirred under the covers. "I'm here. I'm not going to ever leave you again. I promise."

Sarah sat beside Jack in the hard plastic chairs that seemed to line every emergency waiting room. It had been almost two hours since Davey had been brought in. She'd hoped that David would be able to come out and update them, but her patience for waiting till he returned was wearing off.

"Maybe you should go back there and check on them," Jack said from beside her. Her father-in-law had been quiet the whole trip to the hospital and had said only a handful of words since they had arrived.

"I will. Would you like a cup of coffee? I can raid the staff kitchen, they won't mind."

"That would be good," Jack said, then looked down where he had his cowboy hat in his lap. "If Davey's awake, I'd really like to see him."

"I'll be back in just a few minutes," she said as she patted his arm. She knew that Jack was feeling guilty that Davey had been lost while he'd been watching him, but no one could have expected that the boy would take off on an old rundown pony.

After finding a nurse that she recognized, she'd been able to get the information of which room had been assigned to Davey. Opening the door quietly, she saw David messing with the old blanket that covered Davey.

"Yours?" he asked as she shut the door behind her.

"It was Cody's," she said as she looked over the little boy lying on the stretcher between the two of them. Davey's cheeks had lost their bright red color telling her that the fever had broken and his respirations appeared less labored than they had when she had first found him.

"And the house where you found him, it was yours too?" he asked.

"Yes," she said. She'd tried to ignore the existence of that house, her and Kolton's forever home, but after walking through those rooms she knew that it was time for her to face the house and all the memories it held.

"Sarah," said a small voice from the stretcher. Davey's green eyes stared up at her with confusion. "I had a dream and you were in it."

"Hey, Davey," David said to his son. "How do you feel?"

"I'm okay," Davey answered as he looked over at his dad, and then looked back at her. "It was you that I dreamed about. You and Humphrey, and you too Daddy."

"It wasn't a dream," she said, it had been more of a nightmare, but she didn't want to tell Davey that.

"You and Humphrey went on quite an adventure. Do you remember Sarah finding you?" David asked.

"Is it okay to go and get Jack?" she asked and was relieved when David nodded his agreement. She didn't think he held any hard feelings against Jack, but she knew there were some people that would have insisted on blaming him. But not David, he seemed to be insistent that it was his own fault instead.

When she returned, David had set the head of the bed up and was trying to get his son to take a sip from a straw. She felt the older man tense when the boy's eyes dropped down to the bed when he saw Jack come in beside her.

"Do you have something to say to Mr. Jack, Davey?" his father asked.

"I'm sorry, Mr. Jack. I know I shouldn't have gone off without telling you." Sarah saw the boy's eyes shoot to his father. "And I won't do it again."

"That's okay, Davey," her father-in-law said as he moved closer to the little boy's bed.

"Won't do what again?" David asked his son in a stern tone that left no room for the boy to scout around it.

"I won't go off without telling Mr. Jack," the boy looked over at his daddy. A silent message seemed to pass between the two of them. "And I won't go off on my own ever again until my daddy says I'm old enough."

"Why did you leave, Davey?" Jack asked.

"I just needed my daddy, but I promised him that I wouldn't do that again," Davey said, then yawned.

The speech seemed to have taken everything out of the boy as his eyes once more appeared heavy with sleep.

The three adults stood and stared down at him until once more he seemed to have fallen back asleep.

She waited for David to ask her to stay with him, when Jack told her that he was going to head back to the farm, but he didn't. Still, she wasn't ready to leave the two of them yet so she made up an excuse to hang around the hospital a little longer.

"I think I'll get changed and go up on the unit and check on Lindsey and I might as well round on a couple of the new surgery patients too," she said. "Will you be okay driving back on your own?"

"I'll be fine," Jack said. "I've spent many a night waiting for a mare to drop a foal. I'll grab a cup of coffee to go."

She left the two men talking while she went and got Jack a cup of coffee to take with him, then told David that she would check back with him later.

After rounding on two new patients and writing an admission note for Dr. Benton, she went to see Lindsey. Entering the room, she was surprised to see Lindsey was not only awake, but the large ECMO cannulas that had taken the blood from her body and then returned it after oxygenation had been removed. While the little girl's color was still pale, some of the fluid that had been collecting in her body causing the swelling of her face and extremities had decreased, leaving her looking more like herself.

"Hey, Sarah," the little girl said with a small smile.

"Lindsey, I'm so happy to see you," she said as she went to sit down beside her on a chair that she'd last seen Hannah asleep in. "Where's your mother?"

"She had to go to work. I thought she might have been fired again—that's what usually happens when I get sick and she has to spend a lot of time here, but she says her new boss understands."

Sarah didn't know what to say. Had any of them really ever bothered to think about how hard it would be for Lindsey's mother to keep a job while having to go back and forth to the hospital on a regular basis?

She left Lindsey to get some rest and headed back to check on Davey only to find that he had already been moved to the pediatric acute care floor. Deciding that she would look in on him before she headed home, she looked up his room number.

"Hey," she said as she stuck her head in the door to Davey's room to find David standing beside his son's bed watching his son sleep.

"I used to do this all the time. Just sit there and watch him sleep wondering how long I would have him with me. He's been so healthy since the transplant that I've just taken it for granted that he would be okay.

"I dropped my guard, Sarah. I got caught up in my own life and forgot that keeping Davey safe has to be the most important thing in my life right now. It was my responsibility to keep Davey safe. Just mine. And instead of looking after him like I should have, I left him when I knew something was wrong."

Did he really believe that he was in this alone? Didn't he realize how much she cared about his son?

"I understand that you're upset. It's been a rough night, but you don't have to go through this by yourself. I love Davey. Jack loves Davey. We all want to be there to help you."

"Don't you see, Sarah. It's been me and Davey for years now and we've made it work. I'm sorry, it's just better that for right now I spend my time concentrating on Davey."

Sarah stood, staring at him. David hadn't explicitly said that whatever it was that they'd shared was over, but Sarah understood nonetheless.

She took a deep breath and chose her words carefully. "If you truly believe that, David, then I'm the one who's sorry. You can do everything in your power to keep the people you love safe and there are no guarantees in this life. Things happen. It's not anyone's fault, that's just the way life works." Then she held her head high as she turned and walked away, desperate to get out of the room.

She wouldn't let him see her cry. David had stood there and ripped out her heart and he hadn't even realized it.

For the first time since she'd lost Kolton and Cody she had let herself feel hope for a future and all it had gotten her was more pain. Just the possibility of a new family with David and Davey had made her feel alive and now she felt torn in two.

"What's wrong?" Jack asked as she came to sit by him at the table the next morning where he was reading the newspaper. "Is it Davey?"

"Davey's fine," she said, not wanting him to worry. "I'm just tired."

"And since when did your being tired cause you to cry?" Jack asked. "Sometimes just sharing what's troubling you can be a help."

After the death of Kolton and Cody Sarah had spent hours talking to Jack. He'd been the only one to understand what she was going through because her loss had been his loss too.

Pouring herself a cup of coffee from the pot on the table, Sarah told Jack everything. He listened as she explained how she had first seen David that night at the hospital when they had lost Cody and the suspicions she had concerning the donation. She told him about the notes they had both sent to the organ procurement organization and how they were waiting for responses. She admitted to Jack that what she was feeling for David had become deeper than friendship, then ended with how David had pulled away from her because he didn't feel he could have a life himself and be there for Davey.

"Look, David's upset right now. He might not be thinking straight because he's concerned about his son, but I've seen the way he looks at you. He cares for you, Sarah. It doesn't sound like he had much of a relationship with his first wife, not like you had with Kolton, so he doesn't understand the feelings he has for you. Tell me something," he said as he pushed back from the table. "What would you have done if Kolton had tried to push you away?"

"I'd have pushed back at him," Sarah said as she realized where her father-in-law was going with the conversation.

"It seems David's first wife ran at the first sign of trouble. Maybe that's what he's afraid of. Maybe he just needs someone to push back at him instead of running away," Jack said before getting up from the table. "What do you tell your students when they fall off a horse?"

"I tell them to get back up there. You can't let one fall stop you," she said as she smiled for the first time that day.

"Then it's time for you to get back on that horse," Jack said with a smile before he headed out the back door leaving her to consider his advice.

CHAPTER TEN

THE PHONE BESIDE Sarah's bed was ringing. She could hear it, knew that she needed to answer it, but she couldn't seem to find it. She turned over and felt the hard case under her left hip.

"Hello," she said as she hit the button on her phone. Looking outside she realized it was still dark. Had something happened to Davey? Suddenly awake, she grasped the phone and checked the caller ID. It was the hospital. "Hello? David?"

"Sarah? It's Betsy, from the cardiac unit. I'm sorry to wake you, but Dr. Benton said you'd want to know."

"Know what, Betsy? Is something wrong with Davey?" she asked as she jumped out of bed. She was sure she had left a pair of work pants lying out on her bedroom chair.

"I'm sorry, I don't know anything about Davey," the unit coordinator said.

Sarah sat down hard on the chair that she'd been balancing against as she tried to coordinate her legs enough to get them into her pants. "Betsy, it's—" she looked over at the clock by her bed "—four o'clock in the morning—can you please tell me why Dr. Benton wanted me called?"

"Oh, yeah, it's Lindsey. He wanted you to know that they have a heart for her," Betsy said.

"Hang on, just a sec," Sarah said.

She finished pulling on her pants, and then started looking through her closet for a shirt.

"Are you still there?" Betsy asked her as she came back on the phone. "The charge nurse wants to talk to you."

"Sarah, it's Tammy. Sorry about all this confusion, but Dr. Benton said that you could help."

"Of course, what do you need?" She'd be glad to help if someone would just explain to her what was going on.

"It's Hannah. We can't get her on the phone," the charge nurse said. "We're going to get Lindsey ready, but we really need to get her mother here."

Sarah found a pen and wrote down an address. It wasn't far from the hospital, but it wasn't a neighborhood that she was familiar with. "I'm headed out now. Tell Dr. Benton that I'll have her there." She just hoped that it was a promise she could keep.

An hour later, Sarah drove into a small group of apartments that had seen better days, though it was doubtful that they had ever been much to look at. Checking the house number on the piece of paper, she knocked on the door and waited. A startled Hannah came to the door and soon Sarah had her dressed and on the way to the hospital.

"I'm sorry. I worked closing last night, and then I had to study." Hannah said.

"What are you studying for?" Sarah asked, though she had seen the books lying out on the small table in the small living room.

"I'm taking nursing courses," the young woman said, then looked away. "You probably think I'm wasting my time."

"I think that is great. Does Lindsey know?" Sarah asked.

"Yeah, but I didn't want her to say anything," Hannah said.

Sarah pulled into the parking place and turned toward her. "Lindsey loves you and I know she's proud of you. I'm proud of you too. This transplant will change both of your lives and if I can help, I will. I mean that, okay?"

Sarah was beginning to realize that Hannah had been too proud to ask for help or maybe she hadn't felt that she could ask for help. As Sarah watched her head down the hallway at a run toward her daughter's room, she thought of the other person she needed to see that didn't want to accept help.

David jerked awake. He hadn't meant to fall asleep—he'd just been going to rest his eyes for a moment. He looked down at his watch and saw that he'd slept most of the night. Stretching, he stood to check on Davey who seemed to be sleeping comfortably, and was shocked to find Sarah asleep in the chair across from him. He'd assumed that she had gone home hours earlier. After checking Davey's forehead and pulse, he moved over to Sarah.

"Sarah," he said as he squatted by her chair. He watched as her eyes blinked open then widened when she saw him. "What are you doing here?"

"Oh, I'm sorry. I didn't mean to fall asleep," she said, then gasped, "What time is it?"

"It's early. Why?" he asked, then moved away from her, away from the temptation to take her in his arms. He needed to keep her at arm's length until he could learn to control himself better around her.

His life had never been a peaceful one. It had been messy and stressful with an ex-wife that had cared more for her career than for their child who needed a lot of medical attention and care. He had accepted that this would be his life after Davey had been born and Lisa had left. And as Davey had lain there in his crib, not knowing that his mother had walked out on them, he had promised his son that he would always be there for him, that he would make whatever sacrifice he needed to take care of him. Turning away Sarah had to be the hardest sacrifice he had ever made.

"Did Dr. Benton call you?" Sarah asked as she moved over to where he stood beside Davey's bed. "About Lindsey?"

The little girl's name brought him back to whatever it was that Sarah was saying.

"What about Lindsey? Did she have a relapse?" he asked. The girl had seemed to be improving when he had last seen her. Had that been two days ago or had it been three days? The days were all starting to run together now.

"No, it's a heart, David. They have a heart for Lindsey," Sarah said as she grabbed both his forearms with her hands.

"That's wonderful. I know Dr. Benton had his doubts that she'd get a transplant in time, but that doesn't explain why you're here."

"I thought you might want to assist the transplant

team and I knew you'd feel better about it if there was someone to stay with Davey for you," she said as Dr. Benton opened the door.

"I hope I'm not interrupting, but we've got an ETA from Dr. Dreaden and Anesthesia is about to take Lindsey back to the OR," Dr. Benton said.

David looked from the doctor to Sarah.

"I'll be right there," he said, then waited till the doctor had closed the door.

"I'll take care of him, David. Go help with the surgery. You know you want to. We'll both be waiting for you when you get back," Sarah said before taking a seat next to his son's bed.

He couldn't understand what was going on. He thought he had made it clear to Sarah that he couldn't allow himself to make another mistake like he had the night before, but here she was offering to help him once more.

"We'll talk when I get back," she said.

Moving to where Davey slept, David ran his hand through the boy's curls.

He knew he needed to go change into his hospital scrubs, but he couldn't seem to pull himself away from his son. He'd been so scared when Davey had been lost. He had almost lost the boy twice before he had received a transplant and the helplessness he had felt then had been paralyzing. The possibility that he could have to face that again was very real and he had no control over that, but to lose his son because he hadn't been there when his son had needed him was unforgiveable and he wouldn't let that happen again.

"If he wakes up, tell him I'll be back as soon as I can," he said, then left the room.

* * *

Sarah sank into the chair David had occupied earlier. This had sounded much easier while she had been talking to Jack, but coming here and putting her heart back on the line again while she waited for David, while she acted like everything was fine, was the scariest thing she had ever done.

"Sarah," Davey called from the bed. "Where's my daddy?"

Sarah leaned over the bed and smiled down at Davey. David wasn't the only one who had been scared the night the little boy had wandered off and gotten lost. "He had to go help a sick little girl. But he told me to tell you that he would be back as soon as he could. Until then you're stuck with me."

"That's okay. Is my daddy helping the little girl get a new heart like the doctor helped me?" he asked as he sat up in bed. "He says it's very important that you get exactly the right heart."

"It is important and that's exactly what he's doing. Now what do you feel like eating this morning? I have it on good authority that the pancakes are the best thing on the menu," she said as she hit the nurse call button so that she could let the nurse know that Davey was awake.

"Pancakes are my favorite," he said.

"They're my favorite too," she said. "Now the two of us are going to have a long talk about taking horses without permission."

"Am I in big trouble?" he asked. She wanted to tell him no. She had been so happy when she found him that she would have forgiven him for anything, but things could have turned out differently. Davey had to learn that wandering off at any time without letting an adult know where he was going was not acceptable.

"It's not that you're in trouble, it's that you put yourself in danger and you scared me and your daddy."

By the time his pancakes had arrived, they had gone over all the rules of not taking off without telling an adult and not taking an animal that he didn't have permission to take. And he had told her all about his adventure with Humphrey when he'd gone out to find his daddy. An adventure that had caused him to tire.

"And then I saw this big house, but there wasn't anybody there," Davey said, then yawned. "I don't know where all the people were. Do you?"

"I'm afraid there hasn't been anyone living in that house for a long time," she said.

"Why not?" he asked. Sarah watched as his eyes began to close.

"Let's leave that story for another day," she said, and wondered if after the way she and David had left things if there would be another day?

The door opened and she recognized one of the case managers with the organ procurement program as she slipped into the room.

"I don't want to disturb you, but the unit coordinator on the floor told me I could find you here," she said as she looked over at Davey with more than a little curiosity.

"Did you hear that they received a heart for Lindsey?" Sarah asked her.

"I did and I checked on her mother. She's holding up," the woman said.

"The secretary at the office heard I was coming by and asked me to drop this off," she said as she held out a small envelope.

Sarah stared at the envelope. Except for her discussion with Jack, she hadn't thought about the notes she had mailed out to Cody's organ recipients in days.

She took the envelope and thanked the woman then stared at it after the door shut. She didn't recognize the writing on the outside, but that didn't mean anything. She'd decided to mail notes to all the recipients so that didn't mean that this one came from Cody's heart recipient. It could have come from any of the other recipients. There was only one way to find out.

David walked through the waiting room door with Dr. Benton at his side, exhausted but happy. It had been a difficult operation but successful and he was glad that he had been there.

Looking around the waiting room at the families grouped together throughout the room, it took only a minute to pick out Lindsey's mom sitting by herself. He knew that Sarah would usually have made time to sit with her if she hadn't offered to sit with Davey.

"Lindsey?" Hannah said as she walked toward them.

"She's fine," Dr. Benton said, then went on to tell the child's joyful mother what she could expect over the next few hours.

Leaving them to talk, David excused himself and headed to check on his own son.

Sarah stood as soon as he opened the door. He saw the empty breakfast tray across the room and then his son sleeping soundly and he relaxed. Davey was a picky eater when he was sick, but by the empty tray it looked like he was feeling better.

"Lindsey?" Sarah asked.

"She's in recovery," he said, then looked down at the

paper she was clutching in her hand. Were those tears in her eyes?

"Are you okay?" he asked as he moved closer, then stopped when she moved back from him. "What's wrong?"

"I received a note from Davey's heart recipient," she said, then wiped at her eyes.

"It wasn't the one I sent?" he said. Knowing that a part of her had been hoping that it had been.

"No, his name is Joshua and he has blue eyes," Sarah said, then sobbed again. Looking around for the standard cardboard box of tissues that was expected in a hospital room, he found one sitting beside Davey's bed.

"Why are you crying?" asked Davey from the bed. "Did Daddy hurt your feelings?"

"No, your daddy didn't do anything, sweetheart. I just got some news is all," Sarah said as she walked over to where his son lay. He was hit by the perfect picture they made together. With their dark heads bent together the two of them could pass as mother and son.

"I'm sorry you got some sad news," Davey said, as he looked up at her.

"It's not sad news," Sarah told him, "It's just not what I was expecting. It was actually a nice note from a very nice lady. And now that your daddy is back I'm going to run and check on some of the other patients on the floor while you tell your daddy about all the rules of taking a horse we discussed earlier."

David watched as Sarah slipped out of the door before he could think of anything to say to get her to stay.

"Are you sure you didn't do anything to make Sarah cry?" his son asked.

He started to deny that he had said anything that could

have hurt her feelings, but he couldn't. He'd told her in the most painful way that he didn't have a place in his life for her because he had to put Davey first. He'd expected her to accept that things were just too complicated in his life for her. To understand that life with him and Davey would always be complicated. He'd thought she'd leave and not look back, but instead she'd shown up here today and entertained his son so that he could attend a surgery that she knew he'd want to be part of. Sarah was like no other woman he had met and yet he had sent her away. What kind of fool did that make him?

"I don't know, Davey, but if I did I promise I'll apologize," he told his son, then decided it would be best to change the subject. "Tell me what you were doing while I was gone."

"Sarah told me that what I did when I took Humphrey and left without telling Mr. Jack was wrong and that if I ever do anything like that again I won't get to ride any of the horses," Davey said.

"She's right. What you did was wrong," David said as he took a seat beside his son's bed. "You had a lot of people worried about you."

"I think Sarah would be a very good mother. She used to have a little boy, Mr. Jack said, but he had to go to heaven."

"I'm sure Sarah would be a good mother," David said.

"Good, 'cause I think it would be a good thing if you got me a mother," Davey said, then reached for the remote that operated the television.

David didn't know what to say to Davey's announcement. Davey had never said anything before about a mother and he had always assumed that he had accepted that it would always be just him and his father, but apparently he had been wrong. He had more than just himself to think about. Even right then he was being torn between wanting to go check on Sarah and wanting to stay with Davey.

He'd promised his son that he would always take care of him.

And you also promised your son that the two of you would live every day you were given to the fullest. But instead of going out there and doing what you want, you're sitting here, hiding behind your son and living a life of solitude.

Was that what he was doing? Using the excuse of his son needing him to keep himself from getting hurt again like he had been hurt by Lisa? Sarah had been right about living a life alone. That wasn't what he really wanted. He'd been so set on taking care of Davey that he'd isolated the two of them. It wasn't until he had come here and met Sarah that he had opened himself up to anyone else. He had to decide whether he wanted to isolate him and Davey for the rest of their lives or if he wanted to take that leap of faith and learn to trust others. One thing for sure, he wanted Sarah. His heart hadn't been the same since she had walked away from him the day before and he needed to put away his pride and admit that he needed her.

Picking up the phone, he reached out and asked for help, something that earlier that day he'd have sworn he would never do.

David had looked everywhere for Sarah. He'd checked Lindsey's room, but saw only Hannah at her daughter's bedside. Next he'd checked with the other nurses but no one seemed to have seen her. Then it hit him. He remembered when she had told him about the night she'd received the news that her son wasn't going to survive his injuries she'd hid in the pediatric waiting room.

He saw her sitting in a small hidden corner. The sun had set and most of the hospital visitors had left for the day. He tried to remember the night he had sat here, where one of the case managers had found him and given him the news that there was hope for his son. He looked around the room till he found a chair just a few feet from where Sarah sat. Had it been that one?

She didn't look up when he came to sit next to her. He tried to think of what to say, but he couldn't find the words. And then he saw the note that she had held earlier, she still had it in her hands.

"This is the note you should have received," he said as he took the chair beside her. He held out a piece of paper of his own, a note that he'd written her.

"I've already received a note. It's from a nice family. They sent a picture. He's a beautiful little boy. He has blue eyes like Cody's," Sarah said as she stared down at the paper in his hand.

"But this is the one I should have sent you," he said as he tried to get her to take the note from him.

"It's okay, David. I was mistaken about Davey and even though you might not believe it, it doesn't matter. I still love Davey just as much as I did before I received this note," she said.

"I do believe you, Sarah. Look, how about I read this to you?" he said. What if she thought that what he had written was stupid? Why couldn't he find the right words to tell her how he felt?

"Okay," she said as she moved back away from him.

He cleared his throat. "Dear Sarah, I wanted to tell

you thank you for the gift of love that you've shared with me and Davey…"

"But I didn't, David…" she started to say.

"Just wait and hear me out, okay?" he said, then started to read again. "You've shown me a future that I've been too afraid to dream of until now. I hope you'll accept my love in return for yours and agree to a future together with me and Davey. Love, David."

He turned toward her and looked Sarah in the face. He had to face his fear of rejection head on now. But it wasn't rejection he saw in Sarah's eyes before she threw her arms around him and burst out in tears. He knew there were years ahead for them where there would be more tears, some of joy and some from pain, but as long they shared them with each other he knew they would be okay.

EPILOGUE

"PUT HER IN HERE," Davey said as he led the way through the house to his new little sister's room.

Secretly, Sarah had been afraid that bringing Kaitlyn into the same house that she had brought Cody almost seven years earlier would be painful, but instead it had felt right to bring his sister into the same room that had once been her brother's nursery.

After David had accepted a permanent position at the hospital, there had been the decision of where the three of them should live. While she knew they couldn't all move in with Jack, she couldn't bring herself to leave her father-in-law by himself. Her old house had been left empty for so long that there had been a lot of work necessary to get it livable and then there had been changes that both she and David had wanted to make, but when the renovations had been finished and Davey had moved Humphrey to the small stable behind the house they'd all agreed that they had made the right decision to keep the house.

She'd let her memories of Kolton and Cody be clouded by the pain that she had felt when she had lost them, instead of enjoying all the memories they had made together before that tragic day. Since moving back into the house, she had learned to share those good memories with David and Davey, which made her feel even closer to the family that she had lost.

Laying their new daughter in her crib, Sarah and David watched as Davey made faces at his little sister.

"Are you sure she's okay? Her face doesn't look right," Davey said.

He had worried about his sister since the moment they had told him that they were expecting, asking questions about whether she would have to get a new heart like he had. David had been very patient with him and they'd taken him to every obstetric appointment when they were planning to do ultrasounds so that he could see the pictures of his sister as she grew. Sarah herself hadn't worried about the baby as she figured Davey and his daddy were worrying enough for all three of them.

"She's perfect," David said as he stared down at his daughter.

And, surrounded by her new family, Sarah knew things really were perfect.

* * * * *

TEMPTED BY THE BROODING VET

SHELLEY RIVERS

MILLS & BOON

To my fabulous four—I love you all.

To my dad—if you haven't already been kicked out of
heaven then I hope you're smiling down
from a comfy cloud.

To Boo—whose doggy snores I will miss for ever.

To Flo—thank you for your belief and patience.
Without you this book would have lingered
as scattered pieces in my mind.

And finally to all romance readers,
who are the coolest readers in the world!

CHAPTER ONE

LOST.

Kiki Brown's optimism hurtled to her toes as she searched the lush green Dorset landscape. Was it too much to ask for the planets to line up, or whatever they were supposed to do, so one small thing in her life went right?

She had no desire to win the lottery, or spend her life encased in jewels and diamonds, but just once it would be nice if the fates stopped with their constant disasters and sly kicks.

She either kept on walking in the hope that the elusive Fingle Lodge appeared like a rose-covered oasis from nowhere, or headed back to the car in defeat.

She should never have trusted a ninety-eight-year-old's vague pencilled directions. Her godmother struggled to recall her own name sometimes, never mind remembering how to travel to the old lodge house she'd long ago abandoned to weather and time after her beloved husband died.

But the place sounded so romantic, set amongst sloping fields and miles from town. The sole surviving remnant of the vast Georgian estate of a family that had once retained the land and considered it home.

And Kiki's choices were limited after a year living and working in Alaska. A suitcase full of clothes and a redundant engagement ring relegated to the dark depths of her handbag, along with her crumpled tissues and faded hopes, didn't give a girl a lot of choices.

If she didn't find Fingle Lodge soon she would remain homeless and jobless. Something she didn't want and couldn't afford to be. Her savings were small and her options unfortunately not much bigger.

'Okay, Kiki,' she said, in an attempt to boost her flagging spirits. 'Let's find this property. You're not a quitter, no matter what a certain stupid male insisted seconds before you dumped him. You are an intelligent woman and you need no one—especially not a lying cheat.'

Oh, good—now she was talking to herself. Give her a woolly hat, a couple of pretty cats and she'd morph into the stereotypical singleton, living a life filled with nothing but sad memories, bed socks and crocheted blankets to keep her warm throughout the night. Though she did rather like crochet blankets. They reminded her of her godmother.

With another glance around the field, she made a decision. She'd give it another half-mile and then, if she still hadn't found the property, or someone to ask for better directions, she'd turn back. The exercise would do her good, and the spring sunshine was pleasant after months of living in the cold and the snow. She certainly didn't miss that part of Alaska.

She ignored the pinch in her heart, pushed the thought away and continued across the field, dodging the many animal deposits and rabbit holes that scattered the area. Breathing in the fresh air, she let the stress of the last few weeks mentally drift away.

So what if her life had hit a few bumps lately? Who wanted to live in a small town constantly seeing her ex-fiancé slobbering over other women? The same man who had believed it acceptable to drop the lace knickers of half the town's female population months before their wedding. A wedding that, in truth, Kiki had been too much of a coward to call off until complete humiliation and battered pride had forced her into action.

Well, she definitely didn't want *him* any more. Just the thought of the man made her cringe and wonder about her sanity. She'd made some stupid choices in her life, but that one she put down to senseless panic.

She was destined to be single for a while longer. Thirty-two wasn't old. It wasn't the full flush of youth either—but it didn't matter. She didn't even *like* men much, so the loss of yet another one from her life was no big deal. Just one more to forget and move on from. The same sad tune many a woman belted out.

More upsetting was losing her job at the marine research centre. That she *did* regret. But that kind of thing tended to happen when you dumped a man who was not only your fiancé, but also the man who happened to be your boss. She refused to give him the opportunity to abuse his position and make her work life unbearable. And she knew he held a grudge.

Ending their relationship in the middle of the high street, with most of the locals watching on, had ended with both her front and back doors being mysteriously blocked overnight by huge piles of snow and several large truck wheels.

So, with her life in such wonderful disorder, it was important to find Fingle Lodge and get on with her future. Or lick her wounds until they 'scabbed over and hardened', as her godmother had so eloquently phrased it just before she'd handed over the directions and a box of food for the journey.

If Kiki ever found the long-forgotten house she would make it her home for a few months. Somewhere to rest and reassess until she decided what to do and whether she could find a veterinary nursing job locally. She had worked hard to achieve her degree, and had spent six years using it in a city practice before leaving to work in Alaska.

Was that a chimney showing between those trees?

Kiki rushed towards the stile at the edge of the field and climbed over it, almost falling in her rush, thanks to the soles of her wellies slipping on the moss growing along the wooden step.

The adrenaline rush pumping through her veins at the sight of one chimney was quite startling.

Yes, definitely a chimney—and attached to it was a rather stumpy single-storey house with a good section of slipped roof tiles. The woodwork needed a fresh coat of paint, and a dead climbing plant concealed one of the windows with its skeletal stems and leaves. The whole place screamed neglect and despair and looked unloved.

Stumbling forward, she dodged a large muddy puddle and moved to stand in front of an old sign nailed to a worm-riddled gatepost: *Fingle Lodge*.

The last of the tightness in her shoulders eased and she glanced at the property once more. Well, it certainly needed work, but building repairs had never daunted her. Her parents, before their acrimonious divorce during her teens, had spent years renovating properties all over Britain and Europe. Sometimes for paying customers, other times for their own fun. Always for the love of the work.

Kiki had lived in a stately home on the island of Jersey and in a castle in Austria before the age of ten. Unfortunately her parents had always spent money like water in a downhill stream, and had often had to sell each property to increase their dwindling funds before really having time to enjoy the riches of their hard work.

Walking through the gap where she guessed a wooden gate had once swung, Kiki pushed past the overgrown lavender edging the rough flagstone path until she reached the front step.

A dark green-painted front door blocked her entry. Paint peeled off in several places, exposing a light green undercoat. Trying the brass doorknob, she found that, apart from a slight squeak and rattle, it didn't budge— no matter how many times she twisted and yanked on it.

Leaving the step, she walked to the nearest window and peered through the dirt-glazed glass, making out an orange armchair, circa nineteen-thirties, and a yellow-tiled fireplace. She needed to drop in on the keyholder, who apparently lived close by. Hopefully, she might know of a way to get to this place without having to trample through several fields.

She turned and spotted a large barn, several feet away. Built in grey stone, with surprisingly most of its roof still intact, it looked in better condition than the lodge. Intrigued, she wandered over to the building and dragged open one of its huge wooden doors. A strange sound greeted her when she stepped inside. She paused and listened, but no other sound followed. Pulling a face, she guessed either a family of rats or mice lived in its dusty depths.

Screwing up her nose, she took in the abandoned tractor half hidden beneath a grubby moth-eaten bed sheet, several piles of carelessly stacked wooden boxes, a wicker shopping basket filled with dried flowers and a few scattered farm tools. Nothing very exciting or un-expected.

She returned to the doorway, not in the mood to dance around rodents in order to investigate the dark rooms fur-ther in, when the sound came again. This time it sounded strangely familiar.

Kiki paused and frowned. No, it couldn't be… It wasn't possible. But she could have sworn it sounded almost like…

The whimpering sound started once more, this time joined by several high-pitched barks.

Ignoring everything but the barking, Kiki rushed across the uneven dirt floor until she found a locked door in the second section of the barn. Staring at the sus-piciously shiny new metal chain and lock fixed to it, she searched for something to break the padlock. Her god-mother hadn't visited the place in years, so whatever was inside that room had been put there by someone with no right to be anywhere near the property.

Hurrying over to the collection of tools, she found a lump hammer amongst them. Returning to the door, she lifted up the chain and awkwardly hit the padlock with the heavy hammer, relieved when it gave up its stead-fast hold after several hard whacks and bumped to the ground. Luckily, whoever had bought it hadn't spent money on a decent brand.

Throwing down the hammer, she tugged open the door, instantly overwhelmed by the rancid stench inside. Slamming the door shut again, she sucked in several deep breaths before steeling herself and opening it once more.

Six badly malnourished dogs turned to face her. Two

were tied to the wall with frayed old ropes; the other four sat in small tarnished cages not big enough for them to turn around in. All of them stood shaking in a thick layer of their own urine and excrement.

A soft whimpering from the far side of the room caught her attention. Hurrying towards the sound coming from a roughly built enclosure created out of concrete blocks, she peered over the low wall to find three small black and white puppies, barely days old, snuggling into a weary and sick-looking female Papillon.

A horrible realisation dawned on Kiki. An abandoned property, mistreated dogs and a locked door... The whole situation screamed of an illegal puppy farm.

Swallowing sudden nausea, she blinked away the burning sting of tears and forced herself to think. She needed to get help and get it quickly. If this *was* a secret puppy farm, then whoever was responsible might return soon—and she doubted they would be pleased to discover her there, or to find that she knew their secret.

Alex Morsi pushed open the veterinary practice's back door, ignoring the angry meows and hisses that promised feline retribution coming from the cat carrier he carried. For once a smile tugged at his lips, but he controlled it, uncomfortable with outward displays of emotions, and preferring to keep his good mood to himself.

'I don't believe it!' A short, dumpy middle-aged woman with tortoiseshell glasses propped on the top of her grey spiky hair stormed into the room. Her eyes fixed on the complaining cat.

'Morning, Anne,' he greeted her solemnly.

Anne ignored him and demanded, 'How did you manage to talk cantankerous old Mr Evans into letting you have his Ronny? I've tried for weeks and he's always refused.'

The urge to grin almost got the better of Alex as his sense of elation bubbled higher. With practised effort, he curtailed it and instead frowned down at his head nurse. 'I threatened to double his fees if he didn't hand Ronny over. With his large flock of sheep, he can't afford the slightest increase.'

'You're a cruel but brilliant man,' Anne declared with awe. 'You may be blessed with the exotic good looks of a Spanish matador, but you own the mind of a dastardly Irish genius.'

Alex winced at the description, but knew most people thought the same. Sometimes he wished he hadn't inherited his Spanish father's colouring and personality—but then his mother had been a volatile Irish redhead who thrived on drama and tragedy, so he figured he'd got the better trade.

'Allowing this cat to continually mate with the local females is irresponsible,' he said, moving the attention from himself and focusing on the wailing feline doing his best to attack the walls of his plastic prison. 'If Ronny isn't put out of action soon, the town will be overrun with kittens.'

Alex glanced towards the deserted reception area, his eyes narrowing as he noted a missing member of staff. Cold concern crept into his stomach.

'Where's Delia?'

Anne folded her arms and glared at him. 'She resigned yesterday.'

His jaw tightened at the news and he held in a sigh. 'Why?'

'She says you're the devil to work for and she would

rather hopscotch naked through a flooded field with a group of rowdy drunks watching on than spend another minute in your unpleasant company.'

He shook his head, causing his natural loose curls to bounce and move. A sense of injustice replacing his concern. 'I offered her some sound advice and she took it completely the wrong way.'

Anne raised an eyebrow. 'She took it exactly the way you meant it, Alex. She was hoping you would feel sorry for her, but instead you insisted she pull herself together and stop whinging.'

'Her constant moaning and crying gave everyone a headache,' he defended, a stirring of guilt travelling through him.

Perhaps he had been too blunt, but if the woman wanted sympathy she should visit a counsellor or a priest. They were trained to deal with emotional situations. Alex had endured enough female hysterics throughout his childhood to know to avoid it as an adult.

'She's in mourning,' Anne pointed out. 'Her ex-husband has recently died. A little understanding wouldn't hurt.'

'I bought her a condolence card...'

Anne snorted. 'No, you signed the one *I* bought. Delia's mistake was thinking that beneath all your Spanish and Irish ruggedness beats a passionate and sympathetic heart. She soon learnt better, silly girl.'

Alex frowned at the statement. He *did* have a heart, but he'd learnt years ago to keep it hidden and far away from the workplace. What use was he as a veterinarian if he dissolved into tears every time he lost a patient or dealt with a case of cruelty? The best way he could help the sick animals who came through the practice's doors was to keep his head and emotions in check. To be the solid and sensible presence when their owners fell to pieces or looked to him for answers.

And he tried not to get too close to his staff members. It was too easy to give off the wrong messages without meaning to. Women especially were prone to scramble his words and hear only what they wanted. He'd stopped dating a year ago because it had become too much work trying not to say the wrong thing to women who were as complicated as a conundrum and often as annoying.

'I only suggested she do her grieving out of work hours. All she ever did was complain about the man while he was alive. Not once in the six weeks she worked here did she utter one nice word about him.'

'That's irrelevant,' Anne said, though her eyes twinkled with humour.

'No, it's hypocritical.'

'Grief doesn't stay in rigid lines and keep office hours, Alex,' Anne insisted.

'More's the pity,' he muttered. 'I'm your boss—that doesn't mean I want to hear about your lives outside the practice. I'm quite happy not to. Perhaps we should make it a clause in future employee contracts. "Keep all emotions at home where they belong or face the sack."'

Anne chuckled, not in the least offended by his remark. 'How can you be such a caring man when it comes to animals, yet so intolerant of humans?'

He shrugged. 'I like animals. Humans are just a necessary evil I'm forced to endure.'

She laughed and shook her head. 'Fortunately, despite your unusual character quirks and dislikes, I do like *you*. But if you don't stop upsetting the staff we'll be without a full quota and then I will be very unhappy. And you know what I will do then.'

'Find ways to make *me* unhappy,' he predicted, knowing from experience how good she was at it.

'Exactly.' She grinned. 'Now, shall I take care of Ronny while you grab a cup of coffee?'

Alex lifted the cat cage. 'Get him prepped straight away. I want to neuter him before Evans changes his mind and demands him back. I've had him fasting overnight, so there's no reason to delay. This Romeo's days are over.'

Alex glanced through the plastic mesh door at the furious ginger tom cat and couldn't resist a grin. This reprobate had fathered over half the kittens in town, and castrating him would not only be sensible, but medically responsible.

'Good grief,' Anne muttered in shock. 'Did you just smile?'

Alex shoved the carrier at his colleague. 'Don't be ridiculous, Nurse. Have I ever, in the six years we've worked together, done such a thing?'

Anne shook her head but kept staring at him.

Uncomfortable with her stunned expression, Alex headed to his office on the other side of the building. 'Give me a shout when you're ready. I don't want to see anyone until I've dealt with Ronny.'

'Yes, boss. I'll prepare Theatre the minute Leah gets in.'

Dropping into his office chair, Alex ignored the paperwork waiting for his attention and took his phone out of his pocket. Two messages from his aunt, one from the local garage and several from an old girlfriend he hadn't seen in years. He deleted them all, not about to let anyone spoil his good mood.

With a quick look at the day's schedule, he went through his list of patients. A sweet female Bichon was booked in to be spayed. Two rescue Labradors needed dental work and a general check-over before the nearby rescue centre could place them for adoption, and the afternoon consisted of general consultations. A busy day, but nothing unexpected.

A knock on the door caused him to glance up.

'Bit of an emergency just walked into Reception,' Anne said. 'A woman with a seriously neglected dog. You should see the condition of it, Alex. It's dreadful.'

He stood and walked towards her, his pleasure in the morning vanishing more quickly than a meaty treat in a dog's mouth. 'Is the dog hers?'

'She says not.'

'Likely story,' he fumed.

They'd had visits like this before, when a stranger had arrived with a mistreated animal they insisted was not their responsibility.

'Let me see.'

Stepping into Reception with Anne at his heels, Alex was hit by the atrocious odour of animal faeces and wet dog first. The next shock came from the sight of the small, curvy woman holding an old-fashioned wicker basket while a sick-looking Papillon sat at her feet.

'You should be ashamed of yourself,' Alex said, not about to be sucked in by the pretty female or the way her blue eyes widened at his words.

The number one thing he hated was people who ill-treated animals, and by the state of the dog this woman was obviously worse than most. The fact that she caused an odd sensation to flip inside his chest was irrelevant, and probably nothing more than a bout of acid thanks to the bacon and cheese sandwich he'd eaten for breakfast.

'I—I beg your pardon?' the woman stammered, her cheeks turning pink as she stared at him.

Alex set his fists on his hips and continued to glare at her, ignoring the increase in his heartbeat. Let her try and sweet-talk her way out of this. He had the number of a friend who worked for the RSPCA on his mobile, and he intended to use it in the next few minutes.

'You heard fine.'

The way she drew herself up reminded him of an irritated kitten, ready to pounce and dig in her claws. If he hadn't been so angry over the dog's condition he might almost have admired the determined gleam that entered her eyes. Most women tended to simper around him, but he suspected this fair-haired beauty would do anything but.

'Then *you're* the one with the blocked ears,' she snapped, the colour in her cheeks deepening. 'Because I've already explained that this is not my dog—'

'Of course it's not,' he interrupted sarcastically, forcing his thoughts to focus on the situation and not the female.

'I suppose you found it in a bin or along the roadside? I've heard both many times. I've noticed that dog abusers are rarely imaginative.'

He frowned when, instead of defending herself further, she hugged the basket closer and took a step towards him.

'Actually, I discovered her in my godmother's barn.'

'Doubtful, seeing as you're not a local,' Alex snorted.

'How do you know I'm not?'

His eyes raked her from her head to her toes, taking in the fancy green padded coat, the designer jeans and pink whale-patterned wellingtons. They were a definite giveaway. No one around these parts wore anything but green or floral boots.

'I can tell.'

'Are you always this rude and judgemental?' she asked.

Her eyes had narrowed, but she reached down and stroked the Papillon gently, to soothe its whimpering. He begrudgingly liked it that she put the dog's feelings before her own anger.

'Oh, no,' Anne piped up from his side. 'This is him being quite pleasant. Tell me more about where you found this poor soul?'

'She didn't *find* her,' he dismissed, not believing a word the woman said.

'Listen, you arrogant oaf.' The woman stepped closer, though she kept her voice to a low hiss. 'The dog is not mine. I discovered her and several others in a barn.'

'What barn?' he asked, determined to find fault with her tale. Anything to keep his attention diverted from the softness of her skin and the fullness of her lips.

'The place is called Fingle Lodge. It's about a mile from here. It used to be the lodge house on the old Cattleson Estate.'

Alex's suspicions hiked up a level. Fingle Lodge was a property he'd secretly set his heart on owning one day. Once he tracked down who actually owned it now. Surrounded by an ancient wood, it sat in a rare unspoilt band of nature. There was an air of history to the area that intrigued him.

'I know the place. No one has lived there for years.'

'Well, at least you're right about something,' she agreed. 'My godmother owns the property and she's asked me to visit and check on its condition. When I searched the barn I discovered seven dogs and three puppies locked in a room and living in squalid conditions. I suspect someone is using it as a small-scale puppy farm. Why else would they keep them locked up? No one who loves dogs would keep them in such vile surroundings.'

'Puppies?' Alex repeated.

The woman nodded, and gently peeled back the green jumper covering the basket. Three sleepy puppies wriggled inside.

Alex reached into the basket and lifted one out, judging it to be no more than a week old. He gently returned it to the basket with its canine siblings.

'You've only brought Mum and her pups with you,' he pointed out, still not sure he believed or trusted her. Even with the recent introduction of new laws, and the hope of cutting out third party dealers, it didn't mean there weren't still people prepared to ignore it and continue with that side of the appalling puppy trade.

'I couldn't carry them all and fit them into my car,' she explained, in a far from patient tone. 'It's only small and one of my suitcases takes up half of the back seat. I thought it important to bring these four first.'

He searched her face, lingering over her full pink mouth for signs to prove she was lying. But no matter how hard he looked nothing but innocence and truth stared back at him.

Had he judged her wrong? Was there really a puppy farm on his doorstep? The idea made him sick. What monstrosities had these dogs endured so some crook could make easy money. Easy for them, but not for the dogs.

He reached for the dog at the woman's feet, touched when the filthy hound wagged its matted tail and stared at him with hopeful brown eyes. Each of her rib bones protruded through her dirty fur.

Handing the rope to Anne, he said, 'Call Ray at the RSPCA. Get him to meet us at the property.'

'What about PC Foot?' she asked. 'I'm sure he'll want to be informed. You know how he goes on about strong community ties and sharing information—how the police can only be of use if the public lets them.'

Alex nodded. 'Him too.'

He took the basket from the woman, careful to avoid touching her, and handed it to Anne.

'Get Leah to help you with bathing these four. I'll check them over when I get back.'

'What about Ronny?' Anne asked.

'If Evans turns up while I'm out tell him I'll quadruple his bills if he dares to remove Ronny before I've had a chance to neuter him. That cat is not to leave—no matter what he says or threatens.'

'Will do.'

He nodded to the woman who had interrupted his schedule and his day, still not convinced of her innocence. 'You'd better be telling the truth about the dogs not being yours.'

She glared at him. 'I am.'

'Come on, then. I don't have all day to waste. Those other dogs need rescuing from who knows what.'

CHAPTER TWO

HOW UNFAIR FOR the man to own such beautiful brown eyes. Jerks of *his* calibre should be blessed with bland ones—not delectable pools that silently invited a closer inspection.

Kiki gritted her teeth and fought the strong urge not to slap herself on the face for noticing such an inconsequential detail about the man. His eye colour was none of her business and her stupid brain needed to stop with the wayward thoughts and behave for once.

'Where exactly are you going?'

She halted halfway across the car park, frowning as she took in the mud-splattered blue truck he stood beside. The name of the practice emblazoned across the doors was barely legible through the thick coating of grime and dirt. With his brooding looks and tanned skin she'd imagined him owning something flashier, sleeker and cleaner. Something more impractical playboy than sensible, functional vet.

She indicated her aged white Mini, sadly more rust spots than paintwork, but more reliable than a conman's kiss.

'My car, of course. You said you know where Fingle Lodge is, so I'll follow you there.'

Several seconds passed before he shook his head. Those loose curls shifted to frame his face, giving him the appearance of a disreputable angel. A sexy, mischievous one. The type only the most risqué mid-century female artists had dared to imagine through charcoal strokes and lines. The kind best kept hidden from susceptible females easily drawn to such blatant male promise.

'Simpler if we ride together,' he said.

Kiki crossed her arms and lifted her chin. The two of them sharing air space in the same vehicle? Not in this lifetime or any other. Had he forgotten he'd accused her of being a liar and an abuser of animals within five seconds of their meeting? Did he truly believe she'd want to share his company after that? She'd rather have her eyeballs scrubbed with holly leaves, stinging nettles and rose thorns than sit inside his filthy truck.

'I prefer to drive my own car, thanks,' she said, forcing politeness into her tone.

With luck, once they'd rescued the dogs she would never have to see this censorious man again. He proved the old saying about how beautiful people often owned a disagreeable personality true. His personality stank more than rotting food on a hot day. 'The roads are muddy since the last heavy rainfall,' he said, as though she'd not spoken. 'My truck will deal with the local flooded roads better than your car.'

Well, wasn't that just dandy? Not satisfied with accusing her of animal cruelty, he was now insulting her choice in cars. An original British icon, at that. So typical of a man to insist that he knew best. Wanting to organise everything *his* way regardless of other opinions or desires.

Sucking in a deep, calming breath, she spun round

and headed for her Mini. If the man couldn't take a hint, then she refused to stand around squabbling over the merits of their individual vehicles. 'I'm sure I'll manage fine.'

'Instead of arguing we could be helping those dogs,' he called out.

She wasn't the one making a fuss over how they travelled.

Stopping next to her car, she glanced back, shocked when her stupid heart skipped at the sight of him bathed in the warm rays of the late-morning sunlight. For a single brief moment her fingers itched to trace and learn every curve of his flawless bone formation and skim over the soft, plump lines of his mouth.

Convinced the morning's events had sent her gaga, she replied, 'Then stop talking and let's go.'

She opened the driver's door and slid inside, almost screaming when the passenger door flew open and the infuriating man climbed in and settled in the seat next to her. Those beautiful eyes focused on her once more.

'Stubborn.'

Shocked, Kiki blinked several times, trying to absorb the fact that the arrogant man sat uninvited in her car when she had made it clear she didn't want him near.

Narrowing her eyes, she clung to her waning strands of politeness. 'I beg your pardon?'

A small crease materialised between his dark eyebrows as he frowned in her direction.

'I called you stubborn. Are you always so, or is it simply for my benefit?'

Her gaze slid over his too handsome face, taking in the dark bristle that covered his firm jaw. No more than a few days' growth, but a perfect background to show-case his smooth pink lips.

'Dr...'

'Alex,' he supplied. 'My name is Alex Morsi. And you are...?'

Kiki dragged her eyes away from the fascinating curve of his full lower lip and fixed them on the long length of his nose, marred only by the tiniest beauty spot at the top.

'Kiki Brown,' she replied automatically, deciding that the beauty spot actually enhanced his features. It was almost pretty, in a manly sort of way.

'Well, Kiki, as you insist on travelling in your car, let's go.'

Shaking her head, she forced her mind to stop notic-ing things about him and concentrate on getting him out of her car.

'I'm happy to go—once you remove yourself from that seat and get in your own vehicle.'

'What's the problem?'

He really must be obtuse if he didn't realise *he* was the problem. Funny how men frequently created trouble, then put their hands up and claimed innocence, view-ing everything in life from their angle and disregarding someone else's. Especially hers.

'As you've already pointed out,' she said, her patience thinning by the second, 'I'm new in town and, frankly, I don't know you. If you think I'm going to willingly share transport with a stranger, then you're wrong. I've read enough thriller novels and police statistics to know it's never a good idea.'

He offered his hand with a quirk of his lips. 'You can trust me. I'm a vet.'

She ignored his hand and wrinkled her nose, not keen to touch him in any form. A new wave of dislike filled her veins. Men liked to banter the word 'trust' around when it suited them, but they rarely lived by it. Few were acquainted with the true meaning of the word. Certainly not her father, nor her ex. This man would be the same. They always were.

She shook her head. 'In my experience when a man utters those words it always means the opposite is true.'

He nodded towards the practice.

'Go and ask Anne. She'll tell you that you've nothing to fear from me.'

She bristled at his arrogance. Why did men always bring everything back to *them*? She didn't want to share a car with him. Why couldn't he accept that? It didn't mean anything more than what it was.

'I don't fear you, Dr Morsi. I simply prefer to travel alone and for you to do the same. It's no big deal.'

He reached for the seat belt and drew it across his body. The metallic click as he locked it into place echoed in the strained atmosphere.

An irritated heat hummed through Kiki and her mouth fell open at his unbelievable nerve. 'Are you really so thick-headed? Did you not listen to what I said?'

'I did—but as you're talking nonsense I've decided to ignore it. Look, I understand why you're wary, but you've no reason for concern. I promise I hold no improper intentions where you're concerned.'

'But...' The faint spicy scent of his aftershave curled across the gap between them, distracting her thoughts.

Leaning close, he stared at her for several long seconds, before he declared, 'Simply put, Miss Brown, you're really not my type.'

She gasped, not sure whether to be insulted or relieved. Though, oddly, the overwhelming emotion pulsing through her body resembled disappointment. Who was *he* to dismiss her so rudely? This man who accused her of crimes against animals and, uninvited, positioned himself in her car?

'You're too short,' he continued, 'and I'm still not convinced the dogs you brought in aren't yours. Plus, if you recall, I asked Anne to call Ray from the RSPCA and our local police constable, Terry Foot, to ask them to meet us at Fingle Lodge. If I harboured intentions of harming you, would I have arranged for them to meet us at our destination? Or asked a member of my staff to make those calls? Surely those novels have taught you that no one set on menace would make such amateurish mistakes?'

He had a point, but Kiki didn't care. Her dislike for him increased with every word that fell out of his mouth. The less time she suffered his company, the better for her peace of mind and temper. *Wasn't his type?* Good— she didn't want to be Alex Morsi's type and he definitely wasn't hers. No one with a speck of sense would want any interaction with this man.

She shivered at the thought of arousing the man's interest. The sensation was disturbing and unfamiliar. She pitied the unfortunate women he *did* fancy. He probably ordered them around in and out of the bedroom walls. A genuine boudoir dictator.

Her heart thumped as an image of the man naked, wearing just a conceited smile of welcome, fluttered into her mind. With haste, she kicked it out again, blaming its appearance on the stress of the last few months and the delicious notes of his spicy aftershave. What else could possibly trigger such wild and alarming thoughts of a stranger she didn't even like?

'So now we've dealt with your concerns,' Alex said, his voice low and steady, 'shall we go?'

'You truly are a condescending—' she started. But the warmth heating her blood was more to do with her indecent thoughts than his superior, bossy attitude.

'Would you be more comfortable if I sat in the back?' he asked, pinning her with his intense brown stare. 'While we continue to bicker there's every chance the person who placed those dogs in your godmother's barn has returned and found out that Mum and pups are missing.'

She glared at him for several seconds before giving in. She could tolerate anyone for the dogs' safety—even this exasperating man. Their well-being mattered above everything.

Without a word, she tugged on her seat belt, fired up the engine and reversed out of the practice car park.

Never in her life had the urge to cause physical harm to another human being possessed her. Not even her ex's behaviour had instigated such black and brutal emotions. When she'd caught him with another woman, unclothed and doing things he'd had no business doing, she had only felt stupid and, if she was honest, relieved to have a good reason to call off the wedding. Happy to finally escape the trap she had so stupidly placed herself in.

She'd realised a few weeks after their engagement that she'd made a mistake, but the longer it had gone on, the harder she'd found it to disentangle herself. Before she'd had time to get used to the strange weight of the ring on her finger the reception had been booked, the caterers paid and the invitations on order.

But right at that moment she would happily have thrown something large and hefty at the male sitting next to her without a smidgen of guilt. In fact, she suspected she would not only do it, but enjoy it, too.

Gripping the steering wheel, she followed Alex's instructions to the lodge, not bothering to make conversation and determined to concentrate on nothing but the journey through the winding tree-lined country roads.

Some time later, Alex said, 'Take the next turning on the left.'

Distracted by his voice, Kiki glanced across and noticed how big his hands were. Capable hands, able to save precious lives. Hands full of might and ability. For a fleeting moment she visualised his long fingers trailing in an invisible and continual stroke along her body, caressing her sensitive flesh. Teasing her with their light arousing touch…

With a hard slam on the brakes, she brought the car to a stop outside her godmother's property. Much longer and she might have given in to her outrageous thoughts and nuzzled her face into the palm nearest to her.

Turning off the engine, she swallowed hard and fumbled for the door handle. Yes, she was definitely in the middle of a breakdown. She just prayed she could get through the rest of their time together without embarrassing herself completely.

Alex climbed from the Mini, relieved to be free from its restricting confines. Vintage vehicles might be a delight for the eyes and the heart, but compared to their modern successors they lacked basic comfort.

Not that the journey's discomfort had come only from the absence of modern luxuries and decent suspension.

One second longer sitting next to Kiki Brown and her suppressed anger and he might have done something stupid. Something crazy and improper. Like reaching across and touching her.

Slamming the door, he rubbed his jaw, the rasp of the stubble reminding him of the need to shave.

He'd never struggled with the urge to touch an unknown woman before—especially one whose trustworthiness he questioned. Though, in truth, he hadn't touched a woman—stranger or otherwise—in months. Something he needed to rectify if it left him fighting peculiar impulses towards female strangers.

He hadn't lied when he'd stated that Kiki wasn't his type. His preference in girlfriends ran towards the tall, slim and unemotional. Three things Miss Kiki Brown was not. She barely reached his shoulder and her curves promised secrets only intimate exploration would satisfy. And it was clear from her changing expressions that her emotions controlled her every thought and wish.

Sneaking another glance at the female set on disrupting his day, he heard his common sense yelling at him to ignore her. Normally he listened to that reliable internal voice, but when Kiki wasn't grousing, or shooting him silent threats, sadness coloured her blue eyes. Someone had hurt this woman and done a damn good job of it, too.

He frowned and scratched his jaw again, his short nails rough against his chin. Why did he care? His purpose here was to rescue those neglected dogs. Kiki Brown was nothing but a witness and helper in this unfortunate event.

'Is that the barn?' He pointed at the building, reluctant to break the silence between them, but aware one of them had to.

'Yes.'

Kiki led the way over, not waiting to see if he followed. Obviously she was still upset over his sharing her car, but Alex didn't have the time or the desire to concern himself with her bruised feelings. He'd deal with the situation here and then return to the practice. Before the day's end this woman and the unwelcome emotions she stirred would be no more than a memory. One he'd do his best to forget.

'How long do you think the dogs have been here?' he asked.

She shrugged, glancing over her shoulder at him. 'No idea, but a fair amount of filth covers the floor and cages.'

His lips flattened in disgust as he imagined her shock when she found the dogs. He'd dealt with similar situations. Every one distressing and heartrending for the soul. Each one the result of nothing but human callousness and greed.

'Things will improve for them now,' he said, wanting to comfort her, but not sure how.

Instinctively, he reached out and touched her shoulder. She tensed beneath his fingers and shot him a deadly glare. Alex immediately dropped his hand, regretting the innocent action.

Great—now she probably figured him for a sexual predator as well as a potential murderer. No doubt, she'd read books about such men. Thank God he'd given up on women. He'd never had much luck over the years, and now it seemed his skills were as corroded as a tin of rusty scalpels and just about as useful.

Thirty minutes after arriving, PC Foot, tall and bald, wandered over to where Kiki and Alex waited outside the barn. He and Ray from the RSPCA had finally finished viewing the room where the dogs were imprisoned.

'You can remove the dogs now, Alex,' he said, resting his hands on his belt. 'We've taken photos and gathered anything we think is evidence and relevant to the case.'

Alex nodded, but lingered when PC Foot turned his attention to the woman at his side. A trace of suspicion glimmered in the policeman's gaze.

'You say this is your godmother's property.'

'Yes,' Kiki answered.

'But she hasn't lived here for years. Not since her husband died in a boating accident.'

' You're just checking on the place, are you?'

'No, I'm staying here at the lodge for a few months. My godmother's thinking of selling it, so I've agreed to make it a little more liveable and tidy the gardens.'

The policeman frowned. 'You intend to stay here alone?'

Alex bristled at the question. Wouldn't the man's concern be better focused on the crime he was there to investigate than on what Kiki's plans were?

'Yes,' Kiki answered.

'Not a good idea,' he said with a shake of his head. 'This situation is tricky. The people who left those dogs may be part of a gang, or just opportunists out to make money and viewed this property as the perfect dwelling to do so. Either way, they're heartless criminals, and I doubt they will appreciate losing their business thanks to your appearance.'

'Are you saying she's at risk if she stays here?'

Alex finally absorbed the policeman's warning. Had her act of kindness to the dogs placed her in danger?

PC Foot nodded. 'I think it would be best if you didn't

stay on your own. Perhaps a friend can come over for a few nights? Or a boyfriend?'

Kiki dismissed the suggestion. 'I've only recently returned from working in Alaska for a year and most of my friends live in London.'

'Hence the whales?' Alex murmured, glancing at her wellies.

What had happened in Alaska to bring her back to England to live in a shabby house on a deserted estate? A job? A family crisis? A man? Did the person who had caused the pain in her eyes have anything to do with it or someone else?

Kiki glanced his way. 'Sorry?'

Not sure if he had spoken his thoughts out loud, he searched her face for a hint, but only found annoyance. 'Nothing.'

'Would *you* be willing to stay for a few nights, Alex?' PC Foot quizzed.

'Me?' Alex repeated, stunned by the suggestion. Being alone with this woman for hours on end, in the same property, was a terrible idea.

'Gentlemen, I do not need a protector,' Kiki argued. 'I am quite able to look after myself. And I have a mobile to call the police the minute someone drives onto the property.'

The policeman sighed with a resigned expression. 'It will take at least twenty minutes for an officer to get here, miss. I don't want to worry you, but a lot can happen in that time.'

Alex spoke before Kiki could disagree further. He didn't have time to bicker back and forth. Patients awaited him at the practice.

'I can stay over until we're sure there's no further risk.

Once the person who left the dogs realises the place is no longer empty, hopefully they'll keep their distance and move on.'

PC Foot grinned and clapped his hands. 'Good—glad it's settled. Well, folks, I need to get back to the station.'

'But… But…' Kiki stammered.

'I'll keep in touch and let you know how things are progressing,' he added. 'Truth is, we'll probably never find out who's responsible, or be able to bring charges. Don't worry. You can trust Alex to keep you safe.'

Ray finally joined them. 'The sooner we get these poor dogs to the practice, the better. They're all in want of a warm bath and a nice meal. I'll start making calls to find kennels for the night once I've dropped them off.'

Glad to change the subject, Alex said, 'I'll get one of my staff to check the lost dog sites, in case they've been stolen from any owners.'

He moved towards the barn, but Kiki's hand on his arm stalled him. He glanced down at her ringless pale fingers, certain he could feel their warmth through his jacket.

'You really don't need to stay—' she began.

'Miss Brown,' he interrupted, not about to get into another argument. He wasn't exactly thrilled either, but her safety ranked above his own comfort. 'When I offer to do something, I always see it through. Even when the chore promises to be less than agreeable.'

CHAPTER THREE

KIKI'S PLAN TO spend time alone and wallow in her own melancholy was starting to disintegrate quicker than an overcooked pie in a burning-hot furnace. Instead of the relaxed peace and quiet she craved, she was being forced to share her new home with an unwanted houseguest. One she could barely manage to be civil to.

She should have stayed in Alaska. What was seeing an over-sexed ex-fiancé compared to short-term cohabiting with an ill-mannered stranger? At least there she would have been left alone. No one had wanted to spend time with a woman who had publicly rejected a local boy, even if he couldn't be trusted around other women.

Kiki's only bit of luck had come when she'd visited the key-holder and discovered the lodge wasn't as derelict as her godmother had implied. Apparently, until a few years ago, she had regularly rented it out to holiday-makers throughout the summer months. And, although the woman had left the outside alone, she still cleaned the interior every six months or so.

The poor woman had been horrified when Kiki had informed her of the morning's unpleasant discovery in the barn.

After buying several bags of food, Kiki returned to

the lodge in the late afternoon and, after a dust and a general clean, settled into her new abode and started cooking. Not that she could relax. Not with her impending overnight guest on her mind.

Alex Morsi wasn't her idea of good company. The opposite, in fact. Opinionated, bossy, and annoyingly distracting. Much too handsome and quarrelsome. The sooner she convinced him she didn't need a bodyguard in blue scrubs and green wellies, the quicker she could get on with her new life.

She doubted they had much in common other than being in the same line of work. Though she suspected Dr Morsi would consider himself far superior to a lowly veterinary nurse.

A loud knock on the front door caused Kiki to drop her ladle into the saucepan, splashing hot carrot soup over her fingers. Shaking her hand to ease the pain, she grabbed a tea towel.

'Damn.'

Sucking the burn, she left the kitchen. Her footsteps slowed as she walked along the hallway. With a deep breath, she wiped her hands on the towel and opened the door.

Alex Morsi stood on the doorstep, an overnight bag in one hand and a cat carrier in the other. He was dressed in a black hoodie beneath an aged leather biker's jacket. His faded blue jeans emphasised his long legs and old, scuffed black walking boots concluded the casual but elegant outfit.

The man knew how to dress.

Kiki immediately regretted not changing out of the grubby pink dungarees and baggy grey jumper she'd put on earlier to clean the lodge. Next to Dr Perfect Model, she resembled a tramp on a bad day.

Gripping the door handle, she resisted the urge to throw the door shut again and stepped back for Alex to enter. 'You've brought company?'

'His name's Nix and he's a Mini-Lop rabbit. I hope you don't mind? He's not much of a talker. Mostly just twitches his nose and occasionally thumps his feet. He's partial to the odd lettuce leaf, and never goes near cabbage now his doctor has advised him not to.'

She almost smiled at his attempt at humour, but she didn't want him to think she'd softened in her stance towards him. No matter how many jokes or humorous stories he told, she didn't want him or his rabbit for company.

'Okay, I'll be honest,' she blurted out, 'I don't want you here. But, as you are, I'm prepared to make the best of a situation I've reluctantly agreed to.'

The corner of his mouth twitched and his brown eyes twinkled. 'I don't recall you actually agreeing. You did complain, though.'

'I had every right,' she huffed, folding her arms. She'd spent most of her life without a man around to help. And when they had been she'd usually wished they weren't. 'It's not the Dark Ages. A woman can look after herself.'

'I don't question your ability to do so,' Alex said smoothly. 'But Nix and I had nothing else planned for this evening—and, honestly, I've always wanted to see inside this place. I sometimes walk the fields nearby and I've wondered why it's unoccupied.'

Some of Kiki's indignation eased. 'It holds too many painful memories for my godmother,' she said. 'She and her husband lived here for three years before she lost him. When he died in a boating accident not far from here she couldn't bear to return. She says Dorset is where her heart is, but Kent is where her feet will stay.'

'Sad.'

Kiki agreed. 'Especially as she never remarried. She insists her heart died with one man, and there's no point in living with another knowing she'd never love him in the same way.'

'Shame,' Alex murmured, 'when an old place like this is left devoid of love and laughter for so many years. It's almost a sin, don't you think? Especially as the original estate no longer exists, other than the occasional section of rubble penetrating the earth.'

She stared at him, not sure what to say. His comment was unexpected and almost moving. 'That's rather sentimental.'

'From a man like me?' he asked, raising an eyebrow. 'I really have made a bad impression on you, haven't I?'

'W-well...' she stammered.

Would he take umbrage if she told him the truth? That the words 'boorish' and 'rude' entered her head every time he opened his mouth.

'I suppose you think wanting a family and a home is only a female's prerogative? Well, men can want those things, and yet often we're discouraged from admitting it.'

'I know. It's just...' Her words trailed off.

Did he really want a family or did he just have the romantic idea of one? Many men declared they did, but often resented the reality when it didn't include the perfect child. Then they abandoned the first family and tried again with someone else until they finally achieved their wish. Not concerned with the shattered hearts they left behind or the broken lives left to rot after their rejection.

'You didn't think I might?' he asked, misunderstanding her hesitation. 'Don't worry—you're not the first. People often mistake me for some sort of Casanova, just because society's shallowness deems me physically compelling to the female eye.'

'And you're not?' she asked sceptically.

With his handsome face, she figured women stood in queues for the chance of having him as their escort. Sharing a meal with Alex across a candlelit table would certainly put a smile on many women's faces.

He laughed and shook his head. 'I'm not sure I'd know how to start, let alone play the game. Truth is, I'm too old-fashioned for most women's tastes.'

Kiki wrinkled her nose. Did he really think she would believe he was a good guy in a world of bad ones? Most men pretended to be a certain way, but soon changed into the real person they were once they grew bored or content in a relationship. In her experience it was simply a matter of waiting to discover if their words were lies or truths. And they were always lies. Every single time.

She turned away, peeved by the questions the man aroused. What did it matter to her if he was truly what he professed or not? She wasn't interested in men. Right now, all she wanted was to find a position in a local veterinary practice and settle down for a while.

'I need to get back to the kitchen. I've left a saucepan of food heating.'

She hurried along the narrow hallway and found the soup's mouth-watering aroma was filling the house with its comforting scent. It reminded her of all the reasons for her decision to return to England. Terrible homesickness and a yearning for familiar surroundings and sights.

She had never felt completely comfortable in Alaska. It had been as if her subconscious had known it would never really be her home. Possibly her heart had simply yearned for misshapen green fields and the salty crisp scent of the coast.

'Nice,' Alex murmured, stepping into the kitchen a few moments later.

A loud rumble sounded from his stomach, making Kiki's lips tug into a smile.

She glanced up at him after checking the saucepan on the dated gas cooker. 'Hungry?'

He nodded and placed a hand over the flat of his stomach, as though to repress any further appreciative noises. 'A little. I've not eaten since breakfast.'

She fetched two yellow earthenware bowls from an antique pine cupboard. A row of similar cupboards sat under the window that faced the overgrown back garden. On another wall stood an aged walnut dresser she suspected was as old as the property.

She didn't want the man's company, but she refused to be rude. Eating a meal together was nothing but good manners.

'There's enough to share if you'd like some.'

'Thanks. Is there somewhere I can settle Nix?'

She indicated the larder in the corner of the room next to the back door. 'It's empty and clean. Does he need medication? Is that why you've brought him with you?'

'No. He's more of a pet. A few years ago a little girl visited the practice and begged me to keep him because her parents had split up and her mother planned to move to Spain to live. She'd tried to find him a home, but Nix

isn't the cuddly sort and often bites chunks out of anyone who tries.' A smile briefly skimmed his lips. 'She
still sends him a postcard every year on his birthday.'

'He's a house rabbit?' Kiki asked.

Alex nodded. 'He doesn't like his own company in
the evenings. You don't mind, do you?'

She shook her head, surprised this haughty vet owned
a soft heart beneath all his arrogance. He'd taken in a
little girl's pet because no one else had wanted him, and
had brought him here tonight so he wouldn't be lonely.

'No, it's fine.'

Within minutes, Alex had settled the rabbit in the
small room off the kitchen, leaving the door ajar so he
could still see them while they ate their meal.

Setting a couple of warm, fresh baguettes on a well-
used wooden cutting board on the pine table, Kiki
gathered two dessert spoons from a drawer. Not a posh
restaurant, and definitely no candles in sight—thank
goodness—but she hoped they could get through the
meal without arguing.

'I expected the place to be more derelict than this,'
Alex murmured, glancing around the room. His gaze
lingered on the white butler's sink and brass taps.

Kiki signalled for him to sit down while she ladled
out the soup between the two bowls, figuring the lodge
was a safe subject for them to discuss during the meal.

Taking the chair across from his, she said, 'According to the key-holder Mrs Bush, who lives in the blue
cottage down the lane, my godmother used to rent the
place out for holiday lets. It needs a fresh coat of paint
throughout, and some better furniture more in keeping with its architecture, but structurally the building is

sound. It won't take much to revive it and turn it into a small but comfortable home.'

'Are you a designer?' he asked curiously.

She laughed at the notion. 'No. I'm actually a trained veterinary nurse.'

Alex lowered his spoon and stared across the table at her. 'Really?'

She nodded.

'I worked in a busy London practice for several years. I helped out there after school and on weekends, after doing a two-week work experience there. And once I left school, I knew I wanted to work with animals there full-time. I loved it. Though I became a researcher during the past year when I lived in Alaska.'

'Sounds like interesting work.'

She shrugged and lowered her head. Her time abroad had certainly been that. Though the work was the only part she'd truly enjoyed and now missed.

'It was different—and mostly motivating.'

He tasted the soup, then asked, 'What brought you back to England?'

She hesitated, not sure she wanted to admit the truth. Acknowledging failure was never an easy thing to do—especially to a stranger. How to explain getting engaged to the wrong man? It was something she had done without much thought or care. And she'd soon found herself trapped in an association she'd realised she didn't want.

Finally, she shrugged. 'The end of a relationship.'

'Serious?' he enquired.

'We got as far as buying a ring. But it soon became clear that his commitment to the relationship wasn't the same as my own. Though now I see it was always doomed. But that's all in the past. What about you? I see no ring, but that doesn't mean anything. Plenty of men prefer not to wear one.'

He tore off a piece of bread, scattering crusty flakes over the surface of the soup.

'No, I'm not married. Nor have I ever been. Would you be interested in a job?'

Noting the deliberate change in conversation, Kiki frowned. Alex Morsi didn't like discussing himself. Strange, considering every man she knew loved talking about nothing *but* themselves.

'At your practice?' she asked.

He nodded, his attention still fixed on the soup. 'A member of staff recently left, and someone with experience is always useful.'

'How long has the position been vacant?' she asked, dunking a piece of bread into her soup. The mild aroma of garlic and the sweetness of the organic carrots made her mouth water.

'Not long,' he hedged.

Something in his voice made Kiki glance up from her bowl. Alex's closed expression was a sign that there was more to this person leaving than he wanted to share. Did it have something to do with him? She'd bet it did.

'Why did they leave?' she asked, popping the piece of bread into her mouth.

'This soup is good,' he said, keeping his gaze lowered. 'Did you make it yourself?'

She swallowed her food. 'Why are you avoiding answering my question?' she quizzed. 'And, yes, it's homemade.'

'I'm not,' he denied, glancing up.

Now she had his attention she took full advantage. 'So why did the person leave?' she repeated.

His sigh reminded her of someone who'd realised his fate was already decided and had no chance to change the conclusion.

'I suppose the reason is best described as a personality issue with another member of staff.'

'Who?' she asked, already guessing the answer.

Having a conversation with this man was hard, so she hated to think how working alongside him would be. Did his staff tremble in his presence? Or leave because they refused to deal with his brash, high-handed attitude?

Alex cleared his throat and reached for another piece of bread. He took his time buttering it. Making each swipe in time with the ticking of the clock.

'Is that significant?' he asked.

She leaned back in her chair. Yes, he was definitely hiding something. It intrigued her all the more. 'It might be.'

'Okay,' he grumbled, placing the piece of bread back down on the board with a thud. 'According to Anne, the woman found me difficult to work with.'

Kiki didn't bother to hide her grin, enjoying his discomfort. He was both abrupt and direct—she imagined many people found him hard to get along with.

'You *do* shock me, Dr Morsi.'

'You're intent on making me suffer, aren't you?' he asked, smiling back.

Giddiness robbed Kiki of all normal thought as she experienced the effect of his grin. The man was handsome when he frowned, but his unexpected full smile shone with joy when freed.

'Are you sure you can trust me around the animals?' she queried.

The quivering sensation in her chest was lingering.

And, despite being seated, her limbs felt weak and unsteady. What was happening to her? The more time she spent talking to this man, the more she became a heap of hormonal mush.

'Look, I'm sorry I accused you earlier today,' he said.

'You should be,' she replied, but smiled to soften her words.

He chuckled and resumed eating. The shudder of the old fridge and the ticking of the clock were the only sounds in the room. Regardless of their being virtual strangers, an odd contentment fell between them.

'About the job...' she said after several moments, once the strange unsteadiness had finally passed.

Alex lowered his spoon and met her gaze. 'Yes?'

Those beautiful eyes sent another flare of awareness through her body, setting off the fluttering again.

She dropped her gaze to the table. 'I'll think about it.'

'Really?'

She nodded and returned her attention to her food, not looking up again until her heart had returned to its normal beat and the strange sensations in her stomach had disappeared back to the unknown place from where they had so unexpectedly surfaced.

Alex flicked off the bedside lamp and rested against the padded headboard. Although they'd managed to get through the evening without falling out, Kiki's irritation with the situation had thrummed like an uneasy undertone between them. Well, he wasn't overjoyed about spending the night here either. His studio flat above the practice might not be five-star comfort, but at least he slept in a double bed with a lump-free mattress.

Kicking the bedcovers, he pushed deeper into the padding and processed everything he'd learnt about this woman who'd stormed into his practice that morning. Strange, it seemed longer than a few hours ago…

Not only an unemployed veterinary nurse, Kiki had also recently undergone a broken engagement. Evidently the reason for the unhappiness that radiated from her at times.

Was she the one who'd broken things off or her ex-fiancé? Was their relationship over for good, or did she secretly hope the man would travel to England to fix things between them, despite her assertion that the relationship had always been destined to fail?

Wide awake, Alex scratched his chest and stared into the darkness. Who knew what women thought or wanted? He was certainly no expert on the subject. The few relationships he'd shared over the past few years had never progressed further than dinner with no-commitment sex afterwards.

Nix shuffled in his carrier, content to sleep after having the run of the lounge floor for over an hour. That was when the traitor hadn't been snuggled on Kiki's lap, showing no signs of his normal aggressive behaviour.

Alex's gaze shifted to the wall between their bedrooms. Both rooms were situated at the rear of the property. Had Kiki already fallen asleep or was she also pondering the day's developments?

He groaned, not in a hurry to consider the woman being anywhere near a bed or what she might look like in it. After tonight he'd make excuses not to stay over again and find someone else to take his place. Common sense insisted spending further time around this woman promised nothing but problems and trouble.

Suddenly the bedroom door flew open, banging

back on its hinges, and the female tormenting his mind rushed in.

'Did you hear a noise?'

Alex sat up, captivated by the sight before him. Light from the hallway highlighted the short pink nightdress Kiki wore and proved him a liar. Despite his earlier denial, it appeared Kiki Brown was very much his type of woman.

He swallowed hard, and his imagination fired into carnal overdrive as his gaze skimmed over the smooth bare legs and curvy female contours the nightdress lovingly swathed.

He tugged the bedcovers higher, not eager for Kiki to see how much the sight of her affected him physically. Adding horny beggar to his roll of crimes wouldn't benefit either of them.

He coughed and cleared his throat, reluctantly dragging his eyes away. 'Probably mice in the attic.'

'No—outside.' She raced back out of the room. 'I'm sure I heard a car.'

Loosening his hold on the covers, Alex listened, but only the fast beating of his own heart filled his ears. He defied any heterosexual male not to be turned on by the delectable vision who had just left the room. He was just reacting as any man would. It meant nothing. Just a physical response to an attractive woman's body after months of self-imposed celibacy.

Kiki reappeared, placing her hands on her hips, tantalisingly raising the hem of the nightdress an inch higher, unknowingly taunting his already raised interest.

'Why are you still lying there?'

How did he explain to a woman who already had a low opinion of him that the sight of her in such skimpy night clothes had prompted unexpected reactions in his body? Reactions with the potential to embarrass them both.

He opened his mouth, then closed it again. His mind was empty of plausible excuses.

'Come on—get up!'

She tried to grab the covers, but Alex held them tight, feeling slightly ridiculous. 'I can get out of bed without help, thanks.'

She left the room again, flicking off the light in the hall and pitching the lodge into total darkness. The squeak of the lounge door sounded moments later.

Silently cursing, Alex threw off the duvet and scrambled out of bed. *Okay, Morsi, just pretend nothing is wrong.* No reason for Kiki to discover his inability to control his own body. At least she wouldn't be able to see his predicament with the light out. Thank God for that one blessing.

Not bothering to grab his clothes, Alex stumbled to the door wearing no more than his tight black boxers. Normally he didn't sleep in anything other than bed sheets and a duvet, but tonight he'd decided to keep his shorts on.

'Alex?'

'Oomph.'

A small, feminine body smacked into his own before he had a chance to protect himself. Instinctively his fingers flexed against the soft sleek curves beneath his palms, itching to browse and explore the shape further.

'Are you okay?' he asked, hoping she couldn't feel every part of his body the way he could hers. A startled gasp a second later destroyed that hope. With only a thin nightdress and a pair of cotton boxers between them their bodies were keeping few secrets hidden.

'Yes,' she squeaked. 'I'm fine.'

She spun away into the darkness once again, like a night-time nymph set on torturing him. Leaving him aching, lonely and wanting to crawl back under the duvet and not leave until morning.

'Where are you?' he rumbled, rotating his left shoulder to ease some of the tension in it.

'In the lounge,' she called. 'Quick—there's a car outside.'

'Perhaps they're visiting your neighbour.'

'We're the last property in a dead-end lane. If they're visiting Mrs Bush why drive all the way down here? And why do it at this time of night? I'm sure the old lady will be in bed by now.'

Forgetting his discomfort, Alex fumbled through the blackness, hitting a wall before his eyes slowly adjusted to the shadows. Joining Kiki in the dark lounge, he peered out of the window. Sure enough a car waited in the lane and a shady figure walked along the path towards the old barn.

Alex stepped back from the window. 'Stay here.'

'Where are you going?' Kiki asked, her eyes still on the figure outside. A floorboard creaked beneath her feet.

'To speak to our visitor.'

He hurried to his room and grabbed his hoodie off the chair. Tugging it on, he slipped his feet into his boots. Stopping only to grab his phone, he flicked on its torch before heading down the narrow hall towards the kitchen.

'Do you think you should?' Kiki asked from behind him.

Alex paused and half turned, making out Kiki's shape

in the shadows. 'Call the police and tell them you're being broken into.'

'But…' She hesitated, then took a step towards him. 'Shouldn't I come with you?'

'No. Make the call and stay inside.'

Alex continued down the hall. Whoever lurked outside was going to get an unexpected reception. One they weren't going to like. Tonight would be the last time they came sneaking around Fingle Lodge.

Unlocking the back door, Alex felt the cold night air greet his bare legs with a crisp, icy caress. Edging along the stone wall, grit crunching beneath his boots, he'd reached the corner of the building when something touched him on the shoulder. Spinning round, he found himself staring into a familiar female face.

'I've called the police,' Kiki whispered, pulling her coat over her nightdress. Once again, she wore her wellies. 'And they're on their way.'

'Good. Now go inside,' he ordered.

She ignored him and pulled out a pair of woollen gloves from her coat pocket. 'What's the plan?'

'I'm going to the barn and you're going inside.'

'The barn?' she echoed. 'I definitely need to go with you, then.'

Alex clamped down on his irritation. There was an unknown person loitering in the grounds of the property. Someone who thought nothing about hurting and abusing innocent animals. And she refused to listen to sense.

'Kiki, this isn't a pleasure excursion. The person whose dogs we've confiscated is about to find out they're all missing.'

'Rescued,' she corrected.

Gritting his teeth, Alex demanded, 'How do you think he's going to react once he realises they're gone?'

'Might be a woman...' she deliberated. 'I think they'll be very angry.'

'Exactly.'

'But then we're angry, too,' she said, moving past him. 'Come on. Let's show them how angry we are.'

Alex tugged her back and shoved his phone at her. 'Take this.'

She frowned, but reached for it. 'Why?'

'If I need to make a grab for him—or her—I don't want my phone broken in the scuffle.'

Together they made their way to the barn and slipped inside. The bright light from the full moon illuminated the interior, thanks to the large opening once used for lifting hay into the roof space. The smell of damp earth and stale air prickled Alex's nose and he fought the sting of an impending sneeze, not wanting to give away their presence.

Searching the space, he made out the shape of the open door leading to the room where the dogs had been kept. Deep muttering and shuffling came from within, followed by a scraping noise as the person explored the area.

Kiki nudged Alex in the side with her elbow and leaned up to whisper in his ear. Her warm minty breath sent a trickle of awareness over his already heightened senses.

'If I shut the door, can you jam something against it?'

Understanding, Alex touched his mouth to her forehead and nodded. He recalled seeing several planks of wood propped against the wall next to the room. 'Good idea.'

'On the count of three,' she whispered. 'One, two, three...'

Together they rushed forward and slammed the door, trapping the intruder inside. Alex wedged a large heavy wooden plank against the door handle, securing the room and blocking any way for their prisoner to escape.

'We did it!'

Kiki threw herself at him, wrapping her arms around his neck, flattening her body against his in delight. Holding her close, Alex felt the essence of floral shampoo and soft warm woman smother his wits, awakening a strange hunger he'd never experienced before. One he wasn't sure he liked.

'We did.'

A police siren wailed in the distance and muffled yelling sounded from the room, but neither moved or let go. Their whole awareness centred on nothing but the feel and proximity of each other.

Pulling her closer, he tightened his arms. 'Kiki?'

'Yes, Alex?' she gasped.

'Would this be a completely inappropriate moment to kiss you?'

CHAPTER FOUR

'YOU'RE A DAMN FOOL, Morsi,' Alex muttered, squeez-ing the bunch of keys in his hand until the jagged edges cut into his palm. What the hell had possessed him to behave like a first-class idiot with that out-of-nowhere suggestion of a kiss?

Choking on a bitter laugh, he groaned. A kiss? Re-ally? What a Romeo. Old Ronny the cat had nothing on him in the smooth stakes.

He hadn't needed to see Kiki's expression to know the idea of kissing him had repelled her. The speed with which she'd scrambled out of his hold had caused enough sparks to burn down the barn and eradicate his crushed ego along with it.

A car drove by, its loud exhaust breaking into his self-recriminations. He glared after the vehicle's disappearing rear lights, eager to redirect his bad mood somewhere other than at himself. But the shambles of this last hour was no one's fault but his own.

Now he wanted to kick off the day, sink into bed and fall asleep. Just forget it all for a while. Since Kiki Brown had stepped into his life everything had turned into an unbalanced mess.

Slipping the key into the front door lock of his studio

flat, he stepped inside. A cool chill greeted him as he bent and retrieved the blue envelope waiting on the door-mat. Recognising his business partner's printed hand-writing, he shoved it into his jacket pocket. Whatever was inside could wait until tomorrow. Enough already occupied his mind tonight without adding more.

Climbing the five narrow steps to his home—little more than a functional space—he sighed and reluctantly relived the last hour's events.

He'd not hung around after the police had arrived and carted off the intruder. Grabbing Nix and his bag, he'd made his excuses and left. Since the man was under po-lice custody Alex had no reason to stay and risk making a bigger spectacle of himself.

At the top step he came to an abrupt stop. Even in the darkness, with just the street lights shining through the net curtains, he sensed something was off. Though in the shadows he couldn't make out exactly what.

Stepping forward, he paused at a sound he didn't recognise. Tilting his head, he took another step—then stopped.

Why could he hear water running?

Reaching out, he fumbled for the switch and turned on the overhead light. Artificial brightness filled the room, blinding him for a moment. After a few seconds his gaze cleared and he focused on the cheap blue car-pet beneath him.

Lifting his left foot, he slowly lowered it.

Squelch.

He did the same with his right.

Squelch.

Placing Nix's carrier down, he crouched and skimmed

his palm over the short nylon pile, grimacing when his fingers came away wet.

Yep, definitely water. And a lot of it.

Confused, he moved further into the flat, coming to a halt for a second time. Broken plasterboard scattered the vintage rug in front of the television and the bookcase and a steady stream of water ran from a large hole where a big chunk of the ceiling used to be.

Walking closer, he stared up into the attic space and discovered the cause for all the mess and destruction. Water poured from the bottom of a large galvanised tank.

He stepped away from the debris and cursed. How much worse did this night intend to get? Wasn't total humiliation enough, without adding a burst water tank and a destroyed ceiling to the dung heap of his existence?

Grabbing his mobile out of his trouser pocket, he searched for the practice plumber's telephone number. Not caring about the lateness of the hour, he pressed the button and waited. After several unanswered rings he left a message, then threw the phone across the room to land in the middle of his desk.

Locating the mains water tap beneath the kitchen sink, Alex twisted it to the 'off' position and fetched a still boxed carpet cleaner—an unwanted Christmas present from his aunt—from the storage cupboard. Dumping it in the middle of the mess, he returned to the stairs.

Before he dealt with the drenched carpet, he needed to settle the rabbit in his indoor hutch and check downstairs to see if any of the practice ceilings had suffered water damage.

Ten minutes later he left the practice after checking each room. Thank heavens for concrete floors. Not one plastered ceiling showed signs of water damage. One less problem to stress over tonight, when he still had so much to do.

Back in the flat, Alex ripped open the box holding the cleaner, halting halfway through as he felt some of his anger diminish.

Sinking onto the sofa, he rested his head in his hands, digging his fingers through his hair. Heaviness seeped into every muscle of his body. Would the rest of his days be like this? Having to deal with life's problems without the help and support of another person? Never having anyone to talk to other than his staff and the animals he treated? Sorting through daily traumas without someone close to share his concerns and worries?

His fingertips pressed further into his scalp. Was it selfish to want someone to come home to after a day's work? Someone who understood his career and wouldn't complain if he left in the middle of the night for an emergency? Who would welcome him home again at daybreak, with a hot cup of tea and a sleepy smile, even though he returned smelling of animals and covered in stuff best washed off and never discussed?

A special female who enjoyed his company and actually desired his kisses? A woman, in fact, who wanted more than his kisses? Who craved his touch upon her skin and screamed his name during their lovemaking? Someone to share a bath with and argue with over stupid disputes, and then make up sweet and hard? A woman who wanted him with the same passion and intensity with which he wanted her?

Someone kind, sweet…and nothing but a mirage of a hopeless dream.

Rubbing his palms along his face, he leaned forward, feeling bone-tired and so damn lonely. Why was it easy for others to get their dreams, yet he constantly struggled to attain his? Never able to grasp the joys others gained with little effort?

Closing his eyes, he drew in several deep breaths before returning his attention to the cardboard box. He didn't have time for self-pity. His life was nice and calm. Something he'd craved as a boy and accomplished as an adult by moving away from Ireland and his parents. He should be grateful for the peace in his life.

He didn't care that his mother's damning prediction, pronounced in the middle of his tenth birthday party, in front of all his school friends and family members, that he would stay a bachelor for his whole life, appeared to be coming true. But then she also professed that he was the devil's son every time they saw each other.

He stood and removed the cleaner, frowning at all the different nozzles and hoses. Flinging the instruction book to one side, he set about putting the machine together. The sooner he dealt with the water, the quicker he'd get some sleep. Rehashing his rotten childhood was best left for another night.

At least he had one less thing to worry over. After his behaviour tonight, no way would Kiki Brown accept his job offer. Saving him the embarrassment of ever seeing the beautiful, frustrating woman again.

The following morning Kiki stared at the practice entrance, not certain she wasn't making a huge mistake. Yet another mammoth one that she might end up regretting.

Did anyone know the correct protocol for accepting a job after the boss had asked to kiss you? And then done a runner before she could explain why she'd stepped out of his hold before he could attempt to carry out his request.

She wrinkled her nose at the memory, feeling a fresh surge of guilt hitting her hard in the chest. The poor embarrassed man, whom she'd only met several hours before, and most of them had been far from normal or pleasant, had asked to kiss her and she'd reacted as though he carried a foul and infectious disease. Hardly surprising he'd left the house in a whirl of discomfort and excuses, taking his pet rabbit along with him.

A bashful teenager acted with more tact and finesse than she did. No wonder the man had scarpered before the blue lights on the police car had stopped flashing. He'd probably never met a woman more sexually inept and incapable. A true uptight virgin, as her ex had often accused her of being all those times she'd fought out of his pushy hold and reminded him of their mutual decision to wait until after the wedding to consummate their relationship.

She sighed and studied the Tarmac. Was it really a surprise the man had cheated on her? What thirty-two-year-old woman *hadn't* notched up at least one or two sexual partners at her age? Oh, she'd received offers from men over the years, and had occasionally been tempted by them, but something had always prevented her from taking the final step of peeling off her clothes and giving herself to a man. Trusting him with both her heart and body. Putting herself completely in his control.

For her, men were always a great disappointment. Her father's callous treatment of her mother when he'd left the marriage for a younger woman and his appalling behaviour throughout the unpleasant divorce was just one of many examples during Kiki's childhood that had confirmed to her that all men were dishonest, unreliable and incapable of being faithful.

Not wanting to linger further on unpleasant past memories, she returned her focus to Alex Morsi. A man who sent her every sensible thought and doubt reeling far into the ether. Remembering last night and his whispered question sent a fierce but delightful shiver through her body. Because, despite the way she'd drawn out of his embrace, she'd actually wanted to cling to him like a bee on a foxglove and kiss him until he passed out at her feet. Not only to steal his breath away, but selfishly to keep it, too.

And that realisation upset her far more than the man's request or behaviour. She, Kiki Brown, supposedly distraught from the chaos of a recently failed engagement, had desperately longed to plant her lips on Alex Morsi's and kiss him into erotic submission. A man she didn't even like much had made her want to give herself to him completely, without a care or rational thought for the consequences.

She groaned, rubbing her forehead to ease the thumping headache which had plagued her all night, taking with it a decent night's sleep. Instead she'd drifted between consciousness and wonderful fantasies. Fantasies that confirmed she was a wicked female of questionable morals who deserved to be shunned for the wantonness of her desires.

For surely no decent female on the rebound from calling off her wedding to another man complicated her life by fantasising over a stranger? No matter how much she'd liked being in his arms and enjoyed the way the hard contours of his mostly naked form had melded against her own.

It should make no difference if his strong arms wrapped around her had made her feel delicate and safe for the first time in her life. Or if his warm breath whispering against her ear had set off a million quivers and raised her heart-rate to bell-clanging top heights.

No, none of that mattered—because she was sensible and practical Kiki Brown. She'd devoured all the books on moving on after a break-up, and kissing a different man mere weeks after leaving a long-term relationship—even a terrible one—sat at the top of the 'Must Not Do' list. She needed to concentrate on herself—discover her own needs and how important they were to her well-being.

Kiki couldn't recall the exact wording, but the general gist of those books had judged that any new relationship she embarked on should be a long time in the future. The trouble was she wasn't distraught or heartbroken from her failed engagement. How could she be when she had never given her heart to any man—not even her ex-fiancé?

Her mobile vibrating in her coat pocket distracted her wayward thoughts. Retrieving it, she was surprised to see it was a text from a friend in Alaska. She'd meant to call the woman yesterday, to catch up, but with the dogs and everything she'd plain forgotten.

Kiki smiled as she started to read the text, her happiness at this unexpected contact falling away as she stared at the words. She read the text through fast, then more slowly. She read it for a third time, convinced it must be a joke.

Unfortunately, she knew her friend didn't possess much of a sense of humour—which meant the words on the small screen were true.

Her ex had actually married the woman Kiki had caught him with. Her next-door neighbour, who fashioned herself with all the subtleness of a performing drag artist but without any sense of style.

Kiki slipped the phone into her pocket, swallowing hard. Oh, God—what if her friend sent her some wedding photos? Kiki wouldn't put it past the woman to do so without thinking.

She retrieved the phone and sent off a reply, telling her friend in clear terms never to mention the couple again, nor send any evidence of their marriage. Her ex and their relationship belonged in the past. It was a miscalculation she wanted to leave far behind. A mistake of judgement she'd eventually—thankfully—extricated herself from.

Kiki's thoughts returned to the building a few feet away and the man inside. Alex Morsi professed to be a good guy, but she doubted it. Underneath all his gorgeous discomfort hid the real man, who would soon show the true shades of his nature.

She intended to accept his job offer, but to make it clear that any future requests for kisses would be declined and snubbed. She refused to give in to basic physical cravings. They would share nothing but a professional and platonic relationship. No more lapses. No more failures.

She didn't need a man to build a happy future. She refused to become her mother. Wasting her life, longing every day for a man who no longer wanted her or her love. Who'd moved on into his new life with soul-destroying ease.

With her mind clear, and a new fire of determination burning in her stomach, Kiki took a deep breath and marched into the practice—coming to a sharp stop when she found the reception area deserted.

Deflated, she closed the door. 'Hello?'

Several voices drifted from the rear of the building, followed by soft laughter, but no one appeared behind the counter.

After a few seconds Kiki called out for a second time. 'Anyone around?'

Still no one materialised, but the voices dropped to low whispers. Surely someone should be manning the reception desk? What if an emergency came in? A sick cat or a hurt dog which required immediate attention and treatment?

Combing the counter for a bell to ring, all Kiki found was a cash register, several lost dog leaflets and a plastic charity collection box in the shape of a hamster wearing a top hat. Nothing to draw the staff from whatever they were doing.

The giggling from the back increased in volume. Curious, Kiki circled the counter and walked along a short corridor to where a group of women stood in a huddle, peering into an open doorway.

She moved closer and coughed. 'Excuse me?'

A young girl with short green hair turned and grinned. 'Be with you in a sec. Just enjoying the unexpected beauty of this morning's view.'

Kiki frowned, seeing only a yellow-painted wall beyond the girl's head. Not exactly a remarkable vista. 'Is it possible to speak to Alex Morsi?'

A second female chuckled. 'He's a little occupied right at this moment.'

A successful practice required eager and committed staff—not uninterested ones who loitered around making no sense and allowed a member of the public to walk into the back.

Not impressed with the women's attitude, Kiki asked, 'Should I wait in Reception?'

None of the women answered her question.

Not happy to be ignored for the second time, she raised her voice. What sort of business was Alex running? 'With no one out there I wasn't sure if you were open for the day.'

'That's great.' The green-haired girl nodded, obviously more keen to get rid of Kiki than to listen properly. 'Someone will be out in a minute.'

Kiki inched nearer, intrigued by what was holding their attention and causing them to act so unprofessionally. Two of the women shifted and created a gap big enough so that she could see into the room and spot a sleeping male on his side, stretched out on a long trolley. A white sheet covered his lower half, but his upper torso was as bare as nature intended.

Stepping closer, Kiki felt her breath catch and her eyes slowly traced the sexy shape of Alex Morsi's hip, all the way up over each visible bump of his ribs, to finish at his shoulder. Dark hair was scattered across his chest and over his flat stomach. The unexpected glint of a circular nipple ring finally caught her attention.

As if her overactive imagination had needed further material to speculate and swoon over, it seemed Alex Morsi was the perfect vision of male beauty. In fact she doubted there was even a word in the dictionary to describe the exquisite sight before her.

She discreetly licked at the corner of her mouth, in case any dribble had escaped. Breathless, she allowed her gaze to follow the delectable line of the faultless male form once again.

'Yonks since I enjoyed the sight of such a superior

male physique,' said the woman she'd met the day before, called Anne.

Rubbing her damp palms over her black trousers, Kiki whispered, 'Why is he sleeping there?'

'He called me last night to say the water tank in his flat upstairs had burst. My guess is he doesn't want to stay there until it has had time to dry out.'

'Shouldn't somebody wake him?' Kiki asked, noticing the way *all* the women were drooling over Alex. Thankfully, the sheet hid his lower half, otherwise it would be more than the flat upstairs that was drenched. 'I wouldn't like to be gawked at without my knowledge.'

'You're absolutely right,' Anne agreed, then grinned. 'But then very few of us resemble a sleeping Adonis when napping.'

The man stirred, as if subconsciously aware of his audience. He gave a deep groan, and his thick black eyelashes fluttered numerous times before fully opening. For several stretched seconds he stared at them, not saying a word, before suddenly shooting upright.

'What the hell—?'

Kiki bit back a moan at the raspy tone of his voice, stiffening her knees to stop herself from hitting the floor. New shivers of attraction jetted through her core. How was she supposed to stay distant and competent around him when his morning voice set her knees shaking harder than a badly erected tent during a tornado?

'Didn't like to wake you,' Anne apologised. 'Not when you look so adorable.'

He glared at his head nurse and grumbled. 'Ladies, get to work.'

The others dashed off, leaving Kiki and Anne behind.

Alex's gaze shifted to her, his frown deepening. 'Kiki?'

Forcing her eyes to stay on his face, determined not to embarrass herself by blatantly staring at his far too distracting body, she sent him a quick smile. Visually pawing over a man was just unacceptable these days, unless he gave permission.

'I—I'm here to discuss the job you offered yesterday,' she stuttered. 'But if this is a bad time I can come back later.'

Anne turned speculative eyes in her direction. 'Perhaps I can do the interview.'

Alex nodded, tugging his fingers through his curls, looking all the more endearing. 'If you don't mind? Kiki is a trained veterinary nurse.'

Anne grinned and clasped her hands together as though praying. 'How soon can you start?'

Taken aback by the woman's enthusiasm, Kiki shrugged. She had nothing else planned for the rest of the day... 'Immediately?'

'Perfect answer. How good are you at doing a dental on a cat?'

'I've done a few over the years. Do you want to see my CV?'

The older woman shook her head. 'If Alex wants you to work here, then that's all I need to know. Normally he never shows any interest in the staff, or their credentials, so yours must be pretty impressive.'

Kiki frowned, not exactly sure what the woman meant by that remark. She withdrew her CV from her shoulder bag and handed it over. 'I still think you should read it.'

Anne took the folder with a smile. 'You and I are going to get on great. I feel it in my knickers. Come with me and I'll find you a spare uniform.'

Kiki moved to follow, but at the last moment turned

back to the half-asleep man. This time she allowed her eyes to slowly drift downwards. 'Alex?'

His frown returned. 'Yes, Kiki?'

She lifted a finger and pointed. 'That's a very interesting tattoo on your arm.'

A deep blush coloured his skin, increasing his charm. 'Thanks.'

She chuckled and walked away. Such a contradiction of a man. Both beautiful and grumpy. But anyone with a tattoo of a black roaching greyhound couldn't be all bad, now, could they?

CHAPTER FIVE

ALEX GLARED OVER the top of his surgical mask at the woman moving around the operating theatre with a definite satisfied bounce to her mood. He was going to fire Anne if she grinned or hummed one more time. Not only fire her, but suture her mouth together first.

He'd barely washed, dressed and devoured the last mouthful of a cereal bar before the irritating woman barged into his office, shoved Kiki's CV in his face and declared her his new scrub nurse.

Alex detested change. Something his head nurse knew after working with him for years. He especially hated it when nobody listened to his opinion and went ahead and implemented the change. Even more when it concerned a woman he would prefer to avoid. But thanks to Anne and her interference he was now forced to work closely with her whether he wanted to or not.

Clenching his jaw, he ignored the two women in the room and continued with the surgery. *Why* had he offered Kiki a job? Staff hiring came under Anne's responsibilities, but last night during their meal he'd blurted out the offer without thought for the consequences. Making this whole dire situation a creation of his own stupidity.

And where had such cavalier behaviour got him?

Right here in Theatre, removing a large subcutaneous lump from a brown and white collie's hind leg, wondering where the heck his usually well-balanced intellect had gone.

And he mostly blamed the woman across the table for his dilemma. His new scrub nurse rendered him an imbecile every time he spent longer than a few minutes in her company. She wore the utilitarian blue surgical gown, theatre cap and mask with all the allure of a sexy lingerie model, and sent his interest firing to unprofessional places. Places he resented being transported to during work hours.

He needed to get a grip. He'd spent time with beautiful women before—another one would not affect him. If he kept his concentration on his job, then he'd hardly notice her presence.

Yeah, right. Look how well that's going!

Despite being surrounded by theatre equipment, a bright overhead light and chemical odours, she still managed to fill the room with a serene womanly aura and he hated it. God, how he hated it.

He wanted the calm sameness of his everyday work routine restored. He disliked the chaotic state of his thoughts and the way they rushed from questions to doubts and back more questions. What did he care what Kiki thought or did? She was just another member of staff. Her opinion meant no more to him than any of the people who walked along the street. As an employee, she would soon tire of his manner. Women always did.

'Is Thorne working tomorrow?' Anne asked pleasantly from across the room, showing no sign of resentment over their earlier argument. One he'd lost—hence her happy attitude and Kiki's attendance in the room. 'Only he's marked on the rota for the afternoon shift.'

Alex gripped the scalpel and made a straight incision over the top of the lump before answering. 'He's catching the late ferry from the Isle of Wight tonight, weather permitting.'

He suspected the timing of his business partner's trip away had had more to do with wanting to avoid him and less to do with a longing to visit his wife. The letter he'd received last night made it clear Thorne sought to end their partnership after five years and move on with his life.

Alex had half expected the announcement after he'd found out about the other man's recent disastrous affair with a local woman. Talk moved swiftly around a town as small as theirs, and it soon made its way through the practice doors.

'Any news on how his trip went?' Anne asked.

Alex glanced up and caught Kiki's look of confusion. 'Thorne West is my business partner and fellow veterinarian. He's been away for the last couple of days.'

'Does he live on the island?' she asked. 'I have a cousin who spends every summer there. She loves the place. Reckons if it was once good enough for royalty, then it's fine for her.'

Alex shook his head. 'No, he spends most of his time here, but his wife runs a farm on the Isle of Wight. His marriage is going through a difficult patch and he required some time off to sort things through.'

Anne snorted from across the room. 'His marriage has no chance because his wife refuses to leave her goats and cows. Thorne would have more luck gaining true affection from the woman if he grew a set of horns like those rosette-winning bulls she breeds.'

Alex couldn't argue with Anne's disparaging comments. Over the years Thorne's marriage had hit problem after problem, but recently it had seemed neither cared enough to prevent it from further collapse.

'Makes a person wonder whether marriage is worth the bother, doesn't it?' Kiki murmured, her gaze finding Alex's.

He tightened his fingers on the scalpel, intent on ignoring the excited thrill he experienced every time he stared into Kiki's eyes. As a grown man he should be able to control his body's inconvenient reaction to her, yet here he was, acting like a randy animal all worked up after a first sniff of an available female.

'Or if love is even real,' she continued.

He understood her scepticism. Enduring years of his own parents' fights and rows had put him off all things matrimonial for years. Their marriage had been nothing but a battle of wills and barbs of poison. Each filled with hate for the other and for the son who had unwittingly held them together.

'Oh, it can be worth it,' Anne replied. 'When two people are willing to work at the relationship. But long distance isn't worth the bother. A woman wants a man to snuggle up to in the cold dark hours. Someone to lean on and moan to when the day's gone a bit crappy. A helpmate—not some partner who flies in for a quick visit whenever he feels guilty or needs money. And Lise is very good at manipulating when she's in the mood to make Thorne suffer.'

'She's not so bad,' Alex defended.

His head nurse didn't know the truth behind his partner's marriage, or about Thorne's many affairs. Marriage at a young age to an older man as socially outgoing and ambitious as Thorne had created issues from the start for the shy, reclusive Lise. They were simply people married to the wrong person. Same as many misfortunate couples in the world.

Alex returned his attention to the wound, taking his time to separate the mass from the surrounding tissue. In silence, he and Kiki worked together until the excised lump finally sat in a histopathology pot. Kiki removed the blood-soiled swabs from the area after counting them, along with the used instruments. Her movements were accurate and she was confident in the task.

'I understand you're in need of a volunteer for Saturday morning?' she said.

Alex closed and dressed the wound, uncertain what to say. He was booked to pay a visit to a local stud farm, to check over several of their equine residents. It was easier for a practice vet to make the trip out to them on the weekend than to do it on a week day.

'I'm happy to help if everyone else has plans for this weekend,' Kiki added when he didn't reply.

Alex searched Kiki's face, his mind scrambling to find a reason to decline her offer. He could cope with working with her at the practice, when there were other staff members around as a distraction and a buffer, but just the two of them sounded like danger. She disturbed him, and that made her dangerous. All his common sense flew skyward and his attraction to her took over, making him like a hormonal adolescent. All physical with little thought involved.

'A staff member at the farm can help me if I need assistance,' he hedged.

'Are you saying you don't want my help?' Kiki frowned as she gathered everything together.

'Of course he needs your help,' Anne interrupted from across the room. 'Weekends are always hectic at that place, with owners and potential buyers in and out wanting to see the horses. Plus, I know they want Alex to take a look at dear old Horace.'

Alex groaned, dread replacing his annoyance. That horse was a vet's nightmare to treat. Bad-tempered and barely trainable, hc was unfortunately also the owner's oldest daughter's favourite pet.

'It's not necessary,' he insisted, throwing an irritated glance at Anne.

Anne ignored him and moved towards the door. 'He'll be glad of your help, Kiki. I'll write your name on the board so everyone knows the visit's covered. I've a feeling you're going to be a real godsend to this practice. Clever Alex, for hiring you.'

The smug grin she sent Alex's way before she rushed out of the room had him mentally firing her all over again.

Kiki waited until the woman had left before she glared at the infuriating man, and demanded, 'Is this about what happened in the barn last night? Because if it is, we need to talk. I can explain.'

He glanced up for a second, carefully avoiding her eyes, before returning his attention to the collie. 'While we're working, I'd prefer all conversations stayed centred on the patient and its requirements. Unrelated topics should wait until we're finished and out of Theatre.'

Heat rose through Kiki as a taut silence settled between them. She knew she wasn't imagining it. Alex *did* have an issue with her being there. She'd suspected so before they'd entered the operating theatre. He had been courteous and polite around the others, as they gowned and scrubbed in, but now with just the two of them the atmosphere practically blistered with tension.

'I don't believe you,' she said softly.

He stiffened, but only gave a slight nod. 'That's your prerogative, Miss Brown.'

'Oh, stop being so…' She sighed and turned away, biting her tongue to stop herself from saying more.

The man would drive a sane woman up a twisted hill and back down again. So he'd asked to kiss her and she'd hesitated before answering? *Big deal. Get over it.* It hadn't been a full-out rejection.

'So what?' he queried quietly.

'Pompous,' she replied.

Probably not a good move to insult her new boss on the first day, but he'd asked and she wasn't a liar. He was acting like a pompous jerk and the word described him perfectly.

Wasn't it better to sort out whatever his problem was before it developed into a bigger issue and caused more awkwardness? Otherwise she would soon be searching for another job. She refused to work in a bad atmosphere, with a man determined to keep her at a distance for some mysterious reason. She wasn't eager to become his best friend, but surely politeness wasn't impossible whenever they had to work together.

'Pompous?' he repeated, the faint Irish tones in his accent suddenly stronger as they rolled over the word, as though savouring it and not feeling sure whether he cared for the flavour.

Frankly, she doubted it was the first time someone had accused him of being such a thing.

'Yes, Alex. You're acting like a moody child with a cob on. If you'd rather I didn't work here then tell me and I'll search for a position elsewhere. You offered me the job, remember?'

Rolling off his gloves, Alex tossed them into a bin. He frowned before clearing his throat. 'It's not that—'

Kiki didn't give him a chance to continue, not interested in excuses. 'All I know is since I arrived this morning you've behaved as though you wish me anywhere but here. If you'd just let me explain about last night, instead of bristling like a fractious cat...'

He rotated his left shoulder as though it suddenly pained him. 'I just feel...uncomfortable.'

For a moment she thought he meant his shoulder, but then saw his expression. Good grief, could the man make it any clearer that he regretted asking to kiss her? What other reason explained his disagreeable attitude since her arrival? Was he scared she might take it into her head to embrace him in front of the other staff members? Or perhaps try and seduce him in a consultation room when no one was looking?

She'd never attempted such behaviour in her life, and she didn't plan to start with him.

'With me?' she asked, just to be certain.

'I'm not sure how to act around you,' he admitted. 'But, seeing as we're going to be working together, maybe we should just forget that last night I asked to...'

'Kiss me?' she taunted, unable to stop herself from reminding him. A perverse imp filled her with mischief. 'And you held me snugly against your half naked body.'

Alex cleared his throat. 'Yes.'

'Fine,' she said brightly. 'Because until you mentioned it I hadn't considered it a big deal or wasted much thought over it.'

Pleased she'd managed to keep her voice casual and indifferent throughout the lie, she resumed cleaning the area. No reason for Alex to know she'd relived that moment over and over for most of the night. Mentally rerunning each stimulating second until she'd wanted to scream with frustration and track him down to demand he *give* her the proposed kiss.

He frowned at her reply. 'Really?'

She bit hard on her inner lip to prevent a smile. The man certainly didn't like hearing that she found his romantic moves unmemorable.

'If you want to forget what happened—or rather didn't—then just be yourself when we're in the same room. Otherwise people might start to notice and that would create talk.'

'Are you sure I should?' he asked, not sounding convinced.

Unable to stop herself, she laughed. Alex's self-consciousness was rather refreshing and endearing. Not that he was wimpy or lacklustre. No, every time the man forgot his stiff reserve passion smouldered from him. It intrigued her how his personality had two such different sides. Detached, sensible Alex on one, and fiery, nipple-ring-wearing Alex on the other.

'I swear my hesitation had nothing to do with you or your request,' she said. 'It was all me—I promise. So I'll help you on Saturday at the stud farm?'

'Thanks. I'd appreciate it.'

The door swung open and Anne reappeared, stopping

any further conversation. Kiki turned back to the used instruments and continued to clear away.

'Thought you'd want to know, Alex,' Anne said as she prepared to wheel their patient out of the room, 'Leah has phoned all the local guesthouses and hotels and none of them have any available rooms. Apparently they're all booked, thanks to the local literary festival that's on this week.'

Alex tugged the mask from his face. 'Not one?'

'Nope. Your water tank could not have chosen a worse week to burst. If my daughter wasn't over from New Zealand you could have stopped with us. But she and her two friends have taken up the spare bed and the two lounge sofas.'

Alex scrunched the mask into a ball. 'I guess I'll be sleeping on that trolley for a while longer.'

Kiki concentrated on her task and purposely tuned out the conversation. Alex and his sleeping arrangements were not her concern. A few nights sleeping on a trolley wouldn't hurt the man.

He didn't look comfortable, though, her conscience whispered, and she recalled the way his feet had dangled off the end. And a thin cotton sheet wasn't adequate cover at this time of the year, when the nights still held a chill.

'Leah has offered her parents' sofa,' Anne informed him.

'Leah has?' Alex repeated.

The worried note in his voice drew Kiki's interest.

'It's better than nothing,' Anne said, fighting a smirk.

'Doubtful. I think I'll stick with the trolley. Less chance of waking up to discover myself sharing it with several members of her family.'

Curious, Kiki asked, 'What's wrong with them?'

'Everything,' they replied in unison.

'God knows what might happen if I spend the night there,' Alex added.

'They might take him hostage and never set him free.' Anne giggled.

'Leah's a lovely girl, but her parents are overly friendly and welcoming. To the point that it's rather uncomfortable, if not a touch creepy.'

'Oh…' Kiki said.

'I'll tell her you've managed to find alternative lodgings for the next few weeks. Just make sure no one catches you asleep again.'

Relieved, Alex nodded. 'Please do.'

Kiki returned her attention to her chores, refusing to listen to the guilt rising through her. Alex had already admitted he felt awkward in her company, spending time with her under the same roof, even for a short time, would just lead to further discomfort for them both.

Besides, she liked her own company. She hadn't lived with anyone since her mum had passed away five years before. The thought of Alex being at the lodge any time she turned around just made her uneasy. What if she wanted to stroll about in just her knickers and a towel? Not that she made a habit of wandering around in so little, but on occasion it happened—like when she ran a bath and forgot something in her room and needed to fetch it.

No, Alex Morsi was not her problem. He was a grown man. An adult capable of looking after himself. He could rough it for a few nights.

But he did offer you a job when you needed one, her inner voice reminded.

Kiki clenched her jaw, thrusting the reminder away as she concentrated on her chore. Yes, he had offered her a job, but it was obvious he now regretted it. But he had stayed over and prevented her from being attacked by the criminal who might have taken offence to her rescuing the dogs. A criminal whom they'd caught together.

She stopped what she was doing and continued to struggle with her principles. A decent person would at the very least offer him a room. And it would show Alex that she really had no interest in him other than as a co-worker. Also it would prove to herself that she could ignore this stupid attraction and strengthen a work-only relationship between them. A few days faced with how bad they each looked first thing in the morning and they'd soon forget the almost-kiss.

'Look, that bed in the spare room at the lodge is yours if you want it.' Kiki turned to the other two, the words spoken before common sense had a chance to butt in. 'I'm sure we can tolerate each other until your flat is back to normal.'

Alex hesitated, his dark eyes searching her face.

'Wonderful!' Anne cried, looking relieved. 'A perfect solution. And a far better offer than Leah's over-enthusiastic parents' sofa.'

Alex's smile was a mixture of relief and concern. 'Thanks. That's great. For Nix's sake, of course.'

'Of course.' She nodded, then joked, 'This way we won't have to worry about raising a ransom for your safe return.'

She waited until Alex had left the room with Anne and the collie before gripping the edge of the instrument trolley. Silently she willed her racing heart-rate to return to its normal gentle speed.

She would indeed soon be searching for a different job—because if Alex's smiles continued to send her light-headed and unsteady, a whole week of them at work and at home would physically crush her.

And that was completely unacceptable at this stage in her life. Those stupid self-help books said so.

CHAPTER SIX

KIKI PROPPED HER arms against the top rail of the metal fence, her eyes riveted on Alex as he moved the chestnut mare in a wide circle inside the exercise pen at Merryhome Stud Farm. White sand flicked up from the horse's hooves and her muscles moved with grace and beauty as he encouraged her through a slow walk and then into a trot.

The staff at the farm had expressed concern that the horse, named Brandy, was showing signs of lameness. Alex had wanted to observe the animal in motion, and had already had Kiki trotting the mare back and forth on hard terrain to determine which leg had the problem. Now he wanted to assess Brandy on a soft surface.

A sharp bitter wind gusted through the yard, blowing around Kiki and setting off a violent shiver through her body. Hunching further into her thick coat, she prayed the rain would hold off until they'd finished examining all the horses, but the metallic grey sky hinted at it being unlikely. At some point in the next hour she was going to get soaked.

'She's a nice horse, don't you think?'

Startled, Kiki turned to find a silver-haired man standing at her side. The lime-green jumper he wore, carrying the farm's blue horse logo, marked him as a staff member.

She smiled and nodded. 'She seems easy to handle.'

'Don't suppose you're interested in buying her?' the man asked. 'She's as gentle as fluff, but smart like Einstein. A real gem of a horse, she is. I'm not lying when I say if she were a woman I'd consider divorcing my wife and marrying her. Fast over jumps, too. Unfortunately, my daughter's ex-boyfriend is forcing her to sell.'

Kiki smiled at the first part of his statement, but shook her head. While she enjoyed working with horses, she had no dreams of owning one. The responsibility was the last complication she needed. 'Sorry, I'm here to work, not to study the livestock.'

The man raised his thick grey eyebrows. 'You work with Alex, do you? Not seen you before, so I thought you were his girlfriend.'

Kiki turned her attention back to the pair in the ring. Alex's girlfriend? They were barely friends. Though hopefully by the time he returned to his flat in a few weeks they might be. Besides, Alex had made it plain he wasn't interested in her sexually or romantically on her first day, and it suited Kiki fine. Friendship was best between them—less complicated than anything else.

'I'm taking my turn to help out at the weekend,' she explained, gripping the rail. Her frozen hands barely noticed the cold temperature of the metal. 'Being the new girl, I thought it only right.'

Although at this moment she regretted having offered, after waking with a headache and heavy cold. Standing in this open yard, with the wind battering against her back, was stealing any chance of her finding warmth or shelter. She'd stopped feeling her feet ten minutes ago and her cheeks were going the same way. Winter was definitely fighting spring's claim on the weather today.

'I'm Fred. I own this place. Don't suppose you fancy adopting a dog, then? Wife's spaniel's just given birth to six puppies. Already got homes for four—just another two to go.'

As much as Kiki loved animals, her life was too unsettled to take on the obligation of caring for one. Not when she didn't know if she'd be living in the area for longer than a few months. She'd promised to tidy the lodge, but after that her plans were unknown. And until she decided which direction she intended to go with her life, and where she wanted to finally settle, she preferred to stay pet-free. She loved Fingle Lodge, but her godmother wanted to sell it, and paying a mortgage on Kiki's wages was impossible.

'No, thanks.'

'Well, what's the verdict?' Fred asked, his attention shifting to Alex who was now walking towards the gate.

The mare trailed happily at his side, looking keen to return to the shelter of her stable. Kiki understood her eagerness and wished she could join her. Sinking into a mound of straw to thaw out sounded a wonderful idea.

'She's showing lameness when she's in trot,' Alex confirmed, stopping next to them. He patted the mare on the neck. 'And there's heat and swelling in her lower right foreleg.'

'Treat it in the usual way?' Fred asked.

Alex nodded and handed the horse over to a hovering groom. 'To start with. If there's no improvement after a few days, then give the practice a ring and I'll come out and see her again.'

Fred nodded. 'Will do. Just talking to your girl, here.'

Kiki opened her mouth to correct the man again, but before she could utter a word a coughing fit struck. Bending over, she covered her mouth with her hand as it shook her body for several minutes.

'That sounds bad,' Alex murmured with concern.

Kiki straightened and coughed one last time. Fetching a tissue from her pocket, she blew her nose, conscious of the two men watching.

'It's just a cold. Leah was sneezing all day yesterday, and Anne complained several times of a sore throat. I've obviously picked it up from them.'

'Flu's doing the rounds this year,' Fred remarked, shaking his head. 'Can be nasty if you're not careful. Several of the lads who work for me have gone down with it.'

'It's a cold,' Kiki insisted, wishing the two men would turn their attention to a different subject. The urge to cough again tickled the back of her throat, but she swallowed hard, reluctant to give in to it.

Alex frowned, not looking pleased. 'Are you sure you're well enough to be here? We've several horses to check over yet and it's freezing. If you want to go home I can call a taxi for you. I don't mind.'

She waved a hand in refusal, annoyed when the prickle in her throat started her coughing again. 'I'm fine…honestly.'

Unconvinced, Alex stared at her. 'That cough sounds terrible.'

For a moment Kiki thought he was going to pull out his stethoscope and insist on examining her right there in the yard. If he came near her she would shove the instrument somewhere dark and unpleasant. The cough *did* sound chesty, but a silly cold wasn't going to stop her from doing her job.

'Are you worried over my health or concerned I'll pass it on to you?'

'I rarely catch colds,' he replied arrogantly. 'Or flu. I have a very good immune system. I can't recall the last time I was ill.'

She glared at him. Of course he was germ-resistant. No illness would *dare* to infect him. 'Lucky you.'

Fred chuckled at their exchange. 'I guess it's time to see Horace—or perhaps you'd prefer to visit him last?'

Alex pulled a face. 'What's wrong with the old boy?'

Fred stroked a hand over his chin, concern etched over his wrinkled face. 'Hasn't acted like himself since yesterday morning. Think it's best if you check him over—especially as he's getting on in years. My oldest girl will be distraught if anything happens to that old boy. She won her first gymkhana on him. He's the farm's lucky charm.'

'Anything in particular concerning you?' Alex probed.

'Not exactly. Nothing solid. Just a feeling that he's not right. He refused to eat his breakfast this morning. Not like him. Tipped his bucket over every time we offered it. He's playing up like a right grump.'

Alex nodded. 'I've learnt to trust those feelings of yours over the years. They're rarely wrong. But I'm going to require my fingers before Horace can attempt to remove them, so let's deal with the other horses first and leave him to last.'

'The staff will have them all ready for you,' Fred said.

Alex glanced at Kiki, concern still shadowing his gaze. 'Ready?'

She nodded, relieved he didn't mention her leaving

again. Hopefully her cough would settle for the rest of the time they were there.

Wriggling her fingers to encourage some life back into them, she soon accepted that it was hopeless. An iced-over pond had more warmth than her body. She pulled her grey bobble hat further down over her ears.

'Why don't you head over to the stables,' Fred suggested, 'while I go and mix this young lady some of my mother's special remedy. It will soon warm her through. Works every time for flu.'

Kiki was touched by the old man's offer. A hot drink sounded perfect for keeping away the chills and the tremors that now ran through her along with the odd ache. 'It's just a cold.'

Fred placed a hand to the corner of his mouth as if to tell her a secret. 'Here's the thing, missy. It works for colds, too.'

Alex gave Kiki another worried glance once Fred left. 'You look peaky. Are you sure you want to stay?'

For someone with a reputation for being uncaring towards his staff, he was showing a lot of unwanted and unnecessary interest in her. She'd prefer he returned to his normal indifference.

'I'll be fine. It's years since I did any work with horses. Besides, I can't wait to meet Horace. He sounds like a real character.'

'He's more like the devil's charger.'

She laughed, shoving her hands into her coat pockets as another shiver passed through her body. 'That bad?'

'I have the scars to prove it. Be careful *you* don't end up with a few. The horse is not sexist. He'll bite anyone. Male or female.'

* * *

'I feel terrible,' Kiki admitted, staggering from the truck.

Her line of direction rambled from side to side along the garden path at the lodge. Her wellies splashed in the small puddles pooling in the uneven dips. The recently weeded rain-drenched soil on each side of the flagstones expelled a musty, earthy scent that filled the afternoon air.

Alex followed behind her, half smiling at her whiny tone, guessing how much it had cost Kiki to finally admit the truth. Despite her courageous determination, the illness had finally overpowered her body and her spirit.

She'd tried to hide it, of course, but as the morning had stretched on into the afternoon her enthusiasm and movements had slowed, until it had obviously become an effort for her just to stand and hold the horses during the examinations.

Catching her up, Alex wrapped his fingers around her elbow and gently helped her to the front door, pleased when she didn't pull out of his hold. It was a stolen moment of proximity while she was too distracted to notice and put up her usual barriers. A pilfered chance to ignore his scruples and give in to the compulsion to touch her.

'I know you do, stubborn woman.'

Kiki sighed and leaned her head on his shoulder, clearly unconcerned by his damp jacket or the improperness of her action. Illness had obviously rid her of her usual customary hesitation.

Alex eased an arm around her waist, lowering his head until his cheek rubbed the top of hers. He closed his eyes for a second and breathed in. She smelt like freshly washed fruit with the faint undertone of horses.

'I am a professional, Dr Morsi,' she mumbled. 'Just as you are. I can do my job as well on a sick day as a healthy one. But right this minute I simply feel a bit...'

Careful not to smile in case she noticed and took offence, he asked, 'Poorly? Rotten? Terrible?'

Groaning, she leaned further into his side, pressing the soft curve of her hip into the hard bone of his own. She snuggled her face into the dip of his neck, her cold nose and mouth pressing against his warm skin. He didn't mind—he liked her there. She felt right, but at the same time very wrong. Illicit, but coveted.

'Yes, to each one. I swear my headache is set on driving my skull apart into small anguished pieces,' she grumbled.

Helping her avoid the broken edge in the path, he pulled her closer, filled with a need to protect her from harm. A twisted ankle on top of flu would be just miserable. 'Insensitive brute, that headache.'

'Very,' she mumbled. 'You'd probably get on.'

'I rarely get on with anyone,' he admitted, letting Kiki enter the lodge first.

He guided her over the threshold and towards the rear of the building. Once out of her wet clothes, bed would be the best place for his newest employee. Then she could sleep for the rest of the day in warmth, comfort and peace.

Resting a hand on his arm, Kiki asked, 'What about your family? You must get on with them?'

His smile suddenly turned bitter. A familiar reaction whenever he thought of his parents. 'Hardly. My relations would make a year of migraines seem joyful.'

She twisted and swayed towards him, her soft breasts bumping against his chest. Placing a hand lightly on his shoulder, she curled her other arm loosely around his waist and rested her forehead in the centre of his chest. 'You're very comfortable.'

'You'll be more comfortable in bed,' he said gently.

The bad taste on his tongue vanished, to be replaced with the strong flavour of desire. Heat kindled in every nerve in his body. As much as he enjoyed having Kiki lean on him, it didn't help his determination to keep their relationship completely platonic.

Gently turning her around, he leaned close and whispered against her ear. 'Time for bed.'

'No fun your way,' she complained, leaning back against him. 'I can walk backwards, you know? Unless you fancy doing a samba instead?'

He laughed at the ridiculous suggestion, relieved that she'd not caught his comment about his family and was no longer plastered to his front like a warm, alluring extra layer. It wouldn't take long for his body's natural reaction to become obvious to her.

'You're sick, so let's leave the bad dancing for another day.'

'Have you ever tried to samba, Alex? Or how about a waltz?' she asked, twisting again to face him. 'Why don't we waltz our way to my bedroom?'

He smiled at the absurdity of their conversation. Soaking wet, sick and half-cut, Kiki Brown was utterly adorable. 'No, to the first question and not today to the second.'

'You should try it. With the right person it can be really enjoyable. If you ever get the urge to dance just tell me and I'll prove it to you.'

Dancing was the last thing he wanted to perform with this woman. Just holding her close pushed his willpower.

'How much of that tea did Fred make you?' he asked, convinced the remedy the stud farm owner had concocted included more than a good ration of rum. He'd seen an empty bottle on the worktop when he'd returned Kiki's mug to the kitchen in the main house before leaving.

'Several large mugsful,' she answered. 'I didn't like to refuse when he was being so nice and caring. Swears his mother's cure always works. The grooms hanging around the stables agreed when they stopped laughing. I'm not sure what they found funny...'

Holding back his own laughter, he cupped her face, brushing back several damp strands of rain-darkened hair that had stuck to her cheeks with his thumb. 'His mother's medicine is rum, Kiki.'

She blinked up at him, confusion shadowing her eyes. Raindrops still clung to the tips of her dark lashes, giving them a shimmer in the fading afternoon light. 'Rum?'

'Yes, rum.'

'What kind of rum?'

'The alcoholic type,' he said. 'My guess, left over from Christmas or the New Year.'

'I wondered why it tasted funny,' she mused. 'I thought it was one of those horrible herbal teas. Do you think I'm drunk and not ill?'

He spun her again and gently pushed her along. 'I think you're tipsy *and* ill. Come on—to bed.'

She sniggered and relaxed back into him. 'Bet you say that a lot, Dr Morsi. To the boudoir, *mademoiselle*!'

He placed his hands on her hips to keep her steady. 'Actually, you're the first.'

She halted, digging her heels in when he tried to shuffle her on. 'Are you saying you've never helped a semi-drunk and ill female to bed? Not ever?'

'Yes.'

'I think I like being your first,' she said, not complaining when he finally moved her. 'I feel special knowing you've never done this for anyone else.'

'I'm glad,' he said, struggling not to visualise what else he'd like to do for her.

Rainy afternoons were perfect for making love. Whiling away the miserable wet hours in the warmth of twisted sheets and hot sex. How he'd enjoy slowly stripping off each damp piece of clothing from Kiki's body, in between kissing every luscious inch dry...

They finally reached Kiki's bedroom and he opened the door. A large wooden bed, covered with a pink and green floral cover, took up most of the room. A tatty brown teddy sat on top of a pillow, its well-worn furry texture showing signs of an abundance of childhood cuddles and love. Several items of clothing hung on the open pine wardrobe door. His eyes immediately dropped to a fuchsia-pink lace bra dangling on the handle.

Dragging his gaze from the blood-warming underwear, Alex led Kiki over to the bed and lowered her on to the mattress. Drawing her coat zip downwards, he helped her out of the wet garment and discarded it in a soggy pile on the carpet. He'd hang it on a peg in the hall to dry later. Her hat followed a moment after, hitting the floor with a soggy plop.

'Are you going to undress me?' she asked.

Alex swallowed, not allowing the idea to take up further room in his head. What he would like to do was best suppressed. He figured he'd just pull off the top layer of her clothes and leave the rest for Kiki to sort out. Much safer that way.

'No. I don't think so.'

'Wouldn't you like to be my first in that?'

Alex paused in tugging off her wellies, not sure how to reply. Her first in putting her to bed? In undressing her? Seeing her naked? All three brought debauched pictures to mind and dried his mouth until his tongue felt like gritty soil.

'I'm sure your ex-fiancé beat me to it, Kiki.'

She sighed heavily and her shoulders slumped. 'No, he didn't.'

How could any man engaged to such a beautiful woman as the one in front of him not want to see more of her? To search and discover the delicate skin beneath the annoying barrier of her clothes? Surely, they shared an intimate relationship during their time together? He didn't believe her.

'He didn't?' he asked.

She shook her head and collapsed backwards with a small bounce on the mattress. 'No. He wanted to, but I refused to let him.'

Alex stopped removing her clothes and sank down beside her on the bed. He searched her face for signs she was lying. 'You didn't let him undress you? Not ever? How long were you engaged?'

'Five months. Together as a couple for seven. Do you know, sometimes I didn't like him very much? Isn't that terrible? Not liking your own fiancé. Tragic.'

Alex stared down at her, not sure what to say. Why would someone as funny and as affectionate as Kiki find herself in a relationship with a man she didn't like?

'But you planned to marry?' he asked.

'We did.'

He refused to consider why he hated the thought of her feeling anything for another man. It was irrational and ridiculous—and unfortunately very real. Instead, he asked, 'Did you love him?'

She closed her eyes, rubbing her forehead with the base of her palm. 'God, no. Not love. I liked him at first, but once I said yes to marriage I found him kind of annoying at times. Always telling me what to do and what to think. He booked the church and the reception within a week of my agreeing, and he bought my engagement ring without me. Just handed it to me one day while I was in the middle of emptying the rubbish bin.'

She opened her eyes and turned her face his way.

'And, between you and me, I have never seen such an ugly ring in my life. I hate emeralds. Much prefer a sapphire or a ruby. He had an affair, you know…?'

The puzzle pieces kept falling like the rain outside, and with each one Alex's heart wrenched for the female next to him. This sweet, amusing woman deserved diamonds and romance—not ugly jewellery, infidelity and a relationship without love.

'Then he was not only thoughtless but a fool, too,' he murmured, stroking a finger down the line of her jaw.

'He had many, many affairs,' she declared wearily. 'I found out after I dumped him just how many. I mean, I appreciate it can get a little boring in Alaska during the winter, but so many affairs in the few months we were together was rather insulting. It's amazing how people like to admit to knowing things once the man in question is no longer in your life. Some seem to get real enjoyment from it.'

Hatred for the other man and those spiteful people

flooded through Alex as he saw the pain darkening Kiki's irises. 'It must have hurt?'

'Dented the old pride mostly,' she admitted. 'Truthfully, I was glad to have a decent reason to call off the engagement. It was a moment of incredible stupidity to agree to it. I only did it because everyone kept going on about my age, and how I was getting too old to have babies naturally. I guess I panicked. Figured any man would do—even the wrong one.'

'You really didn't love him?' he probed gently.

'It's the very reason why I said yes when he asked. I didn't want to be like my mother. Alone and broken. My father left us when I was thirteen. He had an affair with a woman in the same town and got her pregnant. My mother couldn't have any more children, thanks to medical issues, so he took his chance to have the son he'd always hoped for. He packed his belongings, emptied the bank account and forgot about us.'

'But you were his *daughter*.'

'Girls don't add up to much, according to my father. Easy to forget a daughter when a woman offers you the chance of a son. Sons carry on the family name, don't they?'

'Surely he visited you?' Alex asked. Even if the man hadn't wanted to stay in the marriage, Kiki had still been his child and his responsibility.

Her gaze took on a distant look. 'No. I went to his new house once, after school. My fourteenth birthday. My mum had bought me a second-hand bike. I loved it, and I rode it all the way there and knocked on his door. I didn't want anything from him. I just wanted to see him. I can still hear the sound of the shingle drive beneath my shoes as he dragged me away from the house and threw me on to the street. The scrape of the metal bolt as he locked the gate to keep me out. It took weeks for the bruising on my wrist to fade from where he grabbed me so hard.'

'He turned you away on your birthday and hurt you?'

Kiki sighed. 'He didn't want his new wife to see me. Didn't want me to taint his future with the secrets of his past. He just wanted to forget Mum and I existed.'

'Bastard.'

'He is,' she agreed, a faint smile touching her lips. She reached up and placed her palm against his face. 'So you see, Alex, I learnt as a little girl that love is nothing but a fable people like to use to excuse their abysmal behaviour in hurting others. True love is nothing more than a silly myth.'

'You don't believe in love at all?' he asked softly.

She shook her head. 'That's why I thought getting married to a man I didn't love would work. A man can never truly hurt me if I don't allow him close to my heart, can he?'

Alex's own heart hurt—for the teenage girl so callously rejected on her birthday by her own father, and the woman now too scared to trust in love. 'But it didn't work?'

'Only because my ex insisted on playing around. I don't want a man's love, but I *do* want his respect and fidelity. Next time I'll make sure to pick someone who believes in monogamy.'

'Why not stay single?'

'Because it's lonely sometimes, isn't it? No one to share happy days and fun times can be tiring. I guess I want to be a part of *something*, even if others would consider it far from perfect.'

Kiki shut her eyes again, her hair fanned out in a rather lumpy mess and her nose red from all the wiping and blowing she'd inflicted on it throughout the day. She looked so lovely and vulnerable Alex struggled not to gather her in his arms and hug her close. To shut out her past and only let future good into her life.

He smiled at the unexpected compulsion. Not once in his life had a woman caused such a reaction in him. It shocked him. Confused him. Made him want to leave, but also to lie down next to her and stay. To heal the pain in her heart inflicted by the selfishness of other men and to soothe the pain of rejection—an emotion he understood completely.

Instead, he reached out for her hands. 'Come on, let's get you into bed.'

He struggled through removing her jumper and jeans, but left her remaining clothes when Kiki insisted she didn't want a nightdress.

'You're very diligent in your duties,' she said as he pulled the duvet over her body. 'Are you planning on tucking me in?' She tried to flutter her eyelashes coquettishly, but the left one got stuck shut.

He moved away, but Kiki caught his hand, wrapping her cold fingers round his warm ones. He squeezed them, before placing them back under the cover. He'd pop to the shops and buy a couple of hot water bottles once she fell asleep.

'Not a good idea,' he said.

'Will you ask to kiss me again?' she enquired, staring up at him.

If he kissed her there was no guarantee he'd survive the experience. Kiki was as scarred by her childhood as he was by his own. Sharing anything more than friendship with her would be disastrous.

He forced his lips into a smile. 'No. I always learn by my errors.'

'Shame…because this time I might say yes.'

The hairs on his neck tingled and a warm rush of something he couldn't describe curled through his body. 'I fear missed opportunities might be better between us. Less chance of failure or disappointment on either side.'

She held his gaze and taunted him. 'Where's the fun in that, Alex?'

'I don't *do* fun, Kiki. I'm Mr Boring and Conventional.'

It was safer that way. Less chance of being disappointed or hurt when she let him down. If he gave more of himself she might grow tired of him and mistreat his trust.

Her answering smile held a heart full of mischief. 'I could teach you. I think I'd rather like to. I suspect that under your sensible blue scrubs is a party-loving greyhound waiting to leap out and do zoomies around the room.'

He chuckled, knowing her words were nonsense, but touched that she would say them anyway. 'You think so?'

'Yep.' She lifted her hand again and pointed at his chest. 'He's in there—deep down inside where you've hidden him. I know he is. Don't you think he's in desperate need of some playtime?'

Alex leaned close, his face hovering above hers. His dark eyes searched her blue ones for answers. How would she taste if he gave in to the shot of desire and kissed her? Would it be worth knowing or better to stay ignorant of learning anything more about this woman who tangled his mind?

Nothing of true value could develop between them. They were opposites in all ways. Wasn't it better to leave things as they were and not muddy their relationship further? She had scars on her heart, just as he had on his own. Unfortunate remnants of their less than perfect childhoods.

'Trouble is, Kiki,' he said, his voice deep and hoarse, 'I prefer to do my own teaching.'

'Don't you want to be wicked sometimes?' Kiki asked, licking her lips. 'Give in to emotions instead of allowing all those sensible thoughts to govern your life.'

He tucked the bedcovers under her chin and straightened, determined to end the conversation. Any kind of relationship between them would end in hurt for them both.

'Not if you're likely to sneeze or cough in my face. Time to go to sleep.'

She sighed, not bothering to argue. 'That would be gross.'

He slipped a clean handkerchief underneath her pillow. 'I agree.'

Turning her face into the pillow, she closed her eyes. Several damp strands of her hair fell forward and stuck to the tip of her nose.

'Maybe I'll offer again when I'm less germ-peppered and icky.'

Alex hoped not. Having her healthy and willing would seriously test his control. It was one encounter he doubted he would be able to resist.

He brushed back her damp fringe. 'Go to sleep, sweetheart.'

Her soft snores filled the room moments later.

Alex retreated to the floral chair positioned near the

window and watched this sleeping woman who was becoming so hard to resist. If he didn't guard himself carefully he might end up making a mistake—one he knew would take the rest of his life to get over.

Kiki Brown was not his future, so there was no point in hoping she ever would be.

CHAPTER SEVEN

KIKI PERCHED ON the edge of her bed, toes scrunched into the carpet, trying to decipher the low rumbling tones coming through the bedroom wall. Five minutes earlier Alex's mobile phone blasted out rock music, breaking the lodge's early-morning silence.

Not that the sound had woken her. Over the last week she'd indulged in enough shut-eye to store up a couple of weeks' worth. Instead, she devoted a good portion of the twilight hours to staring into the darkness, contemplating the man sleeping in the next room.

Alex Morsi: her employer and house-sharer. The man who jumbled her feelings until they resembled random peculiar splatters thrown into chaos, and triggered whispers of doubt to pierce her normally orderly beliefs.

Glancing at the bedside clock, she saw the red digits showed six o'clock. Far too early for someone to phone for a casual chat, so whoever was on the other end must have a good reason to call him. All emergency enquires went straight to the practice, where the recently returned Thorne covered the night shift until eight o'clock.

Perhaps a relative from Ireland was phoning with bad news to share? But would they phone so early in the morning when they could call a couple of hours later and catch Alex at work? Maybe the caller was a friend who needed a favour? Or an ex-girlfriend who fancied a pre-work chat and had selfishly rung without considering the hour or the fact he might be in bed.

Her mind whirled with possibilities over the mystery caller's identification, and she found she disliked all probable suggestions. Especially the one involving an ex-girlfriend.

Not that she really cared who listened to Alex's sleepy morning voice, which set off silly flurries like exploding sparkles inside her stomach. They were nothing more than friends, after all. It didn't bother Kiki one tiny smidgen if an old lover phoned him just to relive old times or suggest meeting for a date.

The girls at work insisted the man didn't socialised with anyone, but they could be wrong. Just because he didn't broadcast his love-life to all who were interested, it didn't mean there wasn't someone special in his life. Someone he liked and cared for. Someone he wanted to build a relationship with. A special woman who definitely *wasn't* short, blonde and an emotional vacuum in the love department.

But if such a female existed in Alex's life wouldn't he have declined Kiki's offer to use her spare room and stayed with the woman instead? That was what couples did when one half of the partnership required help. They provided whatever was needed—including a bed to sleep in for a few nights.

She shifted on the mattress, not impressed with the track her thoughts were bumping along. Alex's private life and who he did things with, intimate or otherwise, was not her business. Even if this person phoning so early was, in Kiki's opinion, rude and thoughtless. The man worked hard and deserved to get as much rest as possible. He performed intricate surgery and saved animals' lives. His work was important.

She itched to walk into his room, grab the phone from his hand and tell the person to hang up and stop bothering her boss.

Pushing her hair away from her ear, she tilted her head to hear better, cursing the old building's thick brick walls which made listening in on conversations in adjoining rooms virtually impossible. Perhaps it was a wrong number. It often happened—especially first thing in the morning, when people were half asleep and not concentrating on the numbers they pressed. But then the call would have ended within seconds, so that killed that theory.

Kiki groaned, slapping her hands to her face and collapsing sideways. What was the matter with her? Why was she so obsessed with the man? For days he'd inhabited her every thought.

After a week of his pampering and fussing when her suspected heavy cold had turned out to be full-blown flu, which had confined her to bed in a mass of aches, pains and self-pity, a strange desire to guard him from shameless bothersome strangers had arisen out of nowhere. None of it made sense. Yes, Alex was gorgeous, and had a body she would happily study in great detail if offered the chance, but this full-on attraction wasn't something she had experienced before. It baffled her.

Okay, he had brought her red heart-shaped hot water bottles and kept up a steady supply of paracetamol, fruit drinks and chicken soup. He'd also helped her with bathroom trips when her weakened legs had refused to do more than a shaky stagger. And, yes, such attentive kindness definitely deserved some level of repayment.

But this overwhelming urge to protect him was completely irrational and absurd. She intended to stay single and man-free during her stay in Dorset, so this obsession was intolerable.

She rolled on to her back and stared at the ceiling. Despite Alex's kindness and thoughtfulness over the last few days, she'd also sensed he was trying to push a big wedge of space between them. And she suspected the reason had to do with the confidences she'd shared during that rainy afternoon when they'd returned home from the stud farm.

Neither had mentioned the conversation since, but the easy friendship they'd started to build at work now felt stilted and it was uncomfortable at home. Although they shared evening meals, Alex often retired to his own room not long after the washing up was done.

Did he see her differently now she'd admitted to not wanting a real marriage? View her as an oddity for her unwillingness to share an emotional connection with a man.

Her ex had accepted her reluctance to commit to him emotionally without much fuss. Then again, that relationship hadn't turned out to be very successful, had it?

But since she'd shared the truth with Alex his attitude and behaviour had changed. It was as though he was holding back from her. Set on keeping their relationship firmly in the acquaintance zone, with no chance of it deepening into full friendship.

She sighed, recalling the way he'd smiled when she'd asked if he would kiss her. She'd yearned for him to, and the presence of alcohol in her bloodstream and the onset of flu had had nothing to do with the decision.

The idea of his mouth on hers warmed and excited places deep inside her body she tried not to think about too often. She had the hots for the man, and yet she dared not do a thing about it because she wanted a loveless relationship based on companionship, and Alex deserved to find a woman who loved him fully. It would never be her, because she refused to put herself at risk in such a heart-shattering way.

Dragging the duvet over her body, she let out a long, heavy moan. Obviously her flu-weary brain had weakened her already dodgy judgement in reference to the man. Alex had openly stated his lack of interest in her other than as a work colleague and house-sharer. Nothing had occurred between them to change that. Regardless of that moment when they had almost kissed.

And yet…

She didn't feel indifferent when they spent time together. Her normally solid detachment vanished and left her questioning everything she had formed her life upon.

She rolled over onto her side and buried her face in the feather pillow. The smell of washing powder and warm bed not enough to distract her needy thoughts. She should have kissed him. Just smacked her lips on his without forewarning. Acted on the impulsiveness that often gripped her when they were together. One little kiss to satisfy her curiosity. One small enquiring taste.

She sighed and moved onto her back, the duvet twisting around her body. Alex was probably a terrible smoocher. All slobber, teeth and wet tongue. More drooling dog than amorous male. Not at all pulse-racingly exciting and toe-tinglingly thrilling. Much better not to know than to experience such disappointment and disillusionment.

Of course he might kiss better than any man alive—a virile kissing god who wove sublime magic with his lips and tongue and left women panting, weak and greedy to experience more.

She groaned and yanked the corner of the duvet over her head, squashing the discomforting thoughts and curving into the foetal position to ease the deep, heated ache they stirred. Why torment herself by dreaming of his kisses in all the spots she'd happily let him explore when he clearly lacked any curiosity in doing so?

Alex's low-pitched voice coming through the wall ceased, and a second later she heard the opening of the wardrobe door. Tugging the quilt off, she blew her hair out of her face and listened.

After a few minutes she scrambled out of bed and padded to the door, wrenching it open when a floorboard creaked in the hall outside. 'Alex?'

He was dressed in worn jeans and a rust-coloured knitted pullover, his dark curly hair tumbled all ways, as though he'd recently run both hands through it several times. He halted just beyond her door, a guilty expression on his face.

'What's wrong?' she asked, stepping out into the hallway. She shivered as the cold early-morning air penetrated her thin nightdress. Clasping her arms around herself, she tried to keep her dwindling body heat from fading too quickly and also to shield herself from his view.

Alex retraced a couple of paces until he drew level with her. 'I'm sorry. Did my phone wake you?'

She shook her head. 'Already wide awake.'

He frowned. 'Problems sleeping?'

She shrugged indifferently. 'Too much sleep, I think. My body clock is out of sync, and lying in bed is doing nothing but making me bored and restless.'

And providing unwelcome opportunities to spend time thinking of *him*. Another tremble rushed through her body. What would he do if she threw herself at him? Grabbed hold of his gorgeous face and kissed him hard on his beautiful mouth? Would he resist her then? Politely decline her advances and push her away.

'You're on the mend—just avoid overdoing it,' he warned.

'Are you leaving?' she asked, curious, but unwilling to ask for the reason right out. 'It's a bit early, isn't it?'

He shoved his hands into his front pockets. 'I'm needed at the practice.'

Her body sagged and she fought a smile. No secret meeting to share coffee and cornflakes with some hussy, then. He was just required at the practice, where no female waited to ambush him unless she had four legs and a waggy tail.

'Is there a problem?' she asked, wishing she'd pulled on her dressing gown.

Alex stood less than a step away. A single movement forward and her body would be enclosed by his yummy manly heat. Her nipples hardened at the thought of his breath fanning over the patch of skin on her chest that her old nightdress didn't cover. Of his long fingers slowly but single-mindedly sliding up her leg and further on to her—

She clamped down on those indecent thoughts, swallowing hard and forcing herself to meet his gaze. Tiredness furrowed his handsome features and once again she wanted to scold the early-morning caller for disturbing him. The man really did deserve someone special who cared.

Alex rubbed a hand over his cheek. 'Thorne called. His wife is in hospital and he has to leave for the Isle of Wight immediately. A couple of our overnight patients can't be left unmonitored for long, so I'm going in to take over from him.'

'I'll get dressed and come with you,' Kiki said.

Better to be useful than to suffer another day alone with nothing but scandalous daydreams for entertainment.

Alex reached out, his fingers warm and gentle on her wrist. 'You don't have to.'

'Don't you want me to?' she asked, tired of the unsettled feelings of the last few days. If he didn't want her to join him then he could tell her so.

'It's not that...' He hesitated.

But it was. Kiki could see it in his eyes. It wasn't a figment of her over-active imagination. He truly didn't want to spend time in her company. What stupid mistake had she committed to drive him away? Had she said or done something while she was sick? Or was he just utterly repelled by a woman who wanted to marry but preferred to do it without the hindrance of love?

But, whatever had sent the man into retreat, it needed fixing before their time together at home became intolerable. 'Alex?'

'Yes.'

'Have I offended you in some way?' she asked. 'I understand if the other day...what I told you...makes you feel differently towards me. After all, most single women are desperate to find their perfect partner, aren't they?'

His fingers circling her wrist tightened slightly. 'I don't understand what you're asking.'

She held his gaze. 'Don't you?'

His eyes stayed linked with hers. 'No.'

'Do you think I'm selfish for not wanting love in my marriage?' she asked, half scared of his answer.

Did she really want to know the truth of what he thought? Wouldn't it be better not to know? Easier for them to live and work together without it hanging between them.

He let go of her wrist, but didn't glance away. 'What you want in life is none of my business.'

She nodded, disappointed by his answer. It told her nothing of how he truly saw her. 'You're right—it isn't. But I sense something is different between us.'

'I think,' he said, stopping her from saying more, 'that you believe a loveless marriage will be easier and happier than one filled with love.'

Kiki had seen plenty of evidence over the years of how love was a waste of effort and time. 'I do.'

'But that's not a marriage. It's a friendship.'

She wrinkled her nose, not seeing his point. 'What's wrong with that? Shouldn't every marriage have friendship as a base?'

'Yes,' he agreed. 'But it needs more. It deserves to be more.'

'Why?'

'Because friendship is nice and comfortable and safe.'

As a child she'd enjoyed 'safe' for such a short period, before her father had ripped it away, that she'd happily trade love for the security of that feeling again. No doubt

Alex had a happy family, with parents who adored him. What did he know about being rejected and left alone? Had he listened to his mother cry out her heartbreak at night? Seen the loneliness in her sad green eyes? Lived with the pain of knowing that her love was not enough to make her mother happy again?

'There's nothing wrong with safe,' she said.

Alex shook his head. '"Safe" is a thick coating that covers the tender places inside and hides them from harm and fear. It's a familiar friend who asks nothing from you.'

'Love hurts and destroys,' Kiki countered. 'It steals people's happiness until it's drained everything and leaves them empty.'

'Sometimes,' Alex agreed. 'But other times it's hot and passionate. Electrifying a person with life until it pulses through their soul.'

'Love can hurt,' she insisted, refusing to accept his version of the emotion. Love was nothing but stardust. A faux sentiment.

Alex nodded in agreement. 'As can friendship. But when you mix friendship and love together you have the chance for real happiness.'

'You believe in love, then?'

His defence of the emotion clearly showed he did, and something inside Kiki stung at the realisation. With such opposite beliefs, there was no way for them ever to agree.

'I want to,' he said.

She stepped back to return to her room. What else was there to say?

'If you just give me a few minutes, I won't take long to get dressed. I'm better, and not infectious. Besides, I've a few shifts to make up and I'm bored. So, *so* bored.

If you don't take me with you I might start stripping off that vile wallpaper in the lounge and probably rip out the horrendous tiled fireplace, too. I wonder if the original one is in the barn?'

Alex sighed and half smiled. 'I suppose I can keep an eye on you if you come with me. Make sure you don't overtire yourself. I'll meet you outside in ten minutes.'

Relieved, she smiled and headed back inside her room to dress. Time around other people would clear her mind and bring a familiar routine back to her day. Help to centre her thoughts on important things other than whether Alex Morsi was a kissing god or just a lip-locking loser. Or the disappointing fact that the man she'd hoped would be a good friend considered her nothing but a cold, unemotional fool.

Alex took the scruffy West Highland terrier from his distraught owner and rubbed the dog's left ear. 'Okay, Boo. Let's get you in the back and deal with these bee stings.'

A woman in her sixties, wearing a red and black tartan cardigan and bright orange silk scarf, hovered, clearly ready to snatch the dog out of Alex's arms and run for the practice entrance.

'Is that necessary?'

Alex solemnly regarded her. 'Would *you* like to have a swollen foot or a splinter under your skin?'

Guilt flashed over her worried features. 'Well, no.'

Alex nodded. 'It's the same for Boo, Mrs Church. Dogs who go jumping through lavender bushes risk getting stung. Be thankful it's only a couple of stings we're dealing with.'

'He loves the lavender patch,' his owner said, reaching out to pat her pet. 'Every time my husband and I turn our backs he's in there, sniffing around. We didn't know anything was wrong until we heard him yelp.'

'Maybe you need to dig up those plants and relocate them to a tall pot. Somewhere he can't trample them.'

Mrs Church withdrew her hand. 'I suppose…'

Alex walked away carrying the Westie with him. Kiki patted the woman on the shoulder, not put off by the many white dog hairs that covered her cardigan.

'Better a little soreness than constant pain, hey? Alex will take care of Boo. Why don't you sit down? I'll be back once we've sorted him out.'

The woman grasped Kiki's hand with her bony one. 'It's very strange, you know? He only jumps on the purple lavender, never the pink variety.'

Kiki laughed and drew the lady over to a chair, determined to see her settled before leaving. 'How old is he?'

'Fourteen last February. We've owned him from a puppy. Took him on after our daughter died. Helped with the grief, in a funny way. He doesn't mind when I cry or don't fancy going outside the house. Dear soul, he is. Don't know what we'd do without him.'

Kiki squeezed her hand and left the woman in Reception, talking to Anne, who had asked Leah to fix Mrs Church a cup of tea.

Making her way along the corridor to the consultation room Alex favoured, she wondered if her mother should have taken in a dog when her father had left. Perhaps it would have filled her days with something other than rehashing her rejected love and the task of raising a child alone. The years after had involved them moving from one small flat to another, never finding a real home or a place to fit in and settle. Unable to create close friendships with their neighbours or make friends.

Kiki stepped into the room. Alex held the dog's paw in his hand, gently examining one of the swollen areas.

'How's he doing? Are the stingers still attached?'

'In this one, yes. But not the one on his neck. Boo's something of a regular in the accident and incidents stakes,' Alex said.

'He is?' She stared at the dog, whose large brown eyes looked far too mischievous for his advanced years. Most fourteen-year-old dogs did little more than sleep most of the day, not stamp all over insect-loving plants.

'First time he came in as a puppy, after a large cabbage rolled off the kitchen worktop and fell on his head. Mrs Church was worried about brain damage. Apparently she'd seen a television programme where a dog died of similar injuries.'

Kiki's mouth twitched. 'A cabbage?'

Alex grinned. 'In her defence, it *was* heavy—and about three times bigger than Boo's head at the time.'

'I hate to ask what happened next.'

'If I remember right, he ate an iris rhizome.' At her look of confusion, he explained, 'It's the bulbous part of the flower you half bury in the soil. Another time he chewed half a packet of paracetamol.'

'Goodness. Forget cats and their nine lives. It seems Boo is wrangling for the title of Miracle Dog.'

Alex lifted the Westie and stared into his face. 'He's naughty, greedy, and far too inquisitive, but he helps Mr and Mrs Church get through each day.'

'Their daughter?' she guessed.

Alex raised an eyebrow as he placed the dog back on to the examination table.

'You know about her?'

She shook her head.

'Mrs Church mentioned her daughter's death in passing just now. No details. Just that Boo helps her on the tough days.'

'The girl was on her honeymoon, and instead of enjoying the sand and the Caribbean scenery she ended up in an accident. The hire car was faulty and she wasn't wearing a seat belt. She went through the windscreen.'

Kiki's sympathy for the old lady waiting in Reception increased. 'How awful.'

'For the whole family. Boo is undeniably the most accident-prone and spoilt dog registered with the practice, but I'm happy to tend to him any time Mrs Church is concerned there's something amiss. He does far greater good for the couple than he does harm.'

'Shall I hold him while you remove the stinger?' she offered, moving closer to the table.

Slipping an arm around the Westie, she stroked his head while Alex fetched a pair of tweezers and removed the unpleasant gift left by the bee.

'Good boy. You'll feel much better soon,' she soothed.

Alex cleaned both stings with warm water, followed by a solution of water and bicarbonate of soda.

'There—all done,' Kiki fussed over the dog, stroking him.

Alex cleared the area and disposed of his gloves in the bin. Walking back to the table, he lifted Boo. 'He'll be fine now. Luckily he's showing no signs of an allergic reaction.'

Kiki backed away without glancing at him. 'I'll let his owner know.'

Something in Kiki's voice drew Alex's attention. Concerned, he placed Boo on the floor and moved towards her, touching her elbow. He almost stepped back when without a word she turned into his arms, pressing her face against the curve of his neck.

'Hey, what's wrong?' he asked, enfolding her in his arms.

Was she still upset over their earlier conversation? Had his remarks offended her that much? He'd tried to soften them, but he wasn't used to considering a woman's feelings when he gave his opinion.

God, he wished he had more experience in comforting someone, but it wasn't something he'd experienced much in his life. A cruel word or the sting of a slap had been a more regular occurrence than any kindness or support.

'Nothing,' she mumbled.

He smiled faintly and rubbed his hands over her back, his fingers gently massaging each bump of her spine. 'Not the dreaded *nothing*? Rumour reckons that often makes a person cry without warning and for no reason.'

Kiki giggled at his teasing and pulled back slightly. Wiping the tears from her cheeks, she blushed. 'This is so unprofessional. I never do this normally. It's just sad about Boo's family, and you're being so nice and caring. Utterly sweet, actually.'

'Shh, don't go spreading lies like that,' he said. 'I've worked hard to hone my mean, wicked reputation.'

She sighed and snuggled once more into his hold, the movement sending Alex's nerves shaking and his blood pounding harder than a sculptor's hammer. The woman didn't realise what she did to him every time she sought comfort in his arms. How it left him desperate for more than just a soothing hug.

'They're not lies,' she insisted, rubbing the last of her tears away and stepping back. 'You are a very nice man and you care deeply for others, despite pretending not to. I was just thinking about my mum and how lonely she was after my father left us.'

He reached over to the paper towel machine and awkwardly tugged off a couple of sheets. Handing them to Kiki, he asked, 'Did she never date?'

'She tried, but it never worked out. After a while she retreated into herself. It's been over five years since she passed away, but I still miss her every day.'

'I'm sorry.'

'Thanks.' She wiped her face with the paper towels and sent him a weak smile. 'I really am sorry for crying. I know how much you hate emotional females.'

'Who told you that rubbish?' he asked, suddenly realising that all he cared about was making her feel better. If any of his other staff members had broken down in front of him he would have fetched Anne to deal with them, but Kiki was different. He wanted to hold her and soothe her distress. Give her support when she required it. Whisper sincere platitudes into her pretty ear. Perhaps nibble and kiss it, too. 'My week isn't complete unless I help mop up a woman's tears,' he said.

This time her laughter was stronger and fuller. 'You're so kind, Alex.'

He shrugged, uncomfortable with her praise. Not sure how to react or reply to it. 'It's okay to cry. You're still recovering from flu. Bound to be a bit sensitive and wobbly for a few days.'

She tilted her head and eyed him thoughtfully for a moment. 'Alex?'

Instinctively he tensed at the determined glimmer in her eyes, swallowing hard as a series of strange sensations went off in the pit of his stomach. 'Yes?'

'I want to kiss you,' she declared, dropping her focus to his mouth.

She wanted to kiss him, did she? Not as much as he wanted to kiss her.

He swiped the tip of his tongue over his bottom lip, every inch of his body taut as he balanced the positives and negatives of letting her. What harm would one tiny quick kiss cause? Just a small one... Barely seconds in length and brief in touch...

Undoubtedly a lot, but need whispered her tantalising chant far more strongly than logic's weak tune. That and the seductive sight of Kiki's sweet pink mouth, so inviting and soft. So very kissable. No, reason wasn't talking to him today. Instead desire screamed through him, urging him to act before Kiki changed her mind. To risk the unknown for once. Take the chance for more.

But what if he did something wrong and she pushed him away? Was it worth the risk of her rejection?

'Did you hear me?' she asked.

He sighed, forcing common sense to rule and ignoring the delicious enticement of her arousing words. 'I've heard sickness does that sometimes. Makes people act out of character and do things they wouldn't ordinarily consider.'

'It's not sickness,' she said. 'It's good old-fashioned lust.'

He felt the corner of his mouth tug at her honesty. Kiki always told the truth, even when it was dangerous. And right this second it was as dicey as taking a barefoot stroll along a rickety path of crushed seashells.

'Lust, huh?'

She pushed up on her toes and sited her lips upon his own. Her eyes silently begged him to react to her daring touch, and with the force of a thousand falling stones Alex's control finally gave way.

Thrusting sanity back, he caved in to the madness pounding between them. Capturing her mouth fully, he lifted her closer, all gentleness dying the second Kiki wrapped her arms around his neck and opened her mouth to him.

He devoured her, desperate to savour her flavour. It humbled and inflamed him. Fascinated and enticed him. She tasted of hope, dreams and ecstasy. Of every single thing he wanted but knew he could never have. Of the childhood dreams he'd once kept when the harsh truth of his home life had become unbearable.

'Wow…' she whispered when the kiss ended. Her blue gaze was hazy with desire, her mouth swollen and still so utterly inviting.

'We're going to need to do that again,' Alex growled. 'Lust is always best tasted second time round.'

A sudden loud bark stopped them from continuing. They both glanced down to see their forgotten patient sitting nearby, holding up his injured paw.

With a gasp, Kiki pulled out of Alex's hold. 'Boo, I'm so sorry. How could we forget you?'

Alex ached to pull her back for that second kiss. To continue with the discovery of what riches her mouth held. But Kiki had scooped up the dog, snuggling her reddened face against the top of the terrier's scruffy head.

'I'd best pop him back to Reception. Mrs Church will be worried.'

Without another word or glance, she disappeared out through the door.

Alex stared after the woman who'd just upended his

whole reality with the power of one kiss. A single fault-less kiss he was going to spend the rest of his life remem-bering, eternally tormented by its absolute perfection and the sad, miserable truth that he'd just got bested by a geriatric Westie.

CHAPTER EIGHT

KIKI GAZED AROUND the vast metal barn filled with row after row of animal pens, each holding numerous groups of cattle of various sizes and breeds. When Alex had asked if she wanted to spend their day off together, this wasn't exactly what she'd pictured them doing.

'An auction?'

Alex grinned. 'Yes, it's the perfect way to spend a free morning.'

Kiki dragged her gaze from the grumpy-looking brown and white Hereford bull, loudly complaining of his confinement as he butted the metal sides of the pen several times with his nose.

'We've travelled all this way to come to an *auction*?' she asked.

Alex's grin widened and mischief sparkled in his brown eyes. 'I thought you could do with cheering up after being so ill. Nothing too strenuous—a relaxing day amongst animals instead of a busy one.'

'You're certainly unique with your date ideas.'

She blushed the second the words left her mouth. A *date*? This wasn't a date. Just two acquaintances spending a day together. Yes, they'd shared a kiss—a very nice kiss—before shyness had overwhelmed her and she'd rushed off before they could share another. Neither had mentioned it since, so she figured Alex either regretted it, or considered the whole incident best forgotten—again.

'What I mean is a friend date. You know—seeing as we're friends and…and work colleagues. Friendly colleagues.'

She cringed and shut her mouth, determined not to utter another word. Hail to the queen of rash and stupid. Just cut her tongue out and knock her unconscious before more verbal spillage recklessly exploded from her mouth. Now was the moment to shut up and get her head straight. They were colleagues, and he'd only brought her here because he was kind.

'Exactly,' he agreed, his attention clearly on something other than the hash she was creating, trying to free herself from the ditch of humiliation she'd plunged into.

Relieved he didn't appear to notice her blunder, Kiki studied the animal pens with little interest. 'Is there a particular reason we're here other than as a treat for me?'

'I sometimes come to see what's on offer,' Alex admitted. 'Blame my Irish blood, but horses are my weakness, and sometimes—if you're lucky and know what to look for—you can find a star amongst otherwise average stock.'

She searched the area for anything equine, but all she saw was cattle and three goats, intent on absconding from their pen with the stubborn resolve of escape artists.

'You want to own a horse?'

'Eventually,' he answered. 'Once I find the right property with enough land. Not easy in this part of the world where prices are so high.'

The more time she spent with Alex, the greater he intrigued Kiki and left her eager to discover further details about the man. Each new nugget she uncovered about his life and personality she gathered close and hid away for deliberation at a later time. Why, she refused to ponder—but Alex Morsi was her favourite subject and she couldn't learn enough about him.

'Do you ride?'

He laughed at her question and asked his own. 'Do you *breathe*, Kiki?'

Her thoughts immediately created visions of a topless Alex on horseback, galloping through the rich green Dorset countryside like some dark Lord of the Manor. With a greyhound like the one tattooed on his arm running at the horse's heels. Dressed in nothing but super-tight jodhpurs that clung to his strong firm thighs, outlining every single muscle and solid curve of his lower body. Pearls of salty sweat trickling down the centre of his back to pool in the tempting sexy dip of his...

Good grief! She stopped further contemplation before it became truly X-rated. She already had plenty of material to salivate over without adding more. The man only needed to glance her way with a certain twinkle in his eyes and she turned hot, horny, and ready to strip to her knickers and offer herself as a mid-morning treat.

'Besides, I promised to meet a friend to check over a couple of Shetland ponies he's hoping to buy. You don't mind, do you?'

She sighed, not sure whether to be annoyed or not. But he had catered for her every sickbed whim, so if he really wanted to spend his day off searching for a horse and helping a friend out, who was she to complain?

He reached for her hand and linked their fingers together without taking his eyes from hers. Trying to ignore how nice his hand felt, wrapped around hers, and the erratic hammering of her heart, she stared down at their connected palms.

Did work colleagues and friends hold hands during day trips? She couldn't recall ever doing so with other male friends. And Alex wasn't the outgoing touchy-feely type of man who used physical contact as a form of expression.

Did he *really* want to hold her hand? Well, of course he did, or he wouldn't be doing it. But what did it *mean*? And why was she always so confused?

'I've never been to an auction before,' she admitted.

'Then let's start your education,' he said, tugging her along the busy aisle. 'There's two important things to remember when you're at any kind of auction. Livestock or household.'

She laughed. 'Okay, great master, I'm listening. You may divulge your wisdom.'

He squeezed her hand at her teasing. 'Don't fall in love with anything you can't afford, and when the bidding starts keep your hands below your elbows.'

She shook her head, their hand-holding suddenly feeling intimate and pleasant. 'I'm not interested in taking on any animals. You and Nix are quite enough.'

He glanced down at her. 'I'm touched you regard us so fondly. Come on—I said I'd meet my friend in the other shed.'

Kiki raised an eyebrow and glanced around the busy area. 'There's another one?'

'There's three, but the horses are always kept in Shed Two. Mind the chicken.'

Kiki swerved to avoid the brown chicken strutting along the straw-littered aisle, smiling when it bobbed

under the metal rail holding a group of six young Frie-
sian calves.

'Do you think he fancied a change in conversation?'
she asked, laughing when the chicken decided to use
one calf as a perch.

Alex smirked and pulled her towards the next shed's
entrance. This one held several larger pens, with six
horses in a motley of colours from chestnut to grey.

A man dressed in faded blue combat trousers and a
black T-shirt emblazoned with a glittery oak tree across
its front strolled up to them and vigorously shook Alex's
hand. 'So glad you managed to get the day off.'

Alex made the introductions. 'Kiki, this is Wilf. He
owns a small holding a mile or so from Fingle Lodge.'

'Pleased to meet you, Kiki,' Wilf greeted her. He
dragged a hand through his short red hair, then thumbed
towards the furthest pen in the shed. 'The pair I told you
about, Alex, are over there. Shall we take a peek? I've
heard there's a lot of interest in them.'

Alex nodded and the three of them moved through the
crowd to where the Shetland ponies were held.

Kiki's heart melted at the sight of the toffee-brown
ponies. Both chewed on mouthfuls of hay, contently ob-
serving the world through the long manes that covered
half their faces. 'Adorable' didn't come near to describing how sweet the two ponies were.

Alex ran his expert eye over each one, before entering
the pen and running through some quick checks, searching for any indication of problems with their health and
general well-being. 'They're a nice-looking pair.'

Wilf folded his arms and enthused, 'Turtle's going to
fall in love with them.'

Alex agreed and proceeded to check one of the pony's teeth.

Wilf turned to Kiki with a self-conscious, half-proud grin. 'Turtle's my ten-year-old daughter. She's a true tomboy and gives the lads nearby a good run at rough playing. She's horse mad, though. I want to buy these ponies for her birthday present. She's been a real star since her mum walked out two years ago. She deserves something special and she's keen to start learning competitive carriage driving.'

'She sounds great,' Kiki said.

Wilf's face lit up at the compliment. 'She is. And she thinks her uncle Alex here is a hero. She's already decided to train as a vet when she's older. Says she wants to work with Alex because he's the best vet in the whole of England.'

'Uncle Alex?' Kiki asked, confused. Didn't Alex's family live in Ireland?

'She decided to adopt him the first time he visited the farm because none of her uncles live close by.' He glanced at Alex. 'You're still free for her birthday, aren't you?'

'Of course.'

Wilf smiled at Kiki. 'You're welcome to come, too. It's next month. Alex can give you all the details. Nothing fancy—just a small group of friends and neighbours, sharing cheese and chocolate sandwiches and strawberry sponge cake. All Turtle's favourites.'

Kiki tried to imagine Alex at a child's birthday party, but couldn't. It would be worth attending just to see him in his adoptive uncle role. 'Sounds fun. Thank you.'

Wilf returned his attention to the Shetland ponies,

his expression once again serious. 'Should I buy these two girls or not?'

'They seem fine,' Alex said. 'Does the seller have a good reputation?'

Leaning into the pen to stroke one of the ponies, Wilf nodded. 'Yes. He's already said if I manage to get them he'll let me return them and refund my money if I'm not happy for any reason. He also knows a woman who owns a small carriage and may be willing to give Turtle driving lessons.'

'Sounds good.'

Half an hour later they said goodbye to Wilf, wishing him luck in purchasing the ponies for his daughter. As they passed two men who stood talking at the end of the aisle Kiki felt Alex stiffen and shoot one of the men, dressed in a dirty blue donkey jacket, a hard stare.

Though often abrupt when he chose to be, she had never known Alex to be outright unfriendly. Well, except for when he'd believed she owned those dogs from the barn the first day they met.

'Is something wrong?' she asked.

Alex shrugged and led the way out of the shed. 'The man in the blue jacket rents a farm a couple of miles from the practice. He should be banned from keeping any livestock. When I first moved to Dorset I spent a summer working for a friend at his veterinary practice in the north of the county. That man—Phillips—called me out one afternoon to tend a pregnant sow. I've never seen such a filthy, badly kept farm.'

'What did you do?'

'Treated the animal and reported him. But he managed to squirm his way out of trouble with the help of a good solicitor and an influential in-law with friends in useful places.'

Disgusted that the law could be abused and ignored by people with powerful friends and money to buy their way free from charge, she asked, 'Does that still happen?'

Alex's mouth flattened. 'Too often.'

Wanting to lighten the heavy mood, she quizzed, 'Where are we going now?'

His annoyance seemed to melt away and he reached for her hand once more. 'There's a mare I want to look at over there. I think she may be the one.'

Glad to see his happier mood restored, she clasped his hand, wishing she had the courage to plant another kiss on his lips. Behind the stiffness, Alex really was a kind man. Far gentler than he wanted others to realise. And his love for animals and their safety was unmistakable.

If the man ever fell in love he would worship his wife completely. Kiki almost envied the woman who would earn the gift of Alex's heart.

Shaking away the disturbing notion, she encouraged him. 'Lead the way. I'd hate to get between a man and his ideal horse.'

Thirty minutes later Kiki followed Alex into the third shed, where poultry waited to be sold. They'd passed an ecstatic Wilf on the way, who'd managed to get the two ponies for less than his original budget. Unfortunately the horse Alex fancied had gone for more money than he'd wanted to spend.

She noticed the man Phillips, whom Alex had told her about, chatting with a small group of other farmers next to a row of cages. She pitied the poor animal he made a bid on. From what Alex said, it would be sentencing the animal to a life of suffering and wretchedness.

She also saw an auctioneer, wearing a white overcoat and holding a clipboard, standing next to a cage filled with several brown chickens.

'What's wrong?' Alex asked, his lips tickling the skin of her ear, causing a delightful tingle to glide through her body.

Confused by the pleasurable sensation that always flowed through her every time Alex's hands or lips brushed against her, Kiki frowned. What was it about his warm caresses that felt different from any other male's, effortlessly casting the memory of theirs into insignificance?

Pushing the question from her mind, she tried to ignore the effect his breath triggered and shook her head. 'I'm fine.'

'Enjoying yourself?' he asked. 'Or counting down the minutes until we leave?'

Kiki laughed, realising the truth. Spending time in Alex's company was enjoyable and informative. His in-depth knowledge of what to look for in an animal was fascinating. She also liked the whole atmosphere of the auction, from the smell of the livestock, to the buyers chatting and the auctioneer who made no sense to her uneducated ears.

'It's entertaining.'

'It is.'

She nudged him gently on the arm. 'Shame you didn't get your star horse.'

'There's always next time. I've a close friend who owns a riding school and she's promised to rent me a stable any time I find the perfect one.'

Kiki's stomach muscles tensed and her breath jammed tight in her chest. A friend? How close was this woman? Was the offer of a stable just a ploy to spend time with Alex? Perhaps everyone at work had it wrong and he *did* have someone in his life? A woman he was happy to share more than the odd kiss with?

She forced a smile. 'That's good.'

'Yes, she's a very nice old lady,' Alex agreed. 'She likes to bake me a cake every Christmas and Easter.'

The tightness immediately faded from Kiki's body. How many times was she going to jump to conclusions over the women Alex knew? She had plenty of male friends, but it didn't mean she had ever shared a romantic relationship with any of them. Or wanted to. Though Kiki guessed quite a few of Alex's female friends would happily indulge in a physical relationship with him if given any encouragement from the man.

God, she hated all this up and down spending time with Alex caused. He'd stated that he didn't find her attractive, yet he'd kissed her, invited her out on their joint day off, and was holding her hand as though they were a couple.

His behaviour was as inconsistent and varying as the weather. But she couldn't allow herself to share more than friendship with him because he believed in love and romance, whereas she wanted nothing to do with either.

Yet his mere presence aroused unfamiliar desires and made indecent thoughts float around her mind. It was like an unwelcome disease, and she was suffering its unpleasant symptoms.

The auctioneer had moved along to the next cage, calling out the next lot of ten white ducks. The steward held one up for the bidders to see.

'Do you fancy a cup of tea?' Alex asked. 'The café here makes a decent brew.'

She nodded, her mouth moistening at the thought of a hot drink. With both ends of the building open to the elements, a cold breeze floated through the large shed. 'I'd love one.'

Alex checked his back pocket for his wallet. 'Won't be long. Don't wander off, will you?'

'I promise I'll not move from here.'

She watched Alex push his way through the crowded aisle, occasionally speaking to someone as he passed. He stood out amongst the crowd of farmers and smallholders—not just because of his height, but the confident, easy way he held himself.

Glancing around, Kiki frowned when she spotted the man Phillips again, this time standing close to the auctioneer and his steward. He appeared to be waiting for the bidding to start.

'Who will give me...?' the auctioneer called out.

Kiki's eyes narrowed when Phillips waved in the auctioneer's direction. Did he intend to buy those ducks and keep them in squalor?

She glanced away, digging her hands into her coat pockets. It wasn't her business. She couldn't save every animal who might be at risk. She forced her mind off the bidding and tried not to listen. Perhaps if she recited her shopping list, or counted how many men wore woollen hats, she'd be able to ignore the auction going on around her.

But it was impossible to ignore it when someone with a history of animal neglect wanted to purchase ten innocent, sweet birds.

Alex would know how to deal with this. He'd do

something to prevent the man from buying the ducks—
she just knew he would. Why had he had to leave right
when she required his sensible head?

A second bidder joined in, with a nod at the auctioneer, only for Phillips to come back with a higher bid.
Kiki frowned when, after several turns, the second bidder dropped out.

Clenching her hands until her nails dug into her
palms, Kiki searched in the direction where Alex had
disappeared. If he didn't hurry it would be too late to
stop the sale, and then those ducks would live the rest of
their lives in misery. Ending up in a pie or stuffing the
horrible man's feather pillows.

'Any more bids?' the auctioneer called, saying the
words so fast they were almost incoherent. 'Going
once…'

She stared at the man in the white coat, willing him
to stop talking and call off all bids.

'Going twice.'

Her hand was in the air before sane thought caught up.
If the horrid man wanted the ducks, she'd at least make
him pay over the odds. Hurt him in the wallet, where it
mattered most to farmers.

The auctioneer grinned. 'Wondered how long you intended to leave it. New bidder in at…'

The amount vanished into an indistinguishable figure that Kiki struggled to decipher. Phillips returned
with another bid, but she immediately came back with
a higher one.

'You *do* realise you're paying way too much for those
ducks, don't you?'

Kiki jumped at the unexpected question. Wilf stood
on her left, concern all over his face. Truthfully, Kiki

had no idea how much the bid sat at, because she didn't understand a word the auctioneer said.

She shook her head and returned her attention to the bidding. The ducks' welfare was more important than monetary issues. 'Doesn't matter. I have to stop that man from buying those ducks.'

Wilf raised his eyebrows but stayed silent.

The auctioneer called out. 'The bid is with the lady.'

Phillips hesitated, gripping the catalogue in his large hand. He glared in Kiki's direction before shaking his head and spinning away.

The auctioneer's hammer slammed down on the board. 'Sold to the lady! Congratulations. I hope you enjoy them.'

Wilf left her side and spoke to the auctioneer, mentioning Alex's name. Kiki paid little attention, feeling high on having saved the ducks from harm and filth. They were safe from cruelty and they would live a happy life without becoming someone's dinner. Happiness and relief warmed her insides.

'Sorry I took so long.' Alex handed Kiki a polystyrene cup. A mini-cloud of steam rose from its top. 'The queue carried on out to the car park and then I bumped into a client who wanted to discuss his llamas.'

Taking a sip of her tea, she avoided Alex's eyes. While she'd been saving ducks, he'd conducted a free consultation with a client. Would it be best to tell him about her impulse purchase before or after he took a swig of his drink?

'That's all right,' she said.

His eyes narrowed as he glanced from Kiki to Wilf. Suspicion followed a moment later. 'What have I missed?'

She gave him a sheepish smile, before confessing, 'I think I may have broken one of your rules.'

'What have you bought?' he demanded.

'Ducks,' Wilf supplied unhelpfully. 'Though officially they're in your name.'

Kiki glared at the man, before turning again to Alex. She had hoped to explain what happened first. 'Well, you see…'

'Ducks?' Alex echoed, ignoring her.

'Ten ducks.' Wilf grinned, obviously enjoying Kiki's predicament.

Alex sighed, and when he spoke his Irish accent was definitely stronger. Working and living with the man for the last few weeks, she had learnt that wasn't always a good sign. Most times it happened when something or someone had annoyed or irritated him.

'I only left you for a few minutes…'

Kiki checked her watch. 'Ten, actually.'

'Why?' he asked.

Kiki shrugged. How to explain when she wasn't completely sure what had possessed her either? The urge to prevent Phillips getting those ducks had been stronger than common sense.

'That man you told me about earlier wanted to buy them and I couldn't let him. I can hardly rescue dogs and puppies from puppy farm hell and then allow someone as bad as him to take ownership of ten ducks.'

Alex's anger vanished and she saw tenderness bloom in his brown eyes. The corner of his mouth moved as though he fought to restrain a smile. 'You bought the ducks to save them?'

'Yes,' she admitted. 'I realise you think I am an idiot, but—'

He shook his head and interrupted. 'No, I think you are the sweetest, kindest woman I'm honoured to be friends with.'

So he *did* see them as more than mere acquaintances?

'You're not angry?' she asked, warmed by his compliment.

If he wasn't too upset, then hopefully he wouldn't mind giving the ducks a lift home in his truck. How else was she going to get them back to Fingle Lodge?

'Who am I to deny you the opportunity to prevent *fowl* cruelty?' he said, moving a step closer.

The fondness and pleasure in his gaze caused the hairs on her arms to prickle. He really understood and he wasn't angry. Just another way in which he differed from other men.

'She paid too much for them,' Wilf chimed in, rudely interrupting her happy thoughts.

He stated the price Kiki hadn't been able to interpret. She flinched and mentally calculated the available funds in her bank account. Thank goodness she had enough. She just wouldn't buy much until pay day.

Alex frowned, seeing her expression. Concern entered his eyes. 'Personal question, but can you afford them?'

She nodded, touched by his worry. 'I think so. The auctioneer was really hard to understand...'

'How about we go halves?' he suggested.

She instantly rejected his offer, not keen to inconvenience him with any more than a ride home for her and the ducks. 'You don't need to do that.'

'If I hadn't told you about Phillips you wouldn't have become a duck-defender. I should never have left you alone and vulnerable to temptation.'

'Just be glad the man didn't bid on a pen of cows,' Wilf joked.

The deep rumble of Alex's laughter rang throughout the shed. Several people turned to stare, but Kiki ignored them, captivated by the happiness on Alex's face. So unexpected and uninhibited, it made her heart glow.

If only all men were like him. Most men would have fussed and complained, but Alex had just smiled and understood the importance of the situation. He really was rather marvellous in that way...

'It's not funny,' she complained, trying to keep a straight face. 'What am I going to do with ten ducks?'

'Eat a lot of eggs?' Alex suggested, still laughing.

'I just wanted to save them from that man. After finding those dogs, I suppose I overreacted and didn't consider the practicalities—like where I'm going to put them and what ducks need.'

'Let's finish our tea and then I'll take care of the paperwork.' Grabbing her hand, Alex lifted it to his lips and kissed the centre of her palm. 'Thank you.'

'For what?' she asked ruefully. 'Being a dope and making you laugh?'

'No. For caring enough to want to make a difference. Not many people do.'

She smiled, but bit back a sigh. If only Alex could meet someone who made him laugh out loud every single day. There wasn't a nicer sound than hearing his amusement and seeing his happiness. Both warmed her insides better than frothy hot chocolate.

When he let go of her hand and turned to speak to Wilf, Kiki continued to stare at him. Over the last few weeks Alex had wriggled through her solid self-protection, bypassing the thick wrappings she so determinedly kept around her heart.

And now, the moment she heard his laughter, she realised something she'd never thought possible. She didn't just fancy Alex Morsi. Somehow she had fallen just a little bit in love with the infuriating, wonderful man…

CHAPTER NINE

ALEX RETURNED TO Fingle Lodge late Saturday afternoon, ready to sink into a warm bath. An emergency visit to a local farm to tend the family's sick ewe hadn't ended well. He'd taken one look at the sheep, listened to her symptoms and known he'd have no choice but to put the poor girl out of her misery.

Grumpy, tired and cold, he didn't expect to find Kiki, dressed in ripped jeans, a grey jumper several sizes too big and her whale wellies, dragging garden rubbish into a large pile in the back garden. Since the kiss their relationship had stalled somewhere between caution and confusion. Neither sure what to do or say next.

'You're busy,' he called from the kitchen doorway.

The smell of chicken roasting in the oven behind him stirred his hunger almost as much as the sight of the woman before him. Other than the thick slice of fruit-cake Anne had handed him before he left for the farm, he hadn't eaten anything substantial for a couple of hours.

Kiki stopped halfway across the newly cleared lawn and grinned. 'Figured I should make the most of a dry spring day and start getting the garden into shape. I didn't realise how much rubbish I'd end up with, though.

I thought I'd build a bonfire. The ash will be good for the plants.'

He searched the area, seeing how much work she had already achieved. Gone was the thick layer of rotting leaves that had blanketed the area—instead several bare flowerbeds, enjoying their first glimpse of light for years, now edged the lawn. Plus, a neat stack of logs sat on one side just beyond the patio.

He leaned his shoulder against the doorframe and crossed his arms. Impressed by how much work she'd accomplished. 'It looks much better.'

She laughed and resumed dragging a mid-size tree branch. Its jagged end ploughed a trail through the soft grass. 'It's getting there. How did the visit go?'

He'd called Kiki before he'd left the practice to inform her he'd be late home. Over the last few days they'd shared most of their evenings like a couple, but without the intimacy. Each was hesitant to discuss the complex state of their relationship that was at times thornier and more twisted than the rose growing through the old cherry tree not five feet away.

'Not good,' he said, not wanting to think about the poor animal he'd had no choice but to euthanize. It was a part of his job that he hated, no matter that he'd ended the animal's pain. 'Do you want a hand?'

'Are you sure?' she puffed, flicking her gaze over him. 'You look done in.'

Dismissing the appeal of a bath, he waved away her concern and stepped outside onto the old patio. He wouldn't relax in the bathtub while she worked out here in the encroaching darkness.

'I happen to be a master bonfire-maker. I'm surprised no one at work has mentioned it to you.'

'Great,' she said, leaning the branch against the rest of the stacked wood. 'Probably best to position it over there, in the centre of the lawn. The grass isn't much good, so I can reseed later on. It will be clear of all the overhanging trees, too'

He walked over to her, the bottom of his work boots picking up grass and leaves with each step. 'What can I do?'

'Grab the fallen branches from the apple tree at the bottom end, will you? They're mostly rotten and no good keeping for firewood. If we put them on the bottom of the bonfire, we can add the weeds and dead plants on top.'

They worked together for the next forty minutes, piling wood and garden rubbish into a heap on the lawn. The sky darkened to murky black, until the only light they worked in was the glow from the kitchen and the dark shadows. A bird sang in a nearby tree, keeping them company.

Finally they stood back and regarded the mid-sized pile with satisfaction.

Kiki tugged off her thick gardening gloves. 'Not a bad start.' She fumbled in her pocket for a lighter, found it and tossed it to Alex. 'You can help again.'

He caught the lighter easily. 'Have I impressed you with my fire-building skills?'

'No.' She grinned and pointed at the large log he'd pulled close to the fire. 'But you did uncover the best log to make a seat.'

He laughed and bent in front of the bonfire. Flicking the lighter into flame, he placed it to the rubbish until it caught fire. 'See—this "man must light fire" bit is my speciality.'

She chuckled. 'You're an idiot.'

Perhaps, but he only acted like one around her. Kiki brought out the brighter side of his nature. The part he always kept buried, hidden from others. Maybe she was right when she said he needed to let out his fun side. Take a risk and let her see who he was deep inside.

She glanced towards the lodge and sniffed the air. 'Our food should be ready. How about I dish up two plates and we eat out here by the fire?'

He straightened and tucked the lighter into his jeans pocket. 'Sounds good.'

Sitting on the log seat, Alex watched the dancing and twisting orange and gold blaze work its way between the twigs and branches. From where he sat he could see Kiki moving around the kitchen as she plated up.

What the hell was he doing, spending *more* time with the woman when he should be distancing himself from her? Wasn't he just creating a harder scenario for when he returned to his flat? One day soon Kiki would leave and then his life would return to normal. To the same empty routine he had lived most of his adult years. Why suddenly did it seem so lonesome when before it had never troubled him?

The cold harsh truth whispered on the breeze. He liked Kiki. He liked her a lot. She made him laugh even when she didn't mean to. And, despite his initial reluctance, he enjoyed working with her. Competent, caring, and knowledgeable over new ideas and procedures, she fitted in at the practice.

The staff liked her, too. Anne declared her fantastic almost daily, and she didn't seem to find *him* too annoying or hard to work with. A bonus, considering the number of past staff who had. The clients found her helpful and easy to deal with, often praising her patience and kindness.

Altogether she enhanced his world.

He also enjoyed their conversations and looked forward to seeing her smile every time he walked through the lodge's front door. And tonight—well, tonight he just didn't want to be alone.

He paused in his musing and watched Kiki exit the back door and walk across the lawn, her hips swinging with sexy fluidity as she carried the two plates. Firelight flickered over her face, casting her into both shadow and light.

Handing Alex a plate, Kiki took a seat next to him on the log. Their bodies rubbed at the hip.

'Looks wonderful,' Alex murmured appreciatively, not sure if he meant the food or the female at his side. His knee brushed against her own, sending a spark sizzling through him. One that was hotter than the flames before them.

Kiki stabbed a small golden-brown roast potato with her fork. 'Everything looks good when you're hungry.'

Alex took a bite of chicken so moist and perfectly cooked his tongue melted into flavour heaven. 'I mean it. You're a great cook.'

She turned to him. Several strands of blonde hair had escaped her hairband and framed her face. A smudge of dirt covered her left cheek and her large silver hoop earrings glinted in the firelight. She looked beautiful.

'Thanks,' she said.

Neither spoke again, content to eat the delicious food and enjoy the warmth from the bonfire.

Once their plates were cleared Alex stood, knowing the perfect way to round off their meal.

'What's wrong?' Kiki asked when he reached for her plate.

Sometimes it was as if the woman read his mood—was intuitively able to pick up on his thoughts. 'I need to fetch something. I won't be long.'

Alex entered the kitchen and dumped the plates on the sink drainer. Walking over to where he'd dropped his work bag earlier, he unzipped it and withdrew the bottle of whisky he'd collected from his flat before leaving the practice. Several inches were missing from the top. Grabbing two glasses, he returned outside.

'Are we celebrating?' she asked, spotting the bottle.

Handing Kiki a glass, Alex sat down beside her. Unscrewing the lid, he poured a generous inch of liquid into her glass and then his own. Taking a quick sniff, he clinked his glass against hers. The fire hissed and popped, sending hot ashes into the air.

Raising his glass, he said, 'Here's to clearing the garden.'

Kiki lifted her glass to her mouth, taking her time to breathe in the strong aroma before taking a sip. 'The toast needs to be better than just tidying the garden if we're drinking *this* brand. I didn't realise you liked whisky.'

'I only drink it once a year. I prefer coffee to alcohol.'

She regarded him silently. 'So what shall we toast?'

He swirled the whisky around for several moments, before raising it again. 'How about Happy Birthday to me? Will that do?'

Kiki lowered her glass, her eyes searching his face. 'It's your *birthday*?'

He took a large gulp of his drink, the warm fluid chasing away the lingering taste of their meal. 'It is.'

'Why didn't you say before? I would have baked a cake.'

He dipped his head and smiled faintly. Yes, she would have—out of kindness. 'I like to keep my birthdays low-key.'

Kiki sipped her drink. 'I didn't notice any cards in your office. Are they in your bedroom?'

He shrugged, conscious of her watchful gaze, hearing the silent questions going through her mind. 'I never receive any.'

She lowered her drink and echoed, 'Never?'

He raised his eyes to hers. The steel core he'd formed as a child as the only way for him to cope with his home life hardened. He imagined the thoughts going through her head. What sort of person didn't receive any birthday cards? Someone unlikeable? Someone people didn't care about? Someone no one wanted to be around? Completely unimportant to his family?

'Nope. Never.'

'But what about your parents? Surely they send you one?'

Not in his memory. His birthday had never held any affection or importance for either one of them. Just another day to suffer through in their disappointing lives.

'No.'

Kiki placed her glass down on the ground and shifted on the log. Her knees banged against his outstretched legs with the movement.

'Are you saying your parents *never* send you a birthday card or gift?'

Alex took another swig of his drink, enjoying the burn and the heat in his throat. Nothing removed the bitter taste of life or unpleasant memories better than a well-matured whisky.

'Yes.'

'Why not?' she asked. 'You're their son.'

'That's a fact they'd prefer to forget.'

Her fingers stroking the back of his hand surprised him. The unexpected contact comforted and soothed. He craved the touch, but at the same time resented it. Not wanting her pity because his parents considered him insignificant.

'Your parents don't sound very nice,' she said, her fingers slipping around his hand.

He considered her remark for a moment, unable to deny the truth in it.

Why not tell Kiki the whole unpleasant reality?

'They're not exactly warm and loving. It's the reason I never visit Ireland unless it's for a family funeral.'

She edged closer, the movement causing her thigh to press against his. 'Not even for Christmas or family weddings?'

'Only funerals,' he confirmed abruptly. He attended those out of respect for his aunts, uncles and cousins.

'Did you row?' she asked, her fingers caressing his palm.

The pads stroking against his skin tickled, but also calmed him. 'No, it's more they're not overly fond of me,' he confessed.

He glanced at the fire, not willing to see her reaction to his admission. Would she consider him as unloveable as his parents did? Decide there must be something wrong with him if his own parents didn't care if he breathed or not? Actually, they'd probably prefer to be rid of the physical reminder of their poor choices, if asked.

'How can they not like you?' she demanded. 'You're a very nice man when you're not being arrogant and bossy. And all gorgeously you.'

His fingers on his glass tightened and he glanced down at her. 'You think I'm gorgeous, Kiki?'

'I do.' She nodded. 'But I'm determined to ignore it, so forget I told you.'

Though his heart pinched at her words, he smirked at her confession. Was she struggling not to find him attractive? Fighting against the pull of temptation that had flared between them from the moment they'd met and which continued to grow.

She wiggled on the log; her expression determined. 'I want to know why your parents don't like you.'

Alex grimaced, wishing he'd kept his mouth shut. The woman pushed harder than a priest during confession. He *hated* talking about his parents. He preferred people to think he had no family. It prevented awkward moments like this one. Because while many people regarded their parents with fondness and affection he felt only hollowness when he thought of his own.

'Well, my mother tells me so every time she sees me.'

Kiki gasped, her eyes wide with outrage. 'She tells you she doesn't like you? How horrible. Why?'

He decided to give her the short version of his parents' relationship. 'She was forced to marry my father when she discovered she was pregnant with me. A child she did not want with a man she liked even less. Worse, he's not Irish. Add in the curse of growing up in a staunch and deeply religious household and you have their marriage. It's something she's never accepted.'

'What is your father, then?' Kiki asked.

'Spanish. And he still longs for the woman he lost.

My mother's younger sister. She died, and in grief and stupidity he turned to my mother for one night of sex. Terrible sex, apparently. A mistake he's regretted for over thirty-six—no, thirty-seven years.'

'Well, your mother should have kept her knees together if she didn't want a baby and your father should have worn a condom.'

Alex laughed. 'I'll be sure to tell them next time I'm unfortunate enough to visit.'

Kiki nodded satisfied with his promise. 'Yes, do so. Though if they *had* abstained or used contraception then you wouldn't be here, and that would be a shame.'

Warmth and softness jerked in Alex's heart, easing his discomfort. 'Really?'

She nodded and bumped his shoulder. 'Think of all the animals you've saved and the owners you've made happy because of it. Think of your greyhound.'

'My tattoo?' he asked, confused, wondering if he'd given Kiki too much whisky.

'Yes. Most men choose an ugly picture of a football player or a mass of swirls which make no sense—but you picked a sleeping greyhound. It's lovely.'

'Her name was Nia. A neighbour gave her to me when I was twelve. He'd saved her from the racetrack. He used to help me sometimes if I wasn't sure how to care for or heal an animal. His knowledge surpassed anyone I ever met at college or since. He was a good friend and he never mocked my desire to become a vet.'

'He sounds nice.'

'He was. He never had the chance to become a vet himself, but he helped me achieve it.'

Alex glanced at her face, tensing as two tears suddenly escaped her lashes and rolled over her fire-warmed cheeks. 'Why are you crying?'

'Because I'm sad,' Kiki whispered.

His stomach clenched harder. 'Over what I've told you? Or the animals I've helped?'

She nodded, more tears falling. 'Both. But mostly because your parents are horrible and it's your birthday and you didn't receive a card or present from anyone.'

'Don't cry,' he soothed gently, wrapping an arm around her shoulders. 'There's no need. It's no different for me than any other birthday.'

'But there is a need,' she sobbed against his jacket. 'Your parents don't deserve to have such a wonderful, clever son.'

'I thought I was an arrogant oaf?' he said, reminding her of her comments on the first day they first met.

'Oh, you're that too,' she agreed. 'It's why I like you, though I don't particularly want to. No one's perfect. Especially not you.'

He chuckled, tugging her closer. Resting his face in her neck, he closed his eyes. 'Thanks.'

'You're welcome.'

Drawing away, he felt his stupid heart twist at the sight of her tears. Tears she'd cried for *him*. Because of his childhood. Her gentle sweet nature was an essence he could become addicted to. But he didn't want Kiki crying over his family and the lack of affection he and his parents held for each other. It wasn't important enough for tears—especially not hers.

He smoothed away the moisture. 'Please don't cry. I don't need your sympathy.'

Although he spoke the words softly, she frowned and pulled back.

'I'm not giving you any. It just makes me sad to think you suffer such thoughtless parents. I feel a lot of things for you, Alex. But sorry for you isn't even on the list.'

Standing, Alex reached out a hand to her. He didn't care about cards or presents. What he'd never received, he couldn't miss. But just this once, on this birthday, he'd ask for something only Kiki could give him.

'Will you dance with me?'

She paused for a second, before placing her hand in his and allowing him to draw her to her feet. 'A slow one?'

Guiding Kiki away from the smoky fire and deeper into the cool night shadows, he said, 'I'm a beginner, so best start with something simple.'

'A slow shuffle is perfect for a night like this,' she said, her voice a soft murmur. 'With the rustling leaves and the stars watching…'

He pulled her close, his hand slipping around hers. Every time he held her it just felt more wonderful. As though they fitted. Usually Alex didn't believe in mystical romantic nonsense, but with Kiki he wondered if there was something to the idea.

'I fear you're easily pleased,' he said.

Sliding a hand to his shoulder she shot him a wry glance. 'People often say differently.'

He laughed, and together they gently shuffled on the grass. No rhythm or flair, just the slow swing of their hips, the soft brush of their thighs and the skimming of their clothes.

'So you're hard to please and I'm abrupt?' Alex said, after a few moments. 'Some might believe we'd be a great partnership.'

She chuckled. 'It wouldn't be boring.'

The moonlight on her upturned face released something within him. Something tight and hard that he'd kept tied down for years. God, she was perfect. How could any man hold her and not want to keep her close for the rest of his life?

He lowered his head, letting her sweet smell fill his senses. He wanted to kiss this delightful, graceful woman who made him wish for impossibilities.

Heads close, noses almost in contact, he whispered, 'Kiki?'

Her blue eyes held his for a second before a cloud drifted across the moon, obscuring her expression. Without a word, she slowly let go and stepped out of his hold. Head bent down, she avoided his gaze. 'I'd best do the washing up.'

Disappointment trampled through Alex, crumpling his first and single moment of birthday pleasure. Crushing it until it shattered deep within him.

'Leave it,' he said, his voice hoarse. 'I'll do it once I finish my drink. It's fair, seeing as you cooked.'

Kiki nodded and turned, leaving him alone on the lawn.

Closing his eyes, Alex pushed down on the conflicting sensations swirling through his body. Shutting out the knowledge that, with Kiki in his arms, for the first time in his life his birthday had actually meant something.

Slowly, he opened his eyes. For once the career he loved and had worked so hard to achieve seemed insignificant compared to this woman who had walked into his life and unsettled his tranquillity.

Why had she hurried off tonight? Shyness? Embarrassment? Fear? She'd never slept with her ex so was she still a virgin? Did she fear that he wanted their dance to ultimately lead to the bedroom?

His father had once warned him that only a fool hoped for joy when a woman's impulses were involved. Perhaps he took after the man more than he wished to admit? Wanting a woman who was unreachable.

There was no denying she held strange thoughts about love and relationships. Surely she'd be better off marrying him than sharing a cold liaison with someone she didn't love. At least he would care for her. But he wanted a marriage built on love. He'd promised himself that if he ever found someone to fall in love with he would accept nothing but every piece of their heart.

And what about children?

A flush of longing crept over him at the notion of Kiki pregnant with a child. *His* child. Closing his eyes again, he indulged in the vision of her body large with their unborn son or daughter. She was already beautiful—pregnancy would make Kiki breathtaking.

He dreamed of being a hands-on kind of dad. The type to do his turn with the feeding and the cuddling. To hold his children's hands through every important moment. To wipe away their tears when they were unhappy or hurt and give them strength when life became tough and they needed a helping hand. To build a family on love and true affection. One without the cruelty, fear and pain that darkened his own.

But with only friendship between him and Kiki he'd be a sperm donor father and no more. No better than his own father but without the resentment. A name on the birth certificate and a mention on the family tree.

He'd suffered the sorrow of growing up in an indifferent environment. He'd never willingly inflict the same on his own flesh and blood.

His parents had never even tried to form a relationship to improve the situation and help make life bearable for them all. No, they'd ranted and hidden from the consequences of that one night like two bitter cowards, rattling around a too-large house, carrying a half-empty bottle of gin in one hand and a heart full of regrets in the other. Two lonely hostile shadows, intent on wallowing in alcohol-drenched misery. Content to infest the child they had conceived through one night of drunken sex with their own unhappiness. One parent determined to take her anger out on him, the other preferring to pretend he didn't exist.

Alex rubbed at the sudden pain in his chest. Marriage should be for love and no other reason. Not even to keep Kiki from further disappointment, or the right to enjoy her kisses and more, would he compromise that belief.

Better to protect his heart and stay away from her and the enticing promise of romance when all she was capable of giving him was regret and a half-finished birthday dance.

CHAPTER TEN

'A SCHOOL TALK for our Year Two children.'

The woman who had introduced herself as Miss Ingle, headmistress of the local infants' school, squashed her brown leather handbag while shooting concerned glances at the snoring grey terrier sprawled out in the middle of the reception area's floor. The whites of her knuckles indicated she was no dog-lover.

Kiki tilted her head as she listened, a warm glow filling her at the idea of a group of children being rewarded for being good. During *her* time at school she'd rarely received a gold star.

Miss Ingle flicked one of her mid-length blonde plaits over her shoulder. 'I'm sure they'll enjoy it. They've all behaved particularly well this term. Only one visit to A&E for the teacher this year. A record for this particular group, so I'd liked to reward them with a treat.'

'And you think the children will enjoy a talk from one of our vets?' Kiki asked, but she was already convinced. After all, encouraging children to respect animals and treat them with kindness and compassion was an idea the practice should endorse and encourage.

Miss Ingle beamed, displaying the brace running along her top teeth. 'Absolutely. They're all animal lovers—I checked last week in a class poll. We like to be democratic. Most own family pets—fish, dogs and cats. Only poor Hanna wasn't keen, after an unfortunate incident last summer with Morris, her grandfather's iguana. But according to her parents the scars are no longer visible, and Morris has thankfully recovered from being sat on.'

'Well, one of our vets is away at the moment,' Anne said, flicking a pink biro back and forth. Her glasses sat on the end of her nose and she stared at the headmistress with the same intensity as she did lab results.

'What about Alex?' Kiki suggested, already envisaging him sharing his love and enthusiasm for animals with a younger generation, inspiring them with his wisdom and knowledge, instilling a fascination with the animal world.

Anne twisted in her seat and stared at Kiki. 'Alex? What? *Our* Alex?'

Kiki nodded, still picturing their boss being all clever and wise as he explained the best way to care for a cat or dog, bringing a deeper understanding of animal care into eager young minds.

'You honestly think *Alex* is the best choice to give a school talk?' Anne persisted, raising her eyebrows. 'To children? Impressionable youngsters?'

Kiki smiled, not listening to her colleague's concerns. 'He'll be perfect. Who else is as educated on the subject of animals?'

The headmistress leaned over the desk, her fear of the terrier momentarily forgotten. A red blush rose from the lace collar of her Victorian-style white blouse and moved over her face in seconds.

'May I ask...is he the handsome one? Like the hero

out of a gothic romance novel, with his dark curly hair and wide shoulders? Usually shops at the supermarket on the corner?'

Kiki's eagerness for Alex's involvement in the class talk plummeted at the woman's obvious interest. Glaring at the headmistress, who had practically melted over the desk while describing Alex, she reckoned Anne had a point. Alex anywhere near a school—especially this woman's—was a terrible idea.

'Yes,' Anne chuckled, giving Kiki a sideways glance. 'He's the one.'

'Oh, he'd be ideal,' Miss Ingle gushed, her blush deepening. 'If he does the talk not only will the children be excited, but all our single teachers, too.'

Kiki stiffened, not thrilled at the thought of a bunch of randy teachers salivating over her housemate. Did they sit around at break time, debating the town's handsome single males, scheming ways to entice them into the school building?

Only the other day Alex had endured his own staff lusting at his half-naked body. The man deserved to be treated like a human being—not some hot sex symbol. Even if he *did* have the annoying misfortune to have been born looking like one.

Picking up a pile of leaflets from the counter, Kiki absently tidied them. 'I'm afraid Dr Morsi is very busy at the moment,' she said.

'Nonsense,' Anne dismissed, dropping her pen. She leaned towards the computer. 'I'm sure he would consider it an honour. He loves to do his bit for the community. What sort of date were you thinking?'

Kiki frowned, not recalling Alex ever mentioning doing anything for the community. She often swore if his patients could attend the practice without their owners he'd celebrate for a whole year.

'You really think he might agree?' the headmistress asked, a purposeful glimmer entering her eyes.

Kiki immediately recognised it as trouble for her friend and boss. What was the *matter* with the women in this town? Alex wasn't the only male around. Though he probably did top the list in looks.

Psychic powers weren't necessary to see that this woman was plotting something. For his own sake Alex should stay away from the school and its female members of staff. Who knew what might occur if he was left on his own with a gathering of tenacious women interested in devouring him like a chunky slice of man pie?

Kiki slammed the leaflets down in their spot and lifted a promotional sample of cat food. She pressed it several times, wincing when brown liquid suddenly oozed from the top.

'Alex already does plenty in helping the community's pets,' she pointed out, squeezing the cat food sample again and filling the air with the smell of fish. 'He really doesn't have time for anything else.'

Anne scoffed, her eyes twinkling as she turned from the screen and met Kiki's gaze. 'Not too busy that he can't make room for a thirty-minute talk to the kiddies.'

'He really isn't the right person,' Kiki insisted, determined to regain control of the conversation and nudge it in a different direction. No reason for Miss Ingle to get her hopes up when she had no chance with the man. 'But I'm sure Thorne will be ideal. Once he returns to work we'll contact you.'

'Nonsense,' Anne dismissed, returning her attention to the computer screen.

Miss Ingle clapped her hands together. 'Superb! I'll get my secretary to call and confirm the date and time. She's a whizz at dealing with such things. The children will be *so* excited. And, between you and me, my staff will be ecstatic. He's not married, is he?'

'No,' Anne answered before Kiki could speak. 'Alex is free and single.'

Miss Ingle's blush returned in full startling force. If skin could gush hers would be. 'Oh, how wonderful!'

Kiki's dislike for the woman increased. She glared at her as she waved goodbye, circled the sleeping terrier and headed out through the practice door.

Neither Kiki nor Anne said a word as they watched through the window as the headmistress skipped across the car park to where she'd left her push-bike chained to a lamppost.

'There's no chance Alex will do it,' Kiki maintained, confident in her ability to talk him into refusing.

Anne sniggered. 'But you said he was perfect.'

She glared at the older woman. 'I've changed my mind. It's a disaster in waiting. He'll give the children nightmares for months. Probably be banned from all schools for life.'

Anne tutted and retrieved a romance novel from her handbag. 'Have a little faith, Kiki. You make Alex sound like a monster.'

'He is…unintentionally…at times.'

'No, he isn't,' Anne dismissed. 'He's shy and awk-ward. And I think it will do him good to get away from the practice and see that other things in the world exist— like children and…'

'Women,' Kiki growled. 'Are you really comfortable

sending Alex into a coven of horny teachers? You do realise Miss Ingle is one of *those* women?'

Anne rested her glasses on the top of her head. '"Those" women?'

'Yes.' Kiki nodded. 'The sort who chases a man until she wears him down and digs her claws into him. It's disgusting and unfair.'

Anne stared at her for several long moments before grinning. 'Oh, I see...'

Did she? Kiki didn't think so. Married for over thirty years, Anne had no idea how ruthless some single women were when eligible men with good prospects were concerned. And, despite Alex's personality issues, many women would consider him worthy of pursuing for his bank balance alone. As a major partner in a thriving veterinary practice he wasn't exactly slumming it.

She squeezed the cat food packet once more. 'I'm not sure Alex should be let loose with the likes of Miss Ingle and Co. Anything might happen to him.'

Anne lowered her glasses and shook her head. 'I'm sure he can protect himself from the advances of overeager teachers.'

Kiki gave up. Thrusting the leaking cat food sample at the other woman, she said, 'I think I'll go and see how May's doing with that Myna bird she found.'

Anne took the sample and dropped it into the wastepaper bin under the counter. 'Probably being pecked to bits. That girl never remembers to wear protection when handling birds. I'm not sure whether the swearing was coming from her or the bird when I passed the room earlier.'

Kiki left Reception and decided to go and find Alex instead. She needed to talk to him about the school talk before Anne did. The man needed protecting from desperate teachers. Who knew what might happen to him otherwise?

Alex gently placed the black female cat down on to the examination table in the middle of the practice's cat ward, not fooled by the contented purring coming from her. Experience with this particular patient kept him alert and ready for any sudden movement. Miss Pretty, he suspected, was half-feral and an expert at escape.

She also hated taking her medication. But without it she would become seriously ill—so, despite her reluctance, she had no choice but to endure this procedure twice a day.

'Right, Miss Pretty. Are you going to behave yourself?' he cooed softly. 'Or do you intend to be a bad kitty as usual?'

A soft knock on the open door stopped him from continuing. Kiki stood on the threshold, hands clasped, a pensive expression on her face.

'Hi,' he said, his attention going back to the cat, who'd stopped purring and was now focused on Kiki.

'Can we talk?' Kiki asked, stepping into the room and closing the door without waiting for his answer.

Alex's stomach rolled and the skin on his neck itched. Instinctively he was sure he wasn't going to like the upcoming conversation.

'What's wrong?'

The stiff material of Kiki's burgundy uniform rustled as she moved closer to the table. Though it didn't detract from the pleasing way it sat snug against her curves.

Dragging his gaze away from the captivating sight, he forced his thoughts off Kiki's appearance and back to his patient. He met two large green eyes that seemed to read him and mock him for his improper thoughts.

'Want help?' Kiki asked, nodding towards Miss Pretty and the tablet placed out of the way at the end of the table.

Alex nodded, and waited for Kiki to position her hands on the cat's forepaws to prevent her from attempting a nasty swipe with her claws. The bad-tempered cat had already managed to get a couple of scratches and bites on Leah that morning.

Satisfied Kiki had the cat in a firm hold, Alex grasped the top of Miss Pretty's head and tilted it backwards, using his finger to stroke the fur beneath her lower jaw. 'If you grab the tablet, I'll open her mouth.'

Together they worked until the tablet sat at the back of the cat's tongue. Alex firmly closed Miss Pretty's mouth and gently stroked her throat, waiting until he saw signs that the feline had swallowed it down.

Still keeping hold of the cat, Alex glanced at Kiki, and asked, 'What's wrong?'

For a moment Kiki didn't answer, her expression for the first time since they'd met completely unreadable. Finally she said, 'The headmistress from the local infants'...'

Still listening, but happy that Miss Pretty had taken her medication and wasn't showing any signs of choking on it, Alex carried the feline over to the wall of cages and placed her inside one. The instant he let go the sneaky black cat ran up his arm and onto his shoulder, where she perched for a second before leaping to the floor.

'Damn,' he cursed, grabbing for the cat too late.

Miss Pretty spat out the tablet and raced for a low cupboard on the other side of the room.

'Is this the cat Leah complained about this morning?' Kiki asked, staring at the feline, who now sat on top of the cupboard washing her face.

Alex sighed heavily. 'Yes. Her owner swears she sweet-natured, but I have my doubts.'

'Is he the man who came in with tons of scratches all over the backs of his hands?' Kiki questioned, crossing her arms.

Alex was debating whether to answer truthfully when he noticed how close Kiki was to the door and her chance of freedom. Catching and getting Miss Pretty into a cage would be easier if Kiki stayed and helped—otherwise he was on his own with a very annoyed cat.

He decided to avoid outright lying and hedged. 'I'm not sure...'

Kiki huffed and glanced his way, letting him know she saw through his sudden vagueness. 'Okay. If I go this way, you sneak round to her other side and grab her by the scruff. This kitty needs to learn some manners in acceptable cat behaviour.'

'Good luck,' he muttered.

'We can *do* this Alex,' Kiki insisted. 'We've caught a criminal and outbid a mean farmer. What's a half-wild cat to us? We're professionals, remember? And she is the patient.'

'I like your confidence,' Alex mused, not sounding convinced.

Together they crept closer to Miss Pretty, alert for any sudden movement the cat might make to avoid capture. Thankfully there were no tall cupboards in the room.

Miss Pretty watched them, as if mentally daring them to come nearer.

'Miss Pretty...' Alex coaxed softly, taking another step closer.

The cat ignored him and switched her attention to Kiki, her eyelids narrowing ominously over her green eyes.

'Who's a naughty cat?' Kiki added, moving slowly towards Miss Pretty. 'Perhaps we should try and entice her with a treat?'

'Won't work,' Alex said. 'According to her owner, she's very fussy about what she eats and doesn't really like petting much. Just be careful she doesn't catch you with her claws.'

Kiki took a few more steps, then lunged for the feline, giving Alex his chance to grab Miss Pretty. Fighting off vicious swipes and fierce biting, Kiki distracted the cat for several long, painful seconds before Alex caught Miss Pretty by the back of her neck and subdued her.

Retrieving the abandoned tablet, Kiki shoved it into the cat's mouth while Alex kept a firm hold on her furry body. After making certain the cat had definitely swallowed the pill this time, they returned Miss Pretty to her cage, blocking any second attempt at escape with both their bodies and slamming the door closed.

'Goodness!' Kiki panted. 'That is one grumpy, unfriendly cat.'

Alex nodded, leaning a hand against the cage. 'Sorry, Miss Pretty, but you have to stay there until your owner collects you.'

'You may want to suggest he comes and gets her from here. Save anyone else from having to deal with her bad manners.' She grinned. 'We make a good team, but it might be pushing our luck to mess with Miss Pretty again today.'

Alex smiled, then reached out and touched her cheek. 'She's scratched you.'

Kiki lifted a hand to her cheek and frowned when a streak of blood coated her fingertip. 'Perhaps I should ask my boss for danger money?'

'How about he cleans you up instead?'

Alex guided her over to the sink in the corner of the ward and spent the next few minutes washing the scratch with warm water, before applying a thin coat of anti-septic cream.

'All done,' he said.

Kiki looked up at him, her eyes sparkling. 'No plaster or kiss to make me feel better?'

Alex didn't reply, instead he asked, 'You said you needed to talk to me.'

Kiki nodded, the playfulness leaving her eyes. 'The headmistress of the infant school has enquired whether you might consider giving a talk to a Year Two class. I said you're very busy, but I promised to ask.'

Alex frowned at the request. Why would a teacher ask such a horrendous thing? Surely children preferred the chance of extra playtime over listening to someone who treated sick animals for a living.

'A talk?'

'Yes.'

'About what?' he enquired, glancing towards the wall of cages.

Kiki frowned. 'I'm not sure it needs to be a specific subject. Just a general chat about animals. Apparently the children's behaviour over the school term warrants a treat and she thought of you.'

Rubbing a finger along the collar of his denim shirt, Alex fought the urge to shudder. A talk in front of a group of children sounded as painful as sharing a cage with Miss Pretty. The shudder refused to recede. In fact, a second one joined it. Only sheer determination prevented him from showing his reaction to the woman next to him.

'She wants me to give a talk in front of a classroom of children?'

Kiki nodded, rubbing at a small scratch on the back of her hand. 'She insists the children will love it, but I did explain that you're busy and don't really do talks.'

Alex pulled her hand under the tap, determined to bring the conversation to an end and get back to work. The schoolchildren might love a visit, but he'd hate every intolerable second.

Turning away, he shook his head and grabbed a bottle of disinfectant and a paper towel. 'Sorry, but you'll have to tell this woman I said no. Maybe suggest she try another practice. I'm sure she'll find someone else willing to do it.'

'Perhaps Thorne can do it?' Kiki suggested as she rinsed her hand. 'Once his wife is better and he returns from the Isle of Wight. He really isn't having much luck, is he?'

Alex doubted it, knowing the man wouldn't be invested in the practice for much longer. He'd decided to buy out his partner's share in the business and let Thorne move on. Alex's solicitor was already working on the papers. He needed a partner who concentrated on his work and less on the desires of his latest mistress.

'If any other schools contact us with the same request, tell them no.'

Kiki tilted her head in his direction and bit her lower

lip. 'Don't you like teachers, Alex? Did you have a miserable time at school?'

He coughed, uncomfortable with both her regard and her questions. School had, in fact, offered a sanctuary from his home life.

He wiped over the examination table. 'I loved school. Teachers are not the problem.'

No, but the notion of standing in front of any group of people—even one in which the participants stood miniature in height and were less likely to complain and walk out—was. He did not perform in front of strangers of any age.

His stomach pitched at the thought, arousing appalling memories from his childhood. 'I don't do gatherings of children. *Ever.*'

Kiki's eyes widened at the statement. 'Don't you like children, Alex?'

He shrugged, uncomfortable with the way she stared at him, as if he'd threatened to repeatedly stamp on her favourite possessions. 'I've not thought about it much. No reason to as I'll never marry.'

Saying the words left a sour tang in his mouth, but he refused to lie to himself or Kiki. For him, a wife and family were nothing but an unachievable dream he refused to waste further time on.

For a fleeting moment he'd hoped that Kiki and he... Well, that idea was best forgotten. Even if their attraction refused to cease, she had made it clear she wanted friendship and no more when she'd stepped out of his arms midway through their dance.

'So, it's irrelevant if I like them or not.'

'Why won't you marry?' she demanded, moving to stand on the other side of the table.

Because she wanted a marriage based on friendship, whereas he wanted one based on friendship, sex and love. How could he marry when the one woman he imagined loving refused to permit love into her abused soul?

But he didn't say any of the words in his heart. Instead, he shrugged. 'I like my own company and enjoy the quiet.'

'Rubbish!' she scoffed. 'We share the lodge, remember? You're chatty all the time. And lately you only retire to your room when I go to bed. Hardly the behaviour of a recluse.'

Right now, he'd give anything for her to leave him in peace. Shooting her his best boss glare, he asked, 'Don't you have work to do?'

She ignored his question and persisted with one of her own. 'You don't *really* believe you'll never marry, do you? I mean, it's ridiculous.'

'I'm thirty-seven years old, Kiki, and still single.'

'Hardly old, Grandad,' she mocked. 'I'm thirty-two. Should I order us a couple of walking frames and hearing aids in case we suddenly need them?'

'Tell me—did you speak to your other bosses the way you do me?'

'No…' She smirked. 'But you're my housemate too, so it's different. Look, why don't we leave it a couple of days? You may change your mind and decide you'd *like* to talk to the children. Imagine them as little Turtles multiplied. Children are fun when you get to know them.'

He already knew, seeing as he'd grown up surrounded by a town full of cousins ranging from babies to adults. As part of a large family he'd never lacked playmates to cause trouble and mischief with. It was his home life that had left him lonely.

'I won't,' he insisted. 'Tell the headmistress I'm not free to do the talk.'

Kiki wrinkled her nose. 'But she wants you, Alex.'

'Well, she can't have me, Kiki,' he replied, furious at the old emotions and memories that had been resuscitated by her pushing. Ones he'd long ago suppressed. *Why* did none of his staff understand the employer/employee relationship? If he made a decision they were supposed to respect and abide by it even if they didn't agree.

'But... But...' she stammered, her expression making it clear she intended to argue further.

He raised his hand to stop her from saying another word. 'No, I'm not doing it. Tell the woman to find a policeman. Or perhaps a doctor or a lollipop person. Anyone but me. I'm a vet, not a teacher. I chose to be so because animals don't argue or answer back. I just wish my staff acted the same way.'

Kiki's eyes narrowed. 'They do bite, though.'

'The animals or my staff?' he asked, his imagination immediately conjuring up all the places he'd like to bite *her* while sharing her bed. A different type of heat rolled through him.

Kiki let out a loud huff. 'And you accuse *me* of being stubborn? Well, Alex Morsi, you own the title for being unreasonable and unhelpful.'

Seeing the disappointment on her face, he swallowed the unpleasant taste in his mouth. He hesitated for a second, before asking, 'How many children are in this class?'

Kiki shrugged. 'No idea. Around thirty is the usual number for most classes, I think.'

Thirty small faces staring at him. Thirty individuals

waiting to find fault and ridicule. Thirty loud echoing voices laughing and yelling insults.

No, he couldn't do it.

He blinked several times to clear the sudden flashing stars from his eyes, rubbing a shaky, clammy hand across his brow. 'I'm sorry, but the answer's still no.'

Kiki opened her mouth to argue more, but he shook his head. When he'd left home to attend college in England he'd sworn never to perform in public again. He refused to allow anyone—even Kiki—to talk him into doing something he'd worked hard to avoid.

'I don't do talks of any type.'

She stared at him silently from across the table, digesting his words before she said, 'Forget the talk. I don't want you to do it anyway. But I'm not leaving until you tell me the real reason for your refusal.'

He didn't know whether the soft coaxing tone of her voice or the fact she'd stopped arguing had lessened his resistance to continuing with the conversation, but for the first time in his life he wanted to unburden the secrets entombed deep inside his heart. To finally drag them out from the internal crypt he'd concealed them in long ago.

His shoulders slumped and he raised his eyes to the ceiling. 'I can't stand talking in front of large groups. One to one is fine, but more than a handful is unsettling.'

'I didn't realise…' she said.

He closed his eyes and swallowed hard. 'Was your mother nice?'

'Yes, very.'

He opened his eyes again, his dark gaze holding hers, each syllable waiting on his lips a repugnant ball of acid. 'My mother isn't. She likes to play with people's minds and cause them to suffer. There's something ugly and twisted inside her. A sick need to humiliate others.'

Kiki listened without saying a word.

'All my childhood she enjoyed nothing more than to embarrass and torment me. She got a real kick out of it. Her favourite torture involved forcing me to stand with my toes on a set mouse trap, dressed in my underwear, and recite poetry in front of a crowd of her actor friends. The first time I was four. I wet myself when they laughed at my mispronunciation of "impediments", afraid that at any second my toes were going to be crushed by the metal trap.'

'A mouse trap?'

'Yes—the kind that snaps shut at the slightest touch. I didn't learn until years later that it was useless and broken and wouldn't have done me any physical harm. I was petrified, and that was all my mother wanted.'

Kiki didn't speak.

'I can recite Byron and Shakespeare with ease. Though I always fight the urge to vomit whenever I say or hear the words.'

Even now, all these years later, if he heard the first line of Shakespeare's *Sonnet Eighteen* the memory of warm urine running down his leg overcame him. Not something he would ever forget.

Kiki finally spoke. 'I prefer Anne Bradstreet myself. How often did she make you do it?'

Clearing his throat, Alex lifted the bottle of disinfectant from the table. 'Every time her friends visited the house she'd drag me out of bed in the middle of the night and stand me in the centre of the room while they all stood around laughing and mocking. Torture for a shy, chubby child happier to be alone reading than forced into the company of unfamiliar adults. Most of them were high or drunk and ready to ridicule me over everything from my accent to my weight. If I made a mistake, or forgot the words, she used a scrubbing brush on me. The one used to clean the floors. The bristles were stiff and vicious upon my skin when it was used as a form of punishment.'

Tears filled Kiki's eyes. 'And your father?'

Alex shrugged, not acknowledging the deep pain of his father's indifference and lack of help. 'Too busy drowning his sorrows in the local pub to care about what happened at home. Though I do recall one time when he returned during a particularly horrendous gathering.'

'What did he do?' she asked softly.

Alex hated to destroy the small thread of hope he heard in her voice, but his father had been no help or hero. Not that night or any other.

'He slouched drunkenly in the doorway, watched for several moments, then staggered up the stairs to his bedroom. Though he did tell me about the mouse trap being useless the following day.'

'Oh, Alex...' Kiki rounded the table and reached for his hands. Grasping them tightly, she said, 'I'm sorry. I didn't think when I asked. I just—'

'Assumed I was being awkward for the sake of it?'

She nodded, regret in her eyes.

'I swore when I left Ireland never to allow another person to control me again. Or to put myself in a situation like that.'

Kiki shook her head in disbelief. 'Your parents' mindless callousness and selfishness has robbed them of loving a wonderful son. You're the kindest and gentlest man I know. Don't allow their cruelty to hurt you any longer.'

'Not only a duck-defender, but a vet champion, too?' he said, attempting a joke.

He looked down at her, seeing the compassion in her eyes. How he wanted to pull her into his arms and slowly lick the tears from each corner of her eyes, where they sat like two transparent beads. To melt away her unhappiness and kiss her until they forgot about the past and the future and celebrated the now. To lose his long-hated memories in the velvety beauty of her sweet, tantalising body.

But he didn't reach for her. Instead he gripped her hands and whispered, 'I'm sorry, but I can't do the talk. I just can't.'

CHAPTER ELEVEN

KIKI PLACED HER phone on the wooden table and stared across the staffroom. The smell of coffee wafting from the mug beside her barely registered as she tried to filter the news she'd just received. The ten-minute conversation with her godmother—normally an enjoyable event—had instead left Kiki wanting to curl her lip and snarl like a rage-possessed she-wolf.

Resisting the urge, she shoved her chair back, its rear legs scraping against the tiled floor in a horrendous screech, and stood. The twisting sickness in her stomach had taken away any appetite for the lunch waiting in her shoulder bag.

How *could* he? How could he do this to her? How dared Alex use their friendship to approach her godmother with an offer to buy Fingle Lodge? Sneaking in with a proposal while *she* still resided there? Couldn't she wait a few months for her to finish updating the building before he tried to evict her? Was he so eager to push her out of his life that he would go behind her back and do this?

She grabbed her phone and carried her mug over to the steel sink. Throwing the half-finished coffee down the drain, her fingers shook as she rinsed the cup and left it on the side to dry.

And how dared her godmother agree to consider it without even having the decency to ask if she minded?

The fact that Kiki couldn't afford to buy the lodge was neither important nor relevant. Out of good manners, surely she should have asked how she felt? Her godmother was supposed to be her friend—not striking deals with sneaky, deceitful veterinarians keen to grab themselves a property bargain by any dirty tricks and underhand means.

And to think this morning, after Alex had shared the horrors of his childhood, she'd believed their relationship had strengthened—deepened, even. When the truth was her usefulness to him had run out and now the devious man wanted her gone. Out of his life and out of the lodge.

Her life history was repeating itself—but this time a different man was willing to inflict the mortal wound.

She pushed the thought away and left the staffroom, heading straight for the stockroom, where she knew Alex was hiding, checking over a crate of recently delivered supplies. Normally Leah dealt with the chore, but today she'd booked a dentist appointment so Alex had offered to deal with it.

Since their conversation he'd taken to avoiding Kiki. She'd understood his need to be on his own after opening up his heart, and had respected it. But then her godmother had called, and now the man had some serious explaining to do. This time she was going to demand answers. She refused to be treated in such a shoddy way.

Was it something she did or said that caused men to care so little for her feelings? Why did this always happen, every time she let herself care for a man? First, her father had treated her and her love for him as something unimportant and disposable, then her ex hadn't respected her enough to keep his trousers zipped around other women, and now Alex.

She rubbed her forehead, forcing back the pain of this latest deception. Alex was *not* going to walk away believing he could just cast her out without a care, the same way her father had. She was sick and tired of people always putting their desires before hers. Well, not this time.

She looked forward to hearing Alex's justification for going behind her back to make a deal to acquire ownership of the place where *she* lived. When he'd mentioned on that first night he'd stayed at Fingle Lodge how the property interested him she hadn't realised he meant as his new home.

Opening the stockroom door, she zeroed in on the man bent over the computer positioned on a small desk at the end of the narrow room. Lifting her chin, she fixed all her attention on him, every nerve and hair on her body tingling. He'd better get his excuses ready, because she was ready to see through them.

Alex had taken her offer of friendship and manipulated it for his own means. He planned to make her homeless. Steal the shelter from over her head. Leave her without the warmth of a home just like her father had on the morning he'd left.

Why had she stupidly thought Alex would be different—better, even? Yet again a man had proved he didn't deserve her faith.

However, fools played nicely but enemies played harder. Now they were enemies.

Stalking along the narrow walkway between the

shelving units built on each side, stacked from floor to ceiling with the medical supplies required to keep the practice running smoothly and efficiently, Kiki didn't bother to suppress her contempt as she spat out his name.

'Alex.'

He turned with a frown, before straightening. 'Kiki? Hi.'

She stopped, ignoring the self-conscious expression on his face and the colour creeping under his skin. Their earlier discussion was no longer her concern. He could take his horrible childhood and find some other woman to care over it. She refused to. This was the last time any man was going to use her and then toss her away.

'You devious, untrustworthy rat! Did you truly think I wouldn't find out?'

Alex seemed to listen to her accusation before walking towards her and stopping several inches away. He stared at her for a moment, his eyes narrowing as he digested her words. Finally, he asked, 'Have I upset you?'

Yes—and more.

Just when she'd started to think he might actually be a decent, nice man, reality had shone its ruthless light and showed her the truth. The same way it always did when Kiki hoped for more from a male. The only thing a girl could trust in was reality, ripping away any pretence to expose the repugnant layers that made up a man's character and showed him for the two-faced swine he was.

'Don't you come all innocent with me!' she snapped, taking a step towards him. 'I know what you've done.'

Instead of defending himself Alex folded his arms, the movement pulling the sleeves of his blue scrubs tight. Several inches of dark hair showed, giving a glimpse of his smooth skin underneath.

Not fooled by his guiltless act, she stabbed a shaky finger in the centre of his chest, wincing when she hit bone instead of muscle. 'I *know*.'

Raising both eyebrows, Alex grabbed her finger before she inflicted another bruising assault on his chest. Wrapping his own fingers around it,' he said, 'I'm guessing this has nothing to do with our conversation this morning, so I'll ask again—what is it, Kiki?'

Hating all men and their treacherous natures, she glared at him. If men weren't lying and cheating, they were finding some other way to ruin a woman's life. Cursing her lack of height, she resisted the urge to push herself up on to her toes.

Using her trapped finger, Alex gently tugged her nearer. 'We can spend the next few minutes in a guessing game, but why not cut the twaddle and tell me exactly what terrible crime I've committed?'

Kiki scrunched up her nose, astonished by his lack of shame. She'd expected him to display embarrassment at being found out, but his absence of unease astounded her. The man was unbelievably brazen.

'Don't you try and wriggle out of it!'

'I'd never attempt such a manoeuvre unless I knew what I was apparently wriggling out of first.' He grinned, his eyes sparkling with mischief. 'But then who can guess what I might do?'

The stupid grin ramped up Kiki's pulse, but fortunately it didn't lower her temper. She hardened her soft traitorous side, which sought to weaken at his smile. She couldn't trust him. His deceit over Fingle Lodge proved it. He was just like every other man she had stupidly opened herself to. Only Alex's betrayal was worse, because she'd truly started to believe he was different.

'I'm aware of what you did,' she repeated, sounding unhinged even to her own ears.

But lately that feeling was normal around this man. Since meeting him, everything in her life had changed. All she'd worked so hard to simplify disintegrated in his company. One minute she thought she understood his character—the next he did something so unexpected it crushed that belief to pieces. Destroying her confidence in him. Making her question and suspect everything she'd believed about his trustworthiness.

Alex sighed. 'More clarity, if you don't mind.'

'I know the real reason you've been staying with me at the lodge, pretending to be my friend.'

Her voice broke on the last word, but she ignored it and prayed he hadn't noticed. This morning, when he'd told her about his mother's abuse, she'd hoped... Well, it didn't matter any more. *He* didn't matter to her. She'd endured other men's betrayal, she'd survive his.

The concern in his gaze indicated that he'd heard the break in her voice. 'You do?'

His confusion sounded genuine. She frowned at his hand, still wrapped around her finger and jerked. 'Let go.'

His lips twitched, but he instantly released her. 'Of course. But please try and talk to me without using my body as a target—my chest bone will be grateful for ever.'

She lowered her hand and clenched it at her side. Breathing deeply, she bit back the painful, aching sob that welled in her throat. No, she *wasn't* going to cry in front of Alex. Kick him, maybe, but not cry.

Swallowing the sob down, she said, 'You're nothing but a phony.'

His humour disappeared at the remark and his eyes hardened. 'Strong accusation, Kiki. What reason do you have to allege such a thing?'

She lifted her chin, not about to let doubt into her mind. Her conversation with her godmother proved the truth of his guilt. His friendship and kisses had been nothing but a devious ploy to get the lodge. Every conversation a stride towards his main purpose.

'You searched my phone for my godmother's contact number, didn't you?'

His denial was both immediate and firm. 'I've never touched your phone.'

'How else did you get her number?' Kiki demanded, determined to catch him out on his lie.

Her godmother hadn't visited in years, and most people who'd lived in the area at the time she had, had either died or moved away.

'Whose number?'

Irritated by his playing dumb, she snapped, 'My *godmother's*. The woman who owns Fingle Lodge. The woman you contacted and made an offer to buy it from.'

'Ah…' he said.

What did 'ah' mean? And why wasn't guilt consuming him now she'd confronted him with his misconduct. There wasn't any other way for Alex to obtain that number but from her phone. None at all.

He unfolded his arms and rested his hands on his hips. 'I asked your neighbour in the cottage at the end of the lane.'

Unless he'd done that, of course. Yeah, that was a possibility…seeing as the old lady was the key-holder for the lodge and a very good friend of her godmother's.

Kiki's anger crumbled into a large puddle of humiliation deep enough for her to disappear in. She'd never considered Mrs Bush. A stupid mistake. But it didn't change the fact that Alex had used their association to his own advantage. Offering to let him stay at the lodge after his water tank burst must have seemed like a boon.

'So you didn't search my phone?' she persisted, not ready to accept the truth.

'No.'

'Oh.'

Alex sniggered. 'No apology, Kiki?'

'You're still a sneak for making an offer on my home,' she insisted, grabbing at her diminishing anger.

Okay, so she'd made a tiny little error, but he'd still gone behind her back with the offer.

'But it's your godmother's property—and according to her you're only staying until the renovations are completed. Is it fair for Fingle Lodge to be abandoned once again just because you no longer wish to stay in Dorset? Left to decay like the rest of the Cattleson Estate? Doesn't it deserve to be rescued? So people in the future can live there?'

Stupid tears stung her eyes but she refused to let them fall. Yes, he was right—but did he need to be so keen to get rid of her? *This* was why she refused to let love take hold. Because when a man messed up it only left disappointment and not utter devastation behind. And right at this moment, she wasn't sure what she was feeling.

'I've yet to make a decision about my future. And until I do, or my godmother accepts your offer, Fingle Lodge is *my* home. You're just a lodger.'

The change in Alex came instantly. Before Kiki thought to move he'd closed the gap between them, his large body filling the space until all her senses had no choice but to acknowledge every inch of his intimidating presence.

No longer teasing and light-hearted, his voice now dangerous, he purred, 'Just a lodger, Kiki? You come in here, overreacting to a simple phone call I've made, and then you have the nerve to call me a mere *lodger.*'

She licked her lips, wishing she had kept quiet. The faint smell of his spicy aftershave tickled her nose, arousing prickles over her flesh and making her light-headed.

'Yes, Alex, you're nothing but a lodger—a tenant— whatever.'

His hands circled her upper arms and he shuffled her backwards until her shoulder blades hit the shelving. She gasped and grabbed the front of his top, curling the material into her fists. The heat from his body warmed her fingers, indicating how close they were.

'What are—?'

'Shh,' he ordered, reaching out to push the still-open door shut on the rest of the practice.

It closed with a menacing slam.

Darkness enclosed them, broken only by the light from the computer at the other end of the narrow room.

Kiki gulped, feeling the air suddenly hot and dense. Sweat beaded on her neck and between her breasts as both fear and excitement raced through her body. Obviously Alex planned on some form of retribution.

'You accuse me of stealing your phone and using our friendship,' he murmured darkly, 'even after everything we've done and talked about. Do you honestly believe I'd be so dishonest?'

Shivers roamed over her skin at his even tone. But she wasn't fooled by it. Alex sought payback, and in the next few seconds he would gain it. This time it was his turn not to play nice.

He chuckled softly and shifted closer, not leaving her a millimetre to move. Draining the air until all she breathed was him.

'I was angry, and I thought you were like every other m…' Her excuses vanished as his left hand slowly trailed down her arm to settle possessively on the curve of her waist. The warmth of his brushing fingertips seared through the material of her uniform like scorching flames.

'When are you going to realise there are some people you can trust?' he asked.

Kiki snorted and tried to twist away. But Alex wedged her tight against the shelving, blocking any chance of escape, crowding her with the full impact of his firm body.

His right hand trailed up along her other arm, stopping at her shoulder. The caress was light and enticing. 'You can't live your life never trusting, Kiki.'

She gulped, distracted by his movements and by the certainty that he planned to toy with her. 'It's easy once you learn how. Especially when people keep letting you down.'

He tutted and shifted, his chest rubbing hers. 'But sometimes…like now…you're wrong for thinking the worst. I don't understand how you dare to call me a lodger when we've kissed and danced.'

She preferred not to recall the kiss while she stood there in the semi-darkness, with the hard, muscular outline of his torso pressed against her own. Her nipples hardened, wantonly reacting to the pressure of his weight. Awakening the heat between her legs and every sensitive nerve in her body.

'But it didn't mean anything,' she gasped, as his fingers discovered a sensitive spot on her neck. Not to him anyway. If it had, why hadn't he kissed her again? They shared a home, giving him many opportunities whenever the need came over him. 'You only kissed me because I cried—'

'No, I kissed you,' he interrupted, 'because it's all I think about every time I glance at you. Each time I touch you I mentally undress you, taking every single piece of your clothing from your delectable body, and I imagine what I might discover underneath. I didn't kiss you because you were sad. I did it because I want you.'

She squawked as his left hand slipped to her bottom, curving around the cheek and giving it a squeeze.

'I kissed you,' he continued unevenly, 'because I wanted your full attention and for you to stop thinking of all the reasons why we shouldn't kiss.'

'I see...' she whispered, half her mind on his words, the other half on the hand caressing her bottom.

'I kissed you, Kiki Brown, because you own the prettiest mouth, the dirtiest laugh and I enjoyed doing it.'

He captured her mouth and showed her how much. His lips were warm and full, exploring hers with a thoroughness that staggered and weakened her every thought of resistance. The distant sound of her uniform buttons popping and the tugging of material as he pulled the front apart barely registered as he deepened their kiss. She moaned when seconds later his curious probing fingers slid inside, exploring the contours of her lace-covered breasts and caressing her burning eager flesh.

His hand on her bottom moved to stroke along the length of her outer thigh, encouraging it to lift upwards until it cradled his hip, opening Kiki up to him and rubbing himself against her sensitive heat until she tore her mouth from his.

'I kiss you,' he added huskily, 'because I want to hear you gasp my name, to smell your desire in each sweet aching moan that escapes your lips, and to taste all your stifled passion on my tongue.'

His mouth seized hers again, swallowing every sound his touch sparked, teaching her the unfamiliar, intimate dance of lovemaking with the diligence of a determined tutor.

Minutes later he ripped his mouth from hers, his breath ragged. 'And yet you accuse me so easily and question my integrity. If anyone is guilty of falsehood and playing games, it's you.'

'Me?'

His hand continued its investigation of her breast, gliding over her raised nipple. 'You ran from our kiss and you walked away during the middle of our dance. You didn't care enough to give me the one thing I asked for on my birthday. So, as much as I am tempted to enjoy more of your body, I won't take you here in a stockroom where anyone can hear us.'

Kiki stiffened, digging her fingers into his shoulders. Shame surged through her for the way she had hurt him and let him down. When she'd stepped out of his arms during their dance it hadn't been to deny him, but simply because she hadn't trusted herself not to fall in love with him completely. Each day it was becoming harder to ignore the swelling in her heart and the pleasure she found in his company.

'You won't believe in me because other men have hurt you and humiliated you. I understand your reluctance to trust, but I will *not* be punished when I am not to blame. And I also refuse to be used so you can satisfy your curiosity.'

She didn't understand. 'My curiosity about what?'

'Sex,' he answered harshly. 'I'm the only man you've ever wanted to go further with, aren't I?'

She nodded slowly, then remembered he couldn't see her clearly. 'Yes.'

'You've refused to be intimate with any man—even the one you planned to marry. Yet you'd make love with me here in a stockroom. What makes me so different from your fiancé? From any other man you've kept yourself from loving?'

'I don't know,' she lied, not prepared to tell the truth. That the difference was simply that she'd never loved those other men.

Her fingers searched the darkness for his face. She needed to touch him, to reconnect in some small part with the passionate man of a few seconds ago.

Her fingers finally connected with his warm cheek. Reassured by the solidness of his body against her trembling skin, she begged, 'Please, Alex.'

'You're still that little girl, allowing her father to dictate her life.' Alex touched the side of her head, tapping his fingers against her skull. 'The man may not be in your life, physically pushing your buttons, but he's in *here*. In your mind, controlling each thought and decision you make. You're a grown woman, yet you're still living in the past, running away from the chance of a wonderful future. One with happiness and love.'

'Don't,' she pleaded, not wanting to hear more of her failings.

'Open your heart, Kiki. Otherwise you're never going to change. Your life will stay stuck in the wasteland of fear. Reach for a richer, better life. You insist I shouldn't let the past behaviour of my parents continue to affect me. Isn't it time you did the same?'

He touched her forehead with his own.

'I want to make love with you, but I won't watch you roll out of my bed one morning with a final goodbye on your lips. Those same lips I love to kiss. I won't give you the whole of me and then wait for you to listen once more to that fear you've let control you for so long. I won't give you my commitment and then watch you destroy it. If I ever make love with you it will be when you offer me the same. I deserve nothing less.'

She swallowed, pushing her words out. 'You say commitment, but it sounds as though you really mean love.'

'Perhaps I do,' he said.

Love. Why did it always return to that stupid four-letter word? An emotion she didn't want to acknowledge or trust?

'Why is love so important?'

Alex sighed and planted a soft kiss upon her head. When he spoke his voice was heavy and full of regret. 'I wish you knew the answer.'

The stockroom door suddenly opened, casting bright light over the two of them. Anne stood in the doorway taking in the scene. 'Stocktaking, Alex?'

'Settling staff disputes,' he answered. 'All over now.'

The finality in his words caused a different fear to shift through Kiki. She reached for him but he pulled away, once again putting space between them.

With a last searching glance at her face Alex walked out of the room, leaving the two women staring after him. The squeak of his shoes on the vinyl floor soon mingled with the normal everyday sounds of the busy practice.

'God, he's so infuriating,' Kiki grumbled, snapping her uniform buttons together.

Anne turned and faced Kiki. 'It's the reason we love him, though, isn't it?'

Kiki didn't answer. Heartily sick of love and everything it involved. She'd entered the room determined to confront the man with his supposed wrongdoings, and instead he had cruelly exposed her own. He'd urged her to trust in love—an emotion she'd watched destroy her mother's happiness. If he cared for her, then why did he ask for the one thing she'd sworn she would never be weak enough to give to any man?

'You like her, don't you?'

Alex dropped his keys, his heart somewhere between his mouth and his stomach as he stepped out of the consultation room and into the front reception area. Anne sat behind the desk, a single lamp casting a low intimate light over the writing pad in her hand.

Bending to scoop up the bunch of keys, he said, 'I thought everyone had already left for the night.'

Anne pushed the pad away and shrugged. 'Harry has one of his train meetings, and Dee and her Kiwi friends are at the cinema, drooling over some hot actor whose name my tongue struggles to pronounce. So I decided to stay on and write out a couple of condolence letters to the owners of our recently departed clients. Do I get an answer or accept that earlier groping session in the stockroom as evidence?'

Alex wandered over to the desk, his expression serious. 'Yes, I like her, but it's not important.'

Anne reached across and flicked him on the forehead.

'Don't treat me like a fool, Alex. We've been friends too long.'

Leaning his arms on the top, he frowned. 'I wouldn't dare. You're too vicious when you're annoyed.'

Anne stared at him. 'Since scrumptious Miss Brown joined us you've been acting like a confused man who's discovered that unfamiliar world commonly named as romance. In all the years we've worked together I've never known you to take to a woman the way you have Kiki.'

Alex didn't bother to deny it. The stockroom incident had been a clear sign that something was going on between him and Kiki.

'No one is like her. She's unique.'

Anne studied him over the top of her glasses, a pleased tilt to her mouth. 'I'm glad you realise that. You're not always so observant.'

He knocked his knuckles against the desktop, unsure what else to say. Kiki fancied his body, and the pleasure he could show her, but her heart was so badly damaged she rejected any opportunity to reach for everything he yearned to give her.

'I'm not sure it's going to do any good.'

Removing her glasses, Anne slid them into her blouse pocket. 'When I first met Harry, after one conversation I knew I was going to marry him. Other than the fact we supported the same football team, he gave me a feeling no other man ever had. You know the one?'

Alex closed his eyes and sighed. 'The feeling that they complete you. That everything you'd never appreciated was missing from your soul is there in them.'

'Yes, that's it. No matter what happens in life, you know they're next to you, holding your hand, listening.

You can face any problem, enjoy any pleasure, if they walk the next step with you.'

'But what if their past has inflicted too many hurts for them to see there's a chance to share something special with you? What then?'

Anne didn't answer, instead, she asked, 'What's happened between you? Other than the fact you've kissed her in the stockroom—hardly romantic surroundings.'

'It had its moments,' Alex said with a grin.

Oh, yes, kissing Kiki had certainly had its good points. And the erotic excitement of searching her feminine form in the dark and travelling over places he had only dreamed of touching definitely came under a plus.

Anne glared at him disapprovingly. 'I sensed discord between you both earlier.'

'I made an offer on her godmother's property but forgot to mention it to her. I didn't think it was important.'

Anne flicked his forehead for the second time. 'Honestly—you're not helping yourself, are you? No wonder she's peeved with you.'

Alex rubbed his stinging forehead and added wryly, 'Declining the opportunity to make love to her this afternoon hasn't helped.'

Anne blinked several times before whistling. 'Rather crushing for the girl's ego, Alex. There she has you, all hot and hard, and you go all prim and righteous. Are you saying you haven't succumbed to the sizzling attraction that leaps between you two? Even though you share the same roof and have plenty of occasions for indulging in a night-time vertical dalliance?'

He rested his head on his arms and groaned. 'It's been hard.'

She sniggered. 'I bet. So what are you going to do?'

He lifted his head. 'No idea. I'm a foot deep in trouble and constantly being covered with new layers. Every time we seem to be doing okay, something happens to ruin it.'

Her eyes narrowed with suspicion. 'Why do I get the impression there's more you're not confessing?'

Alex frowned, struggling between the urge to get everything out and his typically reserved nature that made it easier to keep things inside.

'Has Kiki mentioned a school talk?'

Anne nodded. 'I was manning Reception when Miss Ingle called in. Strange woman… I think it's a great idea, though.'

Alex took a step back out of Anne's reach to save his forehead from a third assault. 'I said no.'

Anne's eyes narrowed.

Alex recognised the expression and shifted further away from the desk.

'Why?'

A simple question, yet with so many layers and complexities. How did he make his head nurse understand? He wasn't sure Kiki had. No one truly did unless they'd stood in the same place and faced similar demons.

'I hate talking to groups of people. Really hate it.'

'I hate swede,' Anne replied. 'But Harry loves to grow it, so I eat it without complaint to make him happy.'

'Really?' he asked, not believing her. Normally when she was unhappy Anne made certain everyone within earshot knew it.

She screwed up her nose and confessed. 'All right. I may moan a bit. But he informs me that it's good for me, so I fuss but still eat it.'

'A school talk is a bit different than eating swede,' he pointed out.

'What I mean is sometimes there's no choice but to do something you hate for someone you care about. On our wedding anniversary Harry always takes me to the beach, whatever the weather. He hates the seaside and has an aversion to sand, but he does it to make me happy. For a few hours I can sit on the sand with the wind coming off the sea and remember my childhood holidays.'

'Kiki said she understood why I said no.'

'Good—but don't you think if you do it it would show her that you can put yourself out? Alex, you can be a little unbendable at times. It can't be helped because it's your nature, but if you want to impress the lady you should do something unexpected.'

'Like the talk?'

Ripping out his teeth or sitting through a lifetime of children's TV sounded easier.

'You'd be putting the children's pleasure before your own discomfort. Showing Kiki how you're willing to put yourself out for others even when it's something you hate. That you can be trusted not to let anyone down.'

'I think I'd rather sit on the beach and eat swede for a year.'

Anne left her seat and rounded the counter. Without a word she wrapped her arms around Alex's waist and hugged him close. 'You are the sweetest man I know, but you're lonely. I used to see it in your eyes and hear it in your voice. But since the day Kiki arrived it's disappeared. Be brave. Do the talk for her and show the girl how fabulous you are.'

'She says she doesn't want to fall in love,' he said, not

sure which of them required that cold reminder or why he was telling Anne.

Kiki hated him right now. His bags probably waited on the lodge's doorstep.

Anne snorted, stepping back and patting his chest. 'I think she's already there. What *you* must do is demonstrate unmistakably that you feel the same.'

She loved him.

Kiki scrubbed the thought away and refused to linger on it. But her stubborn mind and the pushy truth refused to stay quiet and she found herself deliberating the notion once more.

She loved sexy Dr Alex Morsi.

She growled under her breath. Fine. So what? It would pass—like her bout of flu or an itchy outbreak of heat rash. She just needed to hold her nerve, suffer the feelings, and wait until her world returned to its regular dull routine. No stupid emotion was going to beat her, especially not *l-o-v-e*.

'You lot don't realise how good your life is,' she said out loud. 'Swimming all day and then waddling around, pecking at the grass, waiting to discover a tasty worm or snail to devour. It's not a hard life—it's an easy one, uncomplicated by the presence of a man.'

Kiki stared at the ten white-feathered ducks who for the last few minutes mostly ignored her presence and muttered rantings. Since bringing them to Fingle Lodge, they'd settled into a routine, in which she cared for all their needs and engaged in one-sided conversations, while they showed absolutely no interest in her other than when she carried the feed bucket.

Checking the water level in the large blue paddling

pool she'd bought from the toy section in the local supermarket, Kiki returned to the rickety wheelbarrow retrieved from the barn for one of the metal buckets filled with clean water.

'We humans deal with extra things you ducks don't worry over. Like bills—the money kind, not your kind. And we navigate complicated friendships with irritating men determined to try our patience who set off our tempers like raging bubbles boiling in a saucepan, and then we face the added problem when our stupid, disobedient feelings develop into more than what we want them to.'

At the low metal drinking trough Alex had bought from a farmer friend, along with several bales of straw, Kiki emptied out the dirty water and replaced it with fresh.

She straightened and glanced at a duck attacking a leaf with its orange bill. 'You just look at a male duck and think, *Is he good enough to mate with or not*? Well, humans view a man and wonder if there's any point in developing a friendship. If it's worth the effort of getting to know him, or if he'll become annoying and boring after a couple of outings, or worse want more than we want to give.'

Like affection, commitment and love.

Kiki dropped the bucket and folded her arms. Damn it, she *loved* Alex. Full, heart-thumping, knee-wilting, soul-wrenching love.

It was one thing to suspect it, but something else to finally admit it.

She didn't want to love Alex. Love hurt and pain always followed it like its obedient servant. Leaving a person vulnerable to another's wants and desires. It tore you apart and left destruction without a care for the damage when it went wrong.

She'd sworn after her father's abandonment never to give a man such power over her life again, and for years she'd firmly kept to the decision.

Until she'd met Alex.

Alex wasn't her father. He wasn't mean and always searching for something better than what he already had. He cared about people—even if he did try to pretend otherwise. He loved them and he gave them his loyalty without conditions or a time span. He was a good man. A decent man. The kind she'd honestly thought no longer existed.

But he did exist and she loved him—despite doing her best not to. Despite a stubborn part of her wanting to believe differently...

She strolled to the wheelbarrow and grabbed a second metal bucket. At the pool, she slowly topped up the water level to give the ducks plenty to swim and submerge themselves in. Within moments, several ducks jumped in for a mid-morning swim.

Staring at three ducks waddling past, wiggling their rear ends in what Kiki considered an impudent manner, she sighed. 'Maybe I'll pack my bags and leave. What reason is there to stay?

If she left today she could visit her godmother in Kent. She brushed away a stupid tear and glared at the scenery. She wanted to live a happy life with a man she *liked*, not loved. But Alex had cursed her with his kisses. Doomed her to a barren existence with those caresses of his mouth. Cast her into a future of disappointment.

How could any other man surpass him, or stir as much

desire within her, now she'd experienced the sweet possibility of what she was missing?

The man insisted on commitment and love. Well, she loved him, but the whole idea terrified her. What if she woke in a few days and found all the love gone—disappeared overnight like an annoying earache? Or what if he changed his mind in a few weeks. What if the attraction fizzled out once they'd made love?

Despite Alex insisting on commitment before they made it into the bedroom, he hadn't actually admitted to loving her, had he? All his demands—yet what did she get in return?

She didn't want the man to break her heart. Yes, she might love him, but she didn't have to do anything about it. She could ignore it and carry on with her life.

She retrieved the buckets and turned to survey the ducks, several of whom had now moved towards the duck house. After a quick count to check for missing ones, she walked towards the gate.

Duck chores done, she left the field, careful to lock the gate behind her. Lifting the wheelbarrow, she headed in the barn's direction.

But she didn't want just the memory of two kisses to keep her warm at night. She wanted Alex and his loving arms to do the job. To wake in the morning and see him across the bed, all sleep-ruffled and sexy. To feel the heat of his body radiating across the mattress to warm her on chilly nights, and hear his sexy voice against her skin when he wished her good morning.

His accusation that she was living in the past and letting her father's rejection mould her choices held a grim grain of truth. Instead of forgetting about the man and leaving him behind, where he deserved to stay, she'd carted him around like a noxious rucksack.

How could she have been so stupid?

Wasn't it better to try and find Utopia than to give in to the fear and never grow or change? Better to risk the chance of happiness than to endure lonely days without the man who made her smile?

The only man she'd ever truly loved.

But what if she offered her heart and he scorned her for thinking they might have a future? What if he didn't believe she loved him? After everything she'd insisted for the past few weeks, who *wouldn't* doubt her sincerity? What if after their conversation in the stockroom he no longer felt the same?

She dropped the wheelbarrow, wiping her hand across her itchy, stinging nose. Okay, if he had changed his mind then she'd find a way to change it back. Fight for possession of his heart. Demonstrate that she was ready to give her full commitment to their relationship.

But first she needed to go into town and do the one thing that would prove her love to him. She just hoped it wouldn't hurt too much.

CHAPTER TWELVE

HE WAS GOING to throw up. Vomit right there in front of everyone. Exhale his half-digested breakfast over a bunch of half-grown strangers in grey school uniforms. In particular, the girl sitting on the left with red ribbons and ladybird slides in her brown hair. She glared at Alex as though she already recognised him as a pathetic failure.

The expression on the girl's face was reminiscent of the looks of disgust and disapproval he'd faced daily from his mother, throughout most of his childhood and his teenage years.

A burning trail of bile hit his throat. Swallowing, he winced as he suffered the sting for a second time.

He coughed and shifted his gaze to the birch tree at the far end of the school's miniature garden. An area had been created out of a hotchpotch of primary-coloured plastic containers, and strange statues had been crafted out of recycled soft drinks bottles and other unidentifiable objects. Each one sprouted a variety of herbs and flowers.

Glancing at the group of children, sitting in a half-circle on a square patch of grass, he let his gaze drift over them once again. Fifteen children in all—not thirty, as Kiki had guessed. The headmistress, Miss Ingle, had stated it was a low-intake year. Still, there were enough staring faces to make him want to spew his guts, like a cat with a serious case of stomach upset.

'Just breathe deeply and count to twenty.'

Advice Anne had thrown over her shoulder before abandoning him to go and sit at the back. Her bright, over-confident smile was a sham to cover the worry they both shared over his natural ability to screw up.

Coming here today concerned more than just the children and the talk. He sat here in front of this class of fifteen pupils to prove that past fears no longer held him in their clutches, and to show Kiki that, even when faced with his idea of hell, he could endure it, survive it, just to please her.

Nothing and no one controlled him. Not the bleak past or the small blonde with attitude and a mouth he wanted to spend the rest of his life kissing.

He'd spent the night on the trolley at the practice instead of returning to Fingle Lodge, figuring that after their argument he wouldn't be welcome. Where their relationship went now was her decision.

Unable to sleep, he'd pondered the conversation with Anne in his head for hours, making a decision, then changing it, until he'd finally settled on one. He'd phoned the school first thing, agreeing to do the talk, but on condition that it took place today. One thing to face the demons—another to drag out the process.

Fortunately the headmistress had agreed, so here he sat, on a plastic chair too small for his body, facing a group of fidgety children whispering behind their small hands, with a cramping stomach and a longing to be somewhere else.

He shifted on the chair, stretching his legs out in front of him. The next thirty minutes promised to push the strength of his constitution to the brink. But he'd get through it somehow—hopefully…

'Is it possible to get some water?' he asked.

Both Miss Ingle and the female class teacher, whose name he'd forgotten, jumped from their seats and raced towards the school kitchen.

Frowning, he glanced again at the children, all waiting with expectant faces. Most of them wouldn't listen. But what if they did?

He stiffened, immediately recognising the old unwelcome voice from his boyhood. Demanding and grating and prone to get on his nerves. Over the years Alex had worked hard to ignore the voice, eventually battering it down until he'd assumed it had left for good.

But here it was, returned and eager to be heard. Sniping and picking. Finding fault with the same whining intensity that had always aggravated the younger Alex.

You're nothing but weak. Useless boy.

He moved his left shoulder—a childhood tic he was prone to whenever he was uncomfortable or tense. He fixed his gaze on a lemon tree planted in a bright yellow pot with blue swirls around the outside.

Just breathe deeply and ignore the voice. It's just stupid memories acting up. Just forget the children are all staring and giggling.

He gripped the notes in his hand, his heartbeat vibrating loudly in his chest. Anne had thought having something to hold would help to keep him focused, but the surgical method for the removal of a foreign body from a dog's intestines was a procedure he'd performed many times over the years, so he wouldn't need them.

His stomach turned and let out another worrying grumble. How soon before he disgraced himself?

Stretching his neck to one side, to relieve the tightness in his shoulder, he glanced towards the sky. Why was he putting himself through hell for a bunch of kids he didn't know?

Oh, yeah. To show the blonde who gave him heartburn that he could face a group of people and not evaporate under the pressure and turn into the scared child again. To face this challenge that pushed him beyond his normal comfortable and content world and win.

He refused to walk away just because it was hard and unpleasant. The time to man up and kick this burden to pieces had arrived.

He rubbed his brow, and the sweat gathering on it. If only Kiki trusted him. Her anger over his offer on Fingle Lodge showed she didn't. Not really. He'd offered to buy the place not because he hoped to get rid of her. He'd happily share it with the stubborn woman if she wished.

He'd asked Mrs Bush for the phone number simply because he'd seen her in her front garden, trimming a clematis, and acted on impulse. But the way Kiki had reacted told him he'd mucked up. Did she really imagine he would force her out after she'd given him a room when he had nowhere else to stay?

Her aversion to trust saddened him. Without it, loneliness would plague her days. But she could trust *him* with everything—including her heart. Hell, he hankered after her heart. To care for it and protect it. Champion her the way she had those ducks.

Miss Ingle returned with the water in a bright red plastic beaker. At her side stood a small blonde girl cuddling a soft toy rabbit, her face stained with tears.

Alex accepted it with a tight smile of thanks. He took a sip, before placing it at his feet.

'Jodie, why don't you sit down next to Fran?' Miss Ingle suggested, giving the child a tender pat on the shoulder.

Then the class teacher introduced him to the group and turned his way with an encouraging smile. He struggled off the chair, cleared his throat and stepped forward.

'Hello, my name is Alex Morsi...'

'Why?' demanded the red-ribbon-wearing mini-replica of his mother, shooting another arrow into his already shaky composure.

When had this talk changed to a question and answer session? Weren't they supposed to sit and listen? Maybe the Victorians had been right with their 'children should be seen but not heard' theory?

'Well, because it's the name my parents gave me.'

No, don't think of them. Don't let their voices in.

Their opinions and criticism didn't matter any more. As a grown man, no one's opinions counted but his own—and a certain pretty blonde's.

'Are your parents dead?' another child asked.

'*Not* a good question, Thomas,' Miss Ingle scolded from the edge of the grass.

Alex retrieved his water and took another sip before answering the boy. 'No, they're not. They live in Ireland.'

When no other questions came forward, he placed the beaker back on the floor and continued,

'I'm a vet. I care for animals. My practice is a mixed one, which means we treat all kinds of animals from cats to cows. Perhaps some of your pets are registered with my practice?'

A small fair-haired boy raised his hand. 'We brought

our guinea pig to you and it died the next day. The medicine you gave him didn't work.'

Alex should have trusted his instincts and stayed away from this school. Now every child stared at him as if he purposely killed the boy's pet.

He focused on a brick wall. *Think of something pleasant, Morsi. Nice and sweet to win them over.*

His thoughts immediately summoned yesterday's kiss in the stockroom, but he backed away from that. This was not the time or place to relive his and Kiki's last exchange.

He glanced down, his eyes falling on the little girl with the toy rabbit. She sucked her thumb and stared back at him.

Dragging the chair he'd recently vacated forward, he placed it closer to the group of children and sat down. Placing the cards on the grass, he pointed to the toy and softly asked, 'Do you mind if I borrow your friend?'

Hesitantly, she silently handed over the furry white rabbit, though her thumb stayed firmly in her mouth.

Alex took the toy and inspected it. It would do perfectly for his purposes. Holding it up, he asked, 'Who knows what animal this is?'

Every child raised their hand. Alex pointed at the boy in front of him.

'It's a rabbit.'

'That's right. *Oryctolagus cuniculus* is its fancy name. Can you all say that?'

As a group they repeated the words, a few giggling.

He smiled, some of his nerves easing. 'Well done. Now, the rabbit has these wonderful long ears.'

He stroked his fingers along the furry ears of the toy... the softness reminded him of Kiki's skin.

'Some people think it's okay to lift a rabbit by his ears, but that's wrong. Do you know why?'

A girl at the back of the group raised her hand. 'Because it will hurt it.'

Alex nodded. 'That's right. You wouldn't like it if every time you moved someone grabbed you by the ears, would you?'

A chorus of 'no' answered him.

'These ears are very sensitive, and the weight of a rabbit's body could cause damage if it was held just by the ears. So I'm going to show you the right way to pick one up. Just in case you ever need to.'

Alex set the toy on his knees and proceeded to demonstrate how to lift a rabbit correctly. Placing one hand under the toy's rear end, he put his other hand underneath its chest and then lifted it off his lap and into his arms. No need to hold it by the scruff when this particular patient was willing and friendly.

A soft 'ooh…' rose from the children as they watched.

Hugging the soft toy in his arms as though it was a baby, Alex continued, 'Rabbits can live between ten to twelve years.'

'That's a long time,' a boy called out from the group.

Alex nodded. 'Most people don't realise how long when they buy them. Does anyone know what rabbits like to eat?'

'Carrots!' several children called out.

He smiled. 'Sometimes they like a piece, now and then, but rabbits prefer grass and hay. And maybe a small amount of those pellets you can buy from the pet shop. They like to drink clean water, too.'

'My auntie's rabbit eats its own droppings,' a tall boy

said, fiddling with his glasses. 'She told me so last time I visited her in the holidays.'

Disgusted groans and laughter rose from the group.

Alex grinned and relaxed further. 'That's right. Rabbits produce two kinds of droppings. One type is hard and the other soft. It's the soft ones they will eat. It's a food source for them.'

'That's disgusting,' declared the girl with the ladybird slides.

'Not to a rabbit,' Alex said, and laughed at her appalled expression. 'Rabbits are very intelligent and curious animals. Although they get scared sometimes when they're worried something might hurt them, but when they feel safe and secure they're capable of being loving and...'

His words trailed off as he realised how similar Kiki's nature was to a rabbit's. She was scared of the unknown and cautious, just as a rabbit considered everything to be either a predator or otherwise harmful until it learnt differently.

And how could Kiki learn that not every male intended to hurt her unless one showed her? She required time and patience in order to see that not every sort of love was the destructive kind. Especially not when it came from someone who cared deeply about her happiness. Someone like him.

The truth hit him harder than a heavyweight's left punch. He loved Kiki Brown. Full-out loved her. Not just *liked*, with an added dollop of sexual attraction, but real love. It was why he yearned for more than a physical connection and refused to make love with her, insisting he wanted her full commitment. Not because he didn't want to be used, but because he needed her love. All of it.

Miss Ingle tapped Alex on the shoulder. 'Are you all right?'

He glanced up at the headmistress, though his chaotic thoughts still centred on another female. He loved Kiki to his very soul, but didn't know what to do about it. How did a man make a reluctant woman fall in love? One stubbornly determined not to?

'I love Kiki,' he stated.

The heaviness in his chest lifted and lightness replaced it. The urge to laugh and cheer gripped him but he held it in, not wanting to scare the children with such odd behaviour.

'You do?' Disappointment clung to the woman's soft tone.

'Yes,' he said. 'Though she doesn't want me to.'

'Is she mad?' Miss Ingle asked.

'I often make her so,' he admitted, with a chuckle. 'People sometimes find me hard to work with.'

Miss Ingle sighed and touched the cameo hanging from a gold chain around her throat. 'How sweet of you to admit your failings. So many people don't. If you love her, then you should tell her. Confess your deepest desires and arrange them in her path for her to see.'

Alex frowned, not convinced the idea was a good one. 'I may lose Kiki for good if I do.'

'Or win her for ever,' Miss Ingle replied. 'Imagine the beauty of finally securing your heart's mate. Of joining so profoundly with another person.'

Alex smiled. Despite the headmistress's eccentric manner, she was sweet. 'You're very kind.'

Miss Ingle beamed. 'And you're a very nice man, Dr Morsi. If it wasn't obvious how much in love you are with the lady you speak of, I'd attempt to turn your head with the sonnets of Shakespeare.'

His stomach turned violently, bringing back the dreaded queasiness. 'I need to find Kiki.'

Miss Ingle agreed. 'You do.'

Remembering their young audience, he hesitated. 'What about the talk?'

'I'll take over,' Anne declared from behind Miss Ingle.

Alex shook his head. He'd come to do the talk and he wasn't going to leave until he finished it.

'Thank you, dear friend, but I think I'll see it through.'

He resumed the talk, giving the children further interesting facts on rabbits and other pets. Instead of the lack of interest he'd feared they would show, all the children sat still, captivated by what they were learning. He finished off by answering some of their questions. Though the one about dinosaurs left him stumped for an answer.

Finally Anne pulled him from the chair and shoved him towards the school entrance. 'If I am to enjoy any harmony at work and keep one of our best nurses, then you need to leave now.'

Handing the toy rabbit back to its small owner, Alex turned to Anne with a grin. He'd done it. For the first time in his life he'd faced a crowd and survived the experience.

'I did it.'

Anne smiled and nodded. 'You did, Alex. I'm so proud of you.'

Alex leaned forward and kissed his friend on the head. 'Thank you.'

Blushing, she brushed him off and ordered, 'Go. And don't bother returning until you find the girl and get her to stay. By any means possible, Alex. Gentlemen never win a woman's heart, but Irish rogues are known to.'

He laughed and saluted her. 'I promise to do my best. Bye, children.'

'Will you come again?' asked the girl with the ladybird slides.

Alex's heart filled with warm delight at the unexpected question. Despite his worries, in the end he'd enjoyed talking to this group of school children.

'Yes, I think I will. Next time I'll tell you all about rats.'

'Rats?' Miss Ingle gasped.

A cheer went up, and with a final goodbye to the women, and a wave to the children, he left the garden and headed for the school gate.

It was time to chase down his woman and offer her his heart. He just prayed she didn't choose to break it.

Kiki slammed her car door and hurried across the school's small car park, searching for Alex's truck amongst the various parked vehicles. When she'd popped into the practice to speak with him Leah had informed her both he and Anne were at the school, giving the talk to the children.

The school? Alex?

After the shock of hearing the news, Kiki had asked Leah for directions to the school and driven straight over. What had caused Alex to change his mind? Yesterday he had been adamant that he didn't want to go anywhere near the building or the children.

Had Anne somehow guilted him into doing the talk? Kiki hated the idea of Alex being forced to do anything against his wishes—especially this.

'Kiki?'

The sound of her name interrupted her searching and she glanced up to see Alex jogging across the car park towards her. The tight set of his jaw gave no clue as to whether he was pleased to see her or not. She straightened her spine and prepared herself for the next few minutes.

He came to a sharp stop in front of her, his brown gaze slowly running over her face with the potency of a lingering stroke. His eyes were intense, as if he sought to read her innermost hopes. She shivered and lifted her chin, courage stirring in her heart.

It was time to fight for their future.

'Alex?' she said. 'What's going on? I went to the practice and Leah said you'd come here to do the talk. Yet yesterday when we spoke you refused. What changed?'

Not answering, he settled his hands on her shoulders with a heavy sigh. His expression was serious. 'Since we've met, I've often found myself challenged.'

She narrowed her eyes, not sure what he meant. Was this another attempt to push her away? Did he doubt that she was capable of affection and love and was now choosing to give up on any relationship between them? Was he taking even his friendship away?

She frowned and stared back at him. 'I don't understand. Do you mean the talk? How did it go?'

He laughed, the sound light and carefree. 'It was fine. Actually, it was great. I *did* it, Kiki. I sat in front of that group of children and talked to them. I think the kids enjoyed it. They want me to go back again.'

She smiled at his happiness. 'They do?'

He nodded. 'I was going to talk to them about the procedure to remove a foreign body from a dog's stomach, but then there was this little girl with a toy rabbit…and I thought, why not use that instead?'

Kiki's eyes widened with horror. 'You weren't *really* going to do your talk on that?'

Confused by her reaction, he asked, 'Yes. What's wrong with it? It's a very interesting procedure.'

Kiki shook her head. Thank goodness for whatever had prevented him from doing a talk on that operation. Otherwise Miss Ingle would have found herself inundated with complaints from the parents of such young children.

'So you changed your mind and used a toy rabbit instead?'

'Yes—a white one—and while I was giving the talk it made me think of you.'

Further confused, she asked, 'I remind you of a toy rabbit?'

He frowned. 'What I mean is the way you are about love. How you view it as something to be wary and suspicious of.'

Kiki's heart sank. 'Oh?'

'But you don't need to be suspicious any more.'

Perhaps this would be the ideal time to distract him, she thought. Until she had a chance to say what she wanted to say first.

But Alex placed his hands on his hips, a strange twinkle in his eyes. 'I must tell you something *very* important.'

Kiki's heart flipped and she resisted the urge to cover her ears. What if she didn't like what he said? Now she'd accepted her love for him, hearing that he didn't feel the same would devastate her.

He shifted closer, until the tips of their shoes touched, and returned his hands to her shoulders.

'Kiki Brown—duck custodian and animal saviour extraordinaire—I love you.'

She bit her lip to stop its sudden tremble. 'You do?'

'I do. And nothing you say is going to change my feelings. They're as real as frost in winter and worms in soil. Run away and find this damn friendship marriage you want with some other man, but no one is ever going to love you with as much of the warm, squishy stuff as I do.'

Speechless, Kiki stared up at him. She'd arrived prepared to beg for his forgiveness and swear her commitment to him, but it seemed he already loved her.

She gulped. 'Oh, Alex, the things you say to keep a scrub nurse.'

He laughed. 'You were right. My parents' marriage prevented me from searching for love. Though no one came along who actually interested me until *you* stormed into my day, clutching a basket of puppies and owning an attitude. You're colour, laughter and warmth. I've lived in dull shades for so long and I'm sick of it. I want vibrant and thrilling. Wild and exciting. I want *you*, Kiki Brown. Today, tomorrow, and for all my life.'

He held out his hand, palm turned upwards.

'Won't you find your courage and live it with me? I know you're scared—just like a rabbit is sometimes—but I'm not a predator. I won't hurt you, neglect you or abuse your love. Be brave with me, sweet girl. Face your fear of love just as I've faced my fear of crowds. Together we can do it.'

She stared down at his hand but didn't take it. Alex's declaration deserved one of her own.

Lifting her eyes, she said, 'You were right too. I allowed my father's rejection to shape and influence my life. His behaviour caused me to live scared, and instead of fighting it I let it grow inside me. But with you it's different. My heart won't let my head take control. It knows what it wants and it's *you*, Alex. I'm tired of being a scaredy-cat. I want to be brave. To build a home and a life with you. Because you make me better. I will *never* make you feel unwanted or inferior. Not ever. I will help you celebrate every birthday the way it should be. Because you're special, Alex, and I am stronger with your love. I'm finally a woman ready to commit to the man I love.'

She placed her hand in his, joining them together for the rest of their days. Sealing a promise no one could break.

'I want to love you for the rest of my life—with every part of my heart and soul. With each heartbeat and breath my love for you grows deeper. So, yes, Alex Morsi. I'll happily hold your hand and ride the wild, bumpy shades of life with you. As long as you vow never to let go.'

A slow smile spread over his handsome face and he cupped her cheek. 'You can trust me. I never make a promise I don't keep. If you want me to love you—which I already do—then I'll love you for ever, I swear.'

A new and welcome peace in her heart spread through Kiki. She squeezed Alex's hand, knowing his words were more than a pledge. They were beautiful, meant and true. This man would destroy himself before he hurt her.

'I know you will.'

Tugging her against his body, Alex ordered, 'Say you love me again. I want to hear it.'

She laughed. 'I love you, Alex. I love you so much.'

'Kiss me, then,' he said.

She raised an eyebrow at his bossy manner, but snuggled deeper into his hold. 'Do you intend to be so very demanding throughout our relationship?'

He answered with a grin. 'Over kisses? Definitely.'

Staring into his handsome face—the face she planned to watch as it aged and changed over the years, to kiss on good days and stroke on bad ones—she felt her heart burst with the most amazing, exciting sensation.

'As I rather enjoy your kisses, I suppose I can get used to that.'

A sudden feeling of tenderness in her chest, reminded her of her surprise.

'I need to show you something...'

Carefully, Kiki pulled her coat open and unbuttoned her blue shirt to reveal the freshly inked tattoo of a small, feminine black greyhound with a pink heart at the centre of its chest. Inside the heart the letter 'A' sat proud.

'His-and-hers greyhounds,' she whispered.

'You and I. Together.'

Alex gently traced her breast, careful not to hurt the sore, sensitive flesh.

'It's beautiful,' he choked. 'Marry me, Kiki. Fill my heart and my days with your love. Let's say goodbye to fear and the past and grasp our happy future together.'

She leaned up on tiptoe and kissed his chin. 'Before or after our next kiss?'

'Definitely after,' he chuckled. 'I'm a patient man, but not a fool.'

And then they kissed, and Kiki knew for the first time in her life that she didn't have to worry or fret—because Alex cherished her heart. And she loved and trusted in her man completely.

EPILOGUE

ALEX OPENED THE gate that separated Fingle Lodge from the surrounding woods—a dense forest planted on the six acres of land they now owned, thanks to Kiki's godmother, who had gifted it to them a few days after their wedding.

Together they walked towards the lodge, the once neglected property they'd lovingly renovated and made their home. A real family home, where nothing but happiness and joy echoed inside the walls.

'I *did* suggest you change into your wellies before we left the house for our walk,' he said, as he helped Kiki edge around a muddy patch.

Kiki glanced down at the mud seeping over her pretty pink ballet flats and smiled. 'I know—but what's a little mud on such a lovely sunny day?'

Alex snorted. '*Not* what you said the other day, when I came home from birthing a calf. You forced me to strip off on the doorstep! If Mrs Bush had visited five minutes earlier she'd have got a shock to go with the pint of milk she popped in for.'

Kiki smirked at the memory. 'You did stink.'

He pulled her close and growled in her ear. 'Not too smelly to kiss you good morning, if I remember correctly. Or for you to try and take advantage once Mrs Bush had left.'

She laughed and leaned her head against his arm. 'You happily joined in. In fact I'm pretty certain it was your wandering hands that actually started it.'

Alex grinned. He loved this woman who filled every day with love and surprise.

Pecking kisses along one cheek, across her mouth, and finishing somewhere under her eye, Alex murmured, 'Happy anniversary, baby.'

Kiki snuggled into his side with a contented sigh. 'To think I arrived in Dorset searching for peace, and instead I found half-starved dogs and a gorgeous vet ripe for falling in love.'

Alex kissed the top of her head. 'We were both lucky that day.'

They'd married exactly two months after declaring their love to each other, in the local register office, and had had a party in the town's village hall.

They'd invited all their friends to celebrate with them—but absolutely no relations.

Kiki's godmother had travelled to Dorset and stayed at a hotel not far away from the church. Taking her role to give the bride away seriously, she'd even given Kiki her antique wedding dress to wear.

It had been a day full of laughter, love and good food. Concerned only with love and friendship.

A snuffling sound from Kiki's front grabbed Alex's attention, pulling it from his wife's beautiful face and those wonderful memories. He smiled as the dark fluffy head peeking out of the top of the pink baby carrier began to move from side to side.

Peering forward, he tried to get a better view of his

child, who humbled him every time he stared into her angelic face. The daughter he'd once believed he would never father.

'Our princess is awake.'

Kiki smiled and nodded, the same look of wonder on her face as she stared down at their child. 'She is.'

As he cupped a hand gently around their eight-week-old daughter's back, his quick glance at his wife caused Alex to sigh at the sight of the tears in her eyes.

'Hormone havoc or baby blues?' he whispered.

She shook her head and smiled. 'Neither—just you, being wonderful and loveable.'

He chuckled and slipped a hand to her cheek, caressing the soft skin with his thumb. 'Not hard, seeing as I love you.'

She grinned. 'I love you more.'

Hugging their child until she was gently sandwiched between them, they said in unison, 'And we love you, too.'

Leaning down, Alex kissed their daughter on the head before capturing Kiki's mouth in a longer, more grown-up version of the kiss.

When he drew back, he smiled down at his girls. 'I'm so glad you agreed to be my wife.'

Tears hovered on Kiki's lashes.

'I'm glad, too. You're a wonderful, loving husband, who is so understanding. Especially about the ferrets. Neeve Louisa Morsi is very lucky to have you for her daddy. I picked well when I chose you.'

Alex grinned. 'My charm and good looks swayed you?'

She shook her head. 'Your Irish kisses, actually. They're irresistible.'

Kiki chuckled as their daughter's snuffling turned to complaining grizzles as her search for food led to frustration.

'Your daughter needs feeding. She's greedy—like her daddy.'

Alex smiled, content and happy with the two most important females in his arms. He'd married a wonderful, loving woman and they had a perfect daughter.

He thanked the twist of fate that had brought Kiki through the practice door after all his years alone. The dogs they'd rescued had found good homes, and one had ended up happily reunited with its original owner—who, amazingly, had still been searching after three years. The reunion between the two of them had brought tears to everyone's eyes—even his.

And Kiki loved him, and they were blessed with a child. Nothing else could make his life better. His life so complete he'd never ask for more. He truly was—

Ferrets? What ferrets? They didn't have any ferrets. Just Nix, and the ducks, and Brandy the horse, and two goats named Bonkers and Ruff...

He'd bet his truck Kiki had bought ferrets off the internet. He'd caught her searching a couple of sites the other night, during a midnight feed. When was she going to accept that she couldn't save or give a home to every animal who looked as if it needed it?

He just thanked God she'd found it in her sweet, gentle heart to save him and give him his.

* * * * *

MILLS & BOON

Coming next month

FIGHTING FOR THE TRAUMA DOC'S HEART
Rachel Dove

Michelle looked at her boss, but he was oblivious.

'So that's it?' she demanded of Andrew. 'I go abroad for four months, to help people who really need it, and then I come back and have to fight for my job, against him?' She hiked a thumb over her right shoulder at her rival.

There was a challenging look evident in Jacob's expression.

'I'm not worried. I like it here, actually, so I say bring it on. What do you say, Mich?'

Michelle stood up straight, drawing herself up to her full height. She tolerated 'Mich' from people she knew and trusted, but his use of it sent a wave of rage charging through her body.

He mirrored her actions, straightening his tie. She was five ten—more when she was out of her trainers and in a pair of heels—but she still had to look up at her suave rival.

'What do I say?' she said to both men, her arms folded to keep her from flailing them about like a child in the throes of a tantrum. She'd never give them the satisfaction. She couldn't be childish about this.

So she'd left, and the place hadn't been able to run on its own. They'd needed Jacob. But now she needed her job—her normality—back. She needed him to leave so she could burrow back into her comfortable life. That was her plan, and she didn't have a back-up. She had to be the victor in this fight. She wasn't sure she would be able to get up again if she got knocked down this time.

'Bring it on. May the best doctor win.'

'In six weeks I'll make my decision about who gets to lead the new trauma centre as head of department,' said Andrew. 'Don't let me down; I need you both at your best.'

'Six weeks of working together...' Jacob smiled, his pearly whites flashing as they caught the light. 'How ever will you resist me, let alone win?'

Michelle looked him up and down pointedly, ignoring the frisson that his sculpted body produced in the pit of her stomach.

'I'll survive, I'm sure.'

She held out her hand, and he shook it, holding it between them. The warmth from his hand pervaded her bare skin.

'We'll see, shall we? This is going to be fun.'

Continue reading
FIGHTING FOR THE TRAUMA DOC'S HEART
Rachel Dove

Available next month
www.millsandboon.co.uk

COMING SOON!

We really hope you enjoyed reading this book.
If you're looking for more romance, be sure to
head to the shops when new books are
available on

Thursday 23rd
July

To see which titles are coming soon, please visit
millsandboon.co.uk/nextmonth

LET'S TALK
Romance

For exclusive extracts, competitions
and special offers, find us online:

 facebook.com/millsandboon

 @MillsandBoon

 @MillsandBoonUK

Get in touch on 01413 063232

For all the latest titles coming soon, visit
millsandboon.co.uk/nextmonth

MILLS & BOON

THE HEART OF ROMANCE

A ROMANCE FOR EVERY KIND OF READER

MODERN

Prepare to be swept off your feet by sophisticated, sexy and seductive heroes, in some of the world's most glamourous and romantic locations, where power and passion collide.
8 stories per month.

HISTORICAL

Escape with historical heroes from time gone by. Whether your passion is for wicked Regency Rakes, muscled Vikings or rugged Highlanders, awaken the romance of the past.
6 stories per month.

MEDICAL

Set your pulse racing with dedicated, delectable doctors in the high-pressure world of medicine, where emotions run high and passion, comfort and love are the best medicine.
6 stories per month.

True Love

Celebrate true love with tender stories of heartfelt romance, from the rush of falling in love to the joy a new baby can bring, and a focus on the emotional heart of a relationship.
8 stories per month.

Desire

Indulge in secrets and scandal, intense drama and plenty of sizzling hot action with powerful and passionate heroes who have it all: wealth, status, good looks…everything but the right woman.
6 stories per month.

HEROES

Experience all the excitement of a gripping thriller, with an intense romance at its heart. Resourceful, true-to-life women and strong, fearless men face danger and desire - a killer combination!
8 stories per month.

DARE

Sensual love stories featuring smart, sassy heroines you'd want as a best friend, and compelling intense heroes who are worthy of them.
4 stories per month.

To see which titles are coming soon, please visit

millsandboon.co.uk/nextmonth